A UNION OF SOULS

"Well, here we are! All alone at last," Joe said with a roguish grin that made his turquoise eyes sparkle wickedly in the gloom of the hallway.

There was something dangerous about his expression that caused prickles of excitement to tingle down Seraphina's spine. "This arrangement is strictly business, I hope you recall, Mr. McCaleb. The marriage service changes nothing," she insisted, alarmed to find her throat suddenly feeling parched.

"Oh no, my dear. You're my wife now, and since this is supposed to be our honeymoon, let's enjoy it, hmmm?"

His voice had grown low and the sensual gleam in his eyes left her in no doubt of his intentions as they raked her from head to toe. It seemed to Seraphina that Joe could see through the layers of clothing to her bared body beneath! He took a casual step toward her and a nervous quiver started in her belly, spreading outward as he came to a halt scant inches away. Though she wanted to back up, out of his reach, she was suddenly frozen to the spot. Lord, why was she so . . . so darned aware of him? It was as if every pore, muscle, and nerve in her body reacted violently to his nearness—tingling and leaping out of control . . .

PENELOPE NERI

Loving Lies

ZEBRA BOOKS
KENSINGTON PUBLISHING CORP.

ZEBRA BOOKS

are published by

Kensington Publishing Corp.
475 Park Avenue South
New York, NY 10016

First printing: June 1987

Printed in the United States of America

Prologue

"Katie, you know how I feel about you! I'd cut off my right hand sooner than do anything to hurt you! You and I have always been close, closer than any brother and sister," Chuck Bushley declared, his handsome, tanned features tense with concern. Irritably, he ran his fingers through his shock of red hair. "But, oh, hell, why can't they get it through their heads that that's as far as it goes, and lay off us?"

Katie went to him and placed a comforting hand upon his rigid shoulder. "Why? Because they don't want to admit it, don't you see? The four of them have been so close themselves, Chuck! We've both heard over and over all through the years we were growing up about the awful times your mama and mine went through together when they were captured by the Comanche back in '63, and how your stepfather and my papa became friends. Sharing hard times like they did brings folks closer to each other than they'd ever grow under normal circumstances. They don't *mean* to pressure us into anything against our will, truly they don't. It's just that they've always secretly hoped that you and I'd be married and join our two families by blood once and for all."

5

Chuck snorted. "I know, Katie. But whether they mean to hurt us or not, the pressure's still there. It's real, all right. And it's not fair, neither to you or me. I'm sick of hearing them say, 'When you and little Katie get married . . .'! No hard feelings, Kate, but sometimes I feel like shouting out loud that it's Seraphina Jones I love, and that you're like my own little sister, if I had one."

Katie nodded in understanding. "I know just how you feel. It's the same back home. It was a relief when school was starting again for the fall, and I could escape it and come back to Boston to Aunt Lucinda's for a breathing spell. But after the holidays, I know it'll all start up again—and there'll be no school to escape to then! This was my last semester, remember? I have a feeling if something's not settled—and soon!—there'll be real pressure brought to bear when I return from Europe. Oh, Chuck, it's no easier for me! Why won't they listen to what *we* want, instead of trying to play matchmaker for us? I'm twenty, darn it! Surely that's old enough to decide for myself what I want to do with my life? Why, I don't even know if I want to get married at all—not to anyone!"

Chuck put his arms around her and hugged her tightly, a gesture of affection that was filled with the gruff tenderness he felt for the slender, black-haired girl. For a few moments, Katie leaned against him, drawing strength from the broad frame that was so dear and familiar.

All at once, the door flew open. Both of them glanced up sharply at the intrusion to see a young, blond-haired woman standing upon the threshold. Her wide blue eyes, so at odds with her somewhat angular features, became even wider with surprise at the sight of the pair by the fireplace. They were, to all appearances, cozily wrapped in an ardent embrace!

6

The pale blue eyes hardened, and a malicious little smile curved her narrow lips.

"Well, well, Miss Katherine Steele and her *dear* friend! Whatever would the Misses Hanover and Merriweather have to say about this little tableau!" she exclaimed smugly.

Katie sighed and drew herself from Chuck's bearhug with no evidence of haste or urgency. "Oh, shut up and don't be such a darn goose, Cecilia! You know very well the Misses Hanover and Merriweather gave their permission for Chuck to take tea with me here."

"Tea? Oh, but of course!" Cecilia retorted rudely. "The rest of us have to follow the dreary Academy regulations to the letter, but our dear Miss Steele is allowed all manner of privileges, isn't she—even to the extent of entertaining her . . . her beaus in Miss Hanover's own sitting room, and letting them take all sorts of . . . liberties while they're here!"

Katie's eyes flashed, their usual gray hue giving way to a more dominant green in her anger. A fiery blush crimsoned her pale golden complexion. "Lord, Cissy, I do believe I already have enough on my mind without your catty interference this afternoon! Don't tempt me, girl," she warned, "or much as I'd hate to do it, I'll let slip a word or two to Miss Merriweather about how you cheated on our final exams—oh, no, missie, don't try to deny it! Everyone knows you wrote the answers on the cuffs of your blouse! And what about that gardener's lad you were meeting in the greenhouse last term? Dick was his name, wasn't it? Or was it Harry . . . ?" Brows arched, she let her voice trail away meaningfully and was gratified to see Cecilia Tallant pale under her rouge and powder.

"You wouldn't—" Cissy whispered, dry mouthed.

"Try me, honey!" Kate retorted in a voice like steel. To her relief, Cissy stifled a sob, whirled about, her skirts rustling noisily, and left without another word, loudly yanking shut the sitting room door in her wake so that the jamb shuddered.

"There. That's better! Now, where were we?" Kate asked Chuck after she had gone. She glanced across the room at him and saw that he was grinning.

"We were discussing your parents, I do believe. Say, you wouldn't really have tattled on her, would you?" he asked, nodding toward the closed door.

"Of course not!" Kate confessed, scornful that he had even had to ask. "You know telling tales isn't my style, Charles Bushley. I just wanted to get rid of her and shut her up as quickly as possible, and threatening her seemed the best way to do it. That little cat! If I'd said nothing, by suppertime the entire Academy would have been buzzing with the news that she'd surprised me in a passionate embrace with you! Now, forget about her, Chuck. We have more important things to worry about than Cecilia Tallant."

She paced back and forth across the carpet, her pale blue silk skirts whispering, her slender fingers twining with the silver and turquoise rings she wore and betraying her underlying agitation.

At just over twenty years of age, she was tall for a young woman, with a slim yet shapely figure and a graceful, assured carriage uncommon in one of her youth—a result, she had decided when the question had arisen, of having enjoyed an active life, riding and walking, without the usual constraints against such vigorous outdoors activities that were placed upon many young women these days. Her eyes were a lustrous gray-green, a color as mercurial as her moods, and could flash with hidden emerald-fire in anger one moment—as they had a little earlier—and glow with the softly luminous ashen hue of twilight gray the next. Her hair was her only true claim to beauty, she had always felt, and she was justifiably proud of it. It was a glorious, tumbling ebony cascade that spilled its inky river clear to her waist when it was unpinned. It also framed her oval face perfectly with the high, exotic cheekbones that betrayed the mixed blood in her veins, as did the pale gold of her complexion and the generous width of her lovely mouth. Today, however, she wore her crowning glory swept up, falling in heavy, glossy black ringlets over one shoulder in the current fashion. The style suited her, though for herself she much preferred to let it simply fall loose and heavy about her shoulders, or to feel it streaming free behind her in the wind.

For several moments, silence reigned in the sitting room, save for the snap and crackle of logs in the hearth, while Katie and Chuck wrestled with their thoughts. Outside, the sun shone brightly on the weathered gray stone walls of the Academy and bathed the sculptured shrubbery and neatly manicured flower beds in liquid gold. Beyond, many people were promenading along the tidy city pavements or strolling in the green parks amongst the flowers and birds, or scanning the busy harbor for a familiar sail. It was July in Boston, but the prestigious school was an ancient, drafty building even so. Her teacher, Miss Hanover, who suffered from rheumatism, poor old dear, and who had graciously permitted Kate the use of her sitting room to entertain her guest, could not abide the chill; hence the unseasonal fire.

Her great-aunt Lucinda suffered from rheumatism these days, also, Kate mused, a result, the fine old lady had declared many times with a surprisingly youthful twinkle in her eyes, of having enjoyed a reckless youth. Dear Aunt Lucinda! How good she and Uncle Bernard had been to her, Katie thought. They had encouraged her to consider their home upon nearby Beacon Hill

9

her own in every way while here at school and away from her parents' ranch in New Mexico, although their own children were her mama's age, and some of their grandchildren as old as she was.

It was in honor of Katie's having completed her schooling and having at last received her coveted certificate as a teacher that Aunt Lucinda had decided to take her and her eldest granddaughter on a grand tour of Europe as a graduation gift. Oh, how she was looking forward to it! In just ten days, they would be on their way. London, Paris, Rome, and Vienna would no longer be mere descriptions in her history books, but alive and real! Imagine, strolling down the Champs Elysees, or listening to the chimes of old Big Ben ring out over London, or touring through Vatican City, or enjoying a gondola ride along the Venice waterways— oh, all of it! And perhaps they'd even—

"Katie!"

Chuck's sudden exclamation broke into her reverie. She flung about from her relaxed pose leaning up casually against the white marble mantelpiece, to face Chuck as he excitedly continued, "Heck, Katie, I've got it, and I can't believe I was such a goldarned fool I didn't think of it before!"

"Got what?"

"A solution to my problem—and yours into the bargain, I reckon. It's so darn simple!"

"Then spit it out, Chuck, and don't keep me dangling!" she urged, knowing Chuck well enough to realize he was purposely drawing out the moment. It was one of his less endearing traits.

Chuck grinned. "Well, shame on you, Katherine Star Dreamer Steele! Your highfalutin, fancy schoolin' hasn't helped your tongue any! Heck, gal! You sound like one of Uncle Luke's *vaqueros!*"

She blushed. "Oh, shush. Never mind that," she

10

scolded impatiently. "Just tell me, darn you!"

"Wee—ll, I was just thinking, how about if Seraphina and me ran away and got married? Before anyone found out we'd eloped, we could be Mister and Missus Larry Charles Bushley. That would solve everything, right?"

She snorted. "It certainly would," she agreed grimly. "It would probably kill Aunt Carol, and Uncle Cay would be fit to be tied! And what about *my* mama and pa? Heck, Chuck! Pa'd be looking for you with a skinning knife if he figured you'd jilted me—taking to the warpath for real!"

"Oh, shucks, be realistic, Katie!" Chuck said in disgust. "What could they really do, once it was over and done with? They'd forgive me; I know they would. I'm the only son they've got, after all, like it or not! And once they'd met 'Phina, they'd love her just as much as I do, and you know it. And as for you—well, you'd be off the hook, and they'd leave off pressing you to get married, at least for a while. Well? What do you think?"

Katie pursed her lips. "I've heard worse ideas," she admitted. "And I reckon you're right about 'Phina. Who could help but love her?" Seraphina Jones was her closest, dearest friend, one of the few truly good people Katie had ever met, and it was no wonder to her that Chuck Bushley loved her so. It had been thanks to Katie that they had met for the first time, right here in this very sitting room, she recalled, thankful now that her aunt Lucinda and Seraphina had disappeared a short while ago in the direction of the Academy kitchens with Miss Hanover to see about the preparations for high tea, which had become customary upon Chuck's rare visits. Their absence had given Chuck the time he so desperately needed to discuss with Katie what was closest to his heart—the subject of Seraphina Jones.

11

Katie had been attending the Boston Academy for Young Ladies as a day student for the past three years, living with her great-aunt Lucinda and great-uncle Bernard Downing instead of boarding, a practice not uncommon among her fellow pupils. About two years ago, a letter had arrived from one of Uncle Bernard's old friends in San Francisco, a fellow by the name of William McCaleb, asking if room could be found to lodge the old man's shy young ward, Seraphina, who had also been accepted as a pupil at the finishing school. Bernard Downing had been only too happy to help his old acquaintance, and Seraphina Jones had been added to the Downing household when the new semester had commenced. Katie and Seraphina had quickly become fast friends, the quiet, shy girl adoring the lively, outgoing, often outrageous Katie, and Katie admiring Seraphina for her totally opposite disposition, which was as angelic as her name implied. Yes, it was all because of his visits to her that Chuck and Seraphina had been brought together and had consequently fallen in love, Katie mused, not without considerable satisfaction, for Chuck and Seraphina were, in her mind, a perfect match.

Carol Cantrell, Chuck's mother, had been a young and lovely widow when she and Cay Cantrell had met. Carol had been expecting her first child and had been desperately lonely. Her husband, Larry Bushley, had been viciously killed a short time before by raiding Indians when their settlers' wagon train had been crossing the Comancheria territory of the Plains en route to the West. Both Promise O'Rourke, Katie's mother, and Carol had been taken captive by the same war party of Comanche Indians. Using their wits and mustering a great deal of courage, Promise and Carol had managed to escape their savage captors. Some while later, Carol had met and married Cay Cantrell, while Promise O'Rourke had wed Katie's father—the half-blooded rancher, Luke Steele, whose Cheyenne blood came from his mother's side.

Chuck had been born that winter, and his stepfather, Cay, had doted on him from the first. Katie had been born the following spring, and Promise and Luke had returned to their cattle ranch, the Shadow *S*, near Santa Fe in New Mexico, while Carol and Cay had headed north into the Colorado Territory, determined to make a living raising horses. Make a living both families had, and a very nice one, too. Now Cay's stepson, whom everyone called Chuck, stood to inherit the Cantrell ranch, the Double *C*, someday, and the famous Cantrell quarter horses that went with it. By anyone's standards, he was quite a "catch," having engaging looks and a good-natured disposition to match his considerable wealth.

But numerous prolonged summer visits back and forth at each other's ranches had quite destroyed the fond hopes none-too-secretly fostered by both the Cantrells and the Steeles that someday the two families would be joined by Katie and Chuck's marriage. The young people had come to know each other *too* well; had grown up with Katie accepting Chuck in her life in the same teasingly affectionate, caring way she accepted her younger brothers, Thomas and Courtney —both named for their grandfathers on either side of the Steele family. The delicious quality of mystery, the gradual learning process, the joy of each new discovery in the other required to set the stage for a heady romance, had long since been lost amidst years of easy camaraderie, familiarity, and childhood tussles. How could she harbor romantic notions about someone she had seen bawling his eyes out after a whupping for trying to play *matador* with Papa's prize stud bull, or while holding that same person's head while he was sick

13

all over your newly polished boots after eating too many *tamales* at one sitting? Chuck had done both, and more! And he had seen her at her worst, too, more times than she cared to count. They felt a fierce loyalty to each other and the deep and abiding bond of love often found between a brother and sister, but the kind of love and physical attraction needed between a man and a woman . . . ? No, sir!

"Well?" Chuck demanded impatiently.

"Well what?"

"Shall I go through with it?"

"Have you discussed it with 'Phina?"

"I hinted at it, sort of. You know how she is, bless her sweet, trusting little heart. She'd go along with it if I talked her into it. With her mama dead, all the family she has left in the world is her guardian, William McCaleb. He's a generous old man, by all accounts, real good to 'Phina in his fashion, but something of a tyrant in the process, from what she tells me. Likes his own way in everything. She's afraid if I ask him for her hand, he might decide against it. It's been said he disowned his only son years back for marrying a play actress against his wishes, so she has reason to think that way. And Seraphina's all he has now. There's no telling which way he'd jump, if it came to the pinch."

"Then you've answered your own question. Go ahead and do it!" Katie urged impulsively. "You and 'Phina have every right to be happy, and if running off and getting married is the only way, then you *have* to do it. And if there's anything I can do, you know without asking that I'll help you."

"Thanks, Katie," Chuck said with a grin, giving her another enormous bear hug. "I knew I could count on you! As a matter of fact, there is something—"

"I knew it!" Katie cut in with a groan. "What is it?"

"I'll need some money. See, Pa gave me enough to

pay my expenses here in Boston while I saw to his business matters, but unfortunately not enough to finance an impromptu elopement! I'll—"

"—pay me back? Oh, don't talk *loco!* I know you will, Chuck."

"Thanks, Katie. Now, we have to figure out how to go about this—make some plans. You can think up some excuse to get Seraphina out from under your aunt's watchful eye for a few hours, can't you?"

She nodded confidently. "Sure. That part of it should be easy. I have some gowns at the dressmaker's that are being altered for our trip to Europe. I could ask 'Phina to come with me on that pretense, and then you could be wait—"

She broke off guiltily as the door suddenly opened again and her great-aunt Lucinda swept into the room, filling it with a lavender fragrance. Neither prissy Miss Hanover nor an Academy maid bearing a heavily laden silver tea tray followed her in. Lucinda Downing's handsome face was unusually grave, Katie observed, a sudden chill of apprehension—foreboding, perhaps?—sweeping through her. Lord, yes, she appeared far more grave than the mundane task of ordering tea would warrant! In her wake trailed Seraphina, her angelic, heart-shaped face damp with tears, her dark eyes enormous and brimming with still more as yet unshed. In her trembling hand, she held a crumpled sheet of paper.

"What is it, Aunt? Seraphina? Oh, dear Lord, 'Phina, honey, sit down before you fall down! You're white as a sheet. Whatever's wrong?" Katie cried, certain beyond doubt now that something was terribly wrong.

Seraphina obediently sat upon the chair Katie had hastily pulled out. Her lower lip quivered and her pale hands trembled. Chuck ached to go to her and envelop

15

her in his strong arms and kiss away her tears—to hold her so she'd stop crying and feel safe and happy once more, whatever it was that was wrong—though of course he could do no such thing with Mrs. Downing standing there.

"I have just received a . . . a telegraph," Seraphina stammered, drawing a lacy handkerchief from her pocket and dabbing at her nose. She held up the rumpled, sodden paper simultaneously. "It was delivered to Miss Hanover's office just a few moments ago while we were ordering the tea tray. Katie . . . oh, Katie, it's about my . . . my guardian, Mister McCaleb. You see, he has . . . has unfortunately p . . . passed away! Oh, Katie, you must help me to pack. There's so much to be done, and so little time in which to do it! I'm to be on the very next ship sailing for San Francisco. It will be the fastest way, Aunt Lucinda says. Uncle William's solicitors have informed me that they have taken care of all the funeral arrangements in my absence, but there is his will to be read, you see, and his house and affairs to be set . . . set in order . . . and I . . . I must leave here at once!" She gave Chuck such a tragic, imploring look that it quite cut Katie to the quick, then Seraphina bowed her head and gave way to her tears.

Katie was immediately at her side, holding her, soothing her dark head and stroking her trembling shoulders as if she were comforting a small child.

"There, 'Phina, honey, don't cry. It will all work out, really it will," Katie crooned reassuringly. "I'm sorry to hear about your guardian, really I am, but he was an old, old man and he'd been ill for some time now, you knew that, so perhaps it was for the best. His pain is ended now. There, there, honey, cry it out. It's you we have to worry about now—what you'll do and where you'll go. I'm sure Aunt Lucinda would let you come

16

back to her home afterward until you decide what to do, wouldn't you, Aunt Lucinda? Soon everything will be back the way it was, you'll see."

Katie met Chuck's anxious blue eyes over Seraphina's shoulder and was shocked by the frustration, anger, and overwhelming disappointment in their depths. Of course, if Seraphina now had to leave Boston for San Francisco, everything he had planned just moments ago to ensure their future happiness would have to be postponed. And there was a chance—a very real one—that nothing would ever again be how it once had been, not for the two of them. San Francisco was so very far away, and no doubt, with her guardian dead, Seraphina would now be a wealthy heiress of some sort—an all too fragile, easily led victim for some western fortune hunter with a kindly manner and a glib tongue. Alone, with no Chuck to look out for her interests and well-being, there was no telling what trouble sweet, trusting Seraphina might get into.

How stupid, how blind she had been not to see the ramifications of William McCaleb's death immediately! Nothing would ever be the same as it had been—no, never again. Oh, poor, poor Chuck! That thought had not even entered her mind until she had glimpsed his anguished expression just now. She held Chuck's gaze and added softly, "I promise I'll help you, 'Phina. We'll *all* help you through this. Katie will make it all come out right, I swear it."

Across the room, Chuck relaxed fractionally and returned Katie's steady, meaningful gaze with a silent nod of thanks—a silent nod that nonetheless spoke volumes.

17

Chapter One

Like an emerald jewel set in the glittering sapphire of the Indian Ocean, the volcanic island of Krakatoa was robed in lush forests and tropical vines. She and the two other small islands that flanked her in the Sunda Straits between Java and Sumatra, Verlaten and Lang islands, had been welcome landmarks to sailors for centuries—their first sight of greenery after sailing endless leagues of ocean. They believed her to be benevolent, an extinct volcanic crater, and would cheer when they sighted her, green and calm, rising from the glassy blue ocean, for beyond Krakatoa lay Java, Garden of the East, and Anjer, where they would halt their journeys to take on a pilot, and perhaps spend a few idyllic days ashore.

Ah, what a delight was Anjer to those sea-weary sailors! Her bay was fringed with lush coconut palms that swayed their fronded headdresses gently in the warm and scented tradewinds. Beyond, the island was thick with abundantly yielding fruit trees known only to the tropics: the jackfruit and the banana, the mango and the plantain. Amongst them, the hibiscus flaunted its brilliant scarlet bugles, and butterflies in confetti swarms flitted lazily to and fro on the moist air.

The red-tiled, white villas of the Dutch with their verandas and picturesque gardens were scattered amidst the rampant vegetation and along the emerald esplanade, shaded with *warignen* trees. Beyond the pretty little town in the wide valley lay the native *kampongs,* villages of thatched bamboo huts, and the colorful Chinese and Arab quarters with their curious little shops and teeming bazaars. At all hours, graceful native women robed in vivid sarongs, as well as little two-wheeled carts drawn by pairs of Brahmin bulls or a single buffalo, could be seen making their unhurried ways to the stalls of the marketplace.

The climate was balmy. The native people were, for the greater part, content with their lot. Though at times they resented laboring for the sultans on the plantations of spices, coffee, tea, and rice, they knew that these various headmen had in turn to answer to masters of their own, the Dutch Resident and his officers. So it had always been, this system of lords and overlords. It made little difference if those overlords were of the white race. A hut could be built in less than a day, for materials were readily available. Fish, rice, fruits, and other foods were plentiful, and the work was not so hard. All in all, it was a good life, save for their lingering doubts about the volcanic island of Krakatoa, to which they continually looked askance. No, they were not as complacent as the Dutch in their attitude toward her.

The natives considered Krakatoa—whose name some translated as "the Crab," though its true meaning had long since been forgotten—the home of *Antoe Laoet,* the Sea Ghost. They believed the wicked spirit lived in the bowels of the earth beneath her and, if he were not properly appeased by sacrifices, would show his fury by causing the very earth to shudder as he belched up fire and smoke. It was a rare, brave

19

fisherman who left his *kampong* and paddled his *prau* to the island for any reason whatsoever. Despite the reassurances of their Dutch overlords that this volcano was extinct, a slumbering relic unlike several of the other, more active volcanoes found in Java that smoked and erupted regularly, to them it was an evil place. In a not too distant time pirates had made the island their lair; they had raided the nearby islands and carried off many of the women. In another time, buried now by the dust of ages and only distantly remembered in legend, it was said the volcano had erupted with catastrophic results and had turned the sea to milky whiteness. It was also prophesied, the wise men warned, that when three thousand rainy seasons had come to pass, the sleeping volcano would once again awaken and bring down terror and destruction upon them all. When it was over, the lands of Java and Sumatra, torn apart by that ancient eruption, would once again be united.

When strange grumblings and mighty roarings were first heard from Krakatoa in the month of May and grew steadily louder through the month of August in that year of 1883, the natives remembered the prophecies, and they trembled.

"Grandfather! Grandfather! I am frightened!"

The old fisherman nodded and drew the small boy to him. The child buried his head against his grandfather's bony brown chest, and soon the old man felt the hot dampness of his tears there.

"Hush, my grandson," he attempted to console the terrified child, his clawlike old hand smoothing the boy's glossy black head. "Have you not felt the rumblings of the volcano many times since you were born?"

"Yes, Grandfather," the boy mumbled between sobs. "But never . . . never like this before. The sounds are so loud—like the roar of the white men's cannon! And last night, the moon—did you see it, Grandfather?—the moon was blue!"

The old man nodded sagely and scooped the child into his arms, carrying him away from the beach and back toward their prosperous little *kampong,* all thoughts of their dawn fishing forgotten. Despite his comforting words, his expression was deeply troubled. The level of the ocean was very high this morning, far higher than was usual for the time of day. And as his grandson had said, the fearful bellowing sounds of loud explosions coming from the volcano Krakatoa in the Sunda Strait, some thirty or so miles away, could be heard clearly even here at Anjer. Though the volcano had been unusually active of late, there had been a peculiar heaviness in his heart for some days now that boded ill and seemed to embody these growlings with an ominously threatening message. He sensed some terrible misfortune about to befall him, his little grandson, his people—a misfortune that he, in his superstitious heart, was certain the whites of the Company must have caused to descend upon them by reason of their warring against the Achtinese. The prophecy of the ancients, he feared, was about to be fulfilled, yet there was nothing he could do to prevent it! Who could avert the will of Allah? He turned in his carrying of the little boy to look back, and he saw now, in the distance, a heavy pall of black smoke and writhing clouds of white steam belching up into the dark sky. Suddenly, jets of orange and red flame roared up hellishly, and a fiery glow of light, like the ruddy glow from a demon's furnace, rested above the distant summit of the Crab, Krakatoa. The repeated, loud explosions had now become a steady, deafening roar

21

that struck terror in his heart.

That same inner sense of impending doom urged him to flee, to get away, far, far away, from the coast. He fancied that above the dull roaring he could hear cries of alarm from the nearby town, women screaming, men raising their voices in terrified prayer. He discarded all thoughts of returning to their *kampong* and instead determined to take his grandson up the low-lying hills and through the rice paddies, toward the village of a distant cousin of his. Surely there they would be safe from . . . *it?*

Breathing heavily, he stumbled along the rocky track beneath the looming coconut palms, wondering uneasily when daylight would break. Surely it was past time for the sun to come up, yet the sky had lightened very little in the past hour save for where the volcano's bloody glow illumined it, and the sun had still made no appearance. His back pained him, but nevertheless he stumbled on, his leaping heart threatening to burst forth from his bony old chest with the effort of carrying the child. Dread had become true fear now. Where was the blessed sun? *Where?*

"Grandfather, when will it grow light?" the boy asked, a quaver in his voice. He had become infected with his grandfather's fear, for all that the old man had tried to hide it.

"Soon, little one, very soon. Come, you must walk yourself now. Grandfather is too old to carry a heavy, big boy like you any farther." He set the boy down and took his young hand tightly in his own, squeezing so hard the boy winced but made no protest. The tightness of his grip was strangely comforting.

"But . . . where are we going? My father's house is that way!" the boy declared, pointing.

"Hush, and walk a little faster. We are going to visit my cousin. You will like him. He has many wonderful

22

stories to tell young ones such as yourself, stories he brings alive with the pretty shadow puppets you are so fond of. Hurry now, my grandson, or you will miss the beginning of the story, yes?"

The boy eagerly trotted along beside him after that, and the old man was relieved, though no less frightened.

The rumblings had grown fainter. The old man heaved a thankful sigh, but his ease was short-lived. Soon, rain began to fall, a strange, clogging rain thickly laden with small particles of ash. A strong wind arose from nowhere, thick with the choking stink of sulphur; a wind that hurled small, hail-like fragments of pumice against their bare chests and faces. Looking down, the old man was astonished to see that where the fragments had touched his clothing, holes had been burned. By Allah, what was wrong with him? He had not even noticed that the fragments were hot! He hurried along, gasping for every breath, the child almost dragged behind him in his haste, the little brown feet scarcely touching the ground. Another dull, roaring sound had begun now, and for the moment the befuddled, frightened old man did not separate the sound from the roaring of his own blood in his ears, pumped furiously by the terrified hammering of his heart.

"Grandfather! Look! *Ayer datang!*" the boy, Djikoneng, screamed.

Turning, frozen for a moment by sheer terror, the old man saw a towering wall of black water racing toward them from the sea, up the slopes at their backs, a black, roaring mountain of water. "Run!" he screamed hoarsely, and flung the boy far ahead of him, forcing his bony old legs to pump like pistons even as he saw the lad scramble to his feet and begin running like the wind for his very life.

The old man ran too, fleeing as fast as his old legs

23

would carry him, trying to outrace certain death as it licked at his heels. But he was too old, too feeble, to outdistance it. The tidal wave, with its dread cargo of small ships, huts, uprooted trees, livestock, and many, many corpses, swept over him, flung him up, hurled him onward, and made him one with it . . .

Djikoneng, silently screaming, his brown eyes round with terror, his hair on end, fled on. A tall palm lay ahead and instinctively he began to climb it, climbing as he had never climbed before, scrambling with bloodied knees and bloodied palms, the image of his poor, fragile grandfather sucked up and swept high by the monster's dripping jaws adding incredible speed and superhuman strength to his climbing. Sobbing now, his lungs afire, he clung to the uppermost fronds of the palm tree and watched and prayed for Allah's deliverance as the wave that had devoured his *kampong,* his family, his friends, the Residency of the Dutch, and the entire region of Anjer swept over him with incredible force—a force that drove all consciousness from him.

When he came to, he was somehow still clinging to the tree. He saw that the water had receded and that—oh, miracle of miracles, praise be to Allah the merciful—he was quite unharmed. Only later was he to learn that he and he alone of his village had survived.

It was Sunday, August 26th, 1883. The volcano mother, Krakatoa, had awakened from her slumber. She had rumbled and smoked and flamed in the terrible final throes of her months-long labor, hurling pumice boulders and ashes for many miles, belching up sulphurous smoke into a sky that glowed red like blood with her flames, and blotting out the sun with her ash and the mud-laden sweat of her unearthly travail.

24

When she was done, her awful labor ended, more than forty villages north of Anjer, Java, were gone, and with them all signs of their habitation. Land formerly under cultivation was now lost beneath the sea as if it had never been, and strange new lands, small islands—the children of Krakatoa—had been born. Portions of coral reefs, torn up by the eruption, were carried miles inland and left there when the waves receded. Thousands of bloating corpses, human and animal, awaited burial in the fierce heat of the tropical sun. Those fortunates who had miraculously survived both fire and flood were pressed into the grisly task as news of the eruption circled the globe. Java, once known as the Garden of the East, was no longer a garden. She had become a charnel house.

But, though capricious Krakatoa had taken the lives of thousands, she had granted a new life to one who had, like Djikoneng, survived her destruction. His name was Joe Christmas.

Chapter Two

Joe groaned and opened one eye. Every part of him ached, throbbed, or smarted. Something wet and sticky that he guessed to be blood had congealed over his left eye, gluing it shut.

Above, the sky was hazy, thickly veiling a sun that had a peculiar greenish hue. Water lapped lazily at his feet and the acrid air came heavy to his nostrils. Neither eased his exhausted body.

He lay very still, unwilling to move lest even the slightest movement should cause the aches thundering through him to become true pain. Instead, he remained motionless, letting the remembrance of what had happened seep back into his consciousness little by little.

Sydney, New South Wales. The name leaped to mind, and with relief he realized that though his body was not, his memory was working just fine, thank you, mate, for he remembered Sydney only too bloody well! Hot on the heels of that, he fancied he could hear Police Sergeant Murphy's voice, as clearly as if even now he whispered in his ear.

Stifling a groan as he attempted to change his cramped position on the wet sand, Joe decided absently that it wasn't all that strange that he should fancy he heard Murphy's voice. After all, it was the same voice he had heard from time to time all the while he had been growing up, on each one of those many occasions he had been hauled down to the police station on some charge or other; it had been a tone filled with regret and edged with stern reproof, and had been coupled with sad blue eyes that had put him in mind of a bloodhound. *Poor old Sarge.* From way back, Joe had known that Sergeant Murphy had had a soft spot for him, and he had played upon it shamelessly, little rogue that he'd been, knowing Murphy would only cuff his ear and send him on his way with a penny or two to soften his gruff words.

But, that last time, the expression in the fatherly sergeant's eyes had turned his blood cold, Joe recalled. The eyes had been bleak as he had glanced up at Joe across the desk, and infinitely weary besides. For the first time in his almost thirty years, Joe had been stunned to realize that Sergeant Murphy had grown old somewhere along the line. The deep furrows that had bracketed his mouth had said so. The generous sprinkling of gray in his black hair, the deep creases in his brow, had confirmed it. For a moment, Joe had felt peculiarly guilty at the part he had undoubtedly played in hastening the aging process in the man he had grown to like and respect.

"You've done it now, Joe, my lad," had come Murphy's melancholy, lilting brogue. "There's not a court in New South Wales will believe ye didn't mean to kill Ned—no, not with your record! Take my advice, lad. If the chance should come up t'get away, take it. Get out of Sydney—get out of the whole bloody country! You've a king-sized chip on yer shoulder, lad, an' I've a notion ye figure the world owes ye somethin' fer yer sorry beginnin's, but, for all that, you've got a quick mind an' a strong back. If you'd only settle down a bit an' stop hatin' the world and everyone in it an' give yerself a chance, you could make somethin' grand o' yerself, I know it. Put yer beginnin's behind ye, an' don't waste what's left of yer life, lad. Don't waste it! We only get the one crack at livin', after all . . ."

Good old Sean Murphy. He'd been a fair dinkum bloke, he had, Joe pondered, Irish mick or no, and had been good to him in his way. Murphy alone had believed in him, had known him well enough to realize that murder wasn't his style, and that Ned's death in that last Bayfront saloon brawl had to have been an accident, pure and simple. Accordingly, Murphy had taken measures to ensure that the "chance" he had mentioned to Joe came up, in the form of a discreetly turned eye and a door "carelessly" left unlocked. Joe had taken the chance for escape without hesitation, knowing Murphy was right. His exploits had been too many, his brawls just too frequent, his card games too notorious. Christ! No jury in Australia would have found him innocent, not with the deck he had had stacked against him! After all, who was he? *A nobody,* that was who, a bloody nameless nobody who had been unloved and unwanted even before the day he was born.

He had been dumped on the steps of a Sydney orphanage on a hot Christmas Eve, wrapped naked and still bloody from birth in a dirty gunnysack without so much as a tag pinned to it to identify him. Accordingly, he had been named, like any stray pup picked up off the streets, by the orphanage woman who had found him. She had likened his fair little head poking up from the sack to that of a baby kangaroo— or "joey," as they were called—peeking out from its mother's pouch, and she had given him the unlikely name of Joe Christmas, Joe for joey, and Christmas on account of the season, for Christ's sake!

He had run away from the orphanage and its Bible-pounding administrators at age eleven and had quickly lost himself amidst the seamier citizens of Sydney who frequented the Bay area. Shortly after, hungry, dirty, alone, and desperately afraid, he had been befriended by the wicked women of a Botany Bay bawdy house and had been raised for the next four years by their madam, "Mother" Polly Mackenzie, who, he reckoned, had come closer to being a real mother to him than the pious ladies of the orphanage had ever proved, and who had been the first person—perhaps the only person—he had ever truly loved, or had loved him in return. Polly Mackenzie had been a true diamond in the rough, but an affectionate woman in her own way, and ambitious for the lad she had befriended and for whom she had felt a fierce, almost maternal, protectiveness. He had been sixteen when Polly had died of a disease so drawn out, so painful and unspeakable, that even her girls would not refer to it. He had decided right there and then that loving someone was too bloody risky. It had made him vulnerable, and he would not risk letting it happen again.

The day after Polly's sorry funeral, he had left Sydney and had set out on his own, turning his hand to whatever work had come his way; he had been both a drifter and a swagman in those rough days, then had found himself jobs at various sheep stations doing the meanest, dirtiest labor, until he had gradually worked his way up to sheepshearer and so on, augmenting his meager wages with his uncanny luck and skill at the poker tables. Some said—though there wasn't an ounce of truth in the tale—that he had also been a bushranger in the bargain, and had ridden with the infamous Kelly Gang. He had always laughed at such wild rumors before, enjoying the notoriety it had given

29

him amongst the girls. But of a sudden, Sergeant Murphy's dire warning had made sense and he had seen his reputation in the unfavorable light in which a judge might see it as he weighed the evidence surrounding Ned's death. He would end up swinging from an oiled noose in the yard of Sydney Gaol for sure this time, he had realized, or else breaking rocks for the remainder of his natural days. Neither had held the slightest appeal for him, and so he had scarpered.

Tough as he had become, his eyes had moistened over later, down by the teeming wharves, when he had fished in the pocket of his moleskin trousers and had found a few pound notes stuffed in his pocket—Sergeant Murphy's parting gift, along with his sound advice, he had known. With the money, he had bought himself a change of clothes, some good, hot tucker, smokes, and a knife, and then he had gone from vessel to vessel in the harbor until he had found a captain who had been none too particular about the men he hired on as deckhands, or their experience at sea, or their eagerness to leave Australia, or much of anything else, for that matter, other than his trusty gin bottle, which had been attached to him as surely as his right hand.

Swarthy as an Arab, short and stocky and with arms of a peculiarly simian length in proportion to his height, Captain Casimir had fixed a bleary, bloodshot eye on him, jabbed a stubby, hairy finger in Joe's direction, and growled thickly, "We go Java; take on spices. You no make trouble, you work hard, I take you on. You give Casimir bad time, then . . . paagh!" He had shrugged and drawn that same stubby finger across his bullish, dirt-seamed throat in a gesture that needed no translation, then had spat over the side.

"Right you are, mate," Joe had agreed solemnly, and that had been that.

The freighter *Neda* had proved as dirty and smelly as

30

her captain, and Joe had wondered at her seaworthiness—or rather, her lack of it. The crew had been little better than the leaky hulk, a motley collection of Malaysians, Caucasians, combinations of the two, and others of indeterminate race and origin. All, however, had been alike in their shifty-eyed demeanor, their air of desperate scrambling to survive, like wharf rats. He had slept, when it had been his turn to sleep, with one eye open and his fist locked firmly around the hilt of his old knife in readiness.

His unrest had abated somewhat when, after several weeks of backbreaking labor stripped to the waist and shoveling coal in the hellhole heat of the boiler room of the *Neda,* they had indeed reached the Spice Islands and taken on cargoes of cinnamon and cloves and pepper. Casimir had grudgingly released his crew for a night's liberty with the snarled order to return by dawn, and the men had swarmed like lemmings to the waterfront saloons and shanties to get drunk and womanize. Joe had left the vessel alone and had shunned both the saloons and the doxies. Brawling and drinking and carousing with the waterfront lovelies had been too much a part of his past. He had wanted more and had been determined to find it. After all, he had mused, Lady Luck *owed* him a break, that tight-fisted, beautiful bitch!

Murphy's words, like burrs under a horse's saddle, had stayed with him, and they had left Joe with a pronounced feeling of guilt. As he had toiled aboard the freighter, he had determined to put his past and his humble beginnings behind him once and for all, as the sergeant had advised, and make something of himself. He was almost thirty years old, and, as Murphy had pointed out, he had a good head on his shoulders. Strewth! What good had that done him? What had he to show for it so far? Little more than a reputation for

31

being sharp with a deck of cards, for being fast on his feet and bloody good with his fists, to which he could only add his skill at shearing other men's sheep, which had become almost legendary in the Outback—where they had dubbed him "Lightnin' Joe"—but which had put money in the station owners' pockets, not his own. And damned little else, that's what! He had had his share of hard times. Enough was enough.

The islands, with their swaying palms and vivid flowers, their smoking volcanic cones, their sunlit coves skirted by turquoise waters rimmed in white surf, their cool, white Dutch buildings, and the indolent grace of the islanders' way of life, had enchanted him and provided him with the much-needed serenity in which to think things through. He had met a pretty young Javanese girl who had worn scarlet hibiscus tucked in her long, dark hair as she sold woven coconut frond hats in a sunlit corner of a market square, and he had relaxed with her and had let himself fall completely under the dreamy spell of the islands while he did so.

Late that night, beneath an absurdly full, golden moon and a star-spangled indigo sky, lying on the warm sand with the slender, velvet-eyed beauty cuddled naked beside him and the scent of blossoms and surf and the fragrance of her musk full and sweet in his nostrils, he had thanked God for Sergeant Murphy yet again, and for the second chance he had given him by letting him escape. Today marked the beginning of a new life, he had promised himself. From here on in, Joe Christmas, foundling, orphanage brat, ne'er-do-well, would finally amount to something, by God, he had sworn, or die in the process!

He had planned then to jump ship when the *Neda* reached India, her next port of call, hopefully with enough money in his pockets to buy passage in steerage on some vessel bound for England. But on further reflection, he had decided against it. What opportunities did the old country have to offer him? Hadn't his ancestors, whoever they were, been laggers in all probability—convicts deported to Australia for their petty crimes? Then why go back there, for Christ's sake, to Mother England, who had washed her hands of him and his kind in the past? Now, America, *there* was the place! Aye, there was a brash, young land that had cut herself adrift from the old ties of England, a land where dreams could still come true and opportunities for wealth and success were still within the grasp of all who were determined and willing enough to work hard for themselves, whatever their origins. That's where he would go—America!

And so the dream had been born, only to become a nightmare less than a month later when the sleeping she-monster, Krakatoa, had awakened.

On August 26th, 1883, her volcanic labor pangs of past months had culminated in a full-blown eruption that had stirred the seas and ruptured the earth's crust, her violent thrashings whipping up great walls of water that could travel for thousands of miles and bring death and destruction to countless innocents in far-flung corners of the globe. One of these had indiscriminately flung Joe Christmas, fugitive, onto what appeared to be a deserted atoll, God knew where.

His thoughts now drifted back to the day the nightmare had begun, so recent yet so peculiarly removed, the memory of it ebbing and flowing like the warm water that lapped at his feet.

The sky had darkened suddenly, although dawn had hardly broken. A muddy rain had begun to fall upon the decks of the *Neda,* and the weight of it had soon threatened to sink the tiny vessel. St. Elmo's fire had licked with eerie, flickering greenish tongues about the masts and spars. The superstitious Malaysian hands had begun praying fervently to their god for deliverance from the "demons" attacking the dirty little vessel, even as they swabbed the decks in a frantic effort to rid them of mud. Casimir, wild eyed and crazed with panic and drink, predictably had sought escape in his bottle, a disgusting, an incompetent coward in a sweat-stained undervest and grimy drawers. He had finally fallen unconscious in one corner of the deck, leaving the first mate in charge, if such as he could be called in charge, for the man was little more competent than his captain.

And then, *it* had come, seemingly out of nowhere—a towering wall of water rearing fifty feet high above the surface of the ocean, swiftly bearing down upon their pitifully tiny ship and the nearby, unsuspecting string of islands they had just left as if it had been some great sea serpent from days of old. There had been hoarse, hopeless screams from the crew then, terror-filled shrieks as the water all about the vessel began to rise and roil, tossing the *Neda* up and down like a cork and catapulting the bodies of men left and right. In the final seconds before impact, Joe had heard his own voice and that of another man shouting hoarsely, urging the mate to steer the ship into the very center of that wall of water—*"For God's sake, straight into it, man; it's the only possible way!"*—but the first mate had refused, babbling to the fear-frozen hands to bring the ship around, out of its path.

Everything had happened so quickly after that. Chaos, utter chaos! The tidal wave, the *tsunami,* had lifted the *Neda* and had flung her over with the mindless fury of an enraged dragon mauling a small, helpless animal in its massive jaws. There had been water—rushing water everywhere—grinding sounds, and shrill cries suddenly and abruptly silenced.

He'd surfaced and found himself clinging grimly to a piece of fractured timber, blood blinding his eyes, a gash above one stinging like blazes from the salt water. Wreckage had littered the foaming swells, as had bodies. A few feet away, he'd seen another man fighting vainly for his life and had managed somehow—he was never to recall exactly how afterward, so confused were his memories—to paddle his way toward him and make a grab for the man's hair just as he began sinking under again, holding him with one arm locked under his armpits until his own arm had gone numb. He'd drifted in and out of consciousness after that, while somehow—a subconscious urge to survive, he supposed—he had maintained his grip upon the piece of the *Neda*'s wreckage.

He had come to again with no idea of time, for the sky had grown darker and the foul, muddy, ash-filled rain still teemed down, and found they were aimlessly drifting, drifting. He had not been able to feel his left arm; the fingers had long since gone numb. But, by some miracle, the man he had saved had still been there. Joe had recognized him then as the fellow they had taken aboard as a passenger back in Anjer, a nice enough bloke about his own age, well dressed but without any fancy airs about him. Though it had also struck him that the fellow seemed an unlikely passenger for the leaky freighter *Neda,* he had quickly discarded such trains of thought as none of his business and had set his mind on the enormous task ahead of him. The man had been hurt badly, Joe had observed. His face was gray, his body limp and a dead weight in his arm. It would be hell to keep his head above water, and the pinkish stain of blood their drifting passage left behind them had made Joe worry about the sharks it might attract.

"Hang in there, cobber!" he had muttered to the unconscious man. "The Lord Almighty didn't intend for us to survive a tidal wave just to become tucker for some great white bastard!"

And so they had drifted on and on and on. The man had come to from time to time, groaning and mumbling a bit before sinking back down into sleep. Joe had known a loneliness in those moments that surpassed even the vast loneliness of the Outback. At least then he had had his blue-heeler, Jimbo, and his horse for companionship, good tucker in his saddle-bag, and smokes in his pocket. Here there was nothing but bloody salt water and rafts of floating pumice—lava flung off from the volcano's eruption and cooled into solid, buoyant masses by the ocean. Some of them were big enough to hold a man, even two, he had realized, hope flaring up like a candle flame inside him, and as soon as the idea had been born, he had determined to put it into action. God knew, it hadn't been easy! Hours had gone by before he had spied another pumice fragment big enough for his purpose, and then still more hours as he paddled futilely after it, alternately weeping and cursing as it drifted on, always just out of reach of his grasping fingers.

And then, at last, he had done it! A large wave had lifted them up and carried them close enough, and he had managed to hook his fingers over the edge and maintain a tenuous, bleeding grip on the crusty pumice. He had had to let go of the injured man to board it, and the effort it had exacted of his exhausted body had almost persuaded him to forget the man, to let him go without a backward glance, once he had lain sprawled and sobbing across it, self-preservation uppermost in his mind—almost.

"Oh, Christ, oh, bloody, bloody hell, I can't leave you, you poor bastard!" he had gasped, and had edged himself over the side of the raft, clawing for the splintered timber even as the unconscious man slipped from it, his arms, which Joe had hooked over the spar, falling free, and his legs dangling limply and shifting like seaweed with the slopping tide.

He had managed to get a grip on the fellow's jacket and, for some time, endless time, had had no strength to do more than simply maintain his grip, letting the pumice raft carry him onward with the man towed behind it. After he had rested some, he had slipped over the side into the choppy water and had shoved and tugged until the injured man had been half on the raft and half off it. During the next hours—day or night, he knew not—he had been able to heave the fellow up to lie beside him. But he was so still and unmoving that Joe, exhausted, crazed with thirst and exposure by now, had wept, believing his frantic labors had all been for nothing. And then, the man had come to, and he had wept again, but this time with joy to find him alive. Just barely, it was true, but alive nonetheless!

He had lost track of the number of days they must have drifted on the makeshift raft, tossed by the capricious waters of the Indian Ocean, the man moaning and screaming from time to time. Joe had comforted him with words, useless words, for there had been nothing else he could do for him. He had managed to bind his mangled thigh crudely with strips torn from his own shirt, but the man had other injuries, he had realized, injuries inside and unseen that he could do nothing about.

And then, through the hazy daylight, he had spied a low, hilly shape against the horizon.

"Land!" he had croaked through blistered, cracked lips, and in his excitement had foolishly shaken the injured man's shoulder, urging him to look, too. Was it a mirage he was seeing, like out in the desert, or truly a low-lying body of land? He had blinked, but the shimmering image had persisted, growing larger and larger as the tide had carried them inward toward a small, white-sanded cove, beyond which the ragged teeth of the reef, littered with dead fish and other debris, jutted above the water. His exultant whoop of joy had been abruptly silenced as the pumice raft, lifted high by the offshore swells, had rammed the first rock, hurtling them both from it and into the water.

Darkness had followed, lasting an indeterminate length of time, a darkness such as Joe imagined death must be like, endless and infinitely painless, until now . . .

The darkness was gone. Pain was again a reality. It thundered in his left arm, howled in his left temple. Memory had returned, too, and with it, the awareness that he was alive; that against all odds, he had survived!

Tears leaked from under the scab of dried blood above his eyes. Christ Almighty, he was *alive!* And as he had survived, so would his dream survive—he swore it.

It was an hour or two before he had enough strength to try standing. When he did, he marveled momentarily at the small island's ability to tilt and lurch, before realizing that it was not the island that moved but his own dizziness that caused it to seem so. He had to move, had to get further up the beach. The tide was coming in, and water filled with debris rose up to his knees. There were dead fish everywhere, he saw, littering the sand; coconut fronds, large pieces of wood and, oh *Christ,* bodies, too—at least half a dozen of them! He turned away and retched into the water, but nothing came up. His belly was empty of everything but brine, and the squeezing convulsions only served to make him feel like death warmed over. Nevertheless, when the wave of nausea had passed, he forced himself to stagger to each bloated, battered body in turn and check to make sure they were really dead. Poor sods!

38

They hadn't stood a chance from the looks of it, he thought, turning away from them and gazing up the beach to the rim of coconut palms that fringed it.

His eyes narrowed. A great twist centered in his gut and wrenched hard at his vitals. There was yet another body up there, a still, pitiful pile of wet rags that he recognized as the young fellow he had tried to save. Christ! It had all been for nothing after all, then. But as he stared dully in that direction, a pale hand moved feebly. At once Joe was off and running, stumbling and tripping over the wet sand toward him, the need for human contact of some kind, *any* kind, in the aftermath of the disaster even stronger than his exhaustion. He dropped to his knees beside the man and saw that his eyes were open, cornflower blue eyes made dull with pain.

"G'day, cobber," he said eagerly and with a foolishly broad, crooked grin. "Welcome back to the land of the living!"

The man smiled weakly, his eyes fluttering closed momentarily before he opened them again. "Living? I'm . . . I'm not so sure, friend," he whispered through cracked lips. "But . . . thanks anyway. You . . . you saved me." His long, slim fingers clawed the air, seeking, Joe knew instinctively, his own rough hand, wanting to clasp it in gratitude.

Joe gripped that pathetic pale hand and squeezed it, the pressure only faintly returned but real nonetheless. "No thanks needed, cobber. Christ! I'm just bloody glad you made it!"

"Me too," the man agreed, managing another weak grin. "Thought . . . thought we'd end up as shark bait."

"You're right there," Joe agreed grimly. "Here, then, let's have a look at you."

With as much gentleness as his massive, callused hands could muster, Joe inspected the man's thigh. It

39

was one hell of a wound, deep and ragged, but the salt water had kept it clean and he'd seen far worse out in the bush. There was a good chance he might have survived it, though maybe with a permanent limp, had that been his only injury. But it wasn't. That thought sobered Joe and effectively wiped the ready grin from his lips. Aye, it was his probable internal injuries that concerned him. Even now, a small trickle of bright red blood was seeping from the corner of the man's mouth.

"Name?" the man croaked suddenly, drawing Joe's concerns back to the present.

"Joe Christmas. Pleased to meet you . . . ?"

"Joel. Joel McCaleb."

Joe rocked back on his heels and ran a hand through his damp, dusty-blond hair, his turquoise eyes now bright again with a suspicion of laughter in their depths. "Joe and Joel, is it, then? Christ, cobber, Someone up there"—he rolled his eyes heavenward—"must have a soft spot for the 'Joes' of this world, wouldn't you say?"

One corner of the man's mouth quirked up. "Amen to that," he murmured faintly, and winced. "But my friends call . . . call me . . . Mac. You . . . call . . . me . . . Mac." With a faint sigh, he drifted off into unconsciousness yet again.

"Mac it is, then, cobber," Joe echoed softly, and felt a lump swell in his throat that he hadn't felt since tears had threatened in his boyhood.

Mac drifted in and out of unconsciousness several times that day. Joe took the opportunity to gather driftwood, no easy task since he had discovered belatedly that his left arm was dangling uselessly and at an odd angle that indicated it was broken. It was nothing short of a miracle that he had been able to use it at all, much less keep Mac afloat for God knew how many hours! Still, he had seen as much before; seen men with broken limbs crawl and hobble across endless stretches of desert when their horses went down, or burned men battling bush fires, not realizing they had been badly burned until after the crisis had passed and they had passed out in sudden agony. Something of a similar nature must have happened to him, he decided, giving him the superhuman strength to do what had to be done. He would have liked to have dragged the bodies up the beach, dug out some shallow graves in the sand, and given the poor blighters a semblance of a decent burial, but that would be out of the question, under the circumstances, and so he set about exploring the coconut grove for anything he and Mac could use.

A straight branch served well enough as a splint for his injured arm, clumsily bound in place one-handed with strips torn from his shirt, but the dull, nagging throb in it refused to lessen. He looked at the heap of driftwood he had collected in hopes of starting a fire, and wondered how in the hell he was to do so, with only one good arm and no matches. His belly growled loudly with hunger, and the dead fish looked more and more appealing as the day wore on, but his stomach heaved at the idea of eating them raw. "You can't be that hungry, old son," he told himself, "else you'd swallow it down, guts an' all, without a qualm!"

As the hazy afternoon faded, the most glorious sunset he'd ever seen in his life, of purple, crimson, rose, and flame, blazed across the horizon and stained the ocean the eerie blood red of the sun. The air grew colder with approaching nightfall as breezes began whispering amongst the ragged palm fronds. Joe peeled off his shirt, long since dried now, and tucked it about Mac, wishing he had a warm blanket for the poor bastard, not to mention a slug of whiskey for them both. He looked dismally at the heaped drift-wood, then back to Mac.

"Sorry, mate, no fire t'night. This here's the best I can do, what with this busted arm and all."

To his surprise, Mac answered him. His voice was weaker now, but by straining his ears, Joe managed to make out the words.

"Matches . . . inside . . ." He jerked his fingers toward his jacket.

"Matches?" Joe leaned over him, slipping his hand inside the inner pocket and withdrawing a bulky, waterproof oilskin pouch from its silk-lined depths. As Mac had promised, there were two boxes of wooden matches inside, a little pouch of tobacco, a sheaf of thin rolling papers, and some folded documents, all miraculously dry as bone. "God Almighty, smokes! You're a bloody marvel, Mac! Mind if I roll myself one?"

"Not . . . not if you share it, Joe," Mac quipped. "God knows, I could . . . could do with a smoke myself!"

"You've got it," Joe promised. He used a match to light the fire first, and it was not long before the heap of driftwood was crackling merrily, orange flames writhing up, orange sparks showering down against the backdrop of the dark-emerald night that ringed them all about. The heat the fire gave off was minimal, but the cheery comfort of its ruddy glow was a balm to Joe's low spirits. A billy of hot water to brew them each a steaming dish of tea would have been just the ticket, he reflected wistfully, but a smoke was almost as good. He carefully shook a little of the tobacco evenly onto the thin paper, licked the gummed edge, and rolled the smoke into a neatly packed tube. He lit it from the fire, unwilling to waste any of the precious matches, and drew a long drag on it, letting the smoke stream slowly from his nostrils before passing the cigarette to Mac and holding it steady between his lips for him to draw on.

"Thanks," Mac murmured gratefully after several long drags, and a shudder ran through him. "Jesus, Joe, I'm so damned cold!"

Joe hesitated only a moment before taking Mac by the shoulders and, with every attempt at gentleness, dragging him closer to the fire. He knew it was dangerous to move someone with internal injuries, but there was something about Mac's ashen color, something dwindling in his eyes, that hinted that whatever he did now would make no difference to the final outcome. At least poor Mac would have a bit of comfort.

"Better?"

"Yeah. Feels good," Mac managed with a grateful smile that faded into a wince of pure agony, which he tried in vain to conceal from Joe.

"Try to get some shut-eye now," Joe suggested, pretending he hadn't seen the grimace, but moved by it nevertheless. "Come daybreak, I'll see if I can't find some fresh water for you, maybe some fish. All the necessaries for a bonzer breakfast! How'd that do you?"

"Sounds good," Mac agreed faintly. "You've . . . been . . . been a good friend, Joe, a real good 'c . . . cobber'—that the right word?"

"Best there is, mate," Joe agreed, cursing the lump that was back again, choking his throat.

"Wish . . . wish I could make it . . . make it up to you."

"Cut it out, Mac. That's what cobbers are for, right? Don't worry about it. Just get some sleep, there's a good bloke. Someday we'll be shouting up a pint in some saloon and laughing our heads off at all this."

Almost an hour passed, Joe guessed. From the silence that had followed his urgings, he thought Mac had fallen asleep as he had suggested. He gazed into the flames or alternately watched the lapping ocean as it curled up the sandy beach, rimmed with white foam stained a peculiar greenish hue by a greenish moon, like something from another world. Where in the hell were they, he wondered? Would there be ships in these waters, looking for survivors and assessing the damage done by the volcano's eruption? Aye, surely there would! Such a disaster could scarcely go unnoticed by the rest of the world. Hundreds must have been killed, left homeless. Yes, he was certain there would be ships, ships with doctors aboard them. Perhaps . . . perhaps if one came soon enough, Mac might have a chance! He decided right there and then to go looking for more driftwood in the morning, and to build the biggest bloody signal fire—

"It's no use, Joe. I can't sleep," came Mac's feeble voice from the darkness. "My gut—it hurts real bad." There was a pause. "Are . . . are you there, Joe?"

"Right here, cobber. Wish to God there was something I could do for you, Mac."

"There is. Talk to me, Joe! Tell me . . . tell me about . . . yourself . . . what you were doing aboard the *Neda*. Just . . . talk. I reckon . . . reckon I could forget about the pain some, if . . . if we talked for a bit."

Joe grinned in the moonlight and firelight. "Then you've got the right man for it, Mac! My Aunt Polly used to say I could talk the hind legs off a donkey, she did!"

And so, in the darkness, Joe's deep voice reached out to comfort the injured man, wrapping his body in the warmth of human contact, his lively tale—told in the rouch vernacular of his native Australia—dulling the pain of Mac's wounds.

He told Mac of his beginnings at the Sydney Foundling Home, and of running away and finding a

44

home—and a unique education!—with the bawds of his "aunt" Polly's bordello; of Polly's death, and of his drifting from sheep station to sheep station; of his wild forays back to Sydney after shearing season with his pockets full of pound notes, and of the gambling, the brawling and drinking in the saloons that had sent him back there, into the Outback, when the money finally and inevitably ran out.

He told him of nights in the Outback when the ivory pallor of the ghost gums gleamed through the darkness, with only his Aborigine companion, Wurarbuti, and his dog and horse for company; of the raucous laughter of the kookaburras and the overpowering scent of the eucalyptus trees that seemed weighed down with blue and green flowers, which would, at a single gunshot, erupt into flight and prove not blossoms at all, but colorful flocks of small parrots or budgerigars; of the seas of golden wattle, yellow as butter in the sunshine. In his hunger, he spoke longingly of camp tucker, of damper bread and jam, kangaroo stew, and roasted galah.

And finally, when there was nothing else left to tell, he told him of that last brawl in Sydney, fought over a pretty little tart named Nancy who had had a roving eye and a low-cut red silk dress, and of how, spoiling for a fight, he had fought Ned Sullivan for her dubious favors, only for it to end with Ned—that poor, unlucky bastard—falling backward, cracking his skull wide open against the corner of the horse trough outside the saloon, and having the bad sense to die of his injuries. He talked of Sergeant Murphy, too, and the Irishman's words of advice, and his decision to take it and get out of Australia and start afresh somewhere else.

"And that's about it, cobber; Joe Christmas's entire bloody life story in a nutshell!" he ended, his turquoise eyes catching the firelight and glinting with a wry merriment that belied his disparaging words. "Not much of a tale, is it? But then, I've turned over a new leaf. From here on in, I mean to make something of myself."

"And you will," Mac murmured. "You're a good . . . good fellow at heart, Joe. I can tell. Like . . . like to help you."

"Come on, Mac, don't, there's a good mate! Don't waste your breath—or your strength—on worrying about me."

"Have . . . have to. Not much time . . . time left. No, Joe, you don't need . . . need to lie to me! If anything . . . happens . . . t'me, there's a letter in . . . in the pouch. Use it, pal! Who's to know? Never . . . never met my grandfather McCaleb. None the wiser. Promise me, Joe, prom . . . promise me!"

"Promise you what, Mac?"

"That . . . that you'll . . . *be* me! Say it, Joe! Maybe . . . maybe I can repay you after all . . . for what you did—trying to save my life. Help you get a start in America. Give me . . . your word!"

He wasn't making sense, Joe realized, and his anxiety, his impassioned speech, had started him coughing. Even in the flickering shadows, Joe saw the further telltale dark trickle that escaped the corner of his mouth, an insidious shadow against the waxy, pale blur of his face. He reached out and squeezed Mac's shoulder. "Hey there, calm down a bit, Mac," he urged gently. "If it's my word you want, you've got it."

Reassured, Mac nodded faintly. His eyes closed.

Joe rolled and lit himself another smoke, shaken by Mac's outburst. When the cigarette was no more than a stub, he tossed it aside and lay down beside Mac, his back turned to the wind, his body forming a living windbreak to shield him, and soon fell into an exhausted sleep himself.

When he awoke at dawn, Mac lay exactly as Joe had left him, unmoving. He touched his waxy cheek and recoiled at the coolness of it. So, that was it. The fight was over. Despite his best efforts, Mac was gone. Joe wept over his still body as he had not wept since they had lowered his aunt Polly into the ground, cursing a God who allowed good men to die while the bad seed flourished. In the course of a few hours, Mac had become friend and brother both, and an overwhelming sense of anger and bitterness, of futility and loneliness and grief, pressed in upon him, too painful to bear.

At length, some sixth sense alerted him to the fact that he was no longer alone. His eyes still misted over with tears, he looked up. Through the haze, he saw a group of natives watching him solemnly and without expression on their brown faces. From behind them came a tall, bearded white man, who strode across the beach with his arm outstretched in greeting.

"Welcome, young fellow!" the man cried eagerly, his accent unmistakably British. "You have the dubious honor of being the sole survivor to reach our fair island unscathed!"

Still fuddled with grief, Joe nodded miserably. "Thanks, mate. But where in the hell am I?" he asked, rising slowly to a standing position.

"Where? Why, this is Christmas Island, my young friend!"

To the Englishman's surprise, the ragged blond fellow began to laugh, holding his sides helplessly until tears rolled down his face. Exposure, possible head injuries, lack of fresh water, perhaps, the man decided professionally, frowning. One or all of them must have caused the poor lad's hysteria.

"I say, steady on; there's a good chap," the old man urged kindly, hurrying toward him.

But Joe, still laughing, waved him away. "Oh,

Christ! Oh, Christ! *Christmas* Island—d'ye hear that, Mac, my old cobber? We're on bloody Christmas Island! The irony of it."

With a grave shaking of his snowy head, the old man gestured to two of the islanders and bade them lead Joe away. He glanced down at the man sprawled lifelessly on the sand and shook his head in pity. Poor young fellow! Yet another to add to the toll of thirty thousand, whose lives had been taken by the eruption of Krakatoa.

He was about to leave when he noticed an oilskin pouch, which he assumed must have dropped unnoticed from the other young man's pockets as he had stood up. He withdrew the contents and quickly scanned the letter inside, which was addressed to one Joel McCaleb and bore a Javan address, before tucking the package into his shirt for safekeeping. Turning to the native headman who hovered at his elbow, he ordered, "See about having that other poor fellow buried, Sing. I'll read a few words over him later. And have Mister McCaleb taken to my hut. The women can prepare him a little food, if they will. Something light and nourishing. Clear broth would be good to start with." So saying, Doctor Hopworth started up the beach toward the coconut grove.

"Very good, Doctah," the native agreed and started toward Mac's body. He knelt at the man's side and made to turn him over on the sand. "Doctah! Come!" Sing cried suddenly, and the white man turned in his tracks and hurried back toward him.

Meanwhile, Joe allowed the natives to lead him to their village like one in a deep trance, or a wooden puppet with no control over its actions. So it would be henceforth. The same hand of fate that had taken so many lives now held the strings to Joe's life. As they were jerked, so would he dance.

48

Chapter Three

It was a dreary, damply chilly Thursday morning in December when Joe disembarked from the *Southern Star,* a vessel of the P. & O. Line, and entered the port of San Francisco, a city he could only dimly discern as hilly in the extreme through the shrouds of damp and clinging fog. His newly "replaced" papers of identification stamped and a warm, if erroneous, welcome "back" to America offered him by the beaming Customs' House official, he bade the ship's captain a hearty farewell and made his way toward the throng of greeters and farewell-wishers of quayside. Steamer Day was as great a day of celebration here as it had proven in the Sandwich Isles, he observed en route, for one and all seemed to have turned out to meet the newly docked vessels.

Joe wove his way through the crowds and thence out onto the wharves proper, where hackney coaches for hire waited amongst the warehouses in a drizzling rain and "runners" from numerous hotels defied the miserable weather to announce the various attributes of their employers' lodging in strident and booming cries.

"Russ 'ouse! Russ 'ouse! Best there is!"

"Occidental Hotel! Occidental, folks—finest in the city!"

"The Lick, can't be beat! Ain't none finer! Lick House, sirs, ladies, Lick House!"

Joe ignored the runners and made his way to the row of hacks, beckoning to the lad he had paid to trundle his steamer trunk on a handcart from the docks to follow him.

"I'm looking for a respectable place to stay for a few days," he told the driver of one likely looking conveyance. "Nothing fancy, but clean, mind you."

"I know just the place, sir," the cabby declared eagerly, clambering down to see the steamer trunk hefted safely into his conveyance, which boasted a fine pair of well-groomed Friesian horses. "Mrs. Barker on Sacramento Street runs a nice little lodging house. Her prices are reasonable and her beds clean. She serves a hot breakfast for them that wants it, too."

"Sounds just the ticket, driver," Joe agreed. "Take the long route to the lodging house, will you? I've a mind to see something of the city before I settle in." Tossing his remaining single piece of baggage inside, he swung himself up into the cab.

Scant seconds later, they were swaying along at a brisk pace, and Joe was looking with keen interest through the hack window at everything they passed. He was here at last, in America, the land of dreams! On occasion over the past months, he'd had to pinch himself to prove he wasn't dreaming. Rereading the letter Mac McCaleb had "bequeathed" to him, however, was usually sufficient to prove he wasn't.

For perhaps the hundredth time, he unbuttoned his tweed overcoat and withdrew the oilskin pouch from the inside pocket of his smartly tailored, silk-lined gray suit, tipped back the broad brim of his black velour hat, and, in the gloomy light of the coach, read it again. The top right-hand corner bore an address that had grown familiar over the weeks, that of Messrs. Silverstein and Caldwell, Montgomery Street, San Francisco, who advertised themselves as partners-at-law. In the left-hand corner was the name Joel McCaleb, *his* name now, and the address given was simply: c/o the Dutch Residency, Anjer, Java. It was dated August 11th, 1883, and the body of the letter contained the following:

Dear Mr. McCaleb,

It is with our deepest regrets and sympathy for your loss that we advise you of the death of your paternal grandfather, William Angus McCaleb, late of this town, who passed away peacefully in his sleep at his residence at the age of seventy-five years after a brief illness.

We are aware that prior to his own death, your father and Mister McCaleb had been estranged, but in his declining years, your grandfather apparently softened his opposition regarding the marriage of your parents and expressed a great desire to meet with you, his only surviving relative and grandson—a desire that his sudden ill health and subsequent death unfortunately denied him. He did, however, dictate a new will and testament, duly witnessed by us, his legal counselors, prior to his demise, in which you are named the major beneficiary of his estate, subsequent to certain conditions that will be explained to you at a later date if you should decide to claim this inheritance.

Mister McCaleb instructed us to enclose a generous bank draft with this missive in the event of his death, to ensure that you are afforded the funds to journey to San Francisco in person for the reading of the will.

We would greatly appreciate a telegraphed reply from you, advising us of your intent in this matter. Meanwhile, we remain your obedient servants, etc.

It was signed by Edward Caldwell. There was a second, briefer letter from the same law firm, obviously in response to a telegraph duly sent by Mac before he left Java, in which Messrs. Silverstein and Caldwell expressed their pleasure at his decision and instructed him to present himself at their offices upon his arrival in San Francisco. It also contained the name of an associate of theirs in Honolulu, The Sandwich Isles, who, they were assured, would make himself available to offer any assistance Joel McCaleb might require. There had also been a very generous bank draft, an advance that Joe had been forced to cash on his arrival in the Sandwich Isles, both to clothe and feed himself there, and to pay for his passage aboard the *Southern Star*.

His penniless state had not seemed unusual under the circumstances of his horrendous experience, which, he had quite truthfully explained, had left him without baggage or indeed any personal effects whatsoever, other than the clothes he stood up in. Accordingly, Mister Jedediah Bishop, Silverstein and Caldwell's Honolulu associate, had been most understanding and sympathetic, and had used every means at his disposal to see him comfortably lodged at the Royal Hawaiian Hotel and suitably outfitted by the finest Chinese tailors the islands could offer.

Any qualms that Joe had harbored regarding his switch of identities were by now thoroughly dispelled. Lapses in his memory since his shocking experience were to be anticipated, kindly old Doctor Hopworth on Christmas Island had helpfully—if unwittingly—advised, and Joe had determined there and then to fall back on this convenient story should his recollections of his "parents" and his former life on Java prove vague. Mac, in those last words they had exchanged prior to his death, had urged him to "be" him, and become Joel McCaleb he would!

San Francisco appeared to be a thriving, boisterous city. Horse-drawn vehicles, their black canopies pulled up against the weather, labored up and down the alarmingly steep, muddy dirt streets, few of which boasted plank boardwalks. Numerous pedestrians in warm coats and with black umbrellas raised against the rain strained up and down the few narrow wooden boardwalks there were, spared the muddy quagmire churned up by the wheels of wagons and horsecars and carriages of varying kinds, while still others rode inside or clung to the rear of clanging cable cars, a peculiar, ultramodern innovation that quite fascinated Joe, who had never before seen their like. He determined at once to ride one as soon as possible, then drew his head back inside the hack.

The driver, Joe suspected, had purposely chosen the most circuitous route both to his destination and about the city in hopes of an even fatter fare, yet Joe chose to ignore this and take the opportunity to see something of the city about which he had thought so much during the past two months he had spent recuperating from his ordeal amidst numerous others on tiny Christmas Island.

All manner of buildings lined the streets they traveled, streets named Kearny, Market, California, Sacramento, and, yes, there was Montgomery Street, where the lawyers with whom he was to meet kept their business offices. Storefronts of every kind as well as churches and restaurants, offices, comfortable resi-

53

dences, and what seemed to Joe an inordinate number of saloons, gambling halls, and dance palaces in proportion to the size of the city huddled in orderly fashion alongside street after street. The architecture, running the gamut from shack to Gothic and every imaginable variation in between, was as diverse as the inhabitants, the gilt and marble plush facades of offices and stores rubbing shoulders with the seamy and the ramshackle planks of one-bit hash houses. There were stockbrokers' and bankers' places of business, assayers' offices, pastel-plastered ice-cream parlors and candy stores, undertakers and restaurants, hotels and grills—more buildings than Joe had ever seen before, and of a variety that dazzled him. Christ, more than that, they *amazed* him, he realized, for he had never imagined to find San Francisco so extraordinarily civilized or so highly populated.

His eyes widened once again as they briskly moved off Dupont Street, around yet another corner, and under a half-moon-shaped gateway. It was as if they had stepped clean into another world, the world of China, of Peking and all the mysteries of the distant Orient!

The buildings here were, perhaps, far shabbier than those they had passed previously, many of them little better than tenements, yet this fault was offset by their colorfulness and the unusual facades they presented. Painted paper lanterns bobbed in the damp breeze, defying the gloom. On many of the clapboard storefronts, writhing dragons of brilliant crimson and gold bared gleaming fangs. Gaudy scarlet pennants fluttered from the eaves bearing bold, sweeping calligraphy in black that announced the store-owners' trades, Joe guessed, though he was unable to read the mysterious Oriental characters. Other, many-storied buildings boasted curling rooftops with gilded eaves,

54

pagodalike in appearance. From some of these, slender Oriental maidens leaned out precariously and, with painted lips and powdered faces, called with singsong enticements to the men in the streets below to come up and join them. On the boardwalks, vendors in conical bamboo hats padded along bearing shallow baskets of silver fish, the baskets suspended from bamboo poles slung over their shoulders. Others sat cross-legged upon stools tending their wares: mysterious herbs and potions, or baskets of fresh brown shrimp from the bay, oysters, heaps of vegetables and fruits of every variety, which seemed to grow here without regard for the seasons. These were being picked over by shrewd Chinese matrons in dark blue trousers and blouses that, to Joe's amused eyes, resembled pajamas more than anything else. On closer inspection, he saw that the collarless pajamalike outfits were worn uniformly by all of the pedestrians hereabout, whether male or female, and were all of the same drab, dark blue color. The men, for the most part, sported western-style derbies—an incongruous accessory—above their long black pigtails, or queues, which were braided with cherry red silk. Many of them puffed on fat cigars.

As they passed, the hack in which Joe was riding barreled through a gigantic mud puddle. At precisely the same moment, an elderly, bearded Chinaman, obviously of some importance, for, unlike everyone else, he wore a fancy lavender blouse with purple froggings and black pantaloons of puffed silk, was making his way down the street. He was followed at a discreet distance by two young women, robed in brilliant silk *cheongsams* embroidered with flowers. They wore silk flowers in their glossy black hair and gossiped behind painted fans as they teetered along on tiny feet, chivied to increase their pace by another, fiercely scowling Chinaman bringing up the rear.

Their charming if gaudy appearance did much to brighten the gloom of the rainy day, and Joe grinned appreciatively and ogled them through the hack window as the girls squealed and giggled on seeing the mud thrown up from the coach splatter the inscrutable old man. The soaking caused him to shake his fist after the coach and its occupant, and to curse them in voluble Chinese, much to Joe's amusement.

The smell of cooking clung in the damp air, an exciting, exotic aroma of foods Joe was certain he'd never tasted before, and one that served to remind him that he was hungry to boot. Clearing Customs and riding the ferry across the bay to the city had taken an eternity, and he hadn't eaten since breakfast. Deciding to dine before he arrived at this Mrs. Barker's establishment, he rapped upon the hack wall. The driver leaned down from his perch and slid aside the partition, craning his head to peer inside.

"Sir?"

"I've decided to grab a bite to eat, driver. Set me down at the next restaurant, will you?"

"Here, sir? But . . . this here's Chinatown! There ain't nothin' but them stinking Celestial restaurants in these here parts. If you'll just hold yer horses a few more minutes, there's a fine white restaurant a ways down, with beefsteaks an' pies an' potatoes an' all. If yer don't mind my saying, sir—"

"But I do mind, mate, since I'm paying your bloody fare," Joe corrected the man mildly. "The next restaurant, if you please."

The driver shrugged and flicked his whip over his horses' rumps, silently brooding, Furrenners was all strange. It was a waste of time trying to figger any of 'em—he should know that by now, yessir! He'd find out soon enough that frequentin' Chinee town didn't do a man no good!

The cab rumbled on a moment or two longer, then came to a creaking halt. Joe ducked his head and looked out. Sure enough, there was a restaurant alongside, with tall columns on either side of the doorway sporting the ubiquitous dragons. Within, he glimpsed several tables spread with snowy cloths. A tempting if unidentiable aroma wafted from the open doorway.

"This do yer?" the driver demanded sourly.

"Just the ticket, mate," Joe agreed with a grin, his mouth watering, and clambered down. He glanced up at the driver, who glowered back, obviously reluctant to linger overlong in this area. "Wait for me, and I'll double your fare."

The man gulped, but greed won out over prejudice just as easily now as it had in the bygone days of the Gold Rush, and at length he nodded. "Yessir."

Joe was about to enter the restaurant's doorway, a low portal for one possessed of his tall, rangy build, when someone came careening around the corner and slammed full force into him, narrowly avoiding hurling him to the mud of the street. Angrily, he looked up into the almond-shaped dark eyes of a Chinese youth who was breathing heavily and very obviously frightened. His anger subsided.

"Steady on, mate! Where's the fire?" he chided good-naturedly.

The slender youth, who could have been no more than seventeen, scarcely gave him a second glance. He darted a hurried look over his shoulder before he flung himself past Joe and across the muddy street, a blur of navy blue trailing a long, black queue. All at once, two other Oriental men, older and burlier by far than the slight lad, stormed around the same corner in hot pursuit, pigtails also flying out behind them. They rapidly overtook the boy. One brought him down in the mire, wiry arms wound about him, but the boy writhed free and managed to regain his footing. With a sharp yell, he leapt into the air and slammed both soles of his feet hard against the chest of one of his attackers, who went down with an explosive "Aaggff!" of pain and fury, losing his black derby. At once the lad whirled about and, with his fingers held ramrod stiff, he chopped the other fellow full in the throat even as he barreled into him.

Joe watched, riveted by the Chinese boy's unusual method of brawling, for though a former brawler himself—and one of no little expertise in such matters—he'd seen nothing like this before! Grinning broadly, he shoved back his heavy coat fronts and hooked his thumbs in his belt, looking on admiringly as the boy struck blow after blow. Each one was accompanied by some of the best, nimblest footwork Joe had ever witnessed, and by a short, enraged yell each time that added force and direction to every chopping blow as he struck out. It appeared very likely the scrawny boy would win despite the odds against him, Joe decided. The older men were bungling fools!

His grin was destined to fade, however, for now a third man, easily near six feet in height, arrived on the scene, wielding a short but stout black billy club. With little ado he, too, set upon the boy, who was now outnumbered three to one. The newcomer succeeded in bringing his cudgel up hard, full into the lad's face. There was a sharp crack. Blood sprayed from the lad's nose, and, simultaneously, Joe erupted, enraged now by the rank unfairness of the fight and quite forgetting the vow he'd made to himself.

The three attackers gaped upon hearing Joe's unexpected roar of outrage behind them. They swung about in the nick of time to see a towering, fair-haired Occidental launching himself through the air in their

58

general direction.

Joe grasped two of the men by their queues and swung them together forcefully. There was a dull thud as skull met skull. Without further protest, the two men slithered down to the mud, leaving Joe, panting heavily, fists clenched, to face the third—and the biggest and ugliest—man.

"All right, chum! Come on! Pick on someone your own bloody size, why don't you?" Joe taunted, beckoning him on, his turquoise eyes dancing with anticipation of the fight, his first since Sydney.

The burly brute muttered something unintelligible in Chinese, and feigned a right hook, coming up instead with his left. Joe was no fool, however, and certainly no stranger to a fight. He recognized the feint for what it was and slammed his own meaty fist in under the man's guard before the other fellow's blow could connect. God Almighty! The Celestial had a jaw like iron, Joe realized, his knuckles ringing, and seemed no more disabled by his most powerful blow than if he'd struck him with a feather! He danced back on his toes, fists raised, catching his breath while the Chinaman warily circled him. With a sudden bellow, the fellow leapt at him, his arms clawing for Joe's throat. This was no time for fair play, nor did this great ox deserve any such delicate considerations, Joe decided grimly. In the last second, Joe nimbly stepped aside and slammed his fist into the fellow's groin as he careened past him, dimly aware, as the great hulk squealed and went down, of the strident sound of whistles nearby, and of someone tugging furiously at his coat sleeve.

"Enough! Come on! We must get away! The police are coming!"

He looked down to see the Chinese lad at his elbow.

"Come *on!*" the boy repeated earnestly and with every evidence of agitation.

59

Joe clamped a hand over his shoulder. "Don't worry, son. I'll speak up for you—tell the coppers what happened. Those bloody thugs attacked you, for Christ's sake! I saw the whole thing."

"It will make no difference, believe me," the lad insisted. "And you will only suffer for coming to my aid. We must go!"

Joe glanced at the three men, all now coming to, then at the street, which had been thronged with onlookers seconds before but was now curiously deserted in the drizzling rain. Even his hack had gone, he realized suddenly. And the sound of whistles was growing closer now.

"Right!" Joe agreed and started after the lad, who was fairly flying down a narrow alley between two buildings.

How far or exactly where they went was never to be clear in Joe's mind afterward. The lad said to follow him, and follow Joe did, more out of curiosity than anything. They blundered their way through dark basement rooms where old Chinamen, sprawled in glassy-eyed stupors, puffed dreamily on bubbling opium pipes, and likewise through others from which the click of the *mah-Jongg* tiles and the high laughter of painted, doll-like Chinese prostitutes lingered in Joe's ears long after they had passed on; through steaming cellar laundries and up into teeming markets, where roasted red duck and *char-siu* pork turned slowly on spits over glowing embers and where bubbling pots of spicy stuffed dumplings gave off their steamy fragrance. Wide-eyed little girls and their mothers gaped as the tall Caucasian stumbled his clumsy way between baskets of turnips or *wong-bok* cabbage, and stall holders yelled curses after the Chinese lad and the *fon kwei* who had upset their wares. On they flew, through narrow alleys and cellars and warehouses where

60

rainbow-colored bolts of silk awaited sale and chests of tea and porcelain and lacquer ware were piled against the ramshackle walls of some rich old merchant's storehouse, until Joe was panting for breath and far too warm in his heavy overcoat.

Just as he was determined to give up their ridiculous flight, they entered the side door of some enormous building and the boy halted. "Wait here," he ordered softly and went through another door without further words. He returned minutes later, beckoning Joe. "It's all right. We'll be safe here for a while. Come inside."

"Inside" proved to be a large theater, the walls embellished with the red and gold and black designs that now seemed familiar to Joe. On the wide stage, which boasted no curtains but was simply an elevated platform, a play was in progress, accompanied by the tinny music of what sounded like cymbals and gongs. There was an audience of sorts, mostly old Chinese men who chatted among themselves as the play progressed with little regard for the performance, and a few women in the upper gallery. The lad gestured for Joe to take a seat—a seat being on the dusty floor—and, somewhat bemused, Joe sat.

"All right, mate," he said at length when they had regained their wind. "What was all that about back there?"

The lad shrugged, turning his almost black, guileless eyes upon Joe. The angelic innocence of his expression seemed incongruous amidst the welter of livid, fast-purpling flesh puffing up around one eye, coupled with his bloody nose. "A little dispute, nothing more," he said offhandedly.

"My arse," Joe countered calmly. "It was more than a *little dispute* that got you that wallop. What did you do? Pick their pockets?"

"No! I'm no thief!" the boy denied indignantly.

"Those oafs were hatchet men from Ah Ping's *tong*. Ah Ping sent them to find me."

Joe sighed. "He wanted to do more than find you, I'd bet! Who's Ah Ping, and what the devil is a *tong?*"

"The *tongs* were once associations of my people who had no family here in America. They helped each other in hard times, you know?" Seeing Joe nod, the lad continued, "But now, the *tongs* serve a different purpose. It is the *tongs* who control the gambling halls here in Chinatown; they who run the houses of prostitution; they who extort money from the shop-keepers for their so-called 'protection.' The *tong* leaders are very evil men who make their wealth from the misery of others. Ah Ping—The Cat—is one of these leaders, and the worst of them all!"

"But why is this Ah Ping after you? Were you double-dealing with him somehow?"

The boy shook his head vehemently. *"Bu-dwei!* Not so! I work for no *tong* bossman! To understand, *fon kwei,* I must explain some of the customs of my people to you. I will try, but understand I must do so quickly, for I do not know how long we will be safe here.

"When times were very bad in our native China," he began, "many of my people came here to America, which we call *Gum San,* the Land of the Golden Mountain, in search of prosperity. Most of those who came were men like my father, who left their wives and young families behind in China, fully intending to find much gold and to return to them in a few years as wealthy men.

"But, it was not as easy to make their fortunes as they were led to believe. When the gold rush started here in California, the Chinese were allowed to work only the claims that the white men had already worked dry. Not only the Chinese but *all* foreigners were forced to pay higher and higher taxes for the privilege of working the mines, leaving them little to live on. Those who were lucky enough to find a little bit of gold often lost it to bandits. Ah, yes, *fon kwei,* my people were fair game for any unscrupulous white man to prey upon, and many of them were brutally murdered and their murderers never brought to justice, for just as it is now, a China-boy could not bear witness for or against a white man.

"My people saw their golden dreams fading, and yet they refused to give up. Besides, they still had to repay the mine owners for the credit extended to them for their passages here from China! And so, they had to find work in other areas—on the railroads, or as fishermen, as vegetable farmers or as servants in the fine houses of the white man—anything that would provide a living and enable them to return to the families they had left behind without losing face. Gradually, many came to accept that they would never see China again, that they must make a new life for themselves here and forget the beloved land they had left behind. So, they worked hard to start the restaurants such as that which you were about to enter, *fon kwei,* or else started laundries—ah, yes, many, many laundries! You see, there were few women in San Francisco back then, but the white men, all busily mining, needed their laundry done. They were willing to pay for it to be done here, rather than send their linens all the way to Honolulu for laundering as they had in the past. One needed only a washtub, soap, an iron, and an ironing board to start such a business, a very small outlay compared to that needed for a restaurant.

"So it was that my father, Chen Shu Yen, started such a laundry, along with my poor mother, Mei Gwi, who did not even carry his name because she was only his lowly concubine, you understand? His *real* and honorable wife yet lived in China! My mother worked many long hours from morning 'til night, even up until the very day she was to deliver her third child. Her time came, but she was old for childbearing then, and far too frail for the birth besides. She and the baby died, leaving myself and my little sister, Chen Mei Ling, alone with our father.

"We worked hard for him, but nothing could please him!" the boy said bitterly. "With our poor mother's death, he saw his hopes for riches dwindle to nothing. After that day, what little money he came by from the work we did he spent in the opium dens and in games of *fan-tan*, until there was nothing left, nothing at all! When I went home last night, he told me he had sold my little sister to Ah Ping, to become a slave girl in one of his happy houses—sold her to make an easy three hundred dollars for his dream pipes! I went there today, to try to get her away from that place, but Ah Ping's men saw me, and I had to run away. They chased after me. The rest you know." He bowed his head and shrugged helplessly, then his chin lifted with a resilience and resolution of purpose that filled Joe with admiration. "Tomorrow, I will try again! Mei Ling is but twelve years old. She is a most excellent sister, an honorable daughter. She does not deserve the shameful life my father would have her live!"

The lad's eyes were filled with tears, which he gamely tried to blink away, Joe saw, and an image filled his mind of another young boy, alone and afraid—an image of himself in the back streets of Sydney with nowhere to turn for help. He squeezed the lad's shoulder. "So that's how it is," he commented softly. "Then I'm glad I was able to help you out, son. Your little sister is lucky to have a bonzer brother like you." He extended his hand. "My name's Joe, Joel McCaleb. And yours?"

"I am called Chen Ming," the boy supplied, clasping Joe's hand and at the same time inclining his upper body in a sketchy bow. "But you may call me Ming."

"And you can call me Joe," Joe said with a grin and a bow of his own. "Now, is there a butcher's around here? I'd say your eye is about ready for a beefsteak, Ming!"

Ming grinned back. "You sure have a lot to learn, Joe! China-boys don't put beefsteak on their black eyes, they eat it! But there's an old herbalist near here. He'll sell me something for my eye—and for your knuckles, too, *fon kwei!*"

"Right you are," Joe agreed, ruefully inspecting his grazed and bruised knuckles. "Lead the way! And while we're at it, cobber, what, in blue blazes, does *fon kwei* mean?"

"It means 'foreign devil,'" Ming supplied, giving Joe a cheeky smile that was made singularly evil in cast by his swollen, rapidly closiong eye, "but I think perhaps you are not truly a devil after all, so I will try not to call you that again, yes? Through here, Joe."

Shaking his head, Joe once more allowed Ming to lead him off through the maze that was Chinatown.

Chapter Four

Joe awoke the next morning in the barren but clean room he had taken at Mrs. Barker's boarding house the afternoon before. He tossed aside the bedcovers and rubbed a hand over his face, yawning. There was a slight throbbing in his knuckles, but other than that, he felt remarkably fit, ready for anything.

Grinning as he remembered the fight the day before, he stepped across the room and rang for water to be brought. While he waited for it to arrive, he set out clean clothes and his shaving gear. He'd best make himself as presentable as he could for the meeting with Silverstein and Caldwell he'd promised himself he'd make today, he decided, glancing in the oval mirror above the dresser. The three weeks he had spent on Christmas Island before the ship came, and then another month spent in the balmy Sandwich Isles recuperating, had delayed it long enough.

A deeply tanned face, topped by a sheaf of dusty-blond hair still rumpled from sleep, considered him calculatingly from turquoise eyes as he combed his hair into a semblance of order. He battled the blond cowlick that fell across his brow until he had tamed it to lie flat and grinned crookedly. "Well, mate?" he asked his reflection. "What do y'think? Passable?" He frowned, then laughed. "What do y'mean it's a face that only a mother could love, cobber? Who the hell asked you, anyway, eh?"

The hot water and towels arrived then, borne by a buxomly pretty if skittish young Irish girl, who eyed Joe's broad and lecherous grin of welcome distrustfully and promptly fled. Chuckling, he stripped to the raw and washed and shaved, whistling as he lathered the pig-bristle brush and painted his jaws with the soap. As he carefully applied the razor, his thoughts went back to Ming. Poor young blighter! Chinese or no, he was only a boy, faced with a dilemma a full-grown man would shrink from. He had a feeling Ming wouldn't give up easily, though, whatever the cost, and he experienced again the surges of admiration Ming had stirred in him at the Chinese theater, mingled with apprehension for the lad who reminded him of himself at that age. Guts and determination were qualities he highly respected, and he'd hate to learn Ming had ended up with his throat slit, floating face down in the bay, the victim of one of Ah Ping's hatchet men. He regretted he'd not had the chance to offer his help, but when they'd parted ways—outside Mrs. Barker's boarding house to which Ming had led him—he'd wished him luck, and without further ado the boy had melted into the dreary, misty afternoon like a shadow.

Inside, he learned from a stout Mrs. Barker that a cabbie had dropped off his bag and steamer trunk, along with a hefty bill for his services. He'd filled out the guest register, paid her for three nights' lodging in advance, plus the cabbie's fare, and watched her sour-lemons expression become an indulgent smile.

"Any chance a bloke could get a hot meal near here, Miss Barker?" he'd asked casually, giving her an engaging wink.

"It's *Mrs.* Barker, Mister McCaleb, not Miss," she'd corrected him gently, but the blush of pleasure that rose up her already florid plump cheeks was a dead giveaway. "I usually only serve breakfast for my guests, you understand, but I could make an exception, just this once, I suppose . . . ? I'll see you to your room, and then you can come down and eat with us in the kitchen, if you wouldn't mind that? It's nothing fancy, though. Just potatoes and some boiled beef and carrots, with apple pie for after, but you're welcome to it . . ."

After supper, which had proved tasty tucker despite Ma Barker's modest disclaimer, he'd gone to bed, and here he was.

Shaved and washed now, he quickly dressed, donning a clean white shirt that fairly crackled with starch and itched like blazes and knotting a gray silk tie in the neck. Satisfied he passed muster, he slipped into the gray suit he'd worn the day before, which Ma Barker, bless her, had had steamed and brushed down. The dark hat with the curled up brim and the heavy overcoat of black and white tweed completed his attire. He left the room and the boarding house, deciding to walk the few blocks to Montgomery Street, where Messrs. Silverstein and Caldwell had their offices, rather than hire a cab. The rain had ceased during the night, and the air, though cold, was only slightly damp. He'd enjoy a brisk walk. His enforced inactivity aboard the *Southern Star* had been contrary to his nature, since he was used to being on horseback outdoors and leading an active life.

Some twenty minutes later, he was being ushered into a plush office that boasted wine red carpeting, glossy, wood-paneled walls, and chairs and desks upholstered in expensive oxblood leather. Legal tomes filled the bookcases that lined the room. As he strode inside, a middle-aged man with a shock of graying red hair rose from his seat behind the desk to welcome him. The man immediately clasped Joe's hand in his own and began pumping it up and down.

"Welcome, my dear fellow. Welcome to San Francisco at last! I can't tell you how glad I am to see you here safe and sound. Why, after your last telegraph from Honolulu, Mister Silverstein and I were afraid we wouldn't be meeting with you until early next year. Krakatoa! What a shocking experience! And the tragic loss of countless lives!" He shook his head sadly. "The eruption's devastating effects have been felt around the world, they do say, but we here are fortunate that they've only resulted in some very splendid sunsets here of an evening, very splendid. Tell me, are you quite recovered from your injuries?"

"Right as rain, Mister Caldwell, and none the worse for them."

"Good, very good," the lawyer declared, drumming his fingers on the desk. "Well, now, since I'm certain you are quite curious to hear what it is that has brought you all this way, we'll get down to business without further ado, shall we?" He glanced up as his secretary, a tall, pallid young fellow, discreetly knocked and entered, bearing a small strongbox. "Thank you, Geoffrey. Just set it here on the desk, will you?" Edward Caldwell fished in his pocket for an enormous key ring, selected one and fitted it into the lock as the secretary quietly left, closing the door in his wake. Caldwell withdrew a sheaf of papers and set them before him. "Well, here we are! This document before me is your grandfather's last will. But before I read it to you, there is something I feel compelled to explain.

"Your grandfather was a good man, you understand, Joel, if somewhat stern in his youth. His bitter disappointment when your father married your mother against his wishes—and who could truly blame him,

69

striking young actress that she was!—caused him to make some rash threats at the time that he bitterly regretted years later, one of those being his vow to your father that he never wished to set eyes on him again, which I'm certain prompted William Junior's departure for Indonesia and his subsequent missionary work for the Presbyterian Church there. As I'm certain you've been told, your grandfather even refused to acknowledge your birth by so much as a letter when your father wrote him from Java of it, am I right?"

"Undoubtedly, sir," Joe murmured with what he hoped was an appropriately grave expression.

"Yes, well, as the years went by, William Senior became a very lonely man. He believed his own family lost to him, and as a consequence he married his housekeeper of many years, a very nice, middle-aged widow of whom he was fond, by the name of Sarah Jones. Sarah had a young daughter by her former marriage, and William was very good to the little girl, very good indeed. After he and Sarah were married, he generously undertook to send Seraphina back east to Boston, to a most highly regarded school for young ladies, to further her education. When Sarah unfortunately succumbed to a female complaint and died two years ago, he arranged for Seraphina to continue her schooling there and to board with the Downings, a reputable family whose granddaughter and great-niece also attended the school, and by whom she would be suitably chaperoned. So it was that he did not see Seraphina following the day of her poor mother's funeral or, alas, in the years following that preceded his own death. Yet he neither neglected nor forgot her, not while he lived, nor after his death. Each month he sent a generous bank draft to cover her living expenses and the little luxuries and folderols young ladies set such store by. These drafts continued until the day he died.

His concern for her continued well-being, orphaned as she unfortunately is, will be made clear to you very soon, Mister McCaleb. Well, I do believe that covers the preliminaries. Now I will read the will itself to you, if you have no questions?" Edward Caldwell hooked a pair of gold-rimmed spectacles over his ears and eyed Joe inquiringly over them as he withdrew William Angus McCaleb's will.

"None, sir. Your explanations have been very concise. I'm . . . heartened . . . to hear that my grandfather had at least a few years of happiness before his second wife died."

"Commendable of you, Joel, very commendable. I'm certain William would have been proud of you, had he lived to meet you."

"Thank you, sir."

Caldwell cleared his throat. "Now, the will. I'll read it straight through, and when I'm done I'll be happy to address any concerns or questions you may have, agreed?" Seeing Joe nod, he continued:

I, William Angus McCaleb, being of sound mind and in possession of my faculties, do hereby bequeath my entire estate in the sum of $5,000 (five thousand dollars), together with such land and property holdings as are in my possession at this date, to wit: the residence at Bayview Drive which is popularly known as the McCaleb residence, and its contents; secondly, a parcel of some twenty-thousand land acres situated in San Juliano County, Southern California, and which are known as the Rancho de las Campanas, to my grandson, Joel William McCaleb, on the condition that the stipulation that follows is duly met, to wit: my only grandson, Joel William McCaleb will, within thirty days of the reading of this, my

71

last will and testament, take as his own lawful wife my legal ward, Seraphina Jones. The deeds and titles to both said properties are duly enclosed, and will be transferred to my grandson in his name immediately following the ceremony, along with said funds. In this fashion, it is my sincere hope to ensure that my dear ward, who impressed me always with her sweet and angelic disposition, is well provided for.

In the event that Joel William McCaleb should have already married, be deceased, or otherwise unable or unwilling to adhere to the stipulations of this document, then the above sum and lands shall become the sole property of the First Presbyterian Church of San Francisco, to be disposed of as they deem fit.

Caldwell concluded, "It is signed by your grandfather and witnessed by both Mister Silverstein and myself." He leaned back in his chair, grasped his lapels, and regarded the young man before him with an expectant expression.

Joe, for his part, felt stunned. Twenty-thousand acres. Five thousand dollars. It was both more—and less—than he had anticipated: more in terms of the size of the bequest, certainly, but less than he had dared to hope for in other ways, what with that stipulation of marriage craftily tacked on the end. Mac had known nothing of that, obviously. *Marriage!* Strewth! No way, Mac! Sorry, old cobber, marriage wasn't for him, not yet! He'd sooner kiss the whole bloody lot good-bye and take his chances on his own than marry some prissy miss he'd never met—nor wanted to, what was more. He was about to open his mouth and tell Caldwell just that when Caldwell raised an admonishing finger to silence him.

"Please, Joel, if you're about to tell me you want no part of this, then don't. Or at least, not for the time being. I'd like you to take a few days to think this through. Then, if the idea still appalls you, I will advise Miss Jones of your decision, and that will be that."

"Seraphina Jones? She's here, then, in San Francisco?"

"But of course! She's been here for several months. We wired the young lady in Boston immediately upon her guardian's death, and then, upon receipt of your telegraph from the islands, we advised her of your imminent arrival. She is presently residing at the Occidental Hotel, and has been supervising the airing and cleaning of your grandfather's residence in preparation for your arrival in the interim."

"She has, has she?" Joe murmured faintly, feeling as if somehow a bale of wool had replaced his thinking equipment. "And what does your Miss Jones have to say about this ... marriage ... Grandfather has so thoughtfully arranged for our mutual benefit? Has she heard the contents of the will yet? Does she know she gets nothing unless we marry?" he demanded through gritted teeth, seeing his dreams falling about him in ashes.

"Of course, my dear boy! And what would you expect any young woman in her somewhat distressed financial state to feel, under the circumstances? She's most eager to meet with you and gain your approval!" Caldwell beamed.

"Is she, now? I see." Joel rose to standing and Caldwell followed suit, craning his head to look up at the tall, lean man who had extended a large, tanned hand in farewell. His firm grip made Caldwell wince. "Well, thank you for everything, sir. You've been most helpful. I'll be in touch shortly and let you know my decision."

73

"I'll look forward to it," Caldwell said. "And Joel . . . I sincerely hope your decision will be the *right* one. The land alone is of considerable value, and quite legally come by. William took his claim before the Land Commission here in San Francisco back in '53 when the ownership of California land, which was then still under Mexican title, became a question of uncertainty and concern. He had to wait seven years for the commission to make a decision, but in the end they granted his claim to the Rancho de las Campanas. You need have no questions on that score."

"Rancho de las Campanas," Joe echoed thoughtfully. "Spanish, isn't it? I'm afraid I don't speak the language. What does it mean?"

"The literal translation from the Spanish is 'Ranch of the Bells,' I do believe. But why it's called that, I have no idea, I'm afraid."

Joe nodded, repeated his thanks, turned on his heel, and left the office.

As he turned onto Montgomery Street, the chill, damp breeze from off the bay was like a sobering slap in the face in comparison to the somewhat pressing atmosphere of the law offices. He kept walking, deep in thought, oblivious to the elaborate offices and buildings at his side, until he found a saloon. Of their own accord, his feet led him through the swinging half-doors and inside.

He shouted up a beer, then drained the glass without so much as blinking before ordering another. While he waited, he drew a smoke from his coat pocket and lit it in the gas flame provided by the proprietor for that purpose. His second drink he carried with him to a small table, where he could peer through a window and watch the many passersby while he nursed it. As he sat there, his thoughts in turmoil, he availed himself of the free lunch the establishment offered its patrons, a San

74

Franciscan innovation of a lavish array of foods calculated to increase the diners' thirst and encourage them to purchase more liquor—a far more lucrative commodity than the food. While he sampled grilled oysters and grizzly bear steak, fried potatoes and eggs, he considered what Caldwell had told him.

Marriage—and within thirty days, too, if he adhered to the conditions of the will! What a lousy prospect, to have some young harridan nagging him, chivying him over this or that, wanting to know where he'd been and with whom and for what reason. He shuddered. Christ, no! Marriage gave him the creeps, pure and simple. Just thinking about it made his blood run cold. He'd seen too many good blokes ruined by marriage, slinking out of the Sydney saloons and hurrying off home with their tails tucked between their legs like whipped hounds, so scared were they of their wives' displeasure. That wasn't for him. He swirled the pale lager beer in the glass and considered its color moodily. What did she look like, this Seraphina, he wondered? It figured she couldn't be much to look at, else the old man would have had no fears for her future. "Angelic," Caldwell had said. Huh! More likely buck-toothed, he wouldn't wonder, with mousy hair and a face that would rival a horse's! Maybe she'd prove enormous, with the suspicion of a swarthy moustache. Neither prospect made him feel any better. He shouted up another beer and downed it quickly, wishing he'd drank whiskey instead of beer. He definitely needed something stronger to dispel the horrible image that filled his mind—that of five thousand dollars and twenty-thousand acres sliding away from him . . .

It was then a sobering thought struck him—one that succeeded in ridding him of the slight fuzziness that had dulled his reasoning process seconds before. Despite what Caldwell had said regarding this Seraphina, there was a better than even chance that the young woman had no more desire to marry *him* than he had to marry *her,* and that she was just after Gramps McCaleb's money, too. She'd never met him, either. Perhaps she already had a sweetheart but was as greedy as he was to receive old Grandpa McCaleb's inheritance so that they could begin a comfortable new life together. Christ! Why hadn't he thought of that before? He and this blasted Seraphina woman could still marry and fulfill the terms of Gramps' will, but what was to prevent them from selling the property immediately afterward, splitting the proceeds, acquiring a divorce, and going their own sweet ways, both the richer for it? *Nothing, nothing at all.* And, unless this Miss Jones was an utter dunderhead, there was a good chance she'd see the sense in it, too, once it was explained, if she hadn't thought of it already. He'd always fancied himself a gambling man, so hell, what was one more long shot? If it paid off, he'd be quids in! The notion was such a glad one, he let out a loud whoop of triumph, causing many heads to turn and several pairs of eyes to regard him with unconcealed curiosity and no little disapproval.

Throwing down a bill upon the table, he retrieved his hat and jammed it on, leaving the saloon for the street once more, whistling now and with a jaunty, carefree swagger rather than with the dragging gait with which he had entered. A broad, crooked grin now tugged at his lips as, head down against the damp wind, he set out to explore the possibilities for celebration of his good fortune that the town of San Francisco might have to offer. First off, he intended to ride one of those jaunty little cable cars up and down a few hills, and then he might even venture into the notorious Barbary Coast area, he decided recklessly. The Barbary Coast was no true coastline, but roughly a six-block area where all manner of rogues gathered, among them the infamous Sydney Ducks—Australian hooligans who terrorized the city by night and whom Mrs. Barker had cautioned him against falling in with, for all that they were his own countrymen. He had a hankering to find out if they were really as tough as they made out, or all bluff, and damned if he didn't feel Lady Luck was smiling on him all of a sudden. What was the saying? "Lucky at cards, unlucky at love." Maybe he could beat the odds this time around and prove a winner at both! After all, it was about time that beautiful bitch, Lady Luck, dealt him a winning hand.

"Mac, my old cobber, if you can hear me where you are, thanks a million!" he murmured as he left the saloon.

Unbeknown to Joe, not many blocks away in a luxurious suite at the Occidental Hotel, a slim, raven-haired young woman had just reached the very same conclusion he had reached. But unlike Joe she was celebrating her cleverness in solitary glee, sipping vintage bubbly champagne from a delicately etched crystal glass, which she had poured for herself from an entire magnum she had ordered sent up by room service. Unaccustomed either to wines or spirits, she was, at that very moment, decidedly tipsy.

They hadn't intended for it to go this far, no sir, she reflected, sprawling across the brocade-covered bed with the glass precariously balanced in her fingers and the frothy white lace of her petticoats—she wore no gown over them—billowing up about her long, shapely, bare legs. Neither of them had ever *imagined* it would go this far, but it had! Until she'd realized there was still a way out of it just a while ago, she'd felt like she imagined a pet rat on a treadmill must feel, going around and around and around with no exit in sight.

She giggled and sipped her champagne, the first she had ever tasted. It was tangy, and the bubbles tickled her nose. The effect was pleasant, too. All the hard edges of reality were softened and pleasantly blurred. In this dizzy state, anything, however improbable, seemed likely.

"Joel William McCaleb. Seraphina McCaleb." She grinned. "What are you like, Joel McCaleb?" she demanded of the opulent but empty suite. "Are you the missionary type—tall and thin with a beard and spectacles? Do you pound on your Bible and preach against hellfire and damnation?" She giggled at the crazy notions her mind came up with. Lord, it didn't really matter if he was as fat as a tub of lard and bald as a coot! Whatever he was like, she would marry him, if that was what it took to see this thing through. She'd promised, and a promise was your sworn word. You didn't break it when fancy struck you, or go back on it when things got rough. Her papa had taught her that much.

The giddy smile she'd worn dwindled momentarily and tears filled her eyes—eyes of a misty, green-flecked gray fringed with curling, sooty lashes that were damp and spiky now. Oh, Papa, you mustn't be angry with me, she implored silently. I tried, I really did, but I just couldn't marry Chuck, however good a match it was, don't you see? Chuck and I, we were like brother and sister. I could *never* think of him the way you wanted me to, never. It was you and Mama who wanted us to marry, and Aunt Carol and Uncle Cay, not me—and not Chuck, either. Chuck's already found the woman he loves, and it isn't me. I had to do this . . . just had to . . .

The crystal champagne glass slipped from her slack fingers to the blue brocade coverlet, spreading a small, dark, wet stain with the remaining few drops of wine that yet lingered inside it. Her flushed cheek cradled against her upflung arm, black ribbons of shining hair spilling about her shoulder, the young woman who called herself Seraphina fell deeply asleep, all notions of supervising the cleaning of the McCaleb residence in preparation for its new owner temporarily forgotten.

Chapter Five

Joe muttered an oath as he attempted—none too successfully—to fit the key in the lock of the door to his room at Ma Barker's. Christ! Surely he wasn't that drunk! A last, clumsy attempt succeeded, to his relief, and the door swung inward slowly. He staggered inside, cursing again as he banged his shin on some piece of furniture or other en route to the bed, where he suddenly sat down, running his hand through his hair.

He had found his way into the Barbary Coast area as he'd planned earlier after leaving the saloon, and he had spent a raucous afternoon and evening prowling the narrow, seedy, but lively streets. Like predatory animals, the waterfront stews slumbered by day, coming to bawdy, lusty life only when darkness shrouded the narrow alleys. Music, loud and brassy, floated from the doorways of taverns and saloons into the streets. Brazenly bare-breasted French and Chilean whores called to him from upper windows as they flaunted their charms, offering him a "touch" for a nickel, and more for a quarter or a pinch of gold dust. He'd been wary nonetheless as he grinned up at them and laughingly refused their bold invitations, for he'd heard of the gangs of crimps and pressmen that frequented the groggeries such as the Goat and Compass and the Fierce Grizzly and the rookeries and the cribs of the whores, on the lookout for unsuspecting men to shanghai and force into reluctant service as crew members on their captains' vessels. After his experiences aboard the dirty little *Neda,* he had no intention of ever going to sea again!

Rubbing seamy shoulders with gamblers who flashed diamond pins from their cravats, and rouged and befeathered tarts who flashed still more, he worked his way through sideshows and small, darkened "theaters" where anything man could imagine and woman could perform could be seen for a dime, his hands in his pockets to keep them from being emptied by the slippery-fingered folk who were everywhere. He'd wound up, finally, amongst that band of notorious villains, the Sydney Ducks, who'd been only too happy to meet with a fellow countryman—or, as they slyly hoped, yet another "green" sucker they could roll for his money. Still feigning the eager-but-bewildered-by-the-big-city air of a new boy in town, Joe had accepted an invitation to play poker and other games of chance with the Ducks, letting them win a few hands to lull them into a false sense of security and raise the ante before he'd shown them what he was really made of, this orphan lad who'd grown up in Botany Bayfront saloons not unlike these gaming halls, and who'd cut his teeth on poker chips. Much to their violent and incredulous displeasure, he'd finally left their tables close to a thousand dollars richer—and with several of the now-ugly Ducks hot on his tail and intent on slugging him at the very least. He'd managed at length to throw off their pursuit though, and here he was, the hefty roll of greenbacks bulging against his hip, his head throbbing with the aftereffects of too much rum and cheap whiskey. Christ! Almost a

81

thousand dollars! Maybe he should stick to gambling and make his fortune that way—

"Must have been some night, eh, *fon kwei?*" a familiar voice inquired from the shadows, startling him. Though the tone was light, there was an edge of something more, something hard and scared sounding to it.

Joe's head jerked up in the direction of the voice. He squinted, plumbing the heavy shadows of his room, cursing the fog that rolled in off the bay and blanketed San Francisco of an evening, allowing no revealing fingers of moonlight to illumine the room.

"Ming?" he asked, his voice surprisingly steady for one who had drunk as much as he had drunk that night, and whose head felt as if miners were digging for gold in his skull. Despite the headache, a certain measure of contentment had settled through him, which the rum, whiskeys, and his winnings had enhanced, but, even so, an alarm bell went off in his head as he caught the undertone in Ming's voice. "What is it? What's up, mate? How'd you get in here?"

Ming stepped from the shadows, a slim, darker silhouette against the gloom. "How doesn't matter. I . . . I came because I need your help, *fon kwei!*" He hung his head, and a defeated sigh escaped his lips as he shrugged. "I went back—I tried to rescue Mei Ling from that place, you know?" Seeing Joe nod, he continued, "But I am ashamed to tell you I have failed yet again. Ah Ping's men, they know me too well! I cannot come within a yard of the House of Happiness without them spotting me. But you—they would not think that you would help one such as I! Will you . . . will you help me, Joe McCaleb?"

The unease that had tightened in Joe's gut since he and Ming had parted ways suddenly dispersed. He was relieved to see the young Chinaman was still safe, for his imagination had conjured up poor Ming suffering a variety of exquisitely painful Chinese tortures, all of which had culminated in his death. He nodded, the fuzziness gone, his drunkenness and the throbbing in his head dispelled by the solemnity and despair of Ming's tone. "Aye, cobber, 'course I'll help you—if I can. What is it you want me to do?"

Ming crossed the room toward him. "Thank you, *fon kwei!* Thank you! I can never repay you—"

"Let's do it first, Ming, old mate. And then—if it all works out right—then you can thank me," Joe cut in softly.

"As you say, Joe," Ming agreed. "I have a plan."

"Let's hear it," Joe instructed, loosening his tie and shrugging off his jacket while Ming began to outline his idea.

"They have taken my little sister, Mei Ling, to the house of Tea Rose, who is the—how you say it?—the madam of the House of Happiness. She is to begin bringing 'joy' to Tea Rose's patrons tonight." Ming shuddered. "I am so very afraid for her, *fon kwei!* I thought perhaps together, the two of us, we could overpower the men who guard the girls and free her?"

Joe's lips tightened, then drew together in a thin, straight slash as he recalled the hard faces of the *tong* hatchet men with whom he had exchanged blows the afternoon before. It was the expression of a side of his new friend's character that Ming had never seen before, a hard, ruthless side. Joe shook his head as he rose and, bare chested now, muscles rippling under taut, tanned flesh, went to the wardrobe and withdrew a clean, dark blue work shirt, which he proceeded to put on. As he changed into heavy cord pants and buckled a wide leather belt around his lean waist, he told Ming, "Forget it. It wouldn't work, chum. They know you've tried to free her once already, right? And

I'd bet they'll be on their toes for a second attempt. No, the only way t'do it is my way! Listen up, cobber, and I'll tell you how . . ."

Less than an hour later, Joe stood before the three steps that led up to the House of Happiness, once a respectable family residence on Walker Street, but now grown considerably shabby and seedy looking. Tinkling sounds and faint bursts of laughter—some high-pitched and feminine, others deep and masculine—carried from within to the foggy street outside. He gritted his teeth and pulled down the brim of his hat to shadow his features, then with a slight stagger his newfound soberness did not warrant, he lurched up the steps to the front door and hammered loudly upon it.

"Open up, there, ye damned Celestial doxies, an' let me in!" He hammered again with a fist of solid oak. "Y'hear me, blast you, let me in! Christ! I'm freezin' my bloody arse off out here!"

The door opened, and Joe saw a giant Chinaman, with his muscular arms crossed implacably over his bulging, massive chest, standing like a great wall before him. His slanted eyes were without warmth, glittering slits of hatred and contempt.

"Pah!" Joe snorted, reeling past the Chinese bouncer and into the house proper. "Ain't no China-boy I'm after! Where're the pretty girlies, eh, mate, tell me that? Some o' the Ducks said there were Chinese girlies to be had here, and I ain't leavin' til I get me one." He stabbed an indignant finger into the massive China-man's chest. "Chop chop, fellah! Fetchee girlie!"

The Chinaman fairly smoldered; it appeared that at any moment smoke might stream from his nostrils. He had reached out a long, bulging arm and extended it in the general direction of Joe's throat when there came a swish of silk at their backs.

"No, Wang. Leave the gent'man be!"

Both men spun around to see a petite but arresting woman standing behind them. Ah, Madam Tea Rose herself, Joe realized with satisfaction. This was more like it! She wore her black hair swept up into a knot at the crown. The knot was ornamented with tinkling strands of beads and several ivory combs. Her diminutive body was robed in a glowing gown of pure, emerald-colored silk, over which embroidered pink tea roses wandered in profusion. Her face, though beautiful, possessed a brittle hardness that made a man recoil rather than want to draw closer to her, Joe decided fleetingly before forcing a broad, foolish grin and lunging toward her, arms outstretched to span her tiny waist.

"Like I told him," he mumbled, swooping her up into the air, "I want a lil' China girlie, and you'll do jus' fine, love, jus' fine!"

"Put me down, you drunken son o' bitch!" the madam hissed, writhing to escape him, her almond-shaped eyes flashing indignantly. "If is a gel you want, I see to it."

"You will?" Joe echoed doubtfully, setting her down as she had requested.

"Sure I will," she assured him arrogantly. "I not doxy! I am Tea Rose, and I am boss lady here. This my house. Now, mistah, what kine gel you like?"

"Get rid o' that monkey over there, love, an' I'll tell you," Joe bantered.

With only a cool nod, Tea Rose dismissed the hulking bouncer, took Joe by the elbow, and led him from the vestibule and into a dimly lit room beyond.

For a second, Joe had the feeling he had somehow stepped into another world. Crimson brocade hangings concealed the walls of what must once have been a staid formal drawing room. Paper lanterns, their shades painted with delicate flowers, softened the harsh amber of lamplight to a rosy, dreamlike pink. Sweet-smelling incense—jasmine, rose, lotus, spices—cloyingly perfumed the air. Joe blinked to clear his vision and saw that upon low sofas spread with glistening silk hangings sat girls, many, many girls, in various lounging poses. Some were barebreasted, while others wore high-collared silk *cheong-sam* gowns like their mistress in varying colors that heightened their dark, petite beauty. Lacquered screens with misty landscapes framed the sing-song girls as if they were exquisite oriental portraits.

"Now, how 'bout Peach Blossom?" Tea Rose queried briskly, indicating one curvaceous yet petite flower with a round, merry face, robed in peach-colored silk. "Very good girl, show you plenty good times, mistah."

"Nah," Joe growled, waving the smiling girl away. He fished in his shirt pocket several unsuccessful times, and finally managed to draw forth a rolled wad of bills, which he flourished before Tea Rose's nose. "She's pretty enough, but she's too bloody old, love." He said the latter in a loud whisper and nudged the madam conspiratorially. "After something sweet, I am, something sweet and . . . and willin' an' eager to learn. See here, I have the ready money t'pay for her, an' all. Fifty dollars, girlie, fifty green ones!" His turquoise eyes glittered. "Very young, very, *very* innocent, and very, very willing—y'know what I mean?"

The madam's black eyes returned the lust-filled glitter of his, yet hers feasted greedily on the sheaf of bills he fanned temptingly before her. "I understand," she said softly. "You want nice li'l virgin girl, yes? Wait, and I see what I can do."

Joe reached out and, lurching just a little, boldly

pinched her powdered cheek. "You . . . you do just that, sweetie. An' don' be too long, now. I'm gettin' kind of . . . kind of . . . anxious . . ."

With a small, tight smile, Tea Rose inclined her head and drifted from the room, leaving Joe to flop down onto a sofa amidst the bevy of giggling Oriental beauties, who at once began to exclaim over his height and his fair hair.

But once outside, all pretense of softness and civility slipped from Tea Rose, and she became the hard, shrewd businesswoman of her reputation. She clapped her fingers, and at once the hulking bouncer, Wang, appeared from nowhere.

"The *fon kwei* with the yellow hair has much money. He wants a virgin, a young one. The Chen girl—she is ready?" Tea Rose demanded in Cantonese.

"But . . . I thought you were saving her for Ah Ping, mistress?"

"And I am, stupid fool," Tea Rose snapped. "But first, I take great pleasure in parting that tall foreign devil from his dollars, yes? Go upstairs and warn pretty li'l Mei Ling again what will happen if she protests. Tell her we'll kill that cursed interfering brother of hers if she so much as squeaks! Tell her she must smile sweetly at the *fon kwei* and offer him tea, as I have taught her. She must make sure he drinks it before he so much as touches her. We will handle it from there, you understand?"

The lout snickered and nodded. "Yes, mistress."

Tea Rose summoned a sugary smile and returned to Joe, who, seeing her approach, extricated himself from the clinging arms of her girls and eagerly dragged himself to standing. A chorus of disappointed groans sounded behind him. Tea Rose did not even come up to his shoulder, he realized.

"I have just the girl for you, mistah," she told him in

her lisping English. "Very pretty, and not a day over eight years old. She is untouched, of course, yes? A virgin, as you requested, just arrive' my house today, an' ve'y eager to learn the delights of love. You ve'y lucky man!"

To Joe's disgust, she simpered up at him. He forced a leer and solemnly handed her the money. "Lead the way, love," he slurred. "There's one little China doll gonna be real happy tonight. Yessir, real happy!"

Up a steep, narrow flight of stairs they went, Tea Rose leading the way, her silk skirts swishing above dainty, black-slippered feet, Joe ducking to avoid the low ceiling as he climbed up behind her. An equally narrow landing led off the stairs, with closed doors on either side. From somewhere, Tea Rose produced a key, went to one, and fitted it in the lock. She swung open the door before her, allowing Joe to pass through and into the room.

"I wish you much joy tonight, sir," she recited as if she'd said the words a million times, and then she bowed and backed out of the room, closing the door in her wake. For a second, Joe remained still, craning his ears. As he had expected, he heard the faint but audible click as the key turned in the lock. For better or worse, he was now trapped.

He glanced up, and he knew with certainty that the sight that met his eyes would remain forever after imprinted in his mind.

Upon the bed, spread with a coverlet of black satin embroidered with golden cranes, was curled a little girl. She wore her glossy, blue-black hair shoulder length, with a fringe of thick bangs that drew one's attention to her lovely, almond-shaped dark eyes, now ashimmer with crystal tears in the light of the single shaded lamp. The *cheong-sam* that seemed molded to her barely pubescent body was a soft, dreamy pink, with delicate flowers of white and silver blooming about the thigh-length slits on either side and encircling the hems. Beneath the gown, she wore matching pale pink trousers and deeper pink velvet slippers.

"Mei Ling?" he asked, his voice hoarse with outrage. A child, she was just a lovely, fragile, innocent *child!* Even were she not Ming's sister, he knew he could never leave the little girl here, at the "tender" mercies of Madam Tea Rose and her clients, when he left tonight.

With a soft sigh of despair and resignation, the little girl rose from the bed and padded toward him, bowing her glossy head low.

"Yes, I am Mei Ling, sir," she acknowledged, her voice barely above a whisper. "The meaning of my name is 'Beautiful Dream' and it is my fondest wish to make all of your dreams beautiful this night, sir."

Her voice broke as she said the words she had been told to say, and he saw that she was trembling. As she lifted her lovely heart-shaped face demurely to his, he saw the faint bluish tinge of a bruise—cleverly lightened with powder—high on her cheekbone, the only visible sign of ill-usage on this otherwise perfect little lotus blossom. Anger roiled through him, anger at the heartless father who had sold her and the filthy animals he had sold her to.

"You're Chen Mei Ling, sister to Chen Ming?"

"I . . . I am," she admitted, fear flaring in her eyes.

"Don't be afraid. I'm a friend. I won't hurt you. Ming sent me to help you escape."

"No . . . that cannot be! You lie!" she cried softly, shaking her head. "My brother . . . the men of Ah Ping's *tong* have him. They will kill him if I do not obey Madam Tea Rose! Now. You will have some tea, yes?" She stumbled away from him to a low, lacquered, black table, where bowls and a steaming pot of tea had been set. The words spilled quickly from her in her pathetic eagerness to please. "We drink tea first, to relax us, yes? Then . . . then Mei Ling will make you ve'y happy."

"No. Mei Ling will escape!" Joe said firmly. "Ming's in the alley below, waiting for you." He strode across the room and tore the black silken covering from the bed. He did the same with the sheets below, knotting the ends together to form a sturdy rope. Mei Ling watched him docilely as he worked, her eyes lustrous, dark pools that seemed peculiarly devoid of emotion.

"You are wrong. I will never escape," she murmured in a sing-song tone. "Mei Ling will not be allowed to escape. They will kill her, kill her brother, kill her most wretched father!"

Joe moved to the window, glancing at her as he passed, certain now her dazed state was due to some drug they had given her. He pulled aside a curtain to expose a dusty window that looked out onto a murky alley below. If all were going well, he mused, by now Ming should be stationed there, having silenced any possible sentries. He tried to raise the window, realizing belatedly it was nailed shut. Ignoring Mei Ling for the moment, he looked about him for something to pry loose the nails, finally settling upon his own knife. The nails gone, he forced up the window, allowing a cool, damp current of air to infiltrate the cloying perfume of the room. He knotted one end of his sheet-rope to a bedpost and tossed the other out the window, then he craned his head through and gave two low whistles into the pitch blackness, which were answered by Ming's single whistle from below.

"You heard that? That was Ming," he told the little girl. He held out his arms. "Come on! In a minute or two, you'll be with him, and safe, I promise."

Mei Ling shook her head and sipped again on the tea she had poured, which, Joe rightly guessed, had also been doctored. Obviously they'd intended to drug him, too, and roll him for the contents of his pockets, he realized grimly. "Come on, Mei Ling!" he repeated sternly.

Again she shook her head and opened her mouth to scream an alarm, her loyalty only to her captors now in her fear for her brother's life. In one lithe move, Joe was across the room and had clipped her gently under the jaw. "Sorry, sweetheart, but Uncle Joe couldn't wait around all night!" he muttered as she crumpled to the carpet like an exotic little marionette with severed strings. Before she landed, he caught her, slung her over his shoulder, and hurried to the window.

He had climbed halfway down into the alley by means of the sheet-rope—which Ming steadied from below—when there was a crash and a yell of outrage from the room above. He looked up and saw two pale moons of faces looking down at him, one that of the madam and the other, her henchman. Shrill commands in Chinese followed.

"Hurry, Joe!" Ming cried. "Madam Tea Rose sent Wang after us and told him to summon others!"

At last, Joe's feet touched solid ground. "Take her and get going!" he snapped. "I'll be right behind you!"

To Ming's credit, he asked no questions that would have taken valuable seconds. He simply took the little girl and began running as he had run from the *tong* members two days before, leaving Joe behind.

Joe hugged the inky darkness of the alley, edging along the side of the building until he reached a side door. Excited voices, muffled by the wooden barrier, reached him, and he grinned in the gloom. If he were not mistaken, it would be from this very door their pursuers would erupt, like hounds in full cry! He looked about, then scrabbled in the refuse at his feet, finding what he needed—a short, stout plank. Grasping it firmly in both hands like a cricket bat, he waited.

He did not have to wait long. The door flew open, and the smell of food and perfume spilled out over the threshold along with three wiry Oriental men, all exchanging excited cries in Cantonese.

" 'Evenin', mates!" Joe roared, lunging into the pool of light. Three aghast yellow faces gaped at him in disbelief, and in that split second Joe swung his makeshift club into three unsuspecting bellies, then brought it up under three unsuspecting chins with a nice, solid thwacking sound. The *tong* goons went down in a messy heap that was wonderfully satisfying, but it wouldn't be long before they were on their feet again, Joe knew. They were stubborn little buggers!

"That should hold you for a few minutes," he muttered. "G'night, mates!"

So saying, he turned and sprinted away through the darkness, moving in the same direction in which Ming had disappeared. Two streets more, and Ming was suddenly running alongside, then ahead of him, Mei Ling jouncing over his scrawny shoulder. Joe halted to catch his breath. "My turn, cobber," he ordered, holding out his arms for the child. Ming willingly relinquished his burden.

On and on they ran, with Ming in the lead weaving down this street and then that alley, bobbing and twisting in the manner of one who knows his way well, while Joe—with Mei Ling slung over his shoulder like a limp but lovely rag doll—padded resolutely after him.

"We must get away from this area—they know it too well!" Ming panted, slithering to a halt before a half-moon-shaped gateway.

"Suits me," Joe rasped.

Mei Ling stirred upon his shoulder. "Ah Ming, my brother, are you there?" she murmured, groggily lifting her head.

"*Shao mei mei*, Little Sister, I am here, never fear! Be

still, now!"

On they ran, their footsteps slapping against the mud and dirt, their breathing hoarse and ragged. Chinatown lay behind them now, and the streets became perceptibly more prosperous in appearance as they fled onward. Gaslights cast bleary amber pools of light onto the ground and reflected in puddles to illumine their path. Set within the narrow pavements on either side of the street, circular skylights paned with sturdy bottle glass glowed yellow with the light of the gas jets in the basements beneath. Like windows into hell, Joe thought absently as they scuttled past. In the near distance, angry cries and shouts floated after them, relentlessly coming closer, ever closer. As Joe had guessed, their pursuers were obstinate fellows.

"This street leads up town," Ming divulged breathlessly, jerking his head toward a street that led off at a right angle to the one down which they ran. "The houses further up the hill belong to wealthy white men. I think perhaps Ah Ping's men will think twice before they follow us there, yes?"

Joe nodded and followed him, crossing the street at a run. Though she weighed very little, in the manner of light things carried for some distance Mei Ling seemed markedly heavier now, and he was eager to take a respite from carrying her and rest his arms. After what seemed an eternity, Ming came to a halt before a rambling, old, two-story house that gleamed a pale yellow in the shadows.

"This house is empty, *fon kwei*," Ming hissed. "There is a broken window in back where the kitchens are. We can get in through there and hide."

Joe had the good sense not to ask Ming how he knew this, and in minutes they were standing in the shrubbery that all but overgrew the rear of the large residence with the dormer windows and ornate

93

gingerbreading that loomed out of the fog and darkness above them. Ming quickly found the broken window and Joe, glad to be relieved of his burden, hurriedly handed Mei Ling to her brother and reached a long arm inside to slide the bolt on the nearby door.

Seconds later, he was opening the door to let the pair in. Mei Ling had recovered somewhat now and was able to stand, and she tottered into the darkened house ahead of her older brother. Once they were all in the kitchen, Joe quietly shut the door behind them. They all held their breath and listened as the sounds of several men running, footsteps racing, reached them, passed by, and continued on. Ming and Joe let out collective sighs of relief.

"Well, here we are," Joe said at length, his voice sounding alarmingly loud on the gloom. "We'll be safe here—for the time being, anyway. I'll look around a bit and see if I can find something in the pantry for your sister to eat, Ming. She'll throw off the effects of whatever it was they gave her faster, with something solid in her belly."

Ming nodded. "I can never repay you, never, *fon kwei*," he said huskily. "You are as fearless as the dragon. You are as cunning and clever as the tiger. You are a friend such as none I have ever had before! You are—"

"You are," came a mocking voice at their backs, slicing through the shadows, "nothing more than a trespasser! Who the hell are you people, and what are you doing here, in my house? Answer me, else I'll blow your goldarned heads off!"

Joe swung his tall, rugged frame about slowly, to find himself looking down the long barrel of a rifle that glinted wickedly in the meager light. It was held by a slim young woman who, if her tone and stance were anything to go by, meant each and every word she said!

Chapter Six

"If you'll put the gun down, I'll explain, love," Joe said levelly, never shifting his narrowed gaze from the pale blur of the young woman's hands, which held the rifle with surprising ease and expertise.

"The hell I will!" she retorted, eyes flashing in the gloom. "I'm still waiting for that explanation, mister!" She threateningly jerked the rifle in their direction, a gesture that made Joe decidedly nervous.

"Please! No! It is on my account we broke in here, missie," Ming hurriedly explained, stepping in front of Joe. "The men of Ah Ping's *tong* were after my little sister, you see, and we had to hide! I believed this house was empty, and hoped to keep her here just until morning! Truly, we . . . we meant no harm!"

"*Tong?* What the blazes is a *tong?*"the young woman demanded impatiently.

"A gang," Joe supplied. "One of the Chinese gangs that operate near here in Chinatown. They had some pretty nasty plans for little Mei Ling, but her brother and I managed to get her away in the nick of time. We're quite harmless, love, so put the gun down, why don't you?" He ventured a reassuring grin, but it had no effect whatsoever on the young woman.

"Uh-uh. You leave, and then I'll put it down. Now, get!"

Joe frowned. In one lithe move, he sprang across the room toward her. He grasped the rifle barrel and with a powerful flex of his muscles wrenched it easily from the girl's fierce grip and angled the long black barrel safely downward toward the flagstones. She made a furious lunge to regain the weapon, but Joe quickly side-stepped and held it out of her reach. "Sorry, love. Much as we'd like to, we can't leave, not just yet. It's too bloody risky," he told her grimly, ignoring the spitting fury in her eyes. He cracked the rifle and pointedly emptied the cartridges onto the floor, where they landed with a series of dull, clinking sounds.

"Why, you bas—!"

"Now, now, don't get your dander up, lady! We'll only be here for a while, then you can have your precious rifle back, I promise. Come on, miss, look at the little girl! She's frightened, tired, and upset. Surely you can't be such a coldhearted bitch you'd send her back out onto the streets like that? Come on, there's a love. See if you can't find her some tucker and a hot cuppa or something, eh?" His voice was gentle now, cajoling almost.

The young woman's rigid posture softened fractionally. "A little girl? Where is she?"

"Right here." Joe reached out and took Mei Ling's chilly little hand in his large one, gently leading her forward from the shadows. As he did so, he discreetly lodged the emptied rifle in the shadows against the wall. "Don't be afraid, sweetheart," he murmured to Ming's little sister. "No one's going to hurt you. The lady looks a lot meaner than she is, I'd say." He grinned crookedly, his teasing tone challenging her to deny the truth of what he'd said.

The young woman had turned away as Joe spoke,

96

and was fumbling with something in the shadows. There was a rasping sound, then a hiss, and then the light of a gas lamp chased away the darkness as she replaced a large milk glass shade over the chimney. The four, momentarily dazzled by the pool of sudden brightness, blinked, then regarded one another curiously.

"Why, heck, she's just a baby!" the young woman exclaimed indignantly, her tone measurably kinder now. "What on earth could she have done to make this . . . gang . . . want to harm her?"

"My father sold her to their boss man, Ah Ping," Ming volunteered. "She was to have served him and the other old goats who come to the House of Happiness—those who have a . . . a fondness for very young girls."

"The House of Happiness?"

"A brothel," Joe supplied bluntly. "It specializes in very young sing-song girls." Seeing she still looked confused, he added, "Whores, love."

"Oh!" the young woman gasped, and in the revealing amber lamplight Joe saw a rush of becoming color pinken her cheeks. "Of all the low-down things to do! She's . . . she's only a child!"

"Precisely. And that's why we just had to get her away. Now do you see?"

"Yes. Of course I do." The young woman went across to Mei Ling and crouched down beside her. "Are you hungry, honey?" she asked gently, brushing dark strands of straight ebony hair away from the tear-streaked little face. Mei Ling nodded shyly, and the young woman hugged her. "Well, I'm afraid I don't have very much to eat here, Mei Ling, but I do believe there's some bread and cheese in the pantry, and probably some coffee. There's no milk or anything, though. Would that do?" She glanced up uncertainly at Joe, then looked quickly away again.

"Just the ticket," Joe agreed, relieved.

"Then I'll see to it, Mister . . . ?"

"Christmas," Joe supplied, not certain why he'd told her his real name, but doing so anyway. "Joe Christmas. And you are . . . ?"

"You can call me . . . you can call me Kate," the young woman returned, demurely lowering her gray-green, long-lashed eyes yet again under the frank, appraising stare he'd given her. Why, she thought, his eyes are the most unusual color I've ever seen! Even by lamplight, they were a rare turquoise hue flecked with gold that struck one as still more vivid, contrasted against the deep bronze of his weathered complexion and the dusty-blond shagginess of his hair and white-blond lashes. He could not truly be termed handsome, or, at least, not in conventional terms of male beauty that demanded regularity of features and chiseled lips and jaw. No, his features were far too rugged and irregular for that. Yet combined, they gave him an attractive, roguish air that was aggressively, deliciously male, and was guaranteed to turn feminine heads for a second glance in his direction wherever he went. Oh, Lord, the way he was staring at her was darned disconcerting, to say the least! His expression made her feel peculiarly breathless, as if she'd run too far and too fast. She was suddenly acutely aware of the quickened tempo of her heartbeat under her ribcage, and the rapid rise and fall of her breasts beneath her gown. She felt heat and color rush headlong to her cheeks as he swept off his hat. Oh, Lord, surely he didn't mean to make fun of her? But no, he inclined his head politely, the very picture of a proper gentleman. Only his eyes belied the proper gesture, for their turquoise gaze never once strayed from her face, and the expression alive in their depths was certainly far from proper. Why, he made her feel quite weak at the knees . . .

"Pleased to meet you, Miss Katie," he drawled, his accent foreign to her ears and as fascinating as the rest of him. "We're grateful for your hospitality, believe me."

To his obvious surprise—and her own—she suddenly laughed, a merry, husky laugh that was very attractive—as was she, Joe realized appreciatively, *bloody* attractive. He stood there, captivated, eyeing the way her loose, raven-black hair threw back the amber glow of the light in glossy blue reflections as it swirled about her shoulders, and the lithe way her trim yet rounded figure moved with unconsciously seductive grace beneath her unpretentious gray gown and a somewhat grimy apron.

"*My* hospitality? Lord, I'm afraid I gilded the lily just a bit, Mister Christmas, thinking you were burglars," she explained in a breathless rush. "You see, this isn't my house, despite what I said. I've just been seeing to the dusting and airing, readying it for the real owner. I was . . . detained . . . elsewhere earlier, and didn't arrive until it was almost dusk. I must have fallen asleep on the sofa, and only woke up when I heard you and your friends break in." She shrugged and gave him a rueful smile. "So you see, I'm only the . . . the cleaning woman, not the owner."

Joe grinned, his turquoise eyes twinkling wickedly. "Miss Kate, you could never be *only* anything!"

She blushed yet again, and bustled away from him into the pantry where she rummaged about for an inordinately long while to regain her shattered composure before returning with a crusty loaf of bread under one arm and a wedge of golden cheese on a blue plate covered with a flowered, blue china dome in the other hand.

"I'll have to start the fire for the coffee—"

"Forget the coffee. It's too much trouble at this late

hour. Water will be fine. Come on, Mei Ling, sit yourself down at the table. You must be sleepy, eh, sweetheart?"

"Yes, sir," Mei Ling mumbled, and Ming went to her and hugged her with a gruff, brotherly display of affection.

"Never fear. You are safe now, *shao mei mei.* I will not let Ah Ping's men take you away again."

Mei Ling nodded solemnly, her trust and belief in her big brother evident as she gazed up at him adoringly. "I know you will not, Ah Ming, my brother."

"What'll you do now?" Joe asked Ming while Kate sliced bread and cheese, almost losing a finger to the sharp blade in her nervousness.

"There is a very kind white woman who cares for girls such as my sister," Ming told him. "She runs a home and school for the unwanted or orphaned daughters of my people, and for unfortunate slave girls who escape their masters. She sees that they are taught to read and write and are properly cared for until they are old enough to marry or gain some respectable employment. Some of them marry very well, too. I plan to take Mei Ling to her. It will be for the best, I believe, for the time being. I have no means to care for her myself, you see."

"Donaldina Cameron's School for Chinese Girls on Sacramento Street?" Kate inquired. Ming nodded. "Yes, I've heard of it. She's a wonderful woman, by all accounts, and her girls are very well cared for. Your sister will be safe with her. But how do you plan to get her there on foot, when those awful *tong* people may still be after you both? Surely they won't have given up looking for you yet?"

Ming shrugged. "It is no problem. I will find a way."

"Well, I . . . I could take her there for you in the

morning, if that would help?" Kate offered impulsively, touched by the charming little girl's plight and her brother's obvious love and concern for her.

"You would do that for us?" Ming cried in astonishment, overwhelmed by her generous offer.

"Of course. Why not? Besides, who'd ever suspect a young white woman like me of harboring a little Chinese girl wanted by the *tong!* Let's see, we can throw my cloak over her shoulders to hide her clothes, and have a hack sent around to whisk her away to Sacramento Street, no one the wiser! That is, if you'd trust me to do it, Ming?" After the "welcome" she'd given them, she doubted it.

Ming looked to Joe, who nodded faintly, and then back to Kate. When he could finally speak, his voice was husky and strangled sounding, "I would trust you, missie, yes. And I . . . I would be forever in your debt!"

"Then it's agreed," Joe said, his voice deep and loud in the weighty silence that followed. "As soon as it's light, I'll leave and send a carriage back here for you ladies. If they tracked us to the house, there's a good chance they'll follow me, hoping I'll lead them to you and Mei Ling. Now Ming, what about you?" He frowned.

"I do not know, *fon kwei.* I fear San Francisco, large as it is, is still too small a city to hide me from Ah Ping's men now! I must go somewhere else, where they cannot find me and my face is not known." He averted his face, no doubt to hide the tears sparkling in their depths, Joe guessed.

"Well, there's time to worry about that later," Kate said firmly, setting a plate of bread and cheese before Mei Ling, and two others across from it for the men. "First things first. Sit down and eat, both of you. It's not much, but it's better than nothing. And I do believe I have almost a half bottle of champagne in the other room, if you'd care for something a little stronger than water to wash it down, Mister Christmas?"

"Why not, love?" Joe replied readily. "After all, Mei Ling's escape is plenty to celebrate, right?" He winked roguishly, his turquoise eyes caressing her face yet again. "And besides, it's not every day a man is lucky enough to meet a beautiful parlor maid called Kate."

"Indeed it isn't!" Kate muttered under her breath as she went in search of the bottle.

Mei Ling fell asleep shortly thereafter, leaving her bread and cheese unfinished. Joe carried her into another room, where dust-sheeted furniture loomed in the gloom like bulky ghosts. He gently set her on a comfortable horsehair chaise and covered her with the cloak Kate gave him for that purpose.

There was only an hour left until dawn, and Joe and Ming passed the time relating the details of their escapades to an incredulous and wide-eyed Kate. Their story drew alternating merry peals of laughter and gasps of horror from her lips and Joe watched the changing expressions on her delightful face with something akin to fascination until it grew light. Used to the bold and brassy women of the saloons and taverns of Sydney's waterfront, or the worn-down, dispirited faces of farmers' and settlers' wives in the Outback, her fresh beauty and the lithe grace that she brought even to the most commonplace movement mesmerized him. He wondered how it would be to hold her warm, female body close against his own, to caress that shining mass of wild black hair, and crush those tempting pink lips beneath his; to feel her come afire and glowing with awakened desire in his arms. Strewth! They were bloody dangerous notions for a man to be having who was bent only on carving out a future for himself, he realized, and accordingly he abandoned them in action.

"Well," he said, glancing toward the kitchen window, through which a bleary dawn was breaking, "I reckon I should be on my way. You'll stay here, Ming?"

Ming nodded. "If I may, until Miss Kate leaves with my little sister, yes. Then I, too, must vanish. It . . . it will not be easy to say farewell to Mei Ling, nor to the two of you who have become such dear friends. Joe, Missie Kate, I have not the words to thank you both—"

"No thanks are needed, Ming," Joe said gruffly. "Isn't that right, Kate?"

Kate nodded readily. "Of course, Ming. I just hope everything works out for you both."

"It will. Of this I am certain. My little mother told me many years ago that before my birth in the Year of the Rabbit, the astrologers predicted a long life filled with good fortune for me. So it is destined! Have no fears for Chen Ming. When next we meet, do not be surprised if I am accounted one of the wealthiest Celestials in Chinatown and am smoking a two-bit cigar! Goodbye, *fon kwei.*"

"Goodbye, Ming. And . . . good luck, cobber," Joe said gruffly. Plucky little blighter, he thought. Inside, he must be wondering if he has any future at all, yet you'd never guess as much from the confident grin he wears.

The pair clasped hands warmly, then Joe got to his feet and strode from the kitchen and through the empty house, headed for the front door. Kate followed him out.

"Wait! Here's the address of this house, Mister Christmas. If you could send a hack for Mei Ling and myself at around eight, say, we'll be ready and waiting."

"Will do."

Hat in hand, Joe stood there, seemingly reluctant to leave. His eyes burned hotly with turquoise fires as they rested upon her face, and he sensed an answering heat in the gray-green eyes that returned his gaze. Not for the first time that morning, he marveled at the strength of his attraction to her. Christ! He'd only met her a few hours ago, but already he felt as if he were leaving someone he'd cared for for years. He had the wildest desire to crush her into his arms and cover the slender, pale-gold column of her throat with hungry kisses; to bury his head against the valley of her breasts and stroke the long and shapely lines of her thighs hinted at beneath the gray folds of her gown; to feel her rosy lips return the heat of his mouth with a flaming desire that matched his own.

"Will I see you again, Kate? I'd sure like to," he asked, despite all his intentions to the contrary, and then he grinned to hide his anxiety that she might refuse. Christ Almighty, had he gone crazy? She was only a chit of a girl! But all of a sudden, it seemed the most important thing in the world that she should say yes! "The least I could do is buy you supper, after the way we broke into your employer's house," he added.

"That's not necessary, really it isn't. You and Ming have thanked me enough. And I couldn't possibly see you again, I'm afraid, Mister Christmas, not for any reason. You see, I'm to be married within the month."

Joe grimaced, an unaccountable lurch of crushing disappointment twisting in his gut. "I should have known a girl like you'd be spoken for. He's a lucky bloke. I envy him, Kate," he added softly. "He must be a dinkum fellow to have a plucky girl like you in love with him."

"Love? Oh, no, Mister Christmas, I certainly don't love him! Why, I don't even *know* him! It's . . . it's

104

just . . . a marriage of convenience, on both sides. Our . . . parents . . . engineered it, sort of." For a fleeting second, there was a look of despair and unhappiness on her lovely face, honest regret in the depths of her gray-green eyes, a tremulous quiver to her temptingly moist, pink lips.

"Then I guess it won't matter if I do this, then, will it?" Joe asked huskily, unable to fight any longer the compelling hunger within him to kiss her, hold her in his arms. He bent his dark-blond head quickly to Kate's raven one before she could realize his intent and escape.

His mouth covered hers, its hungry pressure sending fiery little tingles down to her very toes that seemed to melt her bones clean away and leave her limp and powerless as she leaned weakly against him. The heat of his lean, hard body, so very near, so very, very male, sent excited shivers darting through her. *No! Make him stop! You didn't come all this way just to get involved with a man! Show him the door! Get rid of him now!* Warning bells clamored danger in her mind, but they were alarms she refused to acknowledge in any way as, almost rocking on her heels, too stunned to make any protest, she allowed him to continue his kisses. She was vaguely aware now of the firm pressure of his fingertips gently tracing her spine and the curves of her derrière, the cradling warmth of his other callused palm against the flushed curve of her cheek where he held her head uptilted for his mouth—and of the shameless way her own hands moved upward, with what seemed a will of their own, to twine about his neck and lose themselves in the tousled sea of small blond waves there at his nape. His tongue tip parted her lips and surged hotly between them, exploring and tasting the secret recesses of her mouth in a shocking, intimate way that ignited tickling tongues of fire deep in her

105

belly. She'd been kissed before—oh, yes, several times—but they had been chaste, fleeting kisses given by boys hardly less innocent than she. None of those kisses had even come close to the exciting, blatantly sexual quality of *his* kisses—kisses that shook her to her very core, and left her aroused and aching for more.

"Oh, but you shouldn't have . . . !" she gasped breathlessly when he broke away, stunned by her wanton reaction to this . . . this stranger.

"Oh, but I already did! G'bye, Katie—and thanks!" he murmured huskily, chucking her under the chin. Then he turned quickly from her and strode down the front path, afraid if he didn't leave, and quickly, he'd kiss her again and be utterly lost to stop himself from doing far, far more than just kiss her.

She caught a glimpse of dusty-blond hair lit by the golden torch of dawn in the fleeting second before he turned the corner. Then he was gone.

"Jiminy Christmas!" she whispered to the silent hall, leaning weakly against the balustrade for several minutes until her composure returned. Then she laughed softly at her unconsciously appropriate choice of exclamation. Her eyes were dreamy as she too turned, then reluctantly closed the door behind her.

Joe returned to Mrs. Barker's, whistling jauntily as he strode inside the vestibule. The plump woman eyed him with a disapproving air.

"You're up and about early this morning, Mister McCaleb?" she inquired with a little sniff, undoubtedly well aware that he had been out all night and assuming he'd been drinking and carousing despite her warnings.

"Yes, indeed, lovely lady. There's nothing like a brisk walk in the morning air to set you up right for the day. Puts hairs on your chest, it does." He grinned crookedly and winked and tapped his chest.

"Oh, you young rascal!" Mrs. Barker scolded, all disapproval banished. "Breakfast's in one hour prompt, mind."

"I'll be there," Joe promised and took the stairs three at a time to his room.

It wasn't until some two hours later, as he went out to the street to hail the horse drawn cab for Kate and Mei Ling, that he looked at the scrap of paper he'd tucked in his shirt pocket earlier. He could easily decipher Katie's bold, almost masculine, scrawl. Two hundred Bayview Drive, it said. Something nagged in his mind, some half-forgotten recollection. Damned if that address didn't seem peculiarly familiar, he thought idly, then shrugged off such a notion as he whistled up a passing hack. He'd much rather consider the yielding sweetness of pretty Katie's lips than any address—a sweetness that seemed to linger on his own lips even now, just as the memory of her warm, rounded body trembling in his arms, the fleeting graze of her full breasts against his fingertips, lingered in his mind . . .

Chapter Seven

A week had passed and the old year had given way to the new. Though twice Joe had returned hopefully to the rambling, empty old mansion on Bayview Drive, and once had even visited the Girls' Home on Sacramento Street and spoken with little Mei Ling, now quite happily settled into her new home, neither she nor anyone else there had known where to find Katie, much to his regret, and he had not seen her again since the night he and Ming had broken into the old house.

It was bloody peculiar how that slip of a girl had gotten under his skin; how that single kiss seemed branded into his mind, he thought, disgusted with himself. To date, no other woman had had such an effect on him. "Love 'em and leave 'em longing for more" had always been his motto, and even if he tried, it was a rare woman whose name he could remember a week after she'd warmed his bed. That had suited him fine in the past. He'd told himself he didn't want to be tied down by a woman, and that that was why he'd never stayed with any one woman long enough to get involved. But he had a feeling that wasn't the only reason, not deep down. You were always too bloody scared, Lightnin' Joe, he thought uncomfortably, hating himself—scared of letting go and loving someone, afraid if you did she'd walk out on you, or die, or do something, and leave you feeling like you'd been kicked in the teeth. Then why did his mind refuse to forget Kate? What had her silky black hair and lustrous gray-green eyes done to change him? Why did the image of her lovely face, her defiant stance as she had leveled the rifle at him, the complete and unconditional surrender of herself to his kisses in that fleeting moment they'd shared, continually plague his memory? He cussed and tossed his smoke to the dirt street, grinding the sizzling butt into a puddle under his boot heel. Well, Miss Katie, whatever magic it is you used, you've bewitched me long enough! he announced to himself. It's time now to say good-bye, because I'm about to become a married man, God help me! And with that fervent plea, he determinedly thrust all thoughts of Katie aside and started up the pumice-and-lye-whitened stoop to the offices of Silverstein and Caldwell.

Edward Caldwell, who was in the process of pouring himself a drink when Joe entered his plush office, seemed happy to see him.

"Come in, come in, dear boy! I'd almost despaired of hearing from you, to be honest, and had determined to send a message around to your lodgings by the end of the week to inquire after you. Brandy?"

"Thanks."

"There you go. Now, tell me, Joel, have you come to a decision yet regarding the stipulations of the will?"

"I have." Joe drew a deep breath. "I've decided to go through with it, as my grandfather wished."

"Well, that's splendid, just splendid! I can't tell you how happy I am that you've reached this decision, Joel, and I'm certain you'll not regret it. As I told you before, it's the sensible—and highly beneficial—thing to do.

Now, no doubt you are most anxious to meet with your . . . er . . . fiancée, Miss Jones?"

"I am, very anxious," Joe agreed with a distinct lack of enthusiasm that was at odds with his words. His mouth quirked downward in a grimace that Caldwell, his back to him, failed to see.

"Then let's waste no more time!" the lawyer declared, beaming. "As Providence would have it, Miss Seraphina is here at this very moment, in the room next door with my partner, Mister Silverstein. While you enjoy your brandy, I'll leave you for just a moment and bring her in to meet you."

Joe nodded, somewhat numbed by this sudden turn of events, and Caldwell left him alone.

Oh, Christ, he'd be face-to-face with the old battle-ax in less than a minute! His starched and formal collar suddenly felt overly tight, like a noose. His tie was a garrote, slowly strangling him. He gulped down his brandy as if he were dying of thirst.

The door opened, and he sprang to his feet in jack-in-the-box fashion as Caldwell reentered the office. He ushered in ahead of him a slim, tall woman of indeterminate age—indeterminate because little of her could be seen. She wore a stylishly small black felt hat with a pert, turned-up brim, from which was suspended a concealing, dotted black lace mourning veil, a black cloak over a black silk gown, and black gloves. The small purse and umbrella she carried were also black. All in all, she reminded Joe of a black widow spider— not a comforting image at all, under the circumstances, since that particular species of spider gained its name from its predilection for devouring its mate after the honeymoon was over! Incongruously, the light, airy fragrance of her perfume put him in mind of spring and wildflowers, and was a far cry from thoughts of spiders and widows.

110

"Miss Seraphina Jones, it is my pleasure to introduce you at last to your guardian's grandson, Mister Joel William McCaleb. Mister McCaleb, Miss Seraphina Jones."

The heavily shrouded vision lifted its head, and a small, startled squeak escaped from beneath the heavy folds of her veil. Fright, Joe wondered as he gravely accepted the trembling black-gloved hand she extended, or distaste?

"I'm delighted to meet you, Miss Jones," he murmured as he bowed over her hand.

"And I you, Mister McCaleb," she responded in a faint voice, withdrawing that same hand with disturbing alacrity.

"Well," Caldwell continued, still beaming, "I've no doubt you two young people will wish to waste no time in becoming acquainted, under the somewhat unusual circumstances?" He chuckled. "So, if it meets with your approval, Joel, I thought I'd send my secretary around to make reservations for luncheon for the two of you, at the Auction Lunch restaurant just down the street? I'm certain a delightful repast in pleasant surroundings will do much to put you at ease with each other. The Auction is famous for its delicious fish stew, I might add. I highly recommend it."

"Very thoughtful of you, sir; please do," Joe agreed, wondering desperately if he'd let it go too far to make good his getaway. "Miss Jones, won't you sit down?" He drew forward a chair.

"Thank you, but I . . . I prefer to stand," the young woman replied coolly, her voice muffled by the veil's voluminous folds.

"As you will," Joe said gruffly, nodding to Caldwell as he discreetly left them alone. For several minutes, a weighty and uncomfortable silence hung heavily, like a damp blanket, in the room. Joe coughed. "Might I pour you a brandy, Miss Jones?"

"Oh, please do."

Surprised by her ready acceptance but glad of the chance to move, to do *something,* Joe stood and performed the ritual of pouring the brandy, carrying the snifter carefully to the young woman, who had taken up a position by the lace-curtained windows as if contemplating hurling herself from them to the busy street below. He held out the snifter, intrigued despite his discomfort. She would naturally have to raise her veil to drink, and he was deeply curious to see what she looked like beneath it, after all this.

"Thank you, Mister McCaleb," she said and took the snifter from him.

To his undisguised amazement, she did not raise her veil, as he had anticipated, but slipped the glass beneath its folds and drained the potent contents in a single gulp, before setting down the glass upon Caldwell's desk with a decided thud.

"Oh, Lord!" she exclaimed, fanning herself. "It's quite . . . bracing . . . isn't it? It has a kick like a . . . like a mule!"

Bemused, Joe nodded, doubly intrigued now. "Indeed it has, Seraphina. I may call you Seraphina, I hope?"

"But of course. And I will call you Joel . . . or even Joe, perhaps?"

Was he mistaken, or was there the barest hint of sarcasm in her tone now? Surely not! He'd done and said nothing that he was aware of that could have angered her.

He shrugged. "Either would be dandy by me. Could I take your cloak and hat? It's a bit stuffy in here, wouldn't you say?"

She skittered away from him as if he'd suggested something indecent.

112

"You think so? On the contrary, Joel, I find it rather . . . chilly."

Stalemate, Joe thought, his irritation growing. Undoubtedly she was ugly as sin—he was convinced of that now—and was playing for time. Well, subtlety had gained him damn little. A more direct approach was warranted from here on, he determined.

"Seraphina, forgive me, but if we're to be married, for whatever reason, I must insist you remove your hat and veil! You've seen me, right? And naturally, I'm curious to see you! Surely you can't expect me to marry you sight unseen?"

"Oh? And why not?" she flared, flouncing across the room before whirling about to face him, black veil floating on the air. "Unlike you, I'm in mourning for a man who was . . . was very kind to me while he was alive. If I wish to remain veiled in respect for his passing, I will! Besides, be honest, Joel McCaleb, it doesn't really matter a tinker's damn to you what I look like. You'd marry me anyway, wouldn't you?" she challenged. "It's not a bride you want, but your grandfather's money and land. I'm just a means to that end. Why, I'll bet you don't feel so much as a twinge of remorse that he's dead and gone!"

There was a pause while Joe recovered from her decidedly unladylike speech, and then he decided that equally brutal honesty on his part was the best policy. "Damn it, no, I don't! I had few warm feelings for my grandfather. How could I? Unlike you, I'd never once met the man! And I admit, I was far from overjoyed to find that marrying a woman I'd also never met was a condition of Grandfather's will—I'd be a bloody hypocrite if I said I was! To be honest, I was hoping you'd feel the same about me, and that we could come to some arrangement that would suit us both."

He could tell his words interested her, without

113

having to see her expression. The sudden, tense alertness of her body said so. She fairly quivered beneath her somber garments, the dotted veil trembling.

"Oh. Really?" There was a lengthy pause after Joe nodded. "And just exactly what *arrangement* is it you have in mind?"

"That we marry, of course, and fulfill the stipulations of the will to the letter. But afterward, we could sell the ranch and divide the proceeds, fifty-fifty, right down the middle!"

"And then petition for a divorce, of course?"

"Of course! You'd be free to go your way, and I mine. Come now, admit it, Miss Jones. You strike me as an intelligent young woman. You must have considered that possibility yourself, I'm sure?"

"Oh, yes. More times than I care to count, Mister Joel McCaleb," she responded quickly and with grim humor in her tone.

"Then you must agree the idea has some merit."

"Enormous merit! In fact, I could think of no other way to circumvent the conditions of my . . . my guardian's will . . . and believe me, I've also given it *considerable* thought these past few days!"

"Then what do you say we discuss it over that luncheon Caldwell suggested? And if all appears promising, we'll toast our good fortune—and seal our new partnership—with a bottle of the very best champagne."

There was a pause.

"You're a very greedy, very devious man, Mister McCaleb."

"If I am, then you must be an equally greedy and devious young woman, mustn't you, Miss Jones," Joe retorted. "In which case, we should get along just dinkum for as long as we have to. Well? What do you say?"

"Champagne is my favorite wine, Joel," Seraphina declared, crossing the room somewhat unsteadily toward him on account of the generous brandy she had already imbibed. "Lead the way!"

He offered her his elbow and, teetering just slightly, she accepted.

The waft of springlike perfume tantalized his nostrils and his memory yet again as he led her through the door, and he itched to whisk the heavy veil from her face and see exactly what lay beneath.

The Auction Lunch restaurant, also on Montgomery Street, was crowded with lunching bankers and businessmen, yet it soon became obvious that Caldwell had excellent connections, for even at this late hour, the choice table to which they were led commanded an excellent view of the busy, elegant thoroughfare with its urns and bubbling fountains. The weather that framed the charming scene, however, was as gray and uncertain looking in this month of January as was Joe's mood at that moment.

Deep blue table linens formed a perfect foil for sparkling glass and silverware, and the comfortable straight-backed chairs upon which they sat boasted matching blue upholstered seats. Floor-to-ceiling-length mirrors reflected light everywhere and dispelled the dour gloom of the weather outside. Fine, deep-piled carpeting and exquisite brocade wallpaper added their opulence to the decor, as did the many striking charcoal sketches and oil paintings of gold-rush-era San Francisco in heavy, gilded wood frames. Gas-lit crystal chandeliers twinkled brightly, reflecting in every spotless mirror like rays of pure sunshine.

Though Joe had rarely before dined in such plush

115

surroundings, being more at home with tucker consumed over a campfire out in the bush, he acquitted himself well in ordering their luncheon, silently thanking his aunt Polly for insisting he learn how to deport himself amongst the "toffs." Aunt Polly, bless her, though a whorehouse madam, had been a lady in more ways than many so-called ladies, and she'd done him proud in his education, certain her Joey, as she'd called him, would amount to something one day. They both selected the house specialty that Caldwell had recommended, the fish stew, to begin their meal, while Joe opted for braised lamb chops, accompanied by mint jelly and baby potatoes and pearl onions tossed in a butter and parsley sauce, for his main course. Despite his recommendations, Seraphina wrinkled up her nose at the idea of mutton in any fashion whatsoever, and selected the cold, sliced roasted beef instead.

"Ever tasted lamb?" Joe inquired idly, more as a means of making conversation than anything. "It's tasty tucker when it's cooked right."

Beneath her mourning weeds, Seraphina's slender shoulders gave a delicate shudder of distaste. "I'm afraid not. And nor do I care to! Sheep! Ugh! They're horrible, smelly, dirty creatures! Why, what they do to good grazing land for longhorns is a crime, a . . . a sin!"

"Cattle? Ah. So, you're an expert on cattle ranching, are you then, Seraphina?" His expression was amused.

"Oh . . . no, no, of course not," she hurriedly amended. "But back east I read and heard about the problems between the sheep and cattle ranchers out west, and I must confess, on hearing both sides of the issue, my sympathies lie entirely with the cattlemen."

Joe shrugged. "You're entitled to your opinion, of course. But there's land that won't support cattle, scrub grass that's just made for sheep, which are less finicky,

116

shall we say, than cows. And wool's far more profitable than beef."

"Well, I suppose if the land simply can't support cattle, then sheep might be a worthwhile alternative. A last resort, as it were," she agreed reluctantly, though her tone belied her words. She turned her head as the waiter arrived bearing two steaming, large bowls of soup, crisp sourdough rolls, and pats of butter. "Ah, here's our fish stew!" she exclaimed with what, to Joe's mind, seemed an unnatural eagerness, almost as if she welcomed the interruption and the inevitable change of conversation it produced. She devoted her entire attention to spreading her snowy napkin over her lap, while Joe took up his spoon and began eating.

"Is the stew not to your liking?" Joe asked, nodding his head toward her untouched bowl several minutes later. His own bowl was already half empty. He wondered, faintly amused, how she would handle eating the soup without eating her veil—by requesting a long straw, maybe? He grinned wickedly at the thought, his turquoise eyes brilliant with merriment.

"It does look delicious," she admitted with obvious reluctance.

"It tastes delicious, too," Joe goaded. "You should at least try it."

"Very well," she agreed with a heavy sigh. "But . . . but before I take off my veil, you have to promise me something?"

"If I can. What is it?"

"That you won't change your mind. That whatever I look like you'll still stick to your side of our bargain, *all* of it—the wedding and then . . . then the divorce, as soon as possible?"

"Very well, you have my sworn word," he agreed after a slight pause, certain now that she was horribly disfigured in some way and bracing himself for

117

the sight.

"Shake on it!" she insisted forthrightly and extended her slim, black-gloved hand across the table for him to do so.

He dabbed his mouth with a napkin, pushed back his chair, and stood, taking her hand in his and solemnly shaking it to seal his promise. Her gravity had stirred new feelings in him now, feelings of sympathy, for he had noticed that within the glove her slender hand had been trembling. He'd always favored the underdogs of the world, backed the outsiders in every race. On that score, he hadn't changed. Poor little blighter! What monstrosity would shortly be revealed that could inspire such fear in her? Was she scarred, deformed in some awful way?

With a marked lack of eagerness, she grasped the black veil and slowly lifted it up and away from her face.

Joe's jaw went slack, his mouth dropping open in a manner that was far from elegant. Turquoise eyes widened as, astonished, he gazed back into the gray-green, mysterious eyes and lovely face of *Kate,*—his Kate—the elusive cleaning woman of Bayview Drive, and all the pieces suddenly dropped into place.

What a bloody fool she'd played him for! It had been his house—or rather, his "grandfather's" house, that he and Ming had unwittingly chosen that night for their refuge! And Kate had lied to him, telling him she was Kate when she was in fact none other than Seraphina Jones! The pity he had felt seconds before dwindled. He sat down abruptly, muttering, "Christ!" under his breath, screwing his napkin into a ball, and tossing it irritably onto the table. He hated being made a fool of, and it seemed that he had been this time, and royally.

She grimaced, reading his expression correctly. "Well, don't say I didn't warn you," she reminded him ruefully. "Believe me, I had no idea who you were that night, whatever you may believe to the contrary. And besides, Mister *Christmas,* you weren't exactly honest with me either, were you?" The gray-green eyes, more green now than gray with her mood, glared accusingly into his.

All at once, Joe could see the humor in the situation. For over a week, this Kate had plagued him, memories of a single, sweetly stolen kiss had tormented his thoughts, and he had postponed meeting the mysterious Miss Jones on account of the elusive Kate. And now, when he had despaired of ever finding her again, here she was—and committed to marrying him, what was more! He threw back his head and laughed, a deep rumble of infectious male laughter that drew about more than one female head to look in his direction, there to linger with frank curiosity and appreciation of the rugged, loose-limbed and attractively masculine view he presented.

"Aye, you're right. Christ Almighty! I suppose I wasn't totally honest either, *Katie,*" he agreed at long length, merriment still dancing in his eyes, the perennially crooked grin still twitching the corners of his mouth. "But I *am* totally delighted!"

She frowned worriedly, tiny lines furrowing her smooth brow. "Delighted? Oh, no, Mister McCaleb, that's *exactly* what I was afraid of. You mustn't be delighted, not at all. Our bargain—its terms—must stand. You promised—remember, you shook on it? We'll be married, fair enough, but then afterward, we *must* sell the property immediately and go our own separate ways. If not, I'm leaving—right here and now—and this ridiculous deal's off!"

She sprang to her feet to add weight to her threat, and indeed seemed quite prepared to take flight. Joe reached out and grasped her wrist, yanking her firmly back down to her chair with a grip that made her wince.

"Don't take on! My word's good, love," he reassured her. "Believe me, I welcome the idea of marriage about as warmly as you seem to do! It's just that, what with all the secrecy, I was damned relieved to see it was you, and not some sideshow freak from a carnival! Now, sit down and enjoy your tucker."

She nodded curtly. "Very well. And while we eat, I do believe we should discuss the details of the ceremony and get that formality out of the way. After all, we have only two weeks left before the thirty days William McCaleb stipulated in his will are up. The sooner we set a date, the sooner we can get this whole distasteful business over and done with and go our separate ways. Agreed?"

"Agreed," Joe responded by rote. But as his turquoise eyes roamed her lovely face, committing to memory once more the wide, gray-green eyes with the sooty fringing of lashes, the elegant upsweep of glossy blue-black hair set off today by dangling pendant earrings of turquoise stones, the silly little upturned nose, the arrogant cheekbones, and the lush, inviting pink mouth, business was the farthest thing from his mind. Christ, yes! Eyes half closed and hooded now, he had a sudden, erotic vision of the young woman across the table from him stripped totally nude by his expert—and eager!—hands, her only clothing the luxuriant mass of raven black hair he'd unpinned to spill about her slim shoulders and down over her lovely, bared breasts in a riotous cascade . . . . Oh, Lightnin' Joe, you're an evil-minded bastard, he told himself, endeavoring to concentrate on what she was saying, but still the delicious vision persisted, seemingly painted on his eyeballs. There'd be an invitation in her mysterious eyes and on her lips that he'd be only too willing to accept as he hauled her into his arms and began—

"Now, it was my thought that we could be married at the First Presbyterian Church of San Francisco on Saturday next," her husky voice broke in upon his sensual reverie, rupturing his images, "and spend the following day or two at your grandfather's house while we make arrangements for our journey. How does that sound?"

"Just the ticket," Joe agreed, lying through his teeth as he ogled her unashamedly across the table. She blushed and looked away, obviously disturbed by his frank scrutiny. His lecherous grin broadened as his eyelids drooped once more. He relished her obvious discomfort as the images slowly reasserted themselves. Now he saw her nude yet again, but this time a long, red feather boa coiled snakelike around her creamy hips and waist, its fragile plumes tickling his nostrils in the draft as he dipped his head to press his lips to her silken thighs—

"And then, after all the paperwork is concluded, we could instruct Mister Caldwell to handle the selling of the town house in our absence, and without further ado go to this Rancho de las Campanas and see about selling that, too."

"Bloody marvelous," Joe agreed in a fervent tone, but his gaze was on the swell of her breasts thrusting against the severe black gown, and his thoughts were definitely not on what she had said but on the wicked notion of rolling each delicate nipple between his lips or fingers, or upon his tongue . . .

Again, she colored as if she could read his wayward thoughts, her rosy blush hectic against the cool, mysterious depths of her eyes and the liquid black silk of her hair.

"Mister McCaleb, I don't believe you've heard a damned thing I've said!"

121

The erotic visions burst like pricked balloons. Almost in shock, he glanced across the table and saw her as she really was, arrayed in her mourning weeds without an inch of flesh showing save for her face, and a regretful sigh escaped him. Ah, well. The images had been nice while they had lasted! "I have, too, love," he said in a studiedly casual tone. "I heard every word! We have Caldwell sell the house, go to Southern California and see what Gramps left us by way of land, then see that sold, too, and go on our merry, *separate* ways. Right?"

She nodded, her lips tightly pursed with irritation at his flippancy. "Yes."

"Then it's all settled. Finished. Nothing more to discuss. Waiter!"

"Sir?"

"A bottle of your very best champagne, if you would?"

"Very good, sir."

The bottle arrived, frosty in its silver bucket of ice. The waiter expertly uncorked it with a muted pop of the cork and poured them each a sparkling, bubbly glassful. Joe raised his and nodded to Seraphina to do likewise.

"To us, and to our future . . . prosperity!" he proposed.

"Amen to that," Seraphina echoed as they lightly touched glasses.

Chapter Eight

"Oh!" Seraphina exclaimed, and then she giggled. "The streets just won't stay still, will they, Joe!"

"No, love," Joe agreed amicably, hiding a grin. "The blighters have a nasty habit of moving around just when you don't want 'em to after a few drinks. Seen it happen dozens of times myself. Here, take hold of my arm."

He steadied her by the elbow as, teetering and weaving noticeably, she made her way past the fashionable and opulent facades of Montgomery Street. Outside the Diamond Palace, she came to a swaying halt and blinked as she peered through the polished window at the dazzling array of jewelry—diamonds, opals, emeralds, pearls, and gold—displayed in elegant black velvet cases within.

"That one!" she declared, pointing unsteadily with her index finger at a magnificent opal ring set off in solitary splendor in a small case of its own. She giggled and eyed him slyly. "Just the tick . . . ticket . . . *hick!* . . . wouldn't you say, love?" she teased him, mimicking his Australian twang between an attack of hiccups.

"What I'd say is that you're bloody well pickled, Miss Jones," Joe said amusedly as he engineered her away from the window and on down the street. "Only half a block to the hotel now, love. You can do it!"

"You're a rogue, Mister McCaleb," she told him accusingly, waggling her finger in his face now.

"Oh? What makes you say that?" Joe inquired innocently, carefully steering her around the massed blossoms of a flower seller on the street corner.

"Because you just kept on and on, pouring that champagne . . ."

". . . and you just kept on and on drinking it! I don't recollect having to twist your arm! Come on, turn about, love. Right through here."

She made it through the vestibule of the Occidental Hotel, but that was it. Just inside the polished wood portals, she gave a small sigh. Her hand flew to her face and her eyes went quite blank and staring before rolling up like a panicky filly's. Before she fell, Joe, who had anticipated something along these lines sooner or later, expertly scooped her up into his arms, and carried her across the vestibule to the front desk. Still carrying her and well aware of the raised eyebrows they were drawing, Joe spoke with the desk clerk.

"Miss Jones would like the key to her room, if you will? I'm afraid she's been taken ill and fainted."

"Of course! Here you go, sir, Suite 306! I . . . I do hope the young lady recovers very soon, sir."

"I'm sure she will. Thanks!"

He took the key with difficulty and carried Seraphina through the array of comfortable chaises and large potted plants tastefully scattered about the vestibule, and thence to the elegantly curved staircase. He looked up at the numerous stairs and heaved a sigh. Three hundred and six. Christ! He'd have to carry her up three bloody floors!

Resigned, he started up, pausing to catch his breath at each floor before continuing on and ignoring the startled looks given him by stuffy guests on their way down to the foyer. Thank God Seraphina was as slender as she was! He'd have done himself a mischief if she'd been on the buxom side, he thought wryly.

He was breathing heavily when at last he stood before the door to 306 and set Seraphina down so that she lolled limply against him while he opened the door and flung it wide. Without further ado, he again picked her up and strode into the suite with her in his arms, kicking the door closed behind him. Straightway he carried her through, into the bedroom, and with little ceremony dropped her onto the ornate bed, which boasted a headboard of frenzied cupids darting to and fro blowing impossibly long, heavenly bugles, among which quantities of highly unlikely looking flowers writhed in botanical ecstasy, all of it gilded.

Seraphina sighed and came to, struggling to a sitting position. Her skirts were up about her thighs, revealing a wealth of frothy white petticoats threaded with blue ribbons, a glimpse of lace-trimmed drawers, black stockings gartered in blue and white, and a dainty pair of black, buttoned, high-heel boots. Joe straightened and grinned as he admired the view.

"Where . . . *hick!* . . . where are we, Joe?" she inquired dazedly, looking about her and frowning.

"Your hotel suite at the Occidental. Stay where you are, love, and I'll fetch you some coffee." It wouldn't do to call room service to bring it up, not in her condition, he'd determined. Her reputation would be ruined. Joe didn't know a whole hell of a lot about well-brought-up young ladies, his female companions hitherto having been decidedly less than well brought up and certainly not ladies, but he knew that much.

"Don't want no coffee!" she said petulantly, smothering another hiccup. "Just bring me some more champagne, Joe, do! Oh, Lord, it's wonderful!

125

Everything's just goin' around and around and around
. . . wheee!" She flung her arms wide, as if twirled on
some carousel that only she could see.

"Coffee," Joe repeated firmly, "black coffee," and
beat a hurried exit down to the kitchens.

When he returned several minutes later bearing a
tray with a pot of strong black coffee, he went
immediately to the bedroom. Panic filled him momentarily when he saw that the bed was quite empty. He set
down the tray. Christ, the balcony! But even as he
started toward it, he heard her humming gaily from the
room that led off the bedroom and, following a frothy
lace trail of her discarded clothing, made his way into
the bathroom. There, in an enormous claw-footed
porcelain tub with winking brass fittings, up to her
delectable neck in bubbles, was Seraphina.

For a second, he simply stood there, blinking, for she
appeared to have stepped straight out of his wildest
fantasies at the restaurant. Her naturally pale gold
flesh was rosy now from the heat of the water, all pink
and gold like ripe peaches. Her slenderness when
clothed had been misleading, for he saw now that she
was curved in all the right places, breasts and hips and
bottom far from boyishly slim, but emphatically
female. Enchanting little tendrils of black hair framed
her lovely flushed face, curling with the humidity. Her
nipples played hide-and-seek with the frothy suds in a
way calculated to drive a saint to distraction—and Joe
was of a certainty no saint! The reality of her made
his fantasies pale by comparison, he thought, dry
mouthed. Nude, she was even more tempting, more
innocently seductive, than he had dared to dream! His
erotic visions returned full force, and danced like
sugarplums in his head, tantalizing him with images of
the two of them sprawled across that ridiculously large
bed in the other room. Christ, she was so bloody tipsy,

126

he doubted she'd even know what was going on until it was too late, he thought, licking his dry lips wolfishly in sudden anticipation. Strewth!

"Get behind me, Satan, old mate!" he muttered, remembering for the very first time in at least two decades the stringent moral teachings of the pious old biddies at the foundling home and almost feeling in that weak moment the horned, red-robed demon prodding him in the rear with his sharpened pitchfork to goad him down the path to self-ruin! "I'm not doing it, for Christ's sake, you hear me, cobber?"

But it took enormous self-control on Joe's part to overcome his lust and cast such an underhanded idea aside. Several moments passed by on leaden wings before conscience ruled and his innate sense of fair play and decency reluctantly won out over his baser side. Realizing how dangerously close to taking advantage of her tipsiness he had come, he was suddenly furious, more from his own guilt than true anger at her.

"You bloody little fool! You shouldn't be taking a bath in your condition. You might drown! Get out, right this minute!"

"Right this *very* minute? Like this? O-o-o-h! You naughty, naughty man!" She giggled coyly and cocked her head to one side. "C'mon, don't be such a grouchy ole bear, Joe! The water's so lovely and warm, and the bubbles are wonderful. Why, I feel as if I'm sitting in a glass of champagne!"

"Out!" he repeated sternly, casting about him for a towel. Fresh linens hung in readiness on a brass towel rack, and he snatched one up and headed purposefully toward the tub. "Stand up."

"Yessir," she agreed demurely, giggling as she struggled amongst the slippery bubbles to a standing position. "Anything you say!" Naked as the day she was born save for a few drifts of soap bubbles here and there that were like snowflakes against her rosily flushed body, she stretched out her arms to him. "Oops! I can't seem to stand up. Everything's going 'round and 'round . . . ! Carry me again, Joe!"

Muttering a curse, Joe reached out with the unfolded towel held before him, feeling unaccountably like a Spanish matador extending the cape toward the bull. He wrapped it around her and made to lift her from the tub, immune to her slippery, squirming charms with his newfound sense of honor and decency full upon him. But in the next instant she had coiled her arms ardently around his throat; another, and she had slipped and was dragging him down with her weight, head first into the warm, scented water and the enormous drifts of bubbles.

"Oh, Christ!" Joe spluttered as he resurfaced, all dignity lost.

For a second, Seraphina stared at him incredulously, then she threw back her head and shook her mass of damp black ringlets as peals of merry laughter broke from her rosy lips. "Oh, Joe! You look so darned funny! *Hick!* I haven't seen anything so goldarned funny in years!"

"Cut it out, you tipsy little witch!" Joe seethed, his expression thunderous.

"Oh, don't be sore, Joel, please? I didn't mean to . . . hick! . . . to . . . !" She was off and laughing helplessly again. "It . . . it was . . . the . . . soap and . . . !" Tears rolled down her flushed cheeks as he clambered from the tub, his jacket and pants—everything—soaked, his boots full of water and a cunning little crown of suds clinging to his blond head.

Deliberately ignoring her, pointedly offering her his rigid back and cursing under his breath, he stripped and fastened a second towel about his waist, wringing out his sodden attire as best he could and hanging it over chairs about the suite to drip dry. When it was arranged to his satisfaction, he returned to the bathroom and Seraphina, ignoring her protests and scooping her up from the tub and carrying her back to the bedroom.

"Sleep, young lady, that's the best thing for you," he said through gritted teeth as he set about drying her. Lord Almighty, what had he set himself up for this time, he wondered? He was a strong-willed man, capable of passing all tests of self-denial when he had to, but Christ, he was still a man, still human with human weaknesses for all that, and she was so damned, so *undeniably* female . . . ! She stood there obediently like a contrite child as he toweled her face, her neck, her arms, her legs, yet her nude body was emphatically not that of a child but of a ripe, desirable young woman, from her high, pink-nippled breasts to the curve of her hips and bottom, and all that lay between them. He cursed again as his treacherous body responded predictably to her bare charms, and hoped the towel about his waist would conceal his hugely blatant arousal from her.

"Kiss me, Joe!" she whispered cajolingly, her lovely, flushed face so close to his he could feel her warm breath fanning his cheek, smell the clean, floral fragrance of her flesh full and tantalizing in his nostrils. "Kiss me like you did at Bayview House! Mmmm, it was real nice when you kissed me that time, remember? Do it again, please, Joel?" She riffled her hands through his damp, dusty blond hair, then trailed her fingertips caressingly down to the sensitive hollows at the base of his throat.

Gooseflesh rose all over him, the breath choking him deep in his throat. "Behave, Seraphina, you hussy," he managed, endeavoring to sound stern. But the words came out rather strangled sounding as he moved the

129

towel down to dry her breasts and the almost concave, velvety belly farther below them.

She arched forward and curled her slender arms about his throat, leaning over where he sat upon the bed so that her breasts, with their pert, virginal pink nipples, thrust impudently into his very face. Sweat beaded his brow and slicked his palms instantly. "Please, Joe," she wheedled, pouting. "Just one little kiss, mmm?"

It was no bloody use, Joe thought helplessly, lust roiling through him. He was only a man, with a man's desires, and against her enchanting wiles he was damned, lost before he ever started! "Satan, old mate, I give up! You win, blast you!" he muttered. He let the towel fall unnoticed to the floor and hauled her into his arms, kissing her hungrily while her still damp body squirmed delightedly against his. His tongue outlined her lips and then pressed between them until they parted eagerly under his and he was free to explore the velvety recesses of her mouth at will.

She learned with amazing speed, and in seconds she was returning his kisses measure for measure, her tongue playing, warring teasingly with his tongue, his lips, grazing his teeth in a way that aroused him even more. Perhaps she wasn't as virginal as he had feared, he thought hopefully as his manhood surged against her bare belly. Cradling her in his arms, he fell backward to the bed, Seraphina sprawled half atop him and forcing the air from him in a giddy, breathy rush as they landed.

"Christ, you're lovely, you know that, Seraphina?" he whispered, twining a finger through a dampened tendril of her glossy black hair as he looked up at her from hooded turquoise eyes made darker with desire. "Too bloody lovely by far!"

"And so are *you,*" she whispered back, all merry

130

smiles and luminous gray-green eyes. "A lovely, lovely rascal! Let's kiss again, Joe, mmm? It makes me feel like the champagne—all bubbly and dreamy!"

He willingly obliged, one arm around her, the other hand seeking and finding the warm curve of her breast. He fondled her there, weighing the soft heaviness of her breasts in the cup of his palm, gently drawing the small rose-pink nipples between his thumb and forefinger until they grew harder, tighter. She gasped against his mouth, a low moan of longing breaking far back in her throat that was like the contented purring of a kitten. Her fingers tightened in his disheveled blond hair and over the smooth, sun-bronzed flesh of his well-muscled shoulders.

"So strong," she murmured, and smothered a hiccup. "Just feel those muscles! Mmmm!"

Silently he rolled her over to lie beside him on the brocade coverlet and trailed his lips down from her mouth to rain kisses everywhere upon her bare body. She was lovely all over, he thought, dry mouthed still, looking at her with undisguised desire smoldering in his turquoise eyes like lambent blue fire. The fluid lines and fragrant hollows of her throat led down to supple shoulders and thence to high, rounded breasts, their creamy pallor crowned with rosy steeples. Her waist was slender, her flanks long and sleek, the saucy triangle of hair at the pit of her concave belly a riot of delightful glossy black curls that he burned to fondle. Her long, shapely legs, now sprawled carelessly across his, were as smooth and supple as the rest of her. She was everything he had ever imagined—and more! He dipped his head to her breasts and nipped and nibbled tenderly first at one pert nipple and then the other, darting his tongue against the very tip, swirling it again and again about the puckered crests, inwardly amused as he felt the flutter of a restraining hand cease its protest and fall away to lie tense against his straining flank.

Her breathing quickened until he could feel the wild racing of her heart beneath the flesh of her rib cage, and a warm glow of desire suffused her body beneath his mouth's tender assaults. He leaned back to look at her, to savor again her languid beauty. Her head was to one side now, framed by a tumbled river of black tresses. Her fingers closed and opened on one corner of a plump silk-encased pillow, and for a fleeting second he was reminded yet again of a sleek, contented kitten flexing its claws, marching and purring in undisguised and sensual pleasure. Her eyes were closed, the thick, sooty lashes casting dusky shadows upon her flushed cheeks in the afternoon light that filtered through the lace curtains. Her upper teeth had trapped her lower lip, and her bosom rose and fell rapidly with her breathing as her anticipation and excitement steadily mounted. Suddenly, she turned her head to gaze up at him.

"Teach me, Joe," she whispered. "I don't know what to do—how to please you, you know? T'tell the truth, I've never made love with a man—not once—before, and I don't know what I should—"

Her words acted like a spray of icy water being poured over his head. He drew his hands from her body, though he ached to continue his caresses. "Strewth! I knew it! This is bloody madness, Seraphina! I'd best stop, love, before it's too damned late to stop," he suggested softly, loath to take advantage of her tipsiness and seduce her, though knowing he could do so very easily. Christ, what a turnabout! The women he'd had before had known what they were about well enough, and had been even more eager to begin than he. But he was a shrewd judge of women and was

132

certain that Seraphina wasn't lying. She was both an innocent and a virgin, and that made him wary. If she chose to give herself to him at some point—and he still felt inclined to take her up on the invitation—he wanted her stone-cold sober and fully aware of what she was doing, not to mention the ramifications of it, so there'd be no trouble later. After all, he wasn't the marrying kind. Once their bargain had been met, the proceeds of the deal split straight down the middle, that would be that—'G'd-bye, Lightnin' Joe, it was dinkum while it lasted!' He wanted no messy leave-takings, no tearful accusations, no pleas for him to stay wed to her.

Her heavy-lidded eyes flew open. They were dizzy with desire, he saw.

"Stop. Oh, no, no, don't stop, Joe, don't—"

"Yes, love. It's that bloody champagne. You don't know what you're saying, Seraphina; what you're agreeing to!"

Her hand brushed his thigh, moving higher. "Oh, yes, I do. Yes!" she whispered. "Please . . . ?"

He who hesitates is lost, and Joe was no exception. He hesitated, feeling his resolve melt away to nothing under her eager touch. "You're sure?" he asked her one last time.

"Sure," she echoed, and he sighed with relief and resumed his pleasurable labors. Exploring tanned fingers parted her thighs and stroked up the pliant inner columns to caress their satiny flesh with lazy circling motions until, after endless moments of unbearable delay, he finally reached their joining. She drew an excited, shivery breath as he gently tousled the ebony curls that shielded her womanhood, then brushed them aside before tenderly tracing the outline of her nether lips with a teasing finger. Little whimpers broke from her parted lips, and she arched her hips up to meet the delicious invasion of his hands as he probed

133

gently between the velvety folds and delicately stroked her tender core, then that secret place within. There was an answering moistness to his touch. A long, drawn out sigh escaped her as, breathing raggedly himself now, Joe thrust deeper and deeper into her, capturing her mouth in an ardent kiss even as he did so—a kiss that made all traces of Seraphina's lingering thoughts of resistance and denial melt away. His deep and intimate kiss was a prelude of what was yet to come, she knew; the final unveiling of the mysterious something that took place between a man and a woman. She burned to strip away the veils of secrecy and know at last what that something was . . .

Yet through the delicious, euphoric haze the champagne had created in her, Seraphina recognized that she should by rights put a stop to this, call a halt to his love play before it was too late. Sober and calculating, she had never meant to go this far, never! Not in her wildest imaginings had she ever intended that the marriage of convenience and expediency she had agreed upon with Joe should ever be consummated, never! But what had started out as an innocent game for her, a means to help out two dear friends who were desperate, had, like raging wildfire, grown out of control, fanned by her undeniable attraction to Joe. Dear Lord, she didn't want him to stop, couldn't bear it if he should, not now . . . ! Grasping his shaggy head, she drew it down and kissed him heatedly.

His kisses seemed to sear her swollen lips like the stroke of a brand, sizzling through every part of her until she trembled and quivered as if taken by a fever. A tense knot of heat and expectancy had bunched up in the pit of her belly that screamed to be eased. Oh, Lord! His caresses, every sensual touch of his strong, knowing hands upon her body, made her tingle uncontrollably and yearn for more than mere caresses.

"Joel, Joel, please . . . !" Still whispering his name, she ran her hand down across the broad expanse of his chest, feverishly stroking the thick filaments of gold hair that tapered to a narrow line across his hard, flat belly. She felt him draw an unsteady breath against her cheek as her trembling hand at last enfolded his heated length, the throbbing maleness burning to her touch, a velvety fire encasing the steel within. With faltering fingertips, she gently stroked him there, curious, yes, but hoping somehow to give him the same breathless pleasure he'd awakened in her.

"Christ, Seraphina, cut it out! You'll drive me mad!" he growled against her cheek, his breath hot, his breathing unsteady and thick.

"I surely hope so!" she whispered huskily, wanton with desire. "I *want* to drive you mad—utterly and completely mad, Joel McCaleb!"

The minx was succeeding then, Joe thought dryly, pressing her down to the brocade coverlet, rumpled now, beneath them. Breathing heavily, he rolled atop her and parted her thighs with his knees, remaining poised there between them, braced upon his elbows, without attempting to enter her. Leaning forward, he brushed damp tendrils of her glossy black hair away from her flushed face and gazed deep into the mysterious depths of her dyes—more green than gray in her desire for him.

"There'll be no regrets in the morning, sweetheart?" he cautioned gravely, touching his lips to the tip of her pert little nose. "It'll be too late to turn back then. We don't have to, you know. There are other ways I can please you, without—"

"No, no, I want you to . . . to make love to me, Joel. Please?" she cut in breathlessly, her fingers fastening about his muscled upper arms like slender manacles.

He nodded and kissed her gently on the lips, then

135

dipped his shaggy head again to the hollow of her throat where the pulse throbbed wildly, and then to her breasts, swollen now. "Lie still, then, sweet."

She gasped as he lowered his full weight upon her, crushing her heavily into the depths of the feather bed beneath them, then again as she felt the fiery hardness of him butting against her tender core. He eased forward until he felt the barrier beyond and then, his lips covering hers, their mouths warring in ardent love play, he thrust strongly forward and the barrier yielded easily under his tender onslaught. For a fleeting second, she grew as tense as a bowstring beneath him, then a muffled sob of pain—dammed by his lips— broke from her. Almost immediately, her tension ebbed and she melted in surrender beneath him.

"That's it, sweet," he murmured, cradling her tenderly in his arms. "The hurting part's over with forever." So saying, he eased deeply into her, then slowly withdrew, then repeated his rhythmic thrusts over and over, his unhurried loving easing and deepening his passage, every stroke awakening her innocent woman's body gradually, sweetly, to un-dreamed-of pleasures. No callow boy with his first girl, Joe knew how to please a woman in more ways than Seraphina, innocent Seraphina, giddy in the first flush of desire, had ever imagined! Aunt Polly had seen to that aspect of his education, too, and her "girls" had been more than eager to act as his instructors . . .

It was wonderful, Seraphina thought dizzily, wonderful, wonderful, wonderful! All the whispered confidences the girls at the school had exchanged regarding *it* fell far short of the reality. Why, they—the experienced few who had boasted that they were no longer as innocent and shockingly naive as the rest of them—had implied that *it* was shameful and somehow distasteful, which was certainly not true. No! *No!* It was beautiful, she and Joe moving together as one, their bodies melded into one being in the fluid dance of love that was as ancient as time! How could anything so beautiful, so natural, so good, be thought of as horrid, or in any way distasteful or dirty? Joe's deep and tender thrusts fanned the fires raging through her until she feared she would scream aloud with sheer pleasure, or explode into a million bright fragments. She didn't want it to end, no, not with this peculiar hunger inside her still begging for satisfaction. Instinctively, she arched upward to meet his thrusts, embracing the driving power of his wiry flanks with her long, slender legs to hold him fast within her, to keep him there inside her forever, even as her arms coiled about his neck to twine restlessly in the deep waves of blond hair at his nape. Their eyes locked gazes. Passion mounted. Faster, still faster, deeper and ever deeper, he moved with her, until she felt as if she were drowning in the darkening turquoise pools of his eyes, drowning and not wanting to surface, no, never.

"Joel, Joel, oh, yes, yes!" she cried helplessly as the satisfaction she had craved at last ricocheted through her. She arched beneath him, gloriously transported in her ecstasy, a creature of pure and unashamed sensation as the pulsing waves washed over her and carried her to some other world momentarily—a heavenly, fantasy world where a haze of rose and gold flooded her vision and brilliant rainbows of light dipped and swirled in crazy arcs.

When her eyelids fluttered open seconds later, Joe lay beside her. Somehow, her head was now cradled by his upper arm, her palm possessively flattened against his chest. He affectionately stroked her cheek with a callused knuckle, smiling down at her with the crooked smile she had imagined him smiling so many times since that fleeting kiss at Bayview House.

"Strewth! I reckon we'd better be married as soon as it's humanly possible, wouldn't you say, Miss Jones?" he suggested teasingly, his voice sounding deep and drowsy.

Stunned by her actions—and somewhat sobered by them, too, now that it was over, if the truth were known—she nodded mutely.

The last thing she remembered as she drifted into sleep was the light pressure of Joe's lips upon her closed eyelids, though, of course, she must have imagined it. No, it wasn't real, she decided as exhaustion weighted down her limbs. None of it had been real; it couldn't have been. Tomorrow, she'd wake up alone in her bed in the suite at the Occidental, clutching her pillow. It was only an erotic dream she was having, and soon— all too soon—she'd wake up, wouldn't she . . . wouldn't she . . . ?

Chapter Nine

"You sidewinding, two-faced, conniving son of a bitch!" she screamed, slamming the hefty feather pillow down upon Joe's unsuspecting, sleeping head. "Wake up, you . . . you low-down, dirty rattlesnake! I'll give you ten seconds to get dressed and out of here, and if you're not gone by then, I'm gonna take this gun and blast you in places you never dreamed of being blasted, Mister Joel McCaleb!"

She hurled the pillow aside and cocked the rifle that she held cradled in her other arm, leveling the barrel at his middle. Hectic crimson flamed in her cheeks, the giddy color contrasting vividly with the gray-green, crackling fury of her eyes. She wore a mint green silk robe, hastily dragged on by the looks of it, and her tangled mane of black hair spilled wantonly over her shoulders and halfway down her back. Her wide, sensual mouth was neither wide nor sensual now, but tight and angry, the full lips thinned, a nerve pulsing erratically at her temple as Joe, stretching and yawning sleepily, dragged himself up to a sitting position.

His sensual smile vanished and his turquoise eyes narrowed as he saw her standing over him, the black barrel of the rifle gleaming wickedly in the pale yellow sunlight of morning that lanced through the white lace curtains at the windows. For a second, he thought he must be dreaming he was back at Bayview House again, the night he and Ming had rescued Mei Ling from the House of Happiness.

"What the hell—"

"You heard me, you . . . you womanizer, you! Get dressed and git, you damned polecat! Taking advantage of me—of my condition—that way! Why, hangin' would be too good for you! You should be tarred and feathered and . . . and . . . hog-tied! You should be skinned alive, mister, and your hide nailed to a fence post like the coyote you are!"

She'd obviously run out of insults by now, for she stood there seething silently, her breasts heaving against the silk of her robe, her eyes hurling shards of gray-green glass at him. Joe's expression was slack jawed and incredulous as he reached for his pants on the end of the bed. They were dry now, but wrinkled beyond hope since their soaking the afternoon before.

"*I* took advantage of *you?* Huh! That's a good one, love!" He grinned as he stood and buckled his belt, certain this was some kind of game on her part. "As I recollect it, you were all over me, begging me to kiss you—among other things!" He winked wickedly. "If I'm guilty of anything, it's of obliging you and doing what you wanted me to! Now, put that blasted rifle down before you hurt someone, and let's talk."

"*Obliging* me? Is that . . . is that what you call it? Why you . . . you animal, you . . . *oooh!* If anyone's going to get hurt with this rifle, it's surely going to be you, mister, and that's a promise!" she stormed. "How dare you! How *dare* you!"

Joe tucked in the tails of his shirt, latched his belt, and stepped into his boots. He made no further attempt to argue with her, knowing now the futility of doing

140

so. She was in a fine spate, and anything he said would fall on deaf ears.

"One!"

"I'm leaving, damnit."

"Two!"

He hooked his jacket over his shoulder and stuffed his rumpled rag of a tie into his pants' pocket.

"Three!"

"Seraphina, that's enough, love, you hear me? If you'd just give a bloke a chance—"

"Four!"

He shrugged and headed for the door, then opened it.

"Five! Move on out, you sidewinder!" she threatened.

He gave her a long, unfathomable turquoise stare, then turned curtly on his heel and strode through the door.

"Six! Seven! Eight!" she screamed after him at the top of her lungs, but her furious cries sounded peculiarly hollow, somehow, with him gone. "Nine! *Ten!* Oh, damn, damn!" she muttered, recklessly flung aside the rifle, and sped to the door, craning her head out into the long corridor in time to see Joe's retreating back as he turned to take the stairs down. "Noon, at the First Presbyterian Church on Kearny Street. Be there, Joel, else you can kiss your grandpa's money *adios!* You hear me, McCaleb, you son of a gun?" she screamed after him.

Whether he did or not, he made no sign, for he was gone, she realized. Shoulders slumping now that the initial force of her fury had worn out, she turned back into her suite, slammed the door behind her, and flung herself across the bed, weeping bitterly.

Oh, the shame of it! Despite what she had accused Joe of, the events of the afternoon before had not been totally obliterated by the effects of the champagne, more was the pity. She remembered the *high* points only too well; remembered herself shamelessly begging Joe to kiss her and worse, as he'd pointed out, urging him to continue his lovemaking even when he had sensibly suggested they should call a halt to it! As a result, much of the blazing anger she felt was anger directed at herself, mingled with guilt, for though she'd sooner die than admit it to anyone, even herself, she had enjoyed Joe's loving enormously, and her emotions had been quite out of control. If she was able to recall so much of what had passed between them, despite the euphoric effects of the champagne, then surely she should have been able to say no to the man! Her cheeks burned against the damp pillowcase. What must he think of her? What kind of woman would behave the way she had behaved? A tramp, that was who—she'd behaved no better than those awful painted doxies of the Barbary Coast who enticed men up to their rooms. It was really no wonder he'd taken her up on her brazen offer, none at all, she realized miserably, grinding her knuckles into her swollen eyes. What normal, hot-blooded man would have refused? And Joe was as normal and hot-blooded as any man— and far less a gentleman than most. Oh, Lord, would he be there at the church on Saturday—would he, or had she ruined that, too?

She cried herself out, then wiped her eyes and noisily blew her nose on a lacy scrap of a handkerchief. Well, that was that! Mama had always told her you couldn't erase your mistakes in this world; you could only learn from them and go on, and hopefully do better the next time around. That was what she must do now, make the best of things. If Joe showed up for the wedding on Saturday, there was still a chance she could come out of this relatively unscathed as long as no child resulted from that afternoon's madness. After all, what man could expect a divorced woman to be a virgin? She'd just chalk it up to experience, and make darned sure that if—oh, if!—Joe kept his part of the bargain, he'd never set hands on her again, however delightful those hands might have felt, she amended guiltily.

She slipped out of the robe she'd donned on waking and finding herself quite bare beside Joe in the wide bed, and bathed and washed her hair. As always, such mundane tasks did much to restore her composure, and she felt far better when she was done, her hair swept up neatly and pinned in a regal chignon, a pert green hat with long, elegant plumes set jauntily atop it, a waft of the airy lily of the valley perfume that was her favorite enveloping her in its fresh, woodland fragrance. Defiantly admiring in the cheval mirror the way her tailored green jacket and long green skirt draped her willowy figure as she twirled about, she caught a glimpse of her face and stepped closer to inspect her reflection critically.

Was it just her imagination, or did she look in some way different since last night? Were her eyes not a trifle more knowing, more experienced and seductive than they had hitherto appeared? Were they, perhaps, the eyes of a fallen woman, a decidedly *shady lady,* she wondered, pouting provocatively. "You . . . you Jezebel!" she murmured softly. "You utter Delilah!"

An irrepressible, dreamy smile began at the corners of her wide mouth, but she caught herself in mid-smile and hurriedly smothered it. Forcing a puritanical frown and flicking her head to rid it of such wild and wicked notions, she bent to retrieve her small purse, tossed carelessly under the bed the day before. She was in no mood today to oversee the setting in order of William McCaleb's dusty old mansion. A drive in the brisk air would be far more to her liking.

143

She gazed out of the window, relieved to see that it was not raining. In fact, a bleary sun was endeavoring to shine. Yes, a drive and perhaps a bracing walk would dispel the cobweb of misgivings and self-reproach that clouded her mind. She'd hire a hack and go to that place she'd heard of, the one where the sea lions basked and barked and fought upon the rocks, and then afterward perhaps take luncheon at the famous Cliff House nearby, and hobnob with the writers and artists who congregated there. And, if her stimulating walk along the rugged beach in the brisk cold air did the trick and she still felt she could go through with it, she'd pay a visit to Mister Caldwell at his office and ask his assistance in making the arrangements for the wedding.

And then what? Well, then she'd just have to sit and stew for the three days remaining until Saturday, wouldn't she, wondering if Joel would show up, or if he'd jilt her at the altar after the way she'd shrieked at him and thrown him out of her room after begging him to stay. Lord! It would be the longest three days of her life . . . !

"What time is it now, Mister Caldwell?" she asked the lawyer for perhaps the twentieth time in the past half hour.

Mister Caldwell, splendid in top hat and black frock coat, high collar and gray tie, sighed and fished his gold watch from his inner pocket yet again. "One minute to noon, my dear Miss Jones," he supplied with a long-suffering air.

"Thank you," she muttered, gulping. One minute to twelve! Surely Joe would have been here by now if he intended to come at all. No, he wouldn't—she was convinced of that now. And who could blame him? He'd taken offense at her harangue that morning and decided to throw in the towel, inheritance or no, no doubt convinced that no inheritance, however large, was worth even the briefest marriage to such an . . . an infant as she, she just *knew* it!

"This gown . . . perhaps another would have been better?" she asked Mister Caldwell's diminutive wife, Lavinia, doubtfully, anxiously smoothing the lavender folds of the gown down about her hips. She fidgeted nervously with her pretty bouquet of curly petaled white chrysanthemums that looked, from a distance, like feathers. The high neck of her gown was trimmed with off-white lace. More deep flounces of it frothed over her shoulders and edged the V-shaped lavender silk bodice that outlined her bosom and dipped to a point below her waist. Down the center was a row of tiny pearl buttons, the same buttons that fastened the fitted sleeves from wrist to elbow, above which the cloth puffed out charmingly. A lavender hat about the crown, from the brim of which was suspended a wispy lavender veil that concealed only her eyes, completed her wedding attire.

Lavinia smiled and patted her clammy hand reassuringly. "Nonsense, Seraphina, my dear. You look simply charming! Calm yourself, do, child. There's no cause for alarm. I'm certain your Joel will be here shortly."

Seraphina desperately peered out of the opened doorway and beyond the stuffy vestry to the church proper, while Lavinia busied herself arranging the fall of Seraphina's skirts. The gloomy confines, in which every footfall, every discreet cough, echoed, were filling now with wedding guests. Some had been business associates of William McCaleb's in his lifetime—though fortunately for the young woman awaiting her groom, none had ever had the pleasure of meeting William's young ward before her move to

145

Boston—and others were friends of the Caldwells who had palatial residences on prestigious Nob or Russian Hill. All of them would be celebrating the small but lavish wedding breakfast at the Occidental Hotel that Lavinia Caldwell had arranged would follow the ceremony. What would those satin-gowned dowagers and stuffed-shirted bankers of San Francisco society do if she gave vent to the shrill, panicky scream that was even now building in her throat? Nothing, more likely than not, other than to look away discreetly in that faintly shocked manner such people maintained while viewing the outrageous goings-on of those of lower social status than their own—

"Seraphina, my dear, please stop shredding the petals! Your bouquet will be quite ruined if you don't!"

Seraphina looked down, amazed to see dozens of tiny, shredded chrysanthemum wisps strewn about her feet. Had she really done that? She was so on edge, she couldn't recall! The strains of the organ began then, the music soaring and swelling until the familiar notes of the wedding march filled the church. She let out an involuntary squeak of utter fright. They were already playing—and the groom wasn't even here! She'd die of shame, she just knew it! She glanced wildly about for Lavinia, spying her in conversation with her husband across the small, cluttered room.

"There, my dear, it's time," Lavinia declared, turning to her. "I'll be leaving you in Edward's capable hands now. God bless and every happiness to you and Mister McCaleb!" She reached up on tiptoe and kissed Seraphina's cheek, then was gone.

"Are you ready, my dear?" asked Mister Caldwell, who was to give her away.

"As . . . as ready as I'll ever be, sir," she agreed miserably and accepted the arm he offered her.

Her knees threatened to buckle as they made the

146

long walk arm in arm down the aisle to the distant altar. Her heart almost came up into her throat when she saw a familiar blond figure standing straight and tall and with his back to her before the altar. Joe! He'd come, after all! The realization made her feel dizzy. He was impeccably attired in a dark gray frock coat and seemed so imposing, so tall, that every instinct within her urged her to run! Beside him, obviously his best man, was a short, slightly made, black-haired youth she did not recognize from behind.

Edward Caldwell released her arm as they drew alongside Joel, and she turned slightly and darted a nervous glance up into his face. He appeared stern and unsmiling, and butterflies slipped anxious cartwheels in the pit of her belly. Beyond him, she realized, incredulous despite her nervousness, was a grinning Ming, his pigtail gone and in its place a neatly cropped head of glossy blue-black hair, an obvious copy of Joe's newly shorn locks. Despite this concession, he appeared very young and somehow incongruous with his Oriental features framed by his formal Western attire.

"These are for you," she realized Joe was saying softly, drawing her attention back to him. "I didn't know if you'd have a bouquet." He pressed something into her hands. She glanced down and saw that the "something" was a posy of violets and lily of the valley, still damp with droplets of crystal dew and framed by their own deep green, velvety leaves.

"Oh!" She gasped and looked away, a lump threatening to form in her throat, blinking back tears. The delightful gesture, after the shameful way she had behaved the other morning, was so undeserved on her part that it brought her close to weeping in shame.

The service passed in a daze after that. She heard the minister reciting the vows, heard Joe's deep voice

147

responding without any hint of hesitation or reluctance, and her own voice fainter yet audible in return. Then Joe was taking her clammy, slim hand in his own warm, large one and slipping a heavy band upon her wedding finger.

"I hope it's the right one, love," he whispered and, looking down, she saw the huge single opal set in heavy gold that she vaguely recalled admiring in the windows of the Diamond Palace four days before.

It was more than she could bear! Mutely, she nodded, tears brimming over in her eyes and tracing damp trails down her cheeks. "It's . . . it's *just the ticket,* Joel," she managed, smiling tremulously. "Oh, thank you!"

He squeezed her slender hand in his comfortingly as the minister pronounced them man and wife.

For better or worse, for richer or poorer, for shorter or longer, they were wed—and Joel and Seraphina's inheritance secure.

Chapter Ten

"Joel, stop it, do! You don't have to carry me over the threshold, you darn fool!"

Joe laughed deeply and, still firmly holding his squirming, protesting bride, swept her over the threshold of Bayview House, planted a smacking kiss upon her lips, and then set her down.

"Welcome home, Mrs. McCaleb!" he said, and laughed deep in his throat as he looked down at her.

Seraphina's hat was awry, her skirts and petticoats hiked up about her calves. A rosy blush suffused her cheeks and her eyes sparkled brilliantly with a combination of reluctant laughter and dwindling outrage as she looked up into Joe's smiling face. For a moment, he allowed himself to wonder what it would have been like if this hadn't been just a ruse to get Mac McCaleb's inheritance and Seraphina were truly his bride in every sense of the word. The notion was a strangely appealing one, for despite her childish behavior the other morning, she still drew him like a magnet, and he'd thought of little else but her the past three nights he'd spent sleepless in his room at Ma Barker's boardinghouse, trying to decide whether to go through with the wedding or not. When she was

149

looking up at him the way she was, it was only too easy to forget she'd egged him on to make love to her, then thrown him out on his ear screaming curses at him! Too bloody easy, he thought ruefully.

Edward Caldwell and his wife had followed them through the front door of Bayview House, and the pair exchanged amused glances over the newlywed couple's romantic antics as an embarrassed Seraphina smoothed down her skirts.

"I must say, Joel, that this is turning out far better than I'd ever hoped," Edward commented. "I admit, I had my doubts when William added that stipulation to the will, and I tried several times to talk him out of it. But I must say that now I'm rather glad he wouldn't listen to reason. You make a real handsome couple! I'm sure you know Lavinia and I wish you every happiness together?"

"Oh, yes, every happiness!" Lavinia echoed, dimpling.

"I've taken the liberty of hiring a housekeeper for the remainder of your stay here in San Francisco, a Mrs. Peggy Kelly. She's a wonderful woman, very capable, who used to work for friends of ours on the Hill before they moved back east. She's assured me she'll have no reservations about also acting as your maid, Mrs. McCaleb, should you require her services. Does that sound satisfactory? Seraphina, my dear? Er, Mrs. McCaleb?" he repeated.

Joe squeezed Seraphina affectionately about the waist, grinning broadly. "Wake up! He means you, love! Remember, you're Mrs. McCaleb now—like it or not," he added in a lower tone that only she could hear.

"Oh, of course, Mister Caldwell. I'm sorry; I was miles away! Yes, that sounds wonderful," Seraphina approved, still gritting her teeth over Joe's last words, for they had brought her back to reality with a

150

sickening bump and had destroyed utterly the fantasy she'd given herself over to for the past few hours—the fantasy that she and Joe were really man and wife, in love with each other, and that she'd never even heard of William Angus McCaleb or his darn inheritance, confound the man.

"Splendid!" Caldwell continued. "And now, if we may leave you two ladies for a moment, I'd like to complete our business." He tapped his coat pocket. "I have all the papers here, Joel. All that's needed is your signature upon them."

"Right you are, Mister Caldwell, sir. Won't you step inside the study? Excuse us, ladies." Joe led the lawyer through into the study, leaving Seraphina and Lavinia alone.

"Well! Won't you show me about the house, my dear? I've been longing so to see it. Edward tells me you've done wonderfully putting it to rights since your return from Boston."

"There really wasn't that much to do, Mrs. Caldwell," Seraphina disclaimed. "The furniture had been adequately sheeted after Mister McCaleb's . . . after my guardian's death, and the blinds had been pulled against the sun, so it was really just a simple matter of seeing the rugs taken outside and beaten, and dusting and polishing the furniture and airing out the rooms."

"Such a wonderful old place," Lavinia commented admiringly as Seraphina led her from airy, well-appointed room to room, "and the furniture is so beautifully crafted. European, isn't it?"

"So I believe," Seraphina agreed, intentionally vague. "From his native Scotland, I think. William McCaleb shipped much of it over from there when he emigrated as a young man, I recall your husband telling me. He also mentioned that he believed it was made by my . . . my guardian's own father."

151

"Ah, well, that explains it. They don't make furniture with that amount of love and pride in the craft anymore. I'm certain this gracious old home must hold many, many happy memories for you, my dear," Lavinia said, sighing as she looked about the lovely drawing room with its draperies of deep green and the faded yet still elegant overstuffed chairs of paler green chintz painted with pale pink cabbage roses. Running an admiring finger over a cherry-wood bureau with numerous little drawers, she added, "Won't it be just awful for you to say good-bye to the old place? I always feel that houses are like old friends—they have a heart and soul all their own, and are just as wrenching to part from!"

Seraphina frowned. "We . . . ell, I suppose under other circumstances I might be quite upset, Mrs. Caldwell, but with Joel and I being married . . ." She let her voice trail away meaningfully with the falsehood, and shrugged. "My wishes must be in accord with my husband's now, must they not, and Joel feels that selling the house is really the best thing to do. I'm afraid I must—"

"Oh, but of course, you dear girl. Forgive me. I didn't mean to imply that you should in any way—"

"No, of course you didn't, Mrs. Caldwell; I know that. You've been so kind to me this week! I don't know what I would have done without your expertise in seeing to the wedding arrangements and so forth—and the reception was just delightful. I do thank you, you know, so very much."

"Not at all, child." Lavinia blushed with pleasure despite her denial. "It was the least I could do for you. And I must confess, I fancy I've become something of an old hand at organizing weddings. Both of my daughters were married in the past three years, you know."

152

"Really? No, I hadn't realized that. I'm sure they were the loveliest weddings, however." She cocked her head to one side and listened. "Why, is that Joel's voice I hear? Yes, I do believe it is. They must have finished their business already. This is the last of the rooms. Shall we return to the study?" She took Lavinia Caldwell's arm and skillfully steered her from the drawing room, through the breakfast room, and back out into the long hallway. Joe, though she could not truthfully say she had heard him calling her, and Edward Caldwell were just leaving the study.

"There you are, love!" Joe exclaimed. "Well, everything's settled. The McCaleb fortune is now ours!" He winked at her over the lawyer's shoulder. "Would you care for something to drink, Edward?" he asked, clapping the older man warmly across the back. "A toast to the future, shall we say?"

"No, thank you, really, Joel. I do believe Lavinia and I have enjoyed quite enough toasts for one day; oh, yes, quite enough!" the lawyer said with a chuckle. "We'll be on our way now before dusk. The streets are so boisterous after dark, aren't they? Well, every good wish for the future to the both of you, and I'll be certain to obtain as good a price as I can for this old place and the furnishings. You'll telegraph me when you're settled?"

"We will indeed." Joe shook Caldwell's hand warmly, his liking for the older man evident. "Thanks for everything, sir."

"Not at all, not at all. Come, my dear." He offered his wife his arm and led her to the door. Seraphina and Joe followed. At the doorway, Lavinia kissed Seraphina gently on the cheek. "Good night, dear girl."

"Good night!"

They stood in the doorway and watched until the Caldwell's carriage had driven away and the clip-

153

clopping of the horses' hooves had faded before going inside.

"Well, here we are! All alone, at last," Joe said with a roguish grin that made his turquoise eyes sparkle wickedly in the gloom of the hallway.

There was something dangerous in his expression that caused prickles of excitement to tingle down her spine. "This . . . this arrangement is strictly business, I hope you recall, Mister McCaleb. The marriage service changes nothing," she insisted, alarmed to find her throat was suddenly parched. "If you've read more into it because of what happened the other afternoon, then I'm afraid you'll be quite disappointed."

"Oh, will I?" he taunted, and spread his arms wide, planting a palm on each side of the hallway wall and effectively cutting off her flight—if she'd intended flight. The action caused the giddy flush in her cheeks to fade into a becoming pale pink. "Now, why would I have to be disappointed? What happened between us the other day can't just be forgotten as if it hadn't occurred. You can't turn back the clock, sweetheart, and make believe it didn't happen, whether you want to or not, so . . . why not? Be honest. What have you got to lose? You're my wife now, and since this is supposed to be our honeymoon, let's enjoy it, hmmm?"

His voice had grown low and sensual at the last, a husky tone so reminiscent of that fateful afternoon it made her feel weak with remembrance. The sensual gleam in his eyes left her in no doubt as to his intentions either as they raked her from head to toe. It seemed to Seraphina that he could see through the layers of clothing to her bared body beneath! He took a casual step toward her and a nervous quiver started in her belly, spreading outward as he came to a halt scant inches away.

Though she wanted to back up, out of his reach, she

154

was suddenly frozen to the spot. Lord, why was she so . . . so darned aware of him? It was as if every pore, muscle, and nerve in her body reacted violently to his nearness, tingling and leaping out of control. The scent of his shaving soap was full in her nostrils, a mixture of spices and fresh, tangy lime that was rugged and wholly and undeniably masculine, as was he. This near to him, his slim-hipped torso seemed broader than ever, clothed in the gray formal wear he had donned for their wedding, and she realized that, though she had inherited her mother's willowy build and height, he towered over her, the top of her head barely reaching his shoulder. If he should decide to reach out and drag her into his arms, there would be very little she could do to prevent him!

She drew a shaky breath, drinking in his sensual warmth as she did so, a warmth that rose from him to envelop her like a drug, intoxicating in the extreme. She dared a glance up into his face, seeing every deeply tanned sun furrow, hollow, and angle as if for the first time, and with a crystalline clarity that owed nothing to the gloom of the hall but more to her wide-open senses. He was too damned attractive by far, she thought desperately, weak-kneed. Why couldn't he have been the pious, dry, old stick she had imagined he'd be, instead of this lean, handsome brute? Everything would have been so much easier then. As it was, she was uncertain of herself, unsure whether she could bring herself to refuse him if he should decide to press his attentions on her again—or even if she really *wanted* to refuse him. Or, for that matter, if he'd accept a refusal on her part! No, she wouldn't put it past this man to throw her over his shoulder and stride away with her to his lair, there to do as he would with her. Darn it, that thought should have horrified her, but instead she had the strongest urge to reach up and trace

155

with her fingertip the tiny furrows that winged toward his temples from the outer corners of his beautiful, gold-flecked, turquoise eyes; to smooth back the engaging cowlick of shaggy, dusty blond hair that fell rakishly forward over his broad brow and confess how much she needed him . . . . *Needed* him? Lord, she'd gone *loco,* no doubt about it—

"Seen enough?" he asked casually.

She gasped, blushed, and made to turn her head aside but was restrained by his hand, which came out with lightning speed to trap a smooth black ringlet of her hair where it spilled down over her bosom and jerk her toward him. His warm hand traveled up to her throat and lazily caressed the slender column until her knees grew weaker and she could feel the unsteady throb of her pulse against his callused fingertips.

"Don't, please, Joel, don't!" she whispered breathlessly.

"Hush up," he murmured, finding her hat pin and pulling it free, in the same motion removing the elegant little cloche she'd worn for their wedding and casually tossing it aside.

Bareheaded now, eyes downcast so that her lashes were like sooty half-moons trembling against her cheeks, she stood quivering before him, aware suddenly that he'd taken a step closer now and that he was taking her chin roughly between his thumb and forefinger, tilting her head up for his lips. She saw his head dip, saw his mouth come closer, ever closer, to hers, but it was as if she were still frozen to the spot, unable to move, to think, to do anything but stand there and surrender to his kiss.

His mouth was hard and hot as it staked its claim upon hers, his lips potent with the flavor of brandy and his own exciting, uniquely masculine taste. Her heart suddenly accelerated, seeming ready to leap from her breast. She was certain he must be able to feel its wild hammerings as his hand slipped around her waist and sharply drew her closer to him so that they were pressed together their entire lengths, the heat of his hard thighs and hips burning clear through their clothing to singe her flesh, her breasts crushed against his chest. His other hand burrowed beneath her hair and twined itself lazily through that dark river.

There was no mistaking Joe's desire for her, she thought dazedly, none whatsoever. It was in the almost brutal yet damnably exciting ardor of his lips and his inflaming kisses, in the velvet, vicelike grip of his arms and the masculine hardness of him lodged arrogantly against her hip. The large, callused hand about her waist grazed downward, tracing each knob of her spine through the lavender silk of her wedding gown, stroking the silk-draped globes of her buttocks. The gesture, the possessive and intimate quality of it, finally served to jolt her from the foolish spell she'd fallen under. She came to her senses and violently wrenched herself away from him, ducked under his arm, and fled through the house, up the curved staircase to the bedroom she had chosen for herself, not stopping until she'd flung herself inside and slammed and noisily bolted the door in her wake. From below, Joe's mocking laughter floated upward after her, ringing in her ears, and she covered them with her hands to blot out the sound.

Once inside, it was several moments before she could regain her composure. Her heart still fluttered madly and her limbs felt weak. Perspiration dewed her upper lip, a condition that the Boston Academy for Young Ladies would most certainly have condemned as most unseemly, for well-educated and refined young ladies were merely supposed to glow, were they not—not sweat like lathered horses as she was doing at that moment! The notion made her want to giggle helplessly, a reaction she rightly attributed to her upset and nervous state. Tarnation take the Academy, and the two old spinster biddies, Miss Hanover and Miss Merriweather, who ran it! What did they know about life, about living, anyway, dried up old maids that they were? Nothing, that's what! And despite that incorrigible man's behavior, he *did* make her feel alive, in ways she'd never even dreamed existed 'til now.

Cool logic insisted that no man should hold the power to make her feel this way, especially since she had known him for so brief a time and under such strained circumstances. Nonetheless, the blood in her veins seemed afire, a hot river coursing through her that spread warmth everywhere it pulsed. There was, still, that strange, giddy, restless feeling in her belly that Joe's nearness had seemed to create in her from the first night they'd met in the kitchen of this very house, she admitted, pacing to and fro the length of the room and willing the insidiously pleasant feeling to subside.

Darn the man! Had he no principles at all? Had he clean forgotten this travesty of a marriage they'd entered into was no more than a business deal? He was downright dangerous where decent women were concerned—or, at least, that was what the refined, eastern-educated part of her conscience kept telling her. The other, wilder, less-refined, western side of her character was inwardly smiling—and thrilling to the very danger he represented. Shame on you; shame on you! her conscience nagged, but she ignored the harping. After all, she thought with a secretive little grin, it wasn't really *she* who was guilty of such wicked duplicity of the emotions, no sir. It was all Seraphina Jones's fault—or rather, Seraphina McCaleb's, the shameless hussy! Whatever the outcome of this little scheme, she would at least have some very entertaining

158

memories to hoard in the future, when she finally relented and bowed to her papa's wishes and married some wealthy cattle rancher he approved of, after his shock over Chuck's elopement had worn off, of course. She sighed. Oh, damn! None of this nonsense would have been necessary had she been born a boy! Tom and Courtney had all the freedom in the world to do exactly as they wished, for all that they were younger than she was. No one would ever dream of trying to make them marry anyone they didn't want to.

She realized suddenly that there was a discreet tapping at the door, and her heart skipped a beat, righted itself, and began fluttering like a terrified butterfly all over again, just when she'd believed she was finally under control.

"Damn you, Joel, I warned you, you sneaky polecat! Leave me alone!" she cried, forgetting her refined and well-modulated manner in her anger.

"Sorry, mum, but it's not Mister McCaleb, mum; it's me, Peggy Kelly. Mister Caldwell hired me to see to your needs for the next few days," came a muffled voice from beyond the closed door.

Mrs. Kelly, her new housekeeper! Oh, Lord, what must the poor woman be thinking? She ran to the door, drew the bolt, and flung it wide open.

"Mrs. Kelly, I'm so sorry!" she exclaimed. "Won't you please come in?" She stood aside to permit the housekeeper to enter, seeing a petite, wiry-looking woman with gray-streaked black hair and a pair of twinkling blue eyes that held a somewhat curious expression now, Seraphina fancied—no doubt on account of her strange response to the woman's knocking!

"How do you do, ma'am?" Mrs. Kelly greeted her, extending her hand in a forthright manner that Seraphina warmed to immediately. "I just came

159

upstairs to tell ye I was here an' all, and t'see if there's anything you might be after wanting? Supper's on, and it'll be ready around seven-thirty, ma'am."

"Wonderful, Mrs. Kelly. That sounds just perfect."

Peggy Kelly grinned and smoothed down the starched white apron with the bib front that she wore over her sensible dark dress. "Will ye be after wanting it served ye and t'mister in the dining room, or will the two o' ye be eating up here this evening? I can send it up on trays, if ye'd like. It'll be no trouble, none at all."

Seraphina's spine straightened. "Up here? Why, no, indeed not! We'll dine downstairs, of course, Mrs. Kelly!" she protested indignantly. Whatever was the woman thinking of, to even suggest they might wish to eat supper in her room. She realized then that Mrs. Kelly believed she and Joe to be ordinary honeymooners, and she blushed.

Peggy laughed, a smoky, husky laugh for a woman, and especially for one as diminutive as she was. "Oh, ma'am, to be sure, there's no need for ye to be embarrassed, not with me! I know how it is to be young and in love—though there's them that would doubt it, to see old Peggy Kelly now, no doubt! I'll see the table below set for the two o' ye, then—and meanwhile, should I have some kettles fetched up for your bath?"

"That would be very nice," Seraphina agreed, still bristling. With a firm nod, Mrs. Kelly made to leave. "Wait! One more thing. Where is my . . . my husband?"

"Why, Mister McCaleb went out with that young Celestial rogue just a few minutes ago. I expect he'll be back shortly, though. No need for ye t'fret, ma'am. He'll not be leaving a beautiful little creature like you all alone for overlong, indeed he won't, not on yer honeymoon an' all. Will that be all?" Seeing Seraphina nod mutely, she bobbed a curtsy, smiled again, and left.

160

How dare he? she wondered irritably when she was alone again. They'd not been married over four hours and already he'd gone out gallivanting with his unusual friend! The tiny voice of her conscience that reminded her gently that she had rebuffed his advances, that it had been *she* who had demonstrated in very clear terms that she wished him to leave her be, was quite drowned out by her feelings of indignation. As she undressed, she muttered under her breath, consigning Joe to many, varied and exquisitely uncomfortable fates as she draped her wedding gown over a convenient chair and removed the layered petticoats and the white stockings, the lacy garters and frilly bodice beneath. Clad now in only a beribboned lavender-and-white-striped corset, which exposed the creamy topmost curves of her breasts, and in lacy white pantalets, she took a seat before the dressing table. There she began unpinning her hair, then brushing its silky dark length with furious strokes until she'd reached a hundred, cursing every tangle as she did so.

". . . ninety-seven, ninety-eight . . . !" A knock sounded at the door. "Come in, Mrs. Kelly! One hundred!" she bade the housekeeper without even a glance over her shoulder.

The door opened and someone entered. Seraphina heard the sound of kettles being set down and the enameled bathtub being pulled out from behind the dressing screen.

"Thank you, Mrs. Kelly; you're just wonderful," she called to the woman.

"Wonderful I might well be, love, but I'll be damned if I'm Peggy Kelly!" came Joe's deep, amused voice.

She flung herself about and saw him standing there, his fists on his hips, two steaming kettles at his feet, a bottle of chilled champagne in a bucket cradled with obvious difficulty under one arm. Gone was his formal

161

attire. In its place he wore a clean but simple blue work shirt of rough cotton, the sleeves rolled up to the elbows, the top two buttons casually left unfastened to expose a tanned triangle of hairy chest. His pants were those of any working man, of heavy, dark cord, and tucked into knee-high boots. They were fitted tightly to his muscled horseman's thighs like a second skin, she observed, feeling faint again. His eyes ignited as he boldly appraised her in her scanty, naughty attire, sending her flying across the room in a belated search for her dressing robe.

"Are you deaf, McCaleb, or just plumb stupid?" she yelled over her shoulder. "Didn't I make it real plain down in the hall that I wanted you to leave me be, darn you?"

He set down the champagne and turned again to face her, thumbs tucked jauntily into his belt. "Careful, love," he cautioned. "That classy Academy accent slips just a bit when you're riled up like you are now! Yes, you made it plain enough, but oh, love, your eyes! They tell me something quite different, sweetheart. You want me as bad as I want you. Admit it, Seraphina, and cut out the 'outraged virgin' act you've been playing so that we can enjoy whatever time we have left together! Our marriage today may have been for reasons other than love, but there's no law that says we can't make the most of it while it lasts, is there, instead of carrying on and fighting like cats and dogs? And don't tell me you hated what happened the other afternoon. I know women—and I know better. You enjoyed every bloody minute of it—and so did I. We had something special between us; you know that. Come on, Sera! Let me love you."

His voice was deeper, huskier, as he said these last words, as if he were gentling a frightened wild thing. For a fleeting second, she almost fell into his honeyed

162

trap, for she felt as if she were melting all over at the sound of his soothing voice. Then suspicion replaced the madness.

"Why you . . . you sneaky rattler! Those flowers and the ring I picked out—they were just a part of your plan, weren't they, to soften me up into trusting you again? You didn't believe for a minute that I meant it when I said I wasn't interested, did you? You really expected I'd fall for your wiles and that . . . that coyote smile! Hah! Wrong, you . . . you skunk! Maybe you figure women are just something to be enjoyed like a . . . a grizzly bear steak, or a good smoke, and then *adios,* ma'am, so long and good-bye! Well, let me set you straight, McCaleb. Other women may see themselves that way, but *I* don't! Whatever you may be thinking, what happened the other afternoon between us was a mistake—a big one—and one I don't plan on repeating! No, sir. For a woman—for this one, at least—there has to be love in it when she gives herself to a man, you hear me? And I sure as hell don't love you, McCaleb, any more than you love me! This marriage of ours is a business deal—no more, no less. Quit trying to make something more of it, Joel! That way, no one'll get hurt. When we've sold the land, there'll be no reason for either of us to ever set eyes on the other again, and you'll be glad then that we left it at that. You can take your money and run, and I'll take mine and do the same. Finished—just the way you wanted it at the start. Remember?"

His jaw had tightened, she saw, and there was a coldness to his eyes that hadn't been in them seconds before. Now they were the frosty turquoise of a glacier. "Strewth! What a bloody fool I've been all along! You're right, love, I really didn't see it—leastways, not until now," he said tightly. "All along I thought you were a sweet, innocent young thing, like that night you

163

offered to help little Mei Ling and you called yourself Kate. I was half way to loving you that night. But that sweetness, that innocence, was all an act, wasn't it? That girl wasn't the real you! It was all part of your little scheme, all part of the same plan, the one that arranged my getting into bed with you—right, love— and made damned certain I'd be honor-bound to go through with the wedding? That way, you could virtually guarantee you'd get your greedy little claws into old Grandpa William's money, couldn't you?" He laughed harshly. "You're nothing but a little gold digger, aren't you? Your innocence, in return for half of a small fortune! Not a bad rate of exchange, I'd say, love. The whores on the Barbary Coast spread their legs for far less—and with one hell of a lot more honesty about it!"

Outraged, her hand came up like lightning to slap his hated face with all the force of her wiry female strength behind it. The crack of the blow sounded as if she'd punched a side of raw beef. His head snapped back, and her fingerprints were already rising and livid against the tan of his cheek when he straightened up. His turquoise eyes blazed, and she saw in the instant before he slapped her back, hard, across her own cheek, another Joe—one who was a far cry from the civilized, easy-going gentleman she'd taken him for until now; one who was rough and cruel and deadly dangerous when angered or crossed or believing himself used or betrayed. Tears smarted in her eyes as the slap connected, robbing her of the furious denial she'd intended to hurl back at him, robbing her of all speech whatsoever. She blinked furiously to staunch the yelp of pain that rose on her lips. He'd not have the satisfaction of hearing her cry out, no way, damn him!

"You . . . bastard!" she spat, her eyes those of a wildcat now in her fury. "You're so damned low you're

164

beneath contempt, Joel McCaleb!"

"Why? Because I slapped you? Or because what I said is true?" He shook his head, smiling a mocking smile. "I give as good as I get, Seraphina. Don't forget it! And you earned it. Unlike the men you've no doubt twisted around your little finger in the past, I don't pretend to be a gentleman—"

"You can say that again!" she seethed.

"—just as you're no lady, despite your fine, fancy schooling," he scoffed as if she hadn't spoken. "You could have saved yourself the bother, love. My word's good. I don't go back on it. I would have kept my part of the bargain, without you whoring yoursel—"

Fury choked her. It pounded in her temples, swam in a crimson flood before her eyes. No man had ever spoken to her as he was doing, called her the things he'd called her! Through gritted teeth she spat, "Just shut up, Joel McCaleb! Shut up and get out of my room!"

"Don't worry, I'm going. And . . . what is it you say here out west? Wild horses couldn't keep me here with a conniving, gold-digging little bitch like you!"

"Good! The feeling's mutual! And don't get any notions about sneaking back later on, 'cause I'll be waiting for you with my rifle loaded and leveled."

"Really, love?" He laughed mockingly. "I won't hold my breath, if it's all the same to you. Your type uses other weapons to get what they want . . . right? Besides, you've drawn metal on me twice so far and haven't had the guts to fire. I'd stake money you never will, honey."

Her eyes flashed. "Then you'd lose, so help me!" she seethed through clenched teeth.

He shrugged. "Maybe, woman. But I give you fair warning: if I should ever decide to collect on my . . . downpayment, you won't be able to stop me, I guarantee it." The ring of certainty in his tone was like the grate of chalk on a slate to her ears.

"You think so?" she jeered, her eyes glittering with fury at his arrogance. "Well, let me tell you, mister, it'll be a cold day in Hell before you touch me again, husband or no!"

He suddenly reached out and grasped her wrists, yanking her so forcefully against him that the breath was jolted from her in a gasping rush. He gripped her chin roughly in his fingers to hold her head still while he ravished her lips beneath his brutal mouth. His savage kisses further drained the breath from her and left her dizzy and trembling when he finally pulled back. Insidiously, something was stirring deep inside her despite his roughness. A maddening, tickling sensation was uncurling deep in her belly that craved release. It was a sensation she would never give in to, no, never, she swore, biting down hard on her lower lip.

Insolently, he smiled down at her, and belatedly she realized that as he kissed her, his hand had slipped inside her lace-trimmed corset to fondle her breast. He was idly stroking the creamy flesh there, rubbing the treacherously rigid nipple that had rucked under his touch until it became a hard, aching little peak that was exquisitely sensitive.

"See what I mean, love?" he breathed, mockery in his voice. "Your body knows who's calling the shots here, even if you don't! The next time you take it into your head to threaten me, you'd better make damned sure you carry through—or be prepared to handle the consequences! I'm not some priggish, pimply boy who's afraid of the spoiled little rich girl's temper, y'see."

Her hands flew up to claw at his face, her long nails scoring a bloody trough down his face. "You arrogant son of a bitch!" she panted, her long, midnight hair a tangled mass that spilled over her bare shoulders as she

166

glowered up at him. Her small, clenched fists hammered furiously at his chest. "How dare you speak to me that way! How dare you!"

He grasped her wrists in both of his powerful hands and forced them down to her sides. His face inches from her own, blood trickling down his face, he breathed, "You just don't know when enough's enough, do you, you spoiled little brat? Maybe it's high time someone taught you a lesson!"

For a fleeting moment, there was a glimmer of fear in her eyes, dousing the fury, but she recovered swiftly. "'Someone' meaning you, I suppose?" she retorted, even the defiant tilt of her head a flagrant challenge to his mastery. "Ha! Go ahead, McCaleb! Try it, mister. You'll find you can't tame me with your slaps!"

"Who said anything about hitting you, sweetheart?" he countered softly, lust blazing in his turquoise eyes. With little effort he thrust her backward, sending her sprawling on her back across the bed as her knees buckled. "Why would I beat you, when there's a far more pleasurable way t'tame a woman?"

"Huh! Pleasurable for you, maybe—but not for me!" she denied, trying frantically to scuttle across the bed away from him as, divesting himself of his clothing as he came, he strode toward the bed. Corded muscle rippled down his powerful arms as he tossed his shirt aside, then again as he unbuckled his belt, his eyes impaling her with their lust-filled blaze as he shucked off his pants. His torso was tanned a deep brown-gold, and the light furring of hair across its broad width and down over his hard, flat belly to the thicker golden bush below filled her with horrified fascination as he towered over where she lay huddled. That she had aroused him was only too obvious.

"Of course not, love. If it were pleasurable for you, then it wouldn't be a punishment, now would it?" he answered her in a taunting tone, then he suddenly stretched out alongside her and wound his hand in her black hair, tugging her roughly toward him by it. "Come here, shady lady," he commanded, the timbre of his voice deep and thick with desire. "I'd say half of twenty thousand acres and five thousand dollars leaves me some unused credit, wouldn't you?" he mocked. "I think it's time to collect . . . !"

He hooked his hand over the edge of her clothing and yanked hard. To her horror, the flimsy garment fell away with a ragged, tearing sound, leaving her bared to the waist, breasts jiggling. Her remaining garment followed hot on the heels of the first. Clad only in her white silk stockings and frilly lavender lace garters, she found herself being thrust on her back across the bed. She knotted her fingers in his shaggy blond hair and tore at it in great hanks—though to no avail—as he dipped his head to the valley between her breasts and lapped at the satiny flesh within her cleavage there as if he meant to devour her. His tongue blazed a scorching trail across to her breast. He quickly smothered the soft weightiness with one large hand, leaving only a pert, dusky nipple bared to satisfy his hungry mouth. He drew the sensitive bud between his greedy lips and sucked and flicked and swirled his insatiable lips and fiery tongue tip against and around it until her fingers lost strength and lay slack in his hair and her furious screams died away to helpless little moans. When she was yet gasping from his assault on one breast, he ravished the other in the same way, stroking and kneading each firm, creamy little mound until she felt all will to resist him ebb and a treacherous thrill of pleasure replace her fury.

A low, wicked chuckle sounded deep in his throat, and though the sound of it filled her with fresh outrage, she was helpless to react, to punch, to claw, to fight him off in any way, for his hair was tickling her stomach deliciously now and she was writhing to escape his maddening tongue as he traced the outline of her navel. Her limbs had grown limp, useless, she noted, bewildered by her body's treachery. And then—oh, lord!—and then his lips moved lower and she could feel his heated breath tousling the triangle of black curls below like a hot, inflaming desert wind. He kissed the silken flesh of her inner thighs again and again, teasing the tiny, rose-colored birthmark branded on one with his lips before grasping them, lifting and parting them wider and still wider, then burying his blond head between them and tasting the honeycomb sweetness within.

The throbbing pressure inside her built and spread its pulsing heat through every part of her, centering in her loins as his velvety lips and tongue darted and nibbled and tasted. She wanted to scream, to beg him to give her the release her body craved, but each time she reached the brink, each time she hovered on the precipice, he maddeningly halted, returning his mouth to the hollows of her throat, the valley of her breasts, the quivering plateau of her belly, until she feared she would go mad if he didn't end her torment.

And then, at sweet last, he knelt between her thighs and grasped her buttocks in his large hands, lifting her, opening her, readying her to take him. He drove deep inside her moistness with a powerful, lunging thrust that drove the breath from her in a drawn-out sob, pleasuring himself with hard, plunging thrusts that filled her with shameful yet delicious sensation. He showed her none of the gentleness with which he had taken her virginity that first time, but rather took her with a savage mastery, a sheer male dominance that was every bit as punishing to her pride as he had promised. Yet it was so damnably wild and sweet she never wanted it to end, nor him to stop what he was doing, ever!

Throbbing waves of pleasure engulfed her as she reached her climax, yet still he was not finished with her. Smiling in triumph, he withdrew and turned her smoothly onto her belly, mounting her this time from behind and fondling her swollen breasts as he rode her on and on. He rolled her tender nipples between his thumb and finger. He savagely nipped the seductive, smooth curves of her throat and bared shoulders with his teeth. He kissed her downy nape and her wild, tangled ebony mane until gooseflesh rose all over her. The flickering torment built again in her loins and exploded through her a second time, bringing her dangerously close to fainting from sheer ecstasy, filling her vision with vivid starbursts of light. Her eyelashes fluttered as her eyes closed in exhaustion, sooty half-moon smudges against her rosy cheeks, yet he would not let her escape his taming, not even in sleep.

"Tired, love?" he demanded, yet there was no pity in his tone.

"Yes!" she whispered. "Oh, yes!"

He laughed, ruthless in his triumph as he heard her humbled tone. "And you'll be even more tired when I'm done with you, woman," he threatened. "I paid your doxie's price fair and square, after all, love. A wedding ring and my name, in return for all this!" His hand swept down the length of her body in an insolent, possessive caress that further underlined his mastery of her. "You'd best learn your trade, Sera. A Barbary whore wouldn't fall asleep beneath her man—and neither will you."

Fury swept through her at his insults, and she bucked wildly beneath him, trying to throw him off her. But to her rage, he only laughed at her halfhearted attempts to dislodge him and held her firmly in place as he continued his thrusts again and again.

"That's more like it, love," he mocked as she writhed to escape him, his tone taunting and raspy. Then he suddenly grew still above her and groaned once as he found his own release and fell to her side.

"You animal!" she seethed, rolling as far away from him as the bed would allow. "I hate you! I loathe you!"

"Hate me? Maybe you do, love—but you don't hate the way I make you feel, do you, now?" he countered as he swung off the bed and calmly dressed himself.

As she remembered how she had whimpered and moaned in his arms, a hectic flush rose up her cheeks. She looked away, saying nothing.

"No easy answer, Sera? No more insults? No rash threats?" He grinned his crooked grin. "Then I'd say I won this hand, wouldn't you? My punishment worked!"

He strode to the door, then paused and picked up something from the tallboy nearby. "By the way, I almost forgot. You dropped these in the hall." And with that, he tossed to the bed beside her the sadly wilted little posy of violets and lilies of the valley he'd given her in the church.

She swallowed and gritted her teeth, almost breaking her jaw in the effort it took to control her temper. "Thanks, but no thanks! If I'd realized they had such an expensive price tag attached to them, I'd never have accepted them in the first place. But you see, like a darned fool I thought they were a peace offering—or, at the very least, a kind of apology from you. How wrong I was! Now, if you'll get the hell out of here, I'd still like to take my bath." And scrub away every trace of your loathsome touch, your scent, your lovemaking, *everything,* she added silently, seething.

171

He nodded. "The water's cold now, but go right ahead anyway. It might cool you off! And Seraphina . . ."

"What?" she snapped, dragging the torn remnants of her clothing about her.

He grinned nastily. "I hope you drown, love."

"Go to hell, Joel!"

"That's right where I'm going. To the Barbary Coast. Like I said, at least the women there are honest about what they do, which is more than I can say for you, lady. Enjoy the rest of your honeymoon—and sweet, *lonely* dreams, Mrs. McCaleb!"

He made it through the door just in time to avoid being crowned with a bar of fragrant soap, a well-aimed hairbrush, and a very large, unopened bottle of champagne.

Chapter Eleven

The days that followed and finally stretched into weeks were ones fraught with tension between Joe and Seraphina. Whenever possible, they avoided being alone with each other, exchanging words only when forced to do so. Even those exchanges were stilted and bristling with hostility.

Time and time again, Seraphina wished they could leave, could get to the ranch, get the sale of it over with and go their separate ways. Being around Joe was torture, pure and simple! He'd made it very plain how low he considered her to be, and she knew there was nothing she could say or do to convince him that the conclusions he'd jumped to were false. And nor would she try! His unfairness rankled like poison, but she was too proud, too wounded by what he'd said, too outraged by the things and the motives he'd accused her of, to even attempt an explanation. Let him think what he would, damn him, she thought, still smoldering with anger. She didn't give a darn!

Joe's feelings were not much different from Seraphina's. He told himself he felt nothing but contempt for her, now that he'd figured out her little scheme, and wondered again and again how he could have been such a bloody, trusting fool as to have fallen for it. Ha! And he'd thought he knew women, he mused ruefully! He'd been way off on his estimations of Seraphina; that much was plain. She'd coolly used her body, her very innocence, in an underhanded attempt to blackmail and force him into marrying her so that there'd be no way for him to back out—unless he were an out and out rogue—and her guardian's money would be assured. As far as Joe was concerned, there was only one name for a woman who'd stoop that low, and it was a dirty one. There were whores, and then there were *whores,* Joe thought bitterly, recalling his Aunt Polly—she had been more of a lady than Miss Seraphina Jones could ever hope to be, despite her profession. Christ, he'd be happy when this was all over and he was rid of the gold-digging little bitch!

True, his initial motives for wanting to marry her had been little better than hers for marrying him, but he hadn't set out to seduce her with that end in mind. No, he could say with complete honesty that she'd haunted his thoughts ever since that first night when he'd kissed her sweet lips and called her Katie, and that he'd wanted her since then with a rare, deep craving that had nothing to do with the McCaleb inheritance. Making love to her, for his part, had been the inevitable result of their forced intimacy in her suite, their lack of clothing that afternoon, the champagne they'd drunk, which had lowered his inhibitions and scruples, and the compelling sexual attraction he'd felt toward her from the start. Yes, for him, the desire had been genuine. There, he told himself, lay the difference between them.

He wanted to get out of San Francisco, to ride far, far away from that little bitch whose silken cascade of black hair and lustrous gray-green eyes always made him think of a shady billabong as the sunlight shifted over its surface beneath the eucalyptus trees! Since finding out what she was really like, surely he should have been able to thrust all desire for her from his mind. Aye, he should have—but he hadn't. And his failure to do so hadn't been for want of trying on his part, either. God knew how many eager doxies' swaying hips he'd followed up the stairs to their sad little cribs since his fateful wedding day, each one black haired, many of them far more lovely than Seraphina and a thousand times more eager to please him. But not one among them had served to quench the smoldering fire that lingered within him for more than a few brief moments; a fire that she, damn her, had only to walk into a room to send leaping through his loins!

Could he have been wrong? he'd wondered, hopefully, watching her pale, lovely face covertly from time to time over the days. Could she, as she'd said, simply have drunk too much champagne and allowed herself to get carried away? There were moments when it had seemed not only possible but probable. Catching a glimpse of her guileless and innocently breathtaking face when she had been unaware of his scrutiny, he'd felt an uncomfortable twist of doubt and guilt deep in his gut. Once or twice, he'd decided he was definitely wrong about her, and had half risen to go across the room and offer her his apologies for his accusations. But then she'd looked up, and he'd seen the contempt in her expression, the curl of dislike on her luscious lips. He'd remembered then that she'd made no attempt to deny the things he'd accused her of, and he had decided he'd not been wrong after all . . .

Despite Joe and Seraphina's fervent wishes to leave San Francisco as soon as possible, circumstances conspired against them. Several floods that year washed out the trail the Butterfield Stage normally traveled through the San Joaquin Valley, and twice they bought fares only to have the trip canceled at the last minute on account of the flooding. Joe, though eager to reach the ranch as soon as possible and thence rid himself of Seraphina, whom he now saw as little more than a millstone around his neck, was also forced to delay their journey because of Ming.

After they had said their farewells at the house on Bayview Drive the night they rescued Mei Ling, Joe had not seen or heard from the Chinese youth for almost two weeks. Then, like a lean shadow, he had appeared once more at his lodgings, hungry, exhausted, emotionally drained, with telling dark hollows under his eyes.

"They are everywhere, *fon kwei!*" he had whispered. "Everywhere!"

"The *tong?*"

Ming had nodded. "Yes! There is no place for me to hide from them here in the city. Now that I have crossed Ah Ping, there is a price on my head."

"Then you have to get away. You've no choice."

"This I know, Joe. But . . . where am I to go? My people will not dare hide me. They fear the revenge of the *tong!* And besides, I could not ask them to endanger themselves for my sake. Nor could I hope to find employment in the house of some white man, now that I am wanted. Your people have no liking for Celestials, and even less for those who are sought by the *tong*. They fear and despise us for our differences, for our culture, which is so strange to them."

"Well, cobber, I don't despise you—or fear you either, come to that!" Joe had said with a grin. "I'm to be married on Saturday, and me and the young lady will be leaving San Francisco for Southern California. After that, I don't know what lies ahead, but you're welcome to come along. I could use a sidekick," Joe had added casually, knowing full well the enormous amount of pride Ming possessed.

"Will not your bride disapprove?" Ming had asked, trying to keep the desperate eagerness from his tone, the sudden flare of pure joy from his eyes.

"I doubt it. See, I'm to marry Seraphina Jones, Ming." He had cocked one shaggy blond eyebrow. "When you met her, she called herself Katie."

And so it was that, having no other friends in the city and having taken a genuine liking to plucky little Ming—the first real friend he'd ever had—Joe had asked the Chinese lad to stand up for him at his wedding. Ming, determined to make a go of his life in America, had proudly agreed. He had obviously deemed Joe's request a very great honor, for he had even announced his intention to have the braided queue clipped from his black hair for the occasion, and had asked Joe to act as impromptu barber.

"Perhaps, Joe," he had argued, "if there are less obvious differences between my people and yours, we will learn to accept each other, and live happily side by side, yes? Many of my people are old and set in their ways. It is too late for them to change. They were born in China, and China will always be home to them. But I was born here, and I am American, Joe, for all that the laws of this country deny me the citizenship of my birth. This haircut is but a start. It is my first step on the long road to acceptance." He'd set his jaw in a determined fashion, which had made him seem far older than his seventeen years.

"It'll take one hell of a lot more steps than that, Ming," Joe had warned him, well aware of the enormous difficulties Ming would encounter and reluctant to see his youthful hopes and touching optimism crushed. "It'll take tolerance and understanding and effort—on both sides."

"Ah, yes, that is indeed so. But every journey must begin with a single step before other steps can follow, yes? This will be the first step of Chen Ming! Cut my hair, Joe. Cut it just like yours!"

From then on, Ming had stuck close to Joe and their friendship had been cemented by the deepened understanding they had shared since that day, an understanding that went far below the colors of their skin. Though many of the white men who saw them together in the city clearly assumed Ming was Joe's "Chinee houseboy," Joe and Ming knew their relationship was something far more than that of servant and master. Since they were the only ones whose opinions mattered, they made no effort to correct such mistaken assumptions. But their plan that Ming would go with Joe and Seraphina had been threatened the day following the wedding by the news of Ming's father's illness.

"He has not been a good father to Mei Ling and myself, but despite that, he is still our blood, Joe, and he has no one else to care for him," Ming had told Joe solemnly when the man had first been taken ill. He had hung his head and added with obvious reluctance, "I regret I cannot go with you as we had planned, not unless my father soon recovers, *fon kwei*. You must go to this Rancho de las Campanas without me. If it is still your wish that I do so, I will join you there when he is well again."

"There's no need for that. We'll wait," Joe had reluctantly decided, loath to part with the Chinese youth with whom he had become fast friends and toward whom he felt strangely protective, despite the fact that the delay now meant his uncomfortable relationship with Seraphina must continue indefinitely. The tide of prejudice against the Chinese in San Francisco was growing by leaps and bounds and he was concerned about the boy on two scores now. "The floods should be past history in a few weeks, anyway, and traveling will be easier for Seraphina and Peggy then," he had told Ming. "No, do what you have to do, cobber. I'll wait."

During the next few weeks, Ming had cared for his father as tenderly as the most dutiful son would have done, but not even the finest Chinese physician that money could buy—money pressed on a reluctant Ming by Joe—had been able to cure him, for the heart had gone out of him. The soul had soon followed. Chen Shu Yen had been buried amongst the tinkling bells of the little Oriental graveyard outside San Francisco, from which place his bones would one day be removed, Ming vowed, and returned to the land of China, which his father had continued to consider his homeland until the day he died.

Mei Ling, Ming's little sister, was happy and well cared for now at the Donaldina Cameron Home and school, and Ming no longer had fears for his *shao mei mei* at the hands of the *tong,* though he continued to harbor several for his own neck, since he had crossed powerful Ah Ping and stolen the little girl away. Therefore, it was with a great deal of optimism on his part, and with no regrets whatsoever, that Ming added his lot to that of Joe and Seraphina—as well as to that of Peggy Kelly, who had decided that San Francisco held little attraction for her, either, and had opted to go with them. Smiling broadly, he had arrived on the doorstep of the Bayview Street mansion one morning in April with his meager possessions in a wicker pannier at his feet and had announced that he was now ready to leave with them.

Saying their farewells to the Caldwells for a second time, they departed two days later from the San Francisco depot of the Central Pacific Railroad on

179

K Street, a great adventure for Ming who, though his father had labored alongside many other Chinese to lay the railroad ties for this selfsame railroad, had never ridden aboard a train himself.

Seraphina had made the trip from Boston to San Francisco by ship, and so she was as eager as a little girl on her first trip away from home. Joe and her anger at him were set aside for the time being as she gazed out of the window at the new and exciting terrain of California through which the train steamed and rattled, and she "oohed" and "aahed" with Peggy Kelly over the vineyards and ranches, the orange groves, the wheat fields and the dramatic Pacific coastline that bordered the rails.

In fact, the uneasy relationship that had existed between her and Joe since the night of their wedding eased considerably in those days of travel. It was as if both of them had grudgingly determined that, since fate and promises of great fortune had forced them together, they might as well be civilized about the whole thing and at least maintain an outwardly amicable facade.

Inside, however, Seraphina still felt far from amicable toward Joe. She still smarted from his undeserved tongue-lashing and burned to hurl his accusations back in his damned face and make him eat his words. Gold digger, indeed! But the only way she could do that was to tell him the truth—the *whole* truth—and that she could never do. And so, silently, she seethed. Many times she would look up from an uncomfortable catnap sitting upright on the hard train bench across from Joe and find him staring at her with an enigmatic expression, only to have him quickly look away upon realizing she was awake and staring back. What did that opaque expression mean? she often wondered. Was it hatred? Contempt? Or some-

180

thing else? Was it possible there was also desire for her in his compelling turquoise eyes, or was her imagination playing tricks on her? Whatever it was in truth, those cool, calculating glances never failed to unnerve her. Her palms grew moist. Her throat grew suddenly parched. Her heartbeat quickened.

She suddenly realized one morning as the train puffed steadily across a trestle that she was responding that way because she still felt stirrings of desire for him. *No.* That snake! That sidewinder! She'd be damned if she'd allow herself to want *him,* after the way he'd talked to her, the names he'd called her! She fiercely denied any such emotions and attempted to drown them out by reading, conversation—anything other than dwelling on such a possibility.

Much of the discomfort that was in the air between them, however, was forcibly smoothed over by the presence of Ming and Peggy Kelly, and the pair's continual arguments of their own. Although neither his friend nor the housekeeper would ever admit it, Joe suspected that they actually liked each other and thoroughly enjoyed the verbal sparring that was so much a part of their relationship. An outsider would never have guessed as much, for they bickered constantly, with feisty Peggy calling the Chinese youth "a blatherin', heathen-worshippin' Celestial" and "a Crocker's pet," and Ming terming the housekeeper "a blue-eyed Irish she-demon sent by spiteful gods to torment him and make his life miserable." It was interesting to their companions to note that they dared to address each other so, and even called up the old, heated rivalries between the Chinese railroad workers of the Central Pacific Railroad and the Irish-American laborers of the Union Pacific Railroad, each one maligning the other, yet Joe shrewdly guessed that had the insults been genuinely intended, they would not

181

have dared to voice them. In this, he was correct.

California proved beautiful beyond Joe's wildest dreams, and the clickety-clack of the locomotive over the rails became a song of promise and hope for the future that sang in his heart as he was carried ever closer to his destination.

First explored by the Spanish seaman and navigator, Juan Rodriguez Cabrillo, in 1542, California did not become a matter of concern to the Spanish crown until two centuries after her discovery. Then, fearing both a British advance upon New Spain via the Pacific route after the Seven Years War, and a Russian advance staged downward from Alaska in the north, it became increasingly obvious to the Spanish that the California regions must be colonized by their own people or else there was every possibility that through them they would forfeit control of New Spain. King Charles III of Spain appointed José de Gálvez visitor-general, and in him found the man who possessed the qualities of organization and leadership needed to undertake the task of colonizing California.

Under Gálvez's direction, four colonizing expeditions were sent out from Mexico, two to make the journey across the wilderness by land with Don Gaspar de Portola as their commander-in-chief, and two expeditions in ships to brave the perilous sea routes. The two ships suffered innumerable hardships and losses of life, yet the overland expeditions under Portola safely reached San Diego and established a first small settlement there. Later expeditions sent out from the new settlement were successful in founding yet another colony, this one at Monterey, and thus Spanish control of California was made secure. But it was only with the combination of three institutions—the military fortresses, or *presidios,* the towns, or *pueblos,* and the missions established by various monastic orders—that the new frontiers could be effectively controlled. The Franciscan fathers, under Father Junípero Serra, founded twenty-one missions, each roughly a day's journey apart down the California coast from San Diego to Sonoma. These were founded not only to spread the word of God, but also to provide agencies that could govern and civilize the savage Indians of the territory. And in those early days, Indian attacks upon both *presidios* and missions were all too frequent.

At first, life in the Spanish provinces was simple and unhurried. Cattle ranching was the first main industry, and the huge herds provided most of the small population's needs. The food supply was supplemented by a few ranchers who also began growing grain or kept vegetable gardens and fruit orchards. A thriving—if contraband—trade in tallow and hides was begun with distant New England. The Indians were gradually subdued and brought into the fold of the Christian fathers, and there taught the arts of blacksmithing, tanning, and weaving, at the expense of their own, more simplistic, lifestyles—a state of affairs that would one day prove disastrous to the Indian people of California. Still, such civilized industries were vital to the growing new communities' survival, for the colonies were isolated by sea and desert or mountainous wilderness from Mexico and thus from many of the necessities of life.

Yet as the new *pueblos* that grew up about the missions lost their new-frontier status and became well established and populated, the Spanish Crown determined, in 1833, to put into action its policy of secularization of all missions once a colony was established, a policy that in effect cut off all support of the missions by the Spanish Crown. As a consequence, many of the missions fell into ruin, and the Indian peoples who had come to depend upon them and looked to them for guidance and work—at the expense of their former lifestyles—were scattered, the old ways forgotten, their numbers decimated by battles and the diseases the newcomers had brought to their fair land, and against which they had no immunity. Many tribes simply disappeared as if they had never been, leaving only strange mounds or pictures in stone for those who came after to ponder.

Several small revolutions, minor in themselves but disastrous in their sum total, also broke out among the citizens of the province that year, partly caused by the colonists' dislike of officials sent from Mexico into California to govern them. Mexico was in a precarious position herself at that time, torn by civil war, financially troubled, her military weak and her government best described as turbulent. She could ill afford the time, interest, and financial aid necessary for this distant province that was proving so hard to defend and to control, and simultaneously becoming so attractive to other influences, the United States among them. This was the beginning of the successive events that, decades later, would result in the American expansionist, President Polk, long-anxious to see California annexed to the United States, seizing the opportunity of the Mexican War to establish control over the California province.

Passes over the treacherous and formerly thought impassable mountain ranges had been discovered that would permit migration east to west and populate the new lands, making Pacific California an even more desirable acquisition than early trading had already proved. And with the failure of peaceful attempts to incite the Californians into making a stand for independence from Mexico, war between Mexico and the United States was declared and a military conquest begun. The hostilities came to a close January 13th, 1847, when Andrés Pico, the leader of the last of the California detachments, signed an agreement with John C. Frémont, acknowledging the sovereignty of the United States. Thirteen months later the formal transfer of the territory took place, and, in 1850, following the California Gold Rush and amidst intense debate over the subject of slavery and other matters of import, California was admitted as a state to the Union, and the Stars and Stripes were hoisted and flown over the public square of the first state capital, Monterey.

Monterey was not to be Joel and Seraphina's final destination. Four days after leaving San Francisco, they reached the sleepy but fast-growing *pueblo* of Nuestra Señora la Reina de los Angeles de Porciúncula, Our Lady, the Queen of the Angels of Porciúncula, which was now more commonly known by the simpler name of Los Angeles. All of them were stiff and suffering from aching backs and tender flanks after so many long days of train travel to the coast, then a hot and lengthy coach ride to the *pueblo* after that, and they were relieved to have finally completed the first leg of their journey to Rancho de las Campanas.

Soon after their arrival, they took lodgings at one of the many gracious adobe inns of the *pueblo,* a clean, quiet little *posada* over whose walls rose vines rambled, their fragrance scenting the warm air. The *corredor* was further shaded by several ancient cypress trees, and in the lovely little garden at its heart bloomed olive, orange, and pomegranate trees, great masses of oleander with its red, white, and pink flowers, cape jasmine, and wisteria. After their journey, Casa Catalina was like an oasis in a desert, and Señora Catalina, as the proprietor insisted they call her, seemed a veritable angel. She showed them to their

185

rooms and wished them *Bienvenida* with a warm smile and graciousness that had given Spanish hospitality its renown, bidding Don José, as she insisted upon calling Joe, and Doña Serafina rest and recover their strength by taking a little *siesta* until the late-evening meal.

Early the following morning, Joe gave instructions to Seraphina and the others to prepare themselves for yet another lengthy ride. Meanwhile, he left the inn and strolled through dusty streets lined with little adobe and *brea*-roofed houses shaded by graceful pepper trees, where the hazy yellow sunshine of early morning bathed everything in a sleepy, golden spell. From the church of Nuestra Señora la Reina de los Angeles, the bronze bells in the tower chimed the Angelus. Frail little old ladies in black gowns with black lace shawls veiling their snowy heads came as if from nowhere and hurried across the *plaza* toward the church in response to the bells' summons to prayer. Joe, who had never seen the likes of these devout, quaint little old ladies back in Australia, stopped to watch them before continuing on. Then he found the surveyor's office he had sought across town and received from him directions to the *rancho*.

"Say, friend, what do you plan to do with that land?" the surveyor, an old fellow who sported a long, gray, walrus mustache, inquired after they had consulted several yellowed maps that dated back to the time of the Mexican land grants.

"Sell out, soon as possible," Joe supplied. "If you hear of anyone who's in the market for a place, I'd appreciate it if you'd let me know."

"I'll do that, son." The surveyor grinned slyly. "But I sorely doubt you'll be lucky sellin' that partickler passel of trouble!"

186

Joe frowned. "How's that?"

"Weell, to put it plain, you have yourself a neighbor problem, McCaleb!" The surveyor chuckled. "Yessiree, you sure do! 'Bout the worst there is, in fact. Ain't gonna be easy unloading that land, not even if you was t'passel it up an' give it away."

"Would you care to explain that, mister?" Joe asked, his shaggy brows lowering over narrowed, turquoise eyes.

"Nope! Ain't my place to gossip 'bout folks, like 'em or not. 'Sides, I reckon you'll find out for yourself soon enough, boy," he replied with a wink.

From the cryptic surveyor's office, Joe strolled through the quiet, narrow streets toward Reid's livery stables. The proprietor there seemed friendly enough and more than willing to rent him horses and a buckboard, until he learned Joe's purpose, that is.

"Sorry, McCaleb, but if you want horses, I reckon you'll have to buy 'em. See, I don't lend out my mounts 'less I have a purty good chance of gettin' 'em back!"

Joe's jaw hardened. "Are you saying you think I'm a horse thief, mate?" he demanded, his fists clenched loosely against his thighs.

"Naw friend, cool down there! I jus' think there's a good chance you won't be stayin' in these parts overlong—and a man's gotta protect himself, right?"

"You'd be referring to my 'neighbor trouble,' I take it?"

"Sure am! You won't find anyone in these here parts that would take on Harper Monroe and his boys, unless he was a doggone fool—or didn't know no better." His blue eyes narrowed beneath his broad-brimmed hat. "Which are you, McCaleb?"

"The latter, I guess, mate. Tell me, what's this Monroe got to do with Rancho Campanas?"

"Everything, son! His lands border it, see. His cows

187

use the water like it was their own, and what little grazing there is they reckon is theirs, too. He's the biggest landowner in these parts now, even though he didn't start out that way. See, his other neighbors were only too damned eager in the past to call it quits, pack up and git, once he'd laid down the terms. Indians, Mexicans, even white squatters—it didn't make no never mind t'Monroe. Their land's his now, too."

"Why don't you tell me just what those terms were?"

"Move out—or else," Bob Reid replied with a shrug, his expression grim. "Same terms he gave all the squatters. Doesn't take much of a mind to figger out just what he meant by 'or else,' do it?"

"No, it doesn't," Joe agreed thoughtfully, tucking his thumbs into his belt. "Let's see your horses, Reid. I'll pay cash money for 'em."

He left driving a buckboard and team—his, since he'd paid for them—and with two western-saddled horses, a showy but sound ghostly white gelding he'd purchased for Seraphina to ride and an enormous, rawboned liver-and-white paint stallion for himself. He didn't know if Seraphina could ride, or even if she'd want to if she could, but he figured he'd give her the choice of doing so or riding on the buckboard. After all, the money he'd spent was half hers. He also stopped off at the general mercantile for work clothes and such, and then at the gunsmith's, where he got himself fitted out with a gun belt, holsters, and a pair of black forty-fives. He hadn't liked the sound of Harper Monroe and his "terms" one little bit, and he'd be damned if he'd ride out to the ranch without some means to defend himself, if he had to.

To his surprise on his return to the *posada,* Seraphina seemed not only willing to go out to the ranch but eager. She met him in the dusty street outside the inn minutes after his return dressed for riding in a

188

divided black suede skirt and a crisp jade green blouse with long sleeves. Her black hair had been swept up out of sight under a flatbrimmed, dark green, Spanish-style hat that was braided with silver about the crown and edges. Her hands were encased in tight leather riding gloves and she sported high-heeled, tooled-leather boots inlaid with silver. She looked every bit as coolly remote and tempting in her riding getup as she had in her fancy gowns these past weeks, Joe noted, and grimaced at the sudden hot flood of desire that swept through him. How could she look so goddamned cool and poised and serene when he felt so hot and bothered and edgy around her? he wondered, exasperated.

"My, my, Mrs. McCaleb, you look as if you might actually know one end of a horse from the other!" he was unable to resist saying with heavy sarcasm as she stepped out gracefully into the dusty street to meet him, tapping a braided quirt against the leather of her boots.

"Well, I surely know which end you are, McCaleb!" she retorted waspishly, striding past him to where the horses were tethered at the rear of the buckboard. "Which one's mine?"

"The gray—if you think you can handle him?"

She gave him a withering glance over her shoulder and unfastened the white gelding's reins, running her hand over its lines knowledgeably to check that it was sound—as if she didn't trust him to have ascertained as much—before tucking her toe into the ornate Mexican stirrup and easily swinging astride and into the saddle unaided. From her lofty seat, she looked down at him, her gray-green eyes asimmer with irritation.

"There! Satisfied? You'd be surprised at what us little *gold diggers* can handle, McCaleb. Now, shall we go . . . or stay here yackety-yacking all day?" The white gelding, as impatient as its rider, tossed its head and sidestepped, causing bit and bridle to jingle.

"Keen, aren't you, love?" Joe drawled, tipping back his own new black hat to squint against the brilliant sunshine and look up at her. "Must be the smell of money on the wind, I reckon. It does that to some women—gets them all impatient and as excited as thirsty mares scenting water!"

She smiled sweetly, stroking the gelding's rough-silk mane as if she were caressing her lover's hair. "Really? I'm amazed to hear it, Mister McCaleb! All this time, I stupidly thought it was the stallions that disturbed them! But then, stallions are so *hard* to come by these days, aren't they, when there are so many geldings about?" There, let him make of that what he would, Seraphina thought, inwardly smug as she saw his tanned face pale a little and his ruggedly handsome features tighten in anger.

As she had guessed, the double meaning, and the thinly veiled insult regarding his masculinity inherent in it, had not been lost on Joe. He knew what she was getting at all right, and the barb lodged under his skin, chafing at his pride. Bitch! Didn't that last sly comment of hers prove he'd been right about her all along? If she kept that up, she'd learn soon enough how to tell the geldings from the stallions, by God! Gritting his teeth, he swung about, strode across the street, and mounted his own horse, swinging a long, booted leg over its back.

His flaring anger dissipated once he was in the saddle, for it had been far too long since he'd ridden, not since before he'd left New South Wales, in fact, and riding was something he'd always enjoyed. The fancily carved Spanish-style saddle with its high pommel and ornate silver inlay was a far cry from the simple, flat English saddle he was used to, but he decided he liked it. The stallion felt powerful between his muscular thighs, and he could feel the pent-up energy quivering and dancing through the horse as he wheeled its head about and trotted it back toward Ming and Peggy, who stood waiting uncertainly before the door of Casa Catalina. Peggy carried a picnic basket and a knapsack of provisions under her arm, and Ming, several canteens of water.

"Can you drive a buckboard?" he asked Ming.

"I never have, but I'll give it a try, Joe," the boy said uncertainly, squinting against the sunlight to look up at him. In his blue, western-style shirt and bibbed work pants, he looked even younger than his seventeen years.

"Tsssk! I'll handle the reins, then," Peggy Kelly cut in crossly, tossing her gray head in blatant disgust. She tied the strings to her huge blue calico bonnet with fingers that trembled with irritation. "I suppose 'tis more than could be expected, t'think the likes o' you could handle the likes o' this. Get in, an' let an Irish colleen show ye how it's done, lad!"

"It will be an honor to have such a worthy *elderly* lady instruct this humble China-boy," Ming said solemnly. "And in return for your great kindness, I will endeavor to teach *you* the art of cooking upon our return, Missie Peggy, since it became evident in San Francisco that you are as sadly ignorant of that skill as I am of this!" He inclined his head to the little woman in a gesture of utmost respect, but his black eyes twinkled with deviltry.

Joe, hiding a broad grin, didn't linger to hear the inevitable, furiously explosive retort from the "elderly" Peggy Kelly in response to this. One point for the men! he thought, mentally tallying the score. He gathered the reins in his fist, dug in his heels, and headed the paint out of town after Seraphina.

Chapter Twelve

They rode away from the Coast Range and across the San Gabriel River, traveling through low, dun-colored hills the tawny color and formation of which put Seraphina in mind of a sleeping cougar sprawling across the hazy blue horizon as it basked in the sun after a kill. The low, spare rises were the feline's sleek flanks, with the suggestion of a shiver of powerful muscles rippling beneath the surface; the undulating hills were her full belly and powerful chest. Dark clumps of oak trees, *los encinos,* broke the monotony from time to time, as did the many narrow, rocky streams fringed with willows and straggly cottonwoods that they had to ford or stop at to water the horses and team from time to time. Vineyards, watered by these creeks, were numerous, and spread out around the ruins of what had obviously once been the vast gardens belonging to the missions. Indeed, there was evidence everywhere of the part the missions had once played in the history of California: remnants of the old cactus hedge the mission fathers had grown about their fig and fruit orchards to prevent wild animals—and perhaps local Indians—from sampling the fruits; crumbling adobe walls where once had been shadowed cloisters or refectories or spartan cells. So, too, they saw off in the distance the clouds of red dust thrown up by the hooves of hundreds of head of long-horned cattle that now grazed the ranges, and of the colorful, mounted *vaqueros,* the Mexican cowboys, who herded them for their various *patrones* using trained *bronchos.*

They saw the strange plant that the first pioneers to reach California from the east had named Joshua trees, because of their resemblance to the Biblical prophet at his prayers. These were really not trees but enormous yuccas with spires of lovely, waxen bells that resembled lilies. Several times, they spied deadly rattlesnakes basking on the rocks in the mid-morning sunshine, and gave them wide berth; they saw, too, a few jackrabbits, ground squirrels, and once even an amber-eyed coyote with her litter of yelping cubs resting in the shade of some massive boulders. In some places there were deep rifts in the earth's crust that Seraphina knew must have been caused by earthquakes in past years, for earth-quakes of varying degrees of severity were all too frequent in California. Looking down into the rifts, she could see the many-colored layers of strata, piled one upon the other like the layers of an enormous cake.

It was a strange and exciting land, yet at the same time an achingly familiar one, for much that she saw reminded her sharply of New Mexico and the ranch where she had been raised—and to which she must soon return . . .

"But that's our secret, mmm, Muraco," she whispered, leaning down to murmur in the gelding's ear. The horse, which several miles back she had silently decided to call Muraco, an Indian name that meant "white moon," whickered and tossed its head at the caressing tone of her voice, and she laughed softly as she straightened in the saddle. For all that Joe was an insensitive, arrogant brute, he had chosen her mount well, she had to admit. The ghostly gelding had looks, stamina, an easy, powerful gait, and intelligence, qualities she herself looked for when choosing a horse. She grinned and turned her head aside to look back at the buckboard so that Joe, riding only a few yards off to one side of her, would not see. They were, she'd suddenly thought, also traits she'd promised she'd look for in a man, but with, perhaps, the additional ones of compassion, sensitivity, and, yes, a sense of humor, too! The latter trait was obviously not one Joe possessed. Since she'd retaliated to his sarcasm earlier, he'd not said a word to her, and she'd wanted to laugh at the brooding, furious expression he'd worn ever since.

They crested a low rise, and up ahead on the winding trail Joe reined in his horse and motioned for her to do the same. It was strange, she noticed for the first time, how extraordinarily well he rode, for she would not have expected a man who'd spent his entire life on a small, tropical island to have ridden much, if at all. He *had* spent his life on the island of Java, hadn't he? That was what Edward Caldwell had told her, but then, what did he—or she—really know about Joe? His accent, the way he rode—loose and easy in the saddle like one born to it—made her wonder suddenly if there was far more to his past than he'd told the lawyer. Or . . . had he in fact told the lawyer anything? Hadn't Caldwell simply *assumed* much of what they knew about him? Her attention was abruptly dragged away from this startling train of thought by Joe's shout for her to look up ahead.

In a shallow bluff, protected there from wind and sun, she saw a small soddy. A sorry-looking cow with a lowing calf grazed a small patch of scrub behind it, and two black-haired little boys rough-and-tumbled with a litter of shaggy black and white sheepdog pups in the

194

dust while a woman laboriously scrubbed clothes against a board in a wooden washtub. A few chickens scratched halfheartedly for worms in the dust. The children shouted something on catching sight of them and pointed excitedly in their direction. Their mother straightened and shaded her eyes against the sun to watch them approach. Almost in the same move, she reached to snatch up the rifle that leaned against the bench and held it before her, obviously prepared to defend her home and her little brood if need be as she waited for them to ride closer.

"Let me do the talking, all right?" Joe muttered.

"Go right ahead," Seraphina encouraged him. "You *do* speak Spanish, I take it?"

"Well . . . no. But I suppose you do?"

"Enough. Come on, *gringo!*"

So saying, she touched toes to Muraco and trotted him on ahead.

"Buenos días, señora!"

"Buenos días, señores," the woman replied. Close up, she was short and sturdy, her smooth olive complexion dark from the sun, her handsome black eyes wary and filled with mistrust. She wore her long black hair tidily braided and pinned up. The cotton *camisa* she wore was worn yet clean, the gathered neckline gay with vivid bands of red and blue and yellow Mexican drawn work. The long skirt that brushed her dusty bare feet was neatly patched, as were the clothes of her two young sons. "What is it you want of us?" she demanded in Spanish.

"Want? We want nothing, *señora,*" Seraphina replied in the same fluent tongue. "My . . . husband, Señor McCaleb, and I have ridden out here from the *pueblo* of Los Angeles. We are looking for the *rancho* known as Las Campanas. You know of it, perhaps?"

The woman wetted her lips, her enormous dark eyes

uncertainly going first to Joe, and then back to Seraphina. "Las Campanas? *Sí,* but of course I know of it! This here is all Las Campanas land, *señora!*" She spread her arms wide in an expansive gesture.

Seraphina translated what she had said to Joe.

"Ask her if she knows where the ranch house is, will you?"

Seraphina nodded and complied.

"It is perhaps four miles farther, that way, *señora,*" the woman answered, pointing to the northwest. "My husband, he went that way early this morning to watch over our flock, yes? If you should meet with him, he will tell you which way to go."

"Muchas gracias, señora," Seraphina thanked her.

"De nada, señora," the woman replied, setting aside the rifle now and venturing an apologetic little smile. "You must forgive my bad manners, but . . . but not all the Anglos who come here are good people like yourself. I have my children to protect, my little sons. You are a woman like me. You understand, and you will forgive me, *si?"*

"Claro que sí," Seraphina gently reassured her. "But who are these *gringos* whom you fear? Pardon me, *señora,* but I do not see why anyone should wish to harm either you or your little ones; it appears you have very little for anyone to steal."

"That is so. But Don Harper and his sons, they are very bad men! They want my Esteban and I to leave this land, you see. The last time they came, *señora,* they drove their herds of cattle over the little vegetable garden I had planted, even over our very home! *Mis hijos* and I were forced to run for our lives! *El señor* said that time that soon all the Campanas land will be his, that he will rid the San Juliano Valley of all squatters!" There was bitterness in her tone, and yet also more than a suspicion of stubbornness and

196

defiance. "My Esteban Rodriguez is also a man of determination. He says this will never be; that we will defy *el señor* again and again until he wearies of the game he plays! We have only a few sheep, this little house, nothing more. What could make him hate us so, *señora?*"

Seraphina shrugged. "Greed, by the sound of it, Señora Rodriguez. Some men are that way. A little is not enough for them. They want everything and then still more, and won't rest until they have it all, no matter who's hurt because of their lust for the land, or for gold, or whatever it is they crave. But you can breathe a little easier from now on. You see, Las Campanas belongs to my husband and me now. We mean to sell it, but I am certain whoever buys the land from us will—"

"Sell it? When Don Harper Monroe has sworn that all of Las Campanas will be his one day soon, as so many of the smaller *ranchos* have also fallen into his hands? As you said, what he wants, he will have! Those who are but gentle shepherds like my Esteban have little chance against such a man, however brave, however proud, they might be." She shrugged hopelessly. "It would take a stronger man, an *hombre* as . . . as ruthless and determined as he is to hold this land against him. No, *señora!* I do not believe you will find such a man to buy Las Campanas."

"We'll see about that," Seraphina ended, disturbed by the kindly woman's obvious despair. "Good-bye for now, Señora Rodriguez, and thank you for your directions."

Seraphina motioned to Peggy and Ming, and the buckboard clattered and rumbled, following her and Joe as they rode on a short distance. When they were out of sight of the little soddy, Joe reined in his horse.

"Well? What was all that about?"

"It seems we're already on Las Campanas land, Joel! Señora Rodriguez told me that she and her husband, Esteban, have been herding a few sheep hereabouts and trying to eke out a living for their little family, despite what sounds like some pretty violent opposition from someone called Harper Monroe and his sons. Why, the man stampeded his cattle through their little place and almost killed her and the children!"

"Monroe! Him again!" Joe shook his head and cursed under his breath.

"Then you've heard of him?"

"This morning. And I heard a hell of a lot more than I wanted to, at that," he added grimly.

"Then what she told me is true?" Her gray eyes were wide and dark with alarm as she looked up at him.

"So it would seem. The surveyor back in Los Angeles didn't think I'd have the hope in hell of selling this land, not with Monroe as a neighbor. Seems his reputation is pretty widespread—and damned dirty."

Looking at his grim expression, Seraphina felt a twist of foreboding deep in her belly. "But if we can't sell the land, what will we do? We'll have nothing."

"We'll worry about that if and when it comes to it," Joe said.

A mile or so more, and they saw up ahead the grubby tallow-colored bulks of a few sheep scattered across the dun hills, grazing contentedly on the scrub or resting in the shade given off by one another's bodies. A shepherd, the *pastor* of the small flock, had obviously decided to halt for his midday meal and was squatting before a small fire over which a coffeepot bubbled. A shaggy, black and white sheepdog crouched at his feet. As they rode up, the sheepdog darted forward and began barking furiously. The *pastor* reached for a stout club beside him and sprang to his feet. The wariness in his eyes, the tenseness of his frame, was akin to that

198

Señora Rodriguez had exhibited earlier, Seraphina saw.

"Esteban Rodriguez?" she called.

"*Sí*. Who are you?" the man replied suspiciously.

"Friends," Seraphina reassured him. "Your wife told us where we might find you. May we join you at your fire, *señor?*"

He nodded, yet the club remained firmly in his fist, she noted. "If you are in truth friends, you are welcome," he said softly.

She and Joe dismounted and left their horses ground tied as they went to meet the buckboard, which arrived alongside the small camp amidst clouds of red dust thrown up by the wheels.

"By the Blessed Virgin!" Peggy cried, rubbing her aching rear as she clambered down from the vehicle. Her face was sunburned despite her bonnet. "To be sure, this . . . boneshaker must ha' been invented by the Divil Hisself!" She shot Ming a sly look. "Or a Chinee!"

Ming grinned as he went around the back to get the provisions and the canteens. "Perhaps it is so," he agreed with deceptive mildness. "It is true that my people are very inventive. We possessed all manner of carts and wagons long before other civilizations learned of them. At that time, all wheels in Ireland were square, I have heard. Was that not so, Missie Peggy?" He arched his dark brows innocently, his black eyes half-moons of merriment against his yellow-brown complexion.

"I'faith, it was not! Square wheels, indeed! I've had all I can take o' this young spalpeen, ma'am! I'll not listen to another word out o' that blasphemous, heathen little—"

"That's enough, you two!" Seraphina cut off Peggy's retort, taking the supplies from Ming. "Let's have a bite

199

to eat and then stretch our legs. I'm sure it'll go a long way toward improving our tempers, and I don't know about you two, but I'm more than ready for both!"

Casting Ming a glance that could have killed, Peggy snorted, snatched up the canteens, and followed Seraphina to the fire.

Esteban Rodriguez relaxed considerably after a few minutes of conversation with Seraphina and even more so after, in halting English, he managed a few minutes' exchange of words with Joe. He was a short yet stocky man, with gentle, deep brown eyes and a mop of curly black hair beneath his broad straw *sombrero*. When he discovered that Joe owned the Las Campanas land on which he grazed his sheep, however, he began to stammer his apologies and became visibly upset.

"For myself, my woman, our sons, the sheep are our life, Don José!" he cried, looking earnestly at Joe. "Forgive us for grazing them here, upon your lands, but we have nowhere else to go. There are many of us *pastores* here. We live very simply from day to day. Our needs and those of our sheep are not such great ones. If *el señor* McCaleb could see his way to permitting us to stay, we would offer thanks to God for his compassion—"

Joe was spared answering his plea by the sudden arrival of several more shepherds, bearded men wearing loose white cotton *pantalones, serapes,* and *sombreros,* and carrying wooden staffs and *maletas,* or knapsacks. They halted abruptly when they saw the strange horses and the buckboard and exchanged suspicious glances, but Esteban waved them onward, calling to his companions that Doña Seraphina and Don José came as friends. Reassured, the other shepherds joined them about the fire, eagerly offering to share their *tortillas* and beans, their cheese and their wine with the strange Anglos.

"Ask them how it is they come to be here?" Joe urged Seraphina, and after she'd asked the question, a burly, older man, a Basque who introduced himself as Raoul Garnier, explained.

"Many years ago, this land was owned by Don Miguel de Navidad y Cordero, a *don* from Old Mexico who came here when California was first colonized by the Mexican people. There is an old Spanish saying that wherever the hoof of the sheep touches, the land becomes gold. Don Miguel had faith in this saying, *señores,* and so he decided to raise sheep here—many, many sheep. He had several thousand head of them driven up here from Albuquerque, New Mexico, and was very fortunate that most survived the long, difficult journey.

"Those were the days of what is known as the *partido* system, *señores*. The forbears of these men who sit before you were *partidarios,* each having a part of their *patron's* flock to tend along with their own sheep, which *el patron* gave them to do with as they wished in payment for their herding of his flocks. Side by side, the sheep of the *partidario* and his *patron* grazed the land. Don Miguel became a very wealthy *hacendado,* landowner, in this manner, and so did some of the *partidarios* under him who increased their flocks and were able to buy their own lands for grazing elsewhere. In the shearing time, Don Miguel would send the wool by mule train to Santa Fe, and from there it would be taken east, bringing him *mucho dinero*. And every spring, the sheep would drop still more lambs, many of them twins, until the sheep of Don Miguel were as countless as the stars! Many of their great-grandfathers' fathers were *pastores* for the great Don Miguel, herding his sheep up into the foothills of the Sierra Nevadas in the summer months, and back down into the valley when it was cooler. We here have walked in

201

their footsteps until today."

Joe, who had listened keenly to the man's tale, nodded in understanding. "And what happened to this Don Miguel?"

"Everything went well for him until he married, it is said, *señor*. He returned from a tour of Europe with a lovely woman as his wife, Doña Luisa. However, his bride proved a frail woman, more used to the sheltered life of the city than the life of *una patrona*. When she was carrying their first child, she fell sick and implored *el patron* to return her to her native Madrid in Old Spain. He loved her so very much that he did as she wished and sold the land and the flocks and left with her. Then, for many years after, the land belonged to the Valdez family, and all went on peaceably as before, until the war. After that, the land became the property of an Anglo, a William McCaleb. This was your grandfather, yes, *señor?*"

"You remember him?" Joe asked, curious.

"Very little, I regret, *señor*. I was but a little boy when he lived at Casa Campanas, as were many of the others, too," Raoul supplied, frowning. "Perhaps *el viejo,* the old one, Pedro, over there, can tell you more. You will have to speak loudly, however, *señora* McCaleb, for he is quite deaf these days," Raoul cautioned, grinning.

"Señor Pedro, can you hear me?" Seraphina bellowed.

"Sad, very sad!" old Pedro responded in a quavering voice, looking across the fire at her with tragic, dark eyes. "No one has ever been happy there, and no one ever will. The Indios, now, *they* knew, *sí,* they knew better than those that came after! They stay away from the place. They know the misfortune that befalls everyone who comes to live there is what comes of trying to make the house of God into the house of man,

202

you see." He nodded sagely.

"What is it *el viejo* is talking about?" Seraphina asked, thoroughly confused.

"The *casa*—the ranch house, *señora,*" Esteban explained. "You see, many years ago, the same good fathers who built the missions along the coast also attempted to build a mission inland, three miles or so to the north of here, in the heart of what is now Las Campanas' land. It was not a success. Far from it! *Los Indios* waged many attacks on the mission and some of the fathers were killed. So fierce were they that the building was never completed, save for the magnificent bell tower, which still stands, and a small part of one of the original chapels.

"Among the few Indians the fathers were able to convert was a beautiful *Indio* princess. She fell deeply in love with one of the Spanish soldiers sent here to help the good fathers defend their church, and she wished to marry him before a priest and before God, according to the Christian customs she had been taught prior to her baptism. But alas, the soldier was no man of honor. He wanted the chief's daughter, *si,* but as his lowly *puta,* not his bride! Accordingly, he schemed to take her as his own without the sanctity of marriage. A soldier friend of his masqueraded as a priest and 'married' the pair, and so the princess was happy and lay with her lover each night thereafter, believing they were truly man and wife. Then, when the arrogant, heartless young soldier tired of the dusky princess, he rode north and never returned. Too late, the young woman learned she had been tricked, but by then she was carrying the soldier's child. Her shame soon became evident. The good fathers upbraided her for her sinfulness, and they determined to punish her with heavy penances and hours of prayer and whippings, for the *padres* were stern indeed in those times. Her own father closed his heart and ears to her, for what she had done also went against the strict teachings of their tribe. He bade her leave their people, and even when she begged him on her knees to shelter her, he turned his back on her utterly. He had one of her brothers ride with her far into the desert wilderness beyond the Sierra Nevadas and leave her there at the mercy of the elements and the wild ones, to survive or die as the Great Wise One Above should decree. Before she was taken away, it is said she set a curse upon the mission and the *campanario,* which was its pride. The Indians believe, *señora,* that to this very day the spirit of the lovely Indian princess searches for her faithless beloved, and that because of her heartbreak, only when two who truly love are united in marriage in the chapel of Las Campanas will the bells of the *campanario* ring out across the valley. It is strange, is it not, *señora,* that until this very day, the bells in the *campanario* have not once rung?"

Seraphina nodded, still lost under the spell of the *pastor's* low, musical voice and the melancholy legend. "*Si,* it is very strange," she agreed with a little sigh. "And so sad, too."

Joe, more direct, asked, "Is the ranch house far from here?"

"Perhaps five miles more, *señor.* If you follow this trail through the valley, you will come to a rock shaped like a bird. Its beak points the way. It is a place of great beauty at this time of year, but a place of great sadness, too. Few go there now. It would be better, perhaps, if you and the lovely *señora* did not go, either. You understand, *señor?*"

"You can stay here if you want to, Seraphina," Joe suggested.

Seraphina shook her head. "No sir! Let Peggy and Ming stay here and rest, and we'll ride on ahead. I guess we'll have to camp back here overnight, since it's late afternoon already." Joe nodded agreement. She turned to Esteban Rodriguez and spoke rapidly to him in Spanish. "There, that's settled, then!" she finally announced. "He says he'll be happy to have Ming and Peggy stay here, and will send his eldest son, Antonio, back to his soddy for blankets if we're not back by sundown." She stood, brushed off her skirt, and put on her hat again, running the bead up along the narrow cord that dangled beneath her chin to hold it firmly in place. "Shall we ride on?"

With loose, easy grace Joe stood and strode after her to her horse. To her surprise, he gave her a helping hand up into the saddle.

"Thanks," she told him grudgingly from her high perch.

"De nada!" he shot back.

"Not bad, McCaleb. You learn fast." She grinned down at him, gray-green eyes alive with laughter.

"Faster than you'd ever believe, Sera," he quipped.

"I just bet you do," she said thoughtfully, wondering what new tack he was taking this time and where he hoped it would lead. Was an apology in the offing, perhaps? Let him try! There was no way she'd accept it, she decided resolutely, gathering the reins in her gloved fists. It would take a lot more than a casually extended helping hand to allay her mistrust of this dusty blond wolf, however engaging the grin he shot her and however guileless those sensual, hooded turquoise eyes!

Chapter Thirteen

Four or so more miles of hard riding brought them to the bird-shaped rock, just as Raoul had described. They followed the direction of its beak, and very soon the Casa Campanas lay ahead in the distance, as the Mexican *pastores* had promised. It was quite unlike any other *hacienda* Seraphina had seen.

Casa Campanas stood upon a slight rise that commanded a breathtaking, unbroken view across the valley floor from the Coast Range in the south to the Sierra Nevada Range to the northeast. The sun was almost setting as they headed their horses toward it, flame and gold outlining the saw-toothed, inky mountains and throwing the *campanario,* the bell tower with its three heavy bells, into sharp black silhouette. Rolling seas of wildflowers—purple-blue lupins and silken gold-orange poppies, bluebells and Indian paintbrush—were bathed in the liquid topaz light peculiar to late afternoon and early evening and seemed painted in fine, glowing, old oils by a master artist, their muted colors only further underlining the mystery and majesty of the adobe ranch house. A few twisted cottonwoods and willows straggled along the banks of the narrow river that snaked its lazy way down from the foothills of the Sierra Nevadas, and in the fiery glow of the sunset, the water glinted dully, reflecting the light upon its still surface in occasional molten gold ripples and bloody sunbursts.

"Christ! Will you look at that!" Joe breathed almost reverently, sweeping off his hat and hunching forward over the cantle of his saddle as if he couldn't quite believe his eyes. "It's like a castle . . . or a cathedral . . . or something . . . !"

"So it is," Seraphina murmured softly, equally under its spell. Nothing the Mexican shepherds had described could come close to capturing this! No one could, not with mere words. The drama of the mountains against the gaudy sky, the inky blackness of the *casa grande,* the sea of color that was the wildflower carpet strewn across the valley, possessed a magical beauty that had to be seen with the heart, the soul, and the eyes together. Gazing into the distance, she wondered if Joe could ever bring himself to part with all this, now that it was his. Glancing across at his face, she recognized in his expression a sudden possessiveness and dawning pride that had not been there before, and she experienced the first uneasy twinges of doubt. What if he should decide he wanted to keep the ranch after all? What the devil would she do then? Time was fast running out for her. Two months more, only two months, and the game would be up . . . . He *had* to sell it!

For several moments, they sat astride their horses in silence broken only when one of the horses blew noisily and tossed its head, or when Joe lit up a smoke. Yet even the rasp of the match head striking against his boot could not break the spell for Seraphina. Gazing across the valley to the distant, waiting *hacienda,* she could almost hear again the Spanish words the shepherd, Esteban, had spoken so softly: *"The Indians* say, señora, *that only when two who truly love are united in marriage in the chapel of Campanas will the bells of the* campanario *ring out across the valley."* His words had seemed no more than a fragment of a hauntingly beautiful legend in the brilliant glare of the sunlight. But here, with the cool of the night wind riffling her hair and murmuring through the wildflowers, and with the light fading and the sun fast becoming only a bloody glow upon the distant, ragged ridges, they had taken on new meanings; they seemed no longer a story, but a prophecy. She shivered, gooseflesh crawling down her spine and spreading over her arms.

Joe noted the gesture. "Let's go!"

She nodded without speaking, wishing she could bring herself to ask him outright if seeing the place had changed his intention to sell out. But her fear that his answer would not be the one she wanted to hear made her tongue-tied and the question was never voiced. She kneed her horse forward abreast of his and, side by side, they rode toward the Casa Campanas.

Close up, much if not all of the brooding quality of the unusual ranch house vanished. They tethered their horses to a clump of chaparral and went on on foot, the sound of their boots striking against the rubbled dirt seeming overly loud in the hush.

"Strewth! That Don Miguel had an imagination, didn't he?" Joe said finally, looking up at the *casa*.

She had to admit he was right. The old mission bell tower had been incorporated into the architecture of the house to form a striking facade for the *casa,* the arch with its one bell at the top and two more beneath surmounting wide, hand-planed double doors below it that were studded with black nails in a pleasing geometrical pattern. A fine grit coated the recessed panels, she found, running her hand over the sadly neglected wood. She could just imagine the beautiful old door restored and polished to its former lustre, and for a moment she wished fervently that she could be the one to see to the *hacienda*'s refurbishing. Unlike her tomboy mama, she'd always enjoyed seeing a house put to rights, had discovered what great satisfaction there was to be found in making old things come alive again under her careful hand. It was a trait that her mama'd always said she must have inherited from her grandmother, Mary, who'd died before she was born, since Mama's always preferred riding to chores and housework herself. Darn fool! she scolded herself silently. In a few weeks you'll be gone! What do you care what happens to the place?

The remainder of the house appeared to have been built in the traditional square design of many Spanish houses, the existing bell tower having been incorporated into one of the four sides, with two short rooms leading off it, the whole comprising one side of the square. In the center, there would more likely than not be an open courtyard onto which all the rooms opened, with a wrought-iron gallery for strolling in the cool air of the evening fronting the upper story. Dark beams, the *vigas,* supported the ceiling, and the roofs above were of baked adobe tiles, the red tiles that the Indians had been taught to make by the mission fathers, but many of these had been either lost or stolen over the years.

"Shall we go inside?" Joe asked softly, drawing a heavy, somewhat rusty key from his shirt pocket.

"I guess we should," she agreed.

After a brief battle with the ancient and equally rusted lock, Joe managed to turn the key and shoved hard with his shoulder against the door. The heavy portal swung inward with a loud, protesting groan, and at once there was a flapping of wings and a flash of snowy white, and something swooped over their heads and flew up into the darkening lavender sky. Seraphina squeaked in alarm and clawed blindly for Joe.

"Just a barn owl, love," Joe reassured her, and she knew by his tone that he was amused. "We must have disturbed its *siesta*. What did you think it was—the spirit of the Indian maiden, still searching for her Spanish lover?"

Despite his faintly mocking tone, she knew then that the *pastor's* words had touched him, too, and even now lingered in his mind. The insight made her feel on a more equal footing with him. It was comforting to know she had not been alone in her crazy notions. "For all you know, it may well have been!" she retorted, and heard Joe's low chuckle in response as they stepped inside.

They entered a spacious hallway, and in the dappling of the gray light that spilled through the grilled windows high above, they could see that the white-washed walls that had been added to the bell tower to convert it into a cavernous hall were painted with Indian designs, many of them large, accusing eyes drawn in bright colors that, in the cool and shade, had faded very little.

"That's part of the original mission, isn't it?" Joe asked, looking about curiously.

"I'd say so," she agreed, and shivered. "Lord! I feel as if those eyes are watching us, don't you?"

Joe nodded. "You're right there. And now that I've seen the place, it doesn't surprise me that the Mexicans have crazy beliefs about it! Who wouldn't be superstitious here?" He strode on into the gloom, opening a door at the rear of the hall. As Seraphina had guessed, a wide courtyard or patio opened up beyond it, framed by the remaining three sides of the *casa*. Where once, perhaps, orange trees may have grown in tubs in the courtyard, now there was only dust and a drifting tumbleweed or two, and the pattering sound of some small animal as it fled their intrusion.

"The missions were built like forts this way for protection," she told Joe, "protection against the Indians, that is. They weren't too keen on being baptized at first, and had a tendency to attack the missions to steal the good fathers' supplies!"

"Don't blame 'em, poor devils," Joe said solemnly, though his eyes twinkled. "Being a heathen and following wild, heathen ways is one hell of a lot more fun than prayer and piety! Believe me, I know."

"Oh, I believe it!" she retorted. His teasing banter relieved the tension between them, and Seraphina relaxed and breathed more easily than she had since they'd first spied the house. "I have Indian blood myself, you know," she volunteered. "My father is half Cheyenne."

"Is?"

She reddened in the shadows, furious with herself for her stupid slip. "I meant 'was.'"

"I should have guessed it—all that long, blue-black hair! No wonder you act like a little savage at times!" She caught a flash of white as he grinned.

"It doesn't shock you?"

"Shock me? Don't be a bloody little fool. Why should it? In fact, it kind of makes me envy you, that you knew your parents. See, I never knew my mother or—" He'd been about to say 'or my father,' but managed to cover the dangerous mistake by adding, "—or much about her."

"That's too bad," she murmured, genuinely sympathetic. "I guess I'm . . . I guess I was lucky."

He grunted agreement. "Well, shall we look around before we lose the light?"

The remainder of their tour revealed nothing astonishing; several more large, lofty-ceilinged rooms with attractive dark beaming, all in dire need of cleaning and repair, with bedchambers, dining room, and kitchens among them. Black wrought-iron sconces branched out at intervals from the whitewashed walls, which had turned a mellow beige over the years. There were a few pieces of furniture, but most of it was too badly damaged by time and neglect and weather to offer any hope of salvage.

"Must have been quite a place in its day. I wonder why Grandpa McCaleb left it?"

"Edward Caldwell told me the heart went out of him after his first wife—your grandmother—died, and several years of drought took its toll on his longhorns. He took away your father, William Junior, who was still quite young then, and they went to San Francisco to live."

"Where he later met your mother, Sarah."

"Mmmm? Oh, yes, that's right. She . . . she was his housekeeper."

"I see. Well, that's about it!" Joe declared, looking around one last time. "At least we know what we've got here to sell now. We'd best ride back to camp soon, if we mean to get back by nightfall. You wouldn't want to be lost in the dark with me, now would you, love?" He winked roguishly.

"No, sir!" she retorted quickly. Yet even as she said the words, she couldn't help smiling at his wickedly hopeful tone; couldn't help the nagging little voice of her conscience that whispered that she was lying to him—and to herself. Oh, yes! Despite her anger, despite everything, that afternoon when he'd made love to her at the hotel had come back from time to time and invaded her thoughts, and she had recalled with painful clarity the sensation of his gentle hands caressing her body, the ardor of his lips upon her own. There had been moments, both back in San Francisco and en route here to Southern California, when perversely she'd wanted very much to be alone with Joel, times when his mere presence in the same room had made her heart start that funny skipping rhythm, her nipples swell to hard, aching buds, and—oh, yes—her entire body had cried out for the closeness and intimacy of his. And for the passion—

"Sera?"

She turned in the doorway and looked back at him, her lovely profile framed against the amethyst sky beyond, dark waves of inky hair spilled down from beneath her hat in a soft, ebony cloud to her shoulders. "Yes?"

"What I said on our wedding night, about your being a scheming little gold digger, and the rest of it, remember?" His voice was husky, as if he found it difficult to speak.

Remember? How could she ever forget his hatefulness! "Yes. What about it?"

"Was I right? Did you lead me on that afternoon because of the inheritance?" His tone sounded uncertain now.

She sighed and shook her head slightly. "No, truly I didn't, Joe. If you had only listened to me, I would have told you that then. I'd had far too much champagne that afternoon, and a large brandy, if you recall, neither of which I was used to . . . and I guess . . . I guess I didn't know what I was doing. I suppose, looking back on it, I was as much to blame as you were for what happened—maybe more." It was no lie. Knowing how strong her physical attraction to him had been since that single, stolen kiss at Bayview House, she'd been asking for trouble by letting him ply her with glass after glass of champagne. Once her

213

inhibitions had been quelled by the alcohol, that attraction had been impossible to deny, but so darned easy to surrender to.

"Then I want to apologize for accusing you, Seraphina, and for everything else I said," he continued gravely and with every appearance of sincerity. "See, I'd never met a girl like you before. The women I've been around in the past weren't what you'd call ladies, not by a long chalk, I suppose I thought you were like them, using men to get what you wanted in any way you had to. I figured you'd used me, too, goaded me on to take your virginity just to get your greedy little hands on your guardian's money. Let me tell you, I was damned mad about it!"

"Then we're both guilty!" she confessed, glancing up at him shyly. "You see, Joel, I'd decided that that was why you'd set out to seduce *me*—so that I'd be reluctant to back out of our deal. That's why I was so goldarned mad when I woke up that morning and found myself in bed with you. I thought you'd used me, too!"

She saw the glint in his eyes as he grinned. "Really, Sera? Then I'd say we both need to have a whole lot more trust in each other, wouldn't you, seeing as how we're business partners and all?"

"It surely couldn't hurt any!"

"Fresh start, Sera?"

She hesitated, for there was something there in his eyes, some lambent fire that implied her agreement would mean far more to him than a simple truce. She remembered again the night they had been married and had quarreled, and her glimpse beneath Joe's easygoing, casual facade to another kind of man smoldering just below the surface; a man who took what he wanted with the reckless daring of a gambler; a man made all the more dangerous by the fact that he kept his

214

true nature well under control, until those moments when his emotions blazed forth in savage anger, incapable of being subdued. Was he truly that way—or had that glimpse of another Joe been the work of her overactive imagination and her anger at him? Tingles of doubt shimmied down her backbone as, after what seemed endless moments, she felt compelled to reply softly, "Why not?"

Smiling, he took her elbow and led her back out toward the horses.

She had gathered the reins of the white gelding, Muraco, in her fist and had tucked her toe into the stirrup, preparing to mount, when Joel suddenly took her by the shoulder and turned her about. In that second, looking up into his face, she knew she had been right about him.

"Damn it, Sera, it can't stop there! I don't know about you, but I can't go on like this!" Before she could evade him, his fingers bit like steel into her upper arms and he hauled her hard against his body. For a fleeting second, their eyes met, locked blazing gazes that seemed to charge the air between them with the electricity of sexual tension. In answer to the fierce, blue-fire desire she read in the depths of his, her own senses stirred like smoldering embers fanned into raging flame by a fierce, hot wind.

"No, this isn't meant to happen . . . Joe, don't you see . . . it mustn't happen!" she cried, pressing her hands against his chest. But even as she said the words, she was eagerly melting into the strong arms that reached out to drag her close, was arching her hungry, yearning body to his.

"Tell me one good reason why not, woman? It's what we've both been wanting for a long, long time," he growled but gave her no time to answer him as his lips slanted hungrily across hers. The heated ardor of his kiss, the demanding assault of his tongue, darting, probing, warring with her own, jolted all thought of protest from her mind. She could only surrender herself eagerly, joyfully, to the fury of his passion. The almost brutal urgency of his kisses stirred a response in her loins that refused to be denied, a tingling heat that prickled throughout her entire body to her breasts and the pit of her belly, her toes, even her fingertips.

"These past weeks I've been too bloody proud to admit I was wrong and ask you to forgive me. And there was never a moment to ourselves to tell you how I felt once I realized what a damn fool I'd been," he whispered raggedly when he at last broke away. "God help me, I want you, love! There's no reason or rhyme to it that I can see, but I want you more than I've ever wanted any woman. If you don't feel the same, then for Christ's sake, say so now, before it's too late!"

"Would it make any difference?" she heard herself asking huskily, aware of the challenge implicit in her tone. Oh, she'd grown reckless, heedless of the consequences as wanting swept through her!

He paused, then shook his shaggy blond head, his expression hard and ruthless in his desire. "No, it wouldn't, not now, I admit it. I've wanted you for too many long, lonely nights to give up on you so easily again! Ever since I first kissed you, you've kept me awake at night, filled up my dreams, Sera. It's as if all my life I've been waiting for one woman. Just for you, my lovely, black-haired witch. I see your eyes, the curve of your cheeks, your lips, everywhere I go. I imagine I'm holding you in my arms, but when I wake up, you're not there, and there's this goddamned emptiness inside me. I can't take being around you without holding you, without kissing you, without making love to you! You're mine, Sera—now . . . for always. My woman, my wife, my love! I've never wanted any woman the way I want you, and I'm done waiting for you to come around. Say you feel the same, before I lose what little control I have left,and take you any way I have to! Say it, Sera!" he demanded harshly.

The hands she had pressed so fiercely against his chest to hold him at bay fell away and fastened about his wrists. Their frightened pressure melted into a feverish caress that traveled up the wiry length of his arms to his shoulders. A low moan of anguished surrender broke from her. "Oh, yes, Joel, yes! You don't know how I've . . . oh, Lord, yes, take me, hold me! Don't let me go! Quickly, Joe, before I come to my senses!" she whispered brokenly, and barely had she said the words before he was holding her, sweeping her up into his strong arms, her dark head cradled against his broad shoulder, her arms coiled fiercely about his neck.

Neither said a word as he strode with her away from the horses to the carpet of wildflowers, though she could feel the erratic thundering of his heart beneath her palm where it lay pressed against his broad chest, hear the ragged breathing of his desire. There, in the midst of the silken poppies and the lupins and bluebells, in a spot bowered by overhanging boulders and lit by the silver of the rising moon, he set her down and lay beside her, stroking her cascading midnight hair, caressing the silken, willowy curves of her body as he kissed her again and again, each kiss more intimate, more deeply hungry and possessive than the last; each kiss, each tingling caress, building the heady desire that vanquished her will to deny him. His lips moved down feverishly over her throat like lapping tongues of fire and sought and found the little cleft between her breasts. She was alight and yet drowning, drowning in a sea of molten sensation, and Lord, how she wanted to drown, to burn, to blaze! His kisses were potent magic,

217

and she fell entranced under their virile spell, yielding with every part of herself, her body, heart and soul, as he caressed her, as he tasted the aching peaks of her breasts and devoured her sweet warmth time and time again.

When he'd undressed her, after he'd kissed her bared body everywhere and caressed each trembling inch with lips and tongue and callused, gentle fingertips, he parted her silken thighs and entered her, filled her with his hardness. His broad chest crushed her down into the massed wildflowers beneath them, the scent of the bruised blossoms pungent and green on the cooling night air; it was a scent she would never forget, never, not if she lived to be a hundred. Her fingers twined in spasms of delight about the tender green stems until, as her passion soared, the fragile stalks broke under her impassioned grip and a tide of blossoms spilled from her fists and cascaded about them. He loved her fully, building the rising flood tide of her delight with deep, lunging thrusts of his powerfully muscled flanks that made her cry aloud to the moon and the brilliant, pulsing stars high above with the joyous release that finally exploded through her.

Much later, she lay curled and content in his arms, her cheek pressed against the rough furring of his broad, sun-bronzed chest, his corded, muscular arms coiled loosely about her. The pale moon raced across the starry deep gray sky above, playing hide-and-seek with the scattered clouds. The sharp, fresh scent of wildflowers laden with night dew was full in her nostrils, and in the distance she could hear the yelp of coyotes as they hunted. *Remember!* she told herself, pain twisting in her heart, *remember this night always!* All too soon, memories would be all she had left of Joe . . .

Tears smarted behind her eyelids, and she swallowed

several times in a valiant effort to stop them spilling over. If only everything could have been different; if only she had met Joe under other circumstances, then maybe they might have met and courted and fallen in love like others did instead of being flung together this way by an old man's fancies. If Joe knew—if he ever found out—she knew now that he would never let her go, not willingly! But he mustn't; he mustn't find out! She had to see it through and then hightail it out of here before he so much as suspected he'd been duped! Yessir, even if she *were* dangerously close to falling in love with him and it would break her heart to leave him . . . . Close? Oh, damn, who the heck did she think she was fooling? This went deeper than any mere physical attraction! She was already desperately in love with him—had been since San Francisco, if the truth were known! But she couldn't let that change anything, however much it hurt. She had to leave. The happiness of too many other people depended upon it.

"Sera? You awake, love?" Joe drawled, his voice deep and husky now with sleep, its hard, ruthless edge gone and in its place a tenderness she'd never heard before.

"Mmm. Yes. Well, almost," she murmured, snuggling against him and wishing she could stay there, cuddled close to him that way, forever.

"Get dressed, sweetheart. We've a long ride ahead of us."

"Do we have to go? Can't we stay here for the night"

"We could, if you don't mind being chilled half to death."

"You could keep me warm, Joel." She heard herself say the words and was dimly amazed at their brazenness, and even more amazed that she didn't care. *Time.* There was so little of it left them. She'd make the most of what there was, and to hell with the consequences! she vowed silently.

"There's nothing I'd like better, love. And when you say it that way, all warm and sleepy, I'm tempted! But I have a feeling you might change your mind in the wee hours of morning. It'll get real cold then, and you'll find yourself wishing you had a blanket or two instead of me real soon!"

"Never!" she denied emphatically and yelped as Joe slapped her playfully across the bottom.

"Stop tempting me, sweetheart, and get dressed! Ming and Peggy must be going crazy about now, wondering what's happened to us. For their peace of mind, if not ours, we'd best be getting back." He leaned over and planted a kiss upon her nose. "Come on, there's a good girl. Up with you!"

They dressed in silence, Joe helping her with the buttons of her shirt, fastening each one with a kiss and finally setting her hat atop her tousled black hair with a gruff, "Y'know, right now I'd give anything to be back in Java, love."

"Why's that?"

He grinned, his turquoise eyes catching the silvery moonlight and glinting wickedly. "Because the nights are so damned warm there, we wouldn't have to leave! We got off to a bad start, but I love you, Sera," he murmured, caressing her cheek with a callused knuckle. "I know I've had a damned funny way of showing it these past weeks, but I do. There, I've said it, though I swore I never would. Now, get a move on, woman!"

They rode back to their camp with Seraphina mounted before him on his paint pony, his arms clasped tightly about her, her head resting against his chest. As their horse's drumming hooves marked off the miles to their camp, she wished fervently that their starlit ride through the valley need never end . . .

Chapter Fourteen

Seraphina grazed her hand down over Joe's smooth, bronzed back, a shiver of pleasure spiraling through her as she felt the play of corded muscle ripple under her fingertips in response. He reached over to gather her into his arms and kiss her. As they kissed, his large hand slipped sensually down her own back, dancing playfully over the knobs of her spine and then moving lower to caress the taut swell of her derrière, molding its supple fullness again and again until her excited little gasps broke repeatedly against his mouth.

Oh, how her nipples ached, tingled, seemed ready to explode into frenzied blossom! It was as if they were connected to that secret place between her thighs by an invisible thread in some magical way, for the fluttery sensation of hunger and excitement between her thighs grew more heady and unbearable than ever as Joe pressed her down onto her back upon the feather bed and transferred his maddening, wonderful mouth to each jutting bud, nipping and drawing each one in turn deep into the searing, moist heat of his mouth.

"Sera . . . you little witch . . . Christ, love, you taste like honey, like wild honey and cream . . . !" he murmured, his turquoise eyes now smoky blue with desire. His lips stroked her breasts and her flat, velvety belly with tiny, darting tongues and frothy swirls of fire. Lower his lips moved, until they nestled against the silky riot of curls that concealed her womanhood.

At the sweet, wild assault of his feverish mouth and questing fingers upon her exquisitely sensitive core, she arched upward, fiercely lacing her fingers in his shaggy blond hair, tightening her grip until perspiration glistened in the valley between her breasts and upon her upper lip. She tossed her head from side to side in blissful anguish so that it cascaded across the snow white of the pillow like a raging black silk sea.

"Please, Joe . . . no, you mustn't, mustn't do that ! Oh, Joe, please, no, don't . . . don't . . . don't stop!"

"I won't, love," he whispered huskily. "That's a promise . . ."

He laughed softly in pleasure and triumph as she grew suddenly still beneath his hands and lips and he felt the tiny pulsings and quiverings of her lovely body that betrayed her delight.

"Love you, Sera," he whispered as he slid up the length of her satin body to lie upon her and plant a gentle kiss full upon the crushed flower of her mouth. "Open to me, sweetheart. Let me show you how much I want you, love you, need you." Tenderly he parted her thighs with his knees and raised her hips slightly, the better to enter her, sliding deep inside her and remaining there, poised and quite still, braced upon his elbows, until her long-lashed eyelids fluttered open once more and her arms rose and curled themselves languourously about his neck.

"You're a devil, Joel Mc Caleb," she murmured sleepily, tracing the hard angle of his jaw. "Anything that feels so darn good just *has* to be a sin—and that makes you the Devil, to tempt me so . . . so wonderfully!"

"Then I guess it's time for you to pay the devil his due, love!" he teased, his turquoise eyes glinting in the moonlight, its silvery lustre spangling the dusty blond of his tousled hair. Turning her over smoothly onto her belly, he flexed his lean hips and thrust forward, deep between her thighs. He moved powerfully yet without haste, repeating the sensual plunging again and yet again until the luminous shimmer in her gray-green eyes dwindled, ignited, and became aglow with the new awakening of desire in her, and the heated love words he whispered against her tousled hair drove her to a second moment of madness as he found his own release.

Much later, they lay side by side with their bare limbs intimately entangled upon the white, lace-edged linen sheets of the wide Spanish bed in their room at the *posada*. The moonlight fell through the wrought-iron grills at the window, veiling everything in a silvery gray lace. The past three weeks had been like something out of a dream, Seraphina thought as she hovered on the threshold of sleep—a glorious, glorious dream. The one thing wrong with dreams, however glorious, was that sooner or later one had to wake up and face reality . . .

Soon the only sound was the deep rise and fall of their breathing as they slept, the trill of the cicadas in the oleanders beneath the window, and, from somewhere nearby, the plaintive chords of a softly played guitar.

The brilliant golden light of early morning dawned on a far less intimate scene.

"It's been three weeks, Sera, and believe me, I've tried everything!" Joe was saying, anger in his tone. "Everyone here in the *pueblo* says the same thing—that

223

no one'll buy Las Campanas as long as Harper Monroe is alive, and damn it, love, I think they're right!"

Seraphina tossed aside the covers and sprang from the bed quivering with anger. She was bare beneath the almost transparent lemon yellow silk of her chemise, her raven hair a wanton tangle that spilled halfway down her back, still mussed from his lazy, wonderful caresses of the night before. Her expression, however, was that of a woman hard-pressed and at the end of her patience, an expression far-removed from the languorous picture she'd presented in the wee, dark hours.

"Oh, no you don't, Joe! You may be able to fool yourself, and maybe even Ming and Peggy, too, but you can't fool me! Don't lay the blame for your change of heart on Harper Monroe. I saw your face the very first moment you set eyes on Las Campanas, remember? You won't sell it! You'd never sell it, Joel, not now—not even if someone walked in here right now and offered you a million dollars for it. These past three weeks you've only been going through the motions of wanting to sell it. That nice couple from Minnesota— the Paltierres?—why, they practically begged you to sell it to them, Harper Monroe or no Harper Monroe, and what did you do? You told them the land was grazed out, next to useless! I heard you myself! And do you know why you did that? Because you *want* that land, and all the power that goes with it! Admit it, Joe. It's gone to your head. You want it so bad, you can taste it!"

He flung about, clenching his fists so that the corded muscles rippled up his arms and shivered under the smooth, sun-bronzed flesh of his shoulders and bare torso. His eyes were turbulent, their turquoise hue darkened to stormy lapis lazuli under knotted fair brows. His hair was longer now than it had been the day they were wed, grown shaggy and leonine after

224

several weeks without benefit of a barber's shears. He reminded her of a savage mountain lion, cornered and dangerous as he stalked with lean, virile grace toward her, everything about him bronze and gold in the sunshine that streamed through the leaf-lace of the pepper trees beyond the wrought-iron grilled window.

"All right, damn it, I admit it!" he gritted. "But it's not what you think—no, it's not the power. It's the pride, the owning of it, the chance to make something of it and watch it grow. Las Campanas is *mine!* All your life, you've had everything you've ever wanted. You've only had to crook your little finger to bring someone running to dish up whatever it was you wanted on a platter, a poor little rich girl. Do you know what it's like to grow up never having anything that's your own, *really* your own, to do with as you please? To have to share your clothes, your school-books, your comb—even your goddamned bed!—with half a dozen others?"

"What are you talking about?" she cried, confused.

Joe flicked his head and shrugged, realizing belatedly he was running off at the mouth in his frustration. "Strewth! Never mind all that. It isn't important. I was just talking crazy. Hell! This whole bloody *business* is driving me crazy, you hear me, Sera? Yes, goddamn it, I want that land. And yes, I mean to have it, to make something a man can be proud of from it. Something that's mine and that no one can take from me as long as I live and breathe, so help me God. Something that I'd fight with everything I've got to keep! There, woman! Are you satisfied now that I've admitted it?" he growled, running his hands through his rumpled, dusty blond hair. Muttering a curse under his breath, he reached for his tobacco makings on the dresser and rolled himself a smoke with large, tanned hands that shook with emotion, lighting it and taking a deep drag before exhaling slowly through his nostrils. The act seemed to calm him somewhat.

"And where do I fit into all this, Joel? Las Campanas is my inheritance too, remember? Doesn't what I want count for anything?"

"You know bloody well it does, Sera! Haven't I told you that I love you, woman? That's why I want to build Las Campanas into something for the both of us, Sera, for us—and for any children we might have. Surely that goes without saying. But first, I have to do it for me, for myself, for Joe Chris . . . for Joel McCaleb. I must!" He shrugged. "It's just something I feel here, inside me, driving me, eating away at me! It's been that way ever since I saw the ranch that sundown, and if I don't go after it, I'll be less of a man for it. I can't explain it, love. It just *is!*"

His tone, though aggressive still, implored her to understand what he was telling her. And in that moment, with those words wrenched from deep inside him, Seraphina's worst fears of the past weeks were realized. She'd tried to deny what she'd sensed coming on the wind all along, hoping against hope that she was wrong and that Joe truly intended to sell the ranch as he'd promised. Yessir, she'd been reckless, heedless of the consequences in those first giddy, rosy, whirlwind weeks of loving Joe and being loved by him in return, and had denied even to herself that it would have to end someday. Now, she was only too conscious that her efforts to turn back the clock, to halt time, had failed. Time was running out. In just a few short weeks, Aunt Lucinda would be returning from Europe and her year-long Grand Tour, and her own disappearance would be discovered. It had to end here, now; she knew that—as surely as she knew deep inside that when that moment came, her heart would break.

Earlier that morning, she'd awakened nestled in

226

Joe's arms and realized how very hard it would be for her ever to leave this man. She'd let it go too far, way too far. It had to stop here, now, this very day, for his sake as well as hers, she'd realized. For the past three weeks she'd refused to face facts, burying her head in the sand like an ostrich in the hopes that if she ignored the problem, it would vanish. Her time here was running out, and the problem could no longer be ignored; it had to be dealt with. Accordingly, she'd forced herself to demand that Joe level with her, tell her straight out just exactly what his plans were. Her refusal to accept any hedging or evasiveness on his part had been what had started their furious quarrel. Oh, Lord, until this morning, she'd been hoping that *something* would come up, some miracle to change everything. But it hadn't. He didn't intend to sell the land. He never had, not really, not deep down inside; she'd sensed it all along. He just hadn't been able to admit the truth to her, or even to himself. And if he wouldn't sell Las Campanas, all her plans were dashed. All of it—going to San Francisco, the clever charade she'd played, marrying Joe for the sake of saving Seraphina's damned inheritance—had all been for nothing! No, it couldn't end this way! she thought desperately. She wouldn't let it! She'd put too much into making it work out for it to fail . . .

"If you love me, Joel, you'll find a way to unload it," she said, more harshly, cruelly, than she'd intended. "What about the government? I heard from Señora Catalina that they're looking to buy land for a new railroad. Surely you could try—"

But he was already shaking his head, his expression like a blank stone wall, implacable, granite hard. "No ma'am! There's no way anyone's going to run a railroad through my land, you hear me? Yes, I love you, Sera. But damn it, what about you? Didn't you say you loved me, too? Then prove it! Ask me anything—except that I sell the ranch. Stand beside me, Sera. Help me to do what I have to do to make Las Campanas work. Be my wife for keeps, and forget what we planned back in 'Frisco."

This time it was Sera's turn to shake her head. "No. I can't do that. There are reasons for it I won't explain, but I can't! You gave me your word, Joe," she ended, accusation mingled with desperation in her eyes and in her tone. "You swore it."

"That was before we knew what we had together, before we came to love each other, surely you see that? Sera, they were promises made by two strangers, not by you and me, love," he argued, tossing the butt of his smoke into the brass spittoon in the corner of the room. "How we feel about each other now changes everything."

"Wrong, Joe!" she retorted. "It makes no difference, not in my mind. The deal still stands, Joe, and I intend to hold you to your word."

A long silence followed, a silence in which her last words seemed to echo over and over. The very air crackled with the electricity of their emotions.

"So this is what it boils down to. You're giving me an ultimatum, are you, Sera?" he demanded at length with tangible bitterness in his tone, his lips thinned now with contempt. "You, or Las Campanas?"

She drew a heavy sigh and slowly shook her head, raw anguish in her eyes. "No, not even that, I'm afraid, Joe. My share of the *sale* of Las Campanas, and my freedom—that *was* the deal, wasn't it?"

"For a woman who says she's in love with me, that's a damned strange deal!"

"I don't like it any more than you do, Joe. But that's the way it has to be."

"*Has* to be? Oh, no, I don't think so. We all have

228

choices, and it's plain you've made yours, sweetheart!" He flung about and punched the wall viciously, causing a little shower of white plaster to dislodge before he whirled to face her, eyes blazing. "You know, what we had between us wasn't love—leastways, not on your side, Sera. What was it? A pleasant interlude for a bored little schoolgirl, maybe? Some new sort of thrill? Or an amusing diversion to while away some time, perhaps? Whatever it was, it wasn't love. Love you can't turn off and on, like water from a pump. It's either there, or it isn't. And as far as you're concerned, I'd say it isn't, leastways, not for me. Got someone else waiting for you out there, have you, Sera?" he asked in a hoarse tone, suddenly certain in his heart that she had.

She flinched and looked away, unwilling to let him see the anguish in her eyes and in her agonized expression as she softly mouthed, "Ah. So you've finally figured it out, have you? God knows, it took you long enough! Yes, Joel, that's it. Yes, I do have someone else waiting for me." Better a lie that would end it quickly and cleanly between them like a merciful bullet than a pack of half-truths.

His shoulders slumped. The fire in his eyes dwindled and a curtain dropped over his features, rendering them an implacable mask. "I guessed as much, but I didn't want to admit it, no, not even to myself. I had an idea it must be something like that all along, when you so eagerly agreed to the deal we made, then got so riled up when I made love to you. Of course, that wasn't part of your little plan, was it?" He scowled and muttered an obscenity under his breath. "Christ! What a bloody fool I was to let myself fall for you, Sera, after a lifetime of staying uninvolved. I sure know how to pick 'em, don't I, damned, blasted fool that I am!"

His words were like thorns, each one piercing her heart and drawing blood. But she couldn't allow him to

229

sway her. Gritting her teeth, she forced a catlike smile and met his eyes unflinchingly as she retorted, "Oh, don't be so bitter, Joe. After all, this way you'll have all that precious land to yourself, won't you? Tell you what, you can buy me out, if you want Las Campanas so damn bad." It wasn't what she'd hoped for, but it would be better than nothing.

His jaw hardened. Something cold and heavy replaced his heart. Bitch! Cold, callous, greedy little bitch! Every time he began to trust her, to open up his heart to her, to let himself risk caring for her, she showed her true colors. Ah, hell! It was always that way, sooner or later, when you made the stupid mistake of letting yourself love someone. They either died on you, or killed you inch by inch, until nothing but the hurting was left. Damn her, she was no different. Why the hell couldn't he walk out, turn his back on her and keep on walking? A nerve in his temple danced, but he squared his jaw and steeled his heart and muttered, "If that's how you want it, then fine. You have yourself a deal, Sera. I'll buy you out. I . . . guess you'll be wanting to leave here right away, so I'll contact Edward Caldwell and have him set it all up for us. I'll wire you your share of William McCaleb's inheritance just as soon as I can, and we'll be quits, just like we planned from the first. It may take me a while, but I'll do it somehow, my word on it. Just drop me a line, let me know where to send your share. That suit you?"

Dry mouthed, tears prickling like grains of sand in her eyes, she nodded.

Still reluctant to believe she really meant it, he crossed the chamber and reached out to touch her, to place his large hand upon her shoulder, perhaps even kiss her in farewell, hoping that his touch might sway her. He'd not ask her to stay, nor beg or plead with her. A man had his pride, after all, if little else. Nonetheless, despite everything, he found himself asking huskily, "Sera, love, can't we work this out?"

At the mere brush of his hand, her body responded, seemed to come alive under his fingertips, and hope soared through him. Against the filmy cloth of her chemise, her nipples blossomed into hard, tight buds. Something naked and vulnerable leapt into her eyes and her breathing became suddenly labored and uneven. He noticed—oh, yes, he noticed—and hope burned more fiercely still in his own eyes and heart as he breathlessly awaited her answer. Surely she wouldn't react to him that way if she were really in love with someone else.

"Don't, Joel, don't say anything, don't touch me!" she whispered, her hands raised, palms outward, to ward him off. "Leave things be, as perfect and . . . and unspoiled as they were last night between us. Don't let's do anything that might cause us to part with still more bitterness! I . . . I couldn't bear it!"

His hand wavered in midair, then dropped to his side, floundering as the hope inside him now floundered. "So, last night was good-bye, was it, the grand farewell? And you planned it all along! You little bitch! You should have told me, Sera. I'd have made damned good and sure you had one hell of a night to remember me by. But you see, as it was, last night I still thought we had a lifetime ahead of us to share!"

Tight-lipped, he turned from her and picked up his shirt, shrugging his long arms into it and buttoning it up. When she dared to turn her head to look over her shoulder at him, he was already dressed and striding to the door, his saddlebags hefted over his shoulder, his gun belt riding low on his lean hips. He walked as she had seen gunslingers walk, like men who know their days are numbered and are just waiting for that final,

231

fatal bullet that will end it all.

"I won't be coming back into town for a spell," he said, his voice hoarse. "I guess you'll be gone by then. I'll take Muraco back with me, and leave some money with Señora Catalina for you to be going along with. Good-bye, Sera. I won't tell you to take care of yourself. I have a hunch you'll do that just fine anyway! Your sort usually does. Self-preservation's a strong instinct, I guess."

Her chin came up in a show of defiance, though his words smarted. "You're right. I'll be just fine. Good-bye, Joel. And . . . and good luck. I really mean that!"

"Sure." It sounded like a snarl.

He gave a curt half-nod and was gone, and for what seemed an eternity she simply sat there, dry eyed, and stared at the open door, too numb for tears; choked and aching, yet too resolute to give voice to the silent pleas for him to stay that trembled on her lips. It was better this way, she told herself silently. It would have happened sooner or later. But then, knowing that all along, why did it hurt so darn much now that it had?

It was mid-morning before Joel left the sleepy *pueblo* of Los Angeles, riding the big, rawboned paint pony and leading Sera's gelding, Muraco, behind it. Behind him came the buckboard carrying Ming and Peggy, both uncommonly silent this morning, tools and miscellaneous items—including a crate of laying hens—and enough provisions to last for several weeks. Among them was a bottle or two of whiskey. He had no intention of coming back into town any sooner than he had to, not for anything, and he had a notion he'd be shouting up one of those bottles before the day was through. The several whiskeys he'd already downed like water at a little *cantina* off the plaza after sending the telegraph to Caldwell in San Francisco sat sourly in his gut. Instead of giving him the lift he'd been looking for, they had plummeted him into a mood so morose and black, even Ming hadn't dared to question him or attempt to talk him out of it.

"Seraphina and me are parting ways, mate," he'd told the Chinese boy tersely. "Doesn't seem as if I can sell Las Campanas like I figured, so I plan to see if I can make a go of working it. Are you with me or no?"

"Why, with you, Joe! You know better than to ask," Ming had agreed without hesitation, a little hurt that Joe would have to ask. Still, there were about a hundred questions he'd have liked to ask himself, like why it was Missie Seraphina and his good friend Joe weren't planning to stay together after they'd seemed so happy and in love these past weeks, but he didn't dare. Joe's thunderous expression froze the very questions on his lips. With a shrug, he'd set off for the general mercantile with the list of supplies Joe had requested he purchase.

Peggy, forthright as ever, had heard Joe's bald statement that he and Seraphina were parting ways and that he was giving her and Ming the option of staying or going to the ranch with him, and she had gone straightway to the room he and Seraphina had shared at the *posada* for the past three weeks. The door still stood ajar. She'd pushed it and seen Seraphina sitting on the edge of the bed, staring blindly at the bare whitewashed wall like one in shock.

"Excuse me for botherin' you, mum, but is there anything I can do, you know, t'help?" She had stepped hesitantly into the room, appalled by the young woman's blank expression, the sheen of unshed tears that made her gray-green eyes overly brilliant. "Mister McCaleb told us . . . told us you and he were splittin' up!" Her tone had been incredulous.

233

"It's true," Seraphina had confirmed in a choked voice, her rigid self-control dwindling in the face of the motherly Irish woman's concerned expression. "Oh, Peggy, it was only a matter of time! It was never meant to last, not even this long! We got married for all the wrong reasons. You see, it . . . it was a stipulation in William McCaleb's will that we had to marry in order to claim his inheritance, his way of taking care of Seraphi . . . of me after his death; that's all it ever was. Joe and I planned from the first to see those conditions met, then go our separate ways. Unfortunately, we . . . Joe and I . . ." She had sighed. "Well, that's over and done with now. We've come to the end of the road, and Joe'll go his way and I'll go mine. Did he ask you to keep house for him out at Las Campanas?"

"Aye, mum, he did. But—"

"Then go with him, if that's what you want. He'll need help, all the help he can get. The place hasn't been lived in for years, and men aren't . . . aren't much good at keeping house or at making one into a home." Her lower lip had quivered.

"But, what about you? What will you do, mum? You'll need—"

"No, no, I won't. I won't need a thing, believe me. Joe said . . . said he'd leave me some money. You don't have to worry any about me, Peggy. See, I'm going back where I came from, before 'Frisco."

"Forgive me fer askin', but do ye not . . . do ye not love him, mum?" Peggy had asked in a hushed voice, half afraid she'd gone too far even by voicing the bold question and unwilling to rub salt into a perhaps still-raw wound, for over the past few weeks she'd grown fond of the girl and would never knowingly have said or done anything to hurt her.

Seraphina had squared her shoulders. Her chin had come up resolutely. "Love? Love has nothing to do

234

with it, Peg; that's for other people, not me. It's just . . . just that there's something I have to do, people I love and don't want to hurt. And I will, if I stay here with him."

"And what about yourself, mum? Don't ye have any duty to yerself an' yer own happiness? And to his?"

"No," she had answered in a tone that implied she was trying to convince herself. "We made a deal, Joe and I. He knew what he was getting into, same as I did. Now, go on with you, Peggy. I'll be just fine."

"You're sure?" Peggy had not been deceived by the hardness of her tone, for it had been an eggshell hardness that had seemed ready to crack at any moment.

"I'm sure."

"Then good-bye, mum, and God be with you," Peggy had said with reluctance. The woman had impulsively leaned over and kissed her cheek. Seraphina had squeezed the woman's large, wash-roughened hand in response, feeling an overwhelming urge to bury her face against Peggy's bony shoulder and sob out her hurt. It was an urge she had fought to the bitter end.

Peggy had nodded and left to pack her few possessions, then had joined Ming out by the buckboard.

The twenty-four hours that had followed were lost to Joe forever. Afterward, he could remember nothing after reaching Las Campanas just as the sun had been going down and turning the tall, wild mustard into a brilliant sea of gold before slipping over the distant, darkened buttes. It had been too bloody much like the last time he'd come here and had made sweet, wild love to Sera amongst the wildflowers with the fresh, green scent carried on the night wind that caressed their

235

bodies. The memory had been too much, too overwhelming; his loss too recent and raw. The uncomfortable feeling that in his lust for the land he had lost something worth far, far more and a thousand times more rare and dear was like a sharp spur roweling his heart.

Maybe he should have done what she'd wanted and sold the land to the government for the railroad. Perhaps then he could have talked her into staying with him, and they could have found a likely piece of land together someplace else. But then he remembered. He'd asked her if she had someone else waiting for her, and she had said she had. She'd slept with him, while all the while she'd had some other poor bastard dangling on a string, waiting for her to come back to him. Tramp! Bitch! What did she have instead of a heart—a steel strongbox? He'd wanted to lash the innocent pony into a furious gallop then, and ride him until they both dropped and the pain, the jealousy, and the anger were lost in exhaustion. He wanted to lash out, to hurt someone else to ease his own hurt; to feel the aching, the grieving, quit him in a crimson haze of fists and curses and bloody punches. The old Joe—the Joe he'd been before Krakatoa and meeting Mac McCaleb— would have done just that, acting out his rage without a thought to the consequences, angry at himself and at the world and at Lady Luck, who'd again dealt him a bum hand from the bottom of life's deck. But this time, something held him back; the long-buried remnants of his deeper, finer instincts refused to allow him to unleash his self-control, though he came dangerously close to the edge. That something was the memory of Ned, poor Ned Sullivan, dead back in Sydney—albeit unintentionally—as a result of his uncontrolled rage and jealousy, and the recollection was like a dash of icy water in his face. It served to curb the rage so that instead of brawling or picking a fight as he would have done in the past, he turned the anger inward, on himself. He'd come a long way since Sydney, in more than just miles.

No sooner had they reached the ranch house than he had unlocked the Casa Campanas' portal and curtly bade his subdued pair of companions unload the provisions and find themselves a place to sleep, too lost in his own emotions to truly give a damn what they did or to say anything in answer to the unspoken questions in their eyes. He had helped himself to the bottle of whiskey he'd brought with him, found himself a comfortable spot in one of the musty, dusty old rooms, and proceeded to get good and drunk.

In that, he succeeded very well, waking in the morning over twenty-four hours later and cussing the glaring sunlight that pierced through the grilled windows to blind him and increase the pounding in his skull, cussing Sera, women, and the world in general. Bad tempered, head aching, guts and bladder screaming, jaws thick with a heavy stubble of blond beard, he staggered from the room and wove his way unsteadily along the *corredor,* bellowing for Ming to find him another bottle of whiskey as he went. No one answered his summons, and he was left to go from room to room looking for the boy, growing angrier by the minute.

But instead of coming across Ming, he found Peggy Kelly in what were the kitchens of Las Campanas, and his anger faded and was replaced by shame. The large *cocina* bore little resemblance to the cobwebbed, grimy room he'd first seen in the gloom of early evening with Seraphina. The floor, of large, whitish flagstones for coolness, had been swept clean and, he decided, squinting at it through bloodshot eyes, briskly scrubbed. The cobwebs had been banished, the walls washed. There was a fire of fragrant *piñon* logs

237

crackling in the wide stone fireplace. A coffeepot bubbled over the glowing logs, giving off a mouth-watering, spicy aroma. In the center of the room stood a crude trestle table with the woodsy, resin smell of fresh pine still about it. It had been scrubbed clean and spread with a checkered blue and white cloth. On top of it was set a tin mug, stuffed with a huge bunch of silken, gold poppies, wilting a little now with the heat given off by the fire, and a tin platter of corn bread. Another plate held bacon, and a third crock, golden-fried hashed potatoes.

As he stood there, holding onto the doorjamb for support, drinking in the coziness of the little scene before him, he heard footfalls at his back and turned to see Ming, a load of firewood in his arms, come to an abrupt halt behind him. The lad said nothing. He simply stared at Joe as if he'd never seen him before, a wounded expression in his eyes. It was an expression that Joe had not once seen Ming adopt before, the furtive, wary, disillusioned look of a hound dog who had been whipped by a master he had been devoted to. The look was one that only added to his burgeoning guilt.

Discomfited, Joe looked back at Peggy and saw now that she was staring at him in the same disquieting way. With a sobering rush, it suddenly came to him just how badly he had behaved, leaving the two of them—neither one of whom knew much about roughing it out in the bush, he was certain—to fend for themselves, after they'd loyally agreed without question to come here with him. *You bloody, selfish bastard,* he upbraided himself, and though the effort pained him, he forced a sheepishly crooked grin.

"Well. Seems I'm back in the land of the living, you two!" he began, the shame building inside him. "I've acted like a son of a gun, and I'm sorry. No, don't eye me that way, I mean it! This thing with Sera, it got to me worse than I expected, I guess, but I'm okay now. It won't happen again, Peggy, Ming. My word on it."

It seemed his sincere apology and contrite tone galvanized the pair into action. They both let out collective sighs of relief and began moving again, Ming into the kitchen to stack the kindling alongside the wide hearth, Peggy to the coffeepot over the fire, which she brought to the table.

"You'll be hungry, no doubt, sir?" she said tentatively, and Joe realized she had accepted his apology in her own inimitable fashion. "An' coffee'll be just the thing for that ragin' headache you're after havin', I shouldn't wonder. Sit yerself down, me lad, and I'll fix ye a plate."

Joe sat, mellowing appreciably under her gruffly affectionate tone, noticing for the first time a rough-hewn bench on either side of the table. He took a swig of the scalding black coffee, feeling it burn its sweet, hot way down to his innards, and wolfed down a mouthful of golden, nutty corn bread dipped in hot bacon fat. As Peggy had promised, the food and coffee helped to settle his rebellious stomach. In minutes, he was almost his usual self. "Christ, this is fair dinkum tucker, Peg! And what you've done to this kitchen— why, it's bonzer! And clean as a whistle! There was no furniture here the first time I saw it, either. Where'd it come from?"

"You can thank Ming for the trestles," Peggy said with a disparaging little sniff, yet the smile tugging at the corners of her mouth belied her tone. "It would seem the lad's just a wee bit more useful than I gave him credit for. He rode up into the foothills and cut the timber himself, an' all. Worked on them all day yesterday."

"And did a fine job, too." He patted the sturdy bench

239

upon which he sat. "Solid as a rock. They're just the ticket, Ming."

Ming beamed from ear to ear, his dark, almond-shaped eyes almost disappearing in his pride. "It was nothing, Joe," he disclaimed modestly, yet he was puffed up like a barnyard rooster. "I'm working on a bed for Missie Kelly now. I'll show you, if you like," he offered eagerly.

"Soon as I'm through eating, I'll be right out to see it, that's a promise," Joe said, and meant it.

The next few days were filled with hard work, getting the place in shape for them to live in. Joe welcomed the hard work, for only by exhausting himself during the day could he sleep nights and blot out memories of Sera. He felt the same as a man who had lost a limb. While the limb remained, it hurt like blazes. Yet even after it had been amputated, it still itched, still aggravated. This was exactly the way he felt about the little gold digger. She was gone, but damned if she was forgotten!

Ming and Peggy had gotten off to a good start without him, ridding the *casa* of dust and grit and grime, but much of the work was simply too hard for an aging woman and a seventeen-year-old boy and needed a man's strong back and powerful arms. He had both, and he fell to the work with a will that bordered on compulsion.

He made no attempt for the time being to fix up the entire ranch house, but just enough of the seventeen rooms so that they'd all have a clean and comfortable place to sleep. Peggy said she would see to cleaning the rest in good time, which suited Joe just fine. He found some unused and no doubt forgotten red tiles in a storeroom and fixed the roof just in case it rained. He

240

mixed the whitewash he had brought from Los Angeles, and together he and Ming painted over those staring, accusing eyes drawn by Indian converts decades ago in the hallway under the *campanario,* the ones that had so bothered Sera when he had brought her there that first evening. He helped Ming to finish Peggy's bed, and told him how they could make it more comfortable later by stretching a rawhide across the frame and nailing it in place, instead of using the customary rigid wooden slats. Together they rode up into the foothills and felled timber and hewed posts and built a sturdy, whitewashed corral beyond the *casa* to fence in the mules and horses, and a chicken coop for Peggy's laying hens, and repaired the sagging shed. The immediate cleaning completed, Peg cleared and tilled a small patch of ground beyond the *casa*'s wide rear gateway and sowed seeds for vegetables, which she watered religiously each morning and night until the first tender shoots appeared above the ground.

It was beginning to look more like a home every day, Joe thought, sitting on the corral fence one evening as the sun went down and drawing the makings for a smoke from his pocket. He ignored the nagging little voice in his head that insisted it wouldn't be a home until he had a woman of his own beside him and turned his thoughts to the day's events instead.

He'd spent the morning and most of the afternoon honing Ming's newly acquired skills with the rifle, aiming at bottles set in the ground, or tree branches, for targets, until he was satisfied with the boy's progress for the time being. All in all, they had put in a good three weeks' work, and if Sera had been here to share it all with him, he'd have been a contented man. *If.* Strewth! That was the saddest bloody word in the English language ! No matter how he tried to forget her, he couldn't. With all her many faults, she wasn't the sort of woman a man found it easy to forget, blast her. More times than he cared to count, he'd awakened in the wee hours of the morning and reached out in the darkness to draw her warm, pliant body closer, filled with a compelling hunger to taste her moist lips and inhale the lily of the valley scent of her smooth, silken skin; he ached for the feel of her vibrant loveliness beneath his fingertips and, most of all, for the indefinable yearning he had for her mere presence in his life. It was a hunger that no other woman could come close to satisfying, he admitted to himself for the first time. He craved her as other men craved liquor or gambling or gold, despite his stubborn pride, despite being acutely aware that not only was she not worth the pain and sense of loss he felt for her, but she didn't give a damn for him. "Black-haired witch!" he muttered under his breath. "Get out of my mind, damn you, woman!"

"What did you say, Joe?"

"Aw, nothing, cobber. Just thinking out loud. We've done enough around here for now, I'd say," he told Ming, nodding at the new corral and the ranch house, which now had a decidedly more cared-for appearance. "I think Peggy will be comfortable here for a while, until I can take her into town for the things she's still needing."

"She has a very long list," Ming divulged, grinning. "At the top of it is a milk cow—a newly freshened one. That is what she wants the most. She says she misses fresh-churned butter and milk 'powerful bad'!"

Joe grinned at Ming's not-too-successful imitation of Peggy's lilting brogue, and he tousled the boy's straight black hair. "Does she now? Well, that'll be the first item on my list!" The smile faded. "But meanwhile, I want you to do something for me, if you think you can handle it."

242

"I will try. What is it?"

"I have to leave the ranch house for a while tomorrow, Ming. I didn't want to leave you and Peggy alone just yet, but I have no choice. Remember the shepherds that we met that first day, Esteban Rodriguez, Raoul Garnier, and the rest?"

"Sure I do."

Joe smiled. Ming, like himself, was sounding more western every day. "Well," he continued, "I have a plan to put Las Campanas back on her feet, but to make it work I have to talk it over with them and get their help. If you think you can handle things alone here for a few hours, I thought I'd ride out early tomorrow morning. You'd be in charge of the place and I'd leave you my new rifle, just in case there's any trouble."

"What is this trouble you expect? Trouble with the man they call Harper Monroe?" Ming asked shrewdly.

"Aye, that's it. We haven't seen him yet, I know, but I've a hunch he knows we're here, all right, and has been biding his time. If they run true to form, sooner or later he and his boys'll pay us a visit. If he does come while I'm away, don't take any chances, you hear me? I don't want you or Peggy getting hurt. You don't have to do anything—leastways, I hope not. Just hear him out, and tell him you'll let me know what he says."

Ming wet his lips. "You sound as if you're pretty sure he'll come while you're gone, Joe."

"Nothing's a hundred percent, lad. But I've heard about the way Monroe operates, and I've seen his dirty kind a hundred times. They're cowards at heart—aye, little men who need a bunch of others around them to feel like big men. He looks to make his move on folks when only the women and children are home and can do damn little to defend themselves against him. If he's having us watched—and I'm pretty certain he knows everything that goes on hereabouts—he'll know I've ridden out and that the two of you are alone, and there's a good chance he'll choose that time to make his move. Like I said, be careful."

"I will," Ming agreed solemnly. "Perhaps if he comes, it will be for the best, yes? Bring him out into the open, where we can see what he's up to. A snake is only dangerous when it is hidden and you cannot tell where it may strike, yes?"

"My thoughts exactly, cobber," Joe agreed softly.

"But . . . the shepherds? How will they help with this confrontation?"

"They have nothing to do with that. No, I mean to make them a proposal tomorrow, Ming, one that could make all of us wealthy men and set Las Campanas back on her feet." He grinned, his turquoise eyes devilish in the fiery rays of the dying sun. "Aye, it'll do that, and then some! It'll rock this Monroe back on his bullying heels if he's the sort I think he is. You see, cobber, it has to do with sheep."

Ming frowned. "Sheep?"

"That's what I said. There's only one thing that these cattle barons hate more than squatters, according to what I've heard, and that's sheep ranchers. It's a real pity that sheep are all I know, isn't it, mate? It's liable to make *Señor* Harper pretty riled up, seeing Las Campanas' sheep grazing from wall to wall across what he planned to make his valley!" He threw back his shaggy blond head and laughed deeply, turquoise eyes alive and dancing with wicked anticipation for the first time in many weeks. "Aye, Ming, I plan to sheep ranch. The way I hear it, there's damned good money to be made in wool and mutton for those that aren't scared by the Harper Monroes of this world."

Ming gasped. "You are in truth a devil, *fon kwei!*" he breathed, yet there was, nonetheless, frank admiration in his tone for Joe's daring plan.

244

"So I've been told, many times. In fact, too bloody many!" Joe agreed wryly. "We'll just sit back and see if Monroe finds me as easy to run off as he did those other ranchers and squatters . . ."

From the steely glint in his turquoise eyes, the iron set of his jaw, the determination in his voice, Ming didn't think Monroe would find Joe easy. No, not easy at all!

Chapter Fifteen

If the Church of San Gabriel was the heartbeat of the *pueblo* of Los Angeles, the marketplace in the central *plaza* was its ears, its eyes, and its tongue. But it was not for the sake of listening to or sharing idle gossip that Seraphina went to the market with only an hour to spare before the departure of the stage that would carry her southeast, but to search for a new fan. Her old painted silk one had torn, several of the lacquered wooden ribs had cracked, and the long stage journey south to New Mexico and thence Santa Fe promised to be a hot, uncomfortable one without it. For several days now the weather had been very sultry and what little wind there was brought no relief, for it came up from the arid deserts. Accompanied by Señora Catalina from the inn, who had insisted upon acting as her chaperone on this last-minute shopping jaunt, she made her way through the narrow streets that, even at this early hour, were made hazy with dust thrown up by horses, donkeys, wagon wheels and pedestrians alike.

"I shall miss you so, little one," Catalina declared, her round face solemn as she slipped her arm through Seraphina's and fondly squeezed the girl's slim hand. "Never before did I have the pleasure of knowing an

Anglo with such a rare knowledge and understanding of both my language and my people! If only I could persuade you to stay here in Los Angeles for just a little longer, Serafina, *mi amiga?*" she cajoled, her expression wistful.

"Nothing would please me more, *señora,* if it were but possible," Seraphina replied. "But I regret it is not."

"Ah, *sí.* Your family, it must come first, yes? Well, then so be it! It is the same with my people. When your grandmother is again well, you will return to Las Campanas, and we shall take up our friendship again, *sí?*"

Seraphina nodded, her expression a little guilty. The story of her ailing grandmother had been a barefaced lie, but how else was she to explain her sudden departure to kindly Catalina? She believed in the old ways, very religious, very moral, very Spanish. She would be horrified were she to learn that her beloved Seraphina and her Don José were parting ways.

Catalina rattled on, ". . . but even with the best of good fortune, and constant prayers to the saints and the Blessed Virgin Herself for your dear grandmother's swift recovery, there is no possibility whatsoever that you would be able to return soon, what with the traveling and so on." She sighed heavily. "Alas, you will not be back here until long after the big *fandango* to be held at the *rancho* of Don Harper next month. What a pity, for I did so want you to see it. In truth, Rancho Fuerte is a sight to see—aiee, *díos, qué magnífico!*" In a lower voice she added, "It is said, Serafina *mía,* that everyone from the surrounding *ranchos* will attend the *fiesta* for fear of drawing *el señor's* displeasure by their absence. And, although I am but an impoverished relation, I suppose I shall have to go too, since Doña Anita is my dear cousin and the *pobrecita* is so very unhappy, you understand."

"Relation?"

"Why, yes! Did I not mention before that Harper Monroe is married to my cousin? Her papa was my mother's brother, you see, and my own dear uncle Roberto. Oh, do not look so surprised, *amiga,* for it was certainly no marriage of love! The Anglo *señor* married Anita to obtain my *tío* Roberto's land, nothing more. Señor Monroe was already a widower with four grown sons when he came to the valley, you see, at which time my tío Roberto was having great financial difficulties after several years of drought had laid waste to his fields and vineyards and killed many of his cattle. It was not long after the *señor's* arrival that my cousin Anita's brother, poor Antonio, suffered a tragic accident and was killed. His death destroyed my uncle! Afterward, Tío Roberto was a broken man, for Antonio had been his beloved firstborn and only son. He had hoped that one day Antonio would bring Rancho Fuerte back to its former flourishing state. All his dreams died the day Antonio's horse fell in Canyon Aguila and Antonio was thrown from its back and his neck broken. So, when Harper Monroe requested my uncle's permission to pay court to Anita, he agreed. A year later, he gave her to the Anglo in marriage, and soon after died. Oh, the doctors, they said he died of a stroke to the brain, but we who knew and loved him know better. He died of a broken heart! Now the great Valdez lands—lands that had once belonged to the missions and were also part of the same enormous land grant as your Las Campanas—passed into the hands of Don Harper, where they have remained. And, no doubt, will remain until his death places them in the hands of one of his hateful sons."

"I see. I gather from your tone that you have little liking for your cousin's husband or his children?"

"Liking? Pah! Does the lamb love the buzzard that

248

tears and devours it, *amiga?* No, I do not like him. Rather, I loathe that . . . that *gringo!* Nor does Don Harper have any liking for any of my people, let alone his own poor, innocent wife, Anita, to whom he has ever been cruel and unjust. No, he despises us all! She was simply a means to an end. It was the land he wanted and will always want, as much of it as he can get; the accursed land that has already been watered by the lifeblood of too many over the ages!"

Was Joel McCaleb a Harper Monroe in the making, Seraphina wondered fleetingly, recalling the expression on Joe's face when he had spoken of the Las Campanas ranch as his own? She shuddered at the unbidden thought, though the sunlit square was hot and the sun beat down upon the flagstones. In subdued silence now, both momentarily lost in the uneasy trains of thought their conversation had set in motion, they continued on, lingering at each stall that might offer for sale a fan such as Seraphina needed.

The *plaza* was thronged with marketgoers and little stalls under awnings of woven tule reeds. Peasant women were everywhere, laughing, gossiping, haggling. The young ones were like exotic, brightly feathered, chattering birds in their scarlet *rebozos* and *camisas* and swirling embroidered skirts, golden hoops dangling from their earlobes; the old ones all dressed in the same rusty black, dowdily feathered crows made all the duller, more wrinkled looking in vivid contrast to the young and beautiful maidens of the *pueblo.* Amidst the crowds, a few women stood out for their aristocratic bearing, their fine silken gowns, and the quality of the delicate lace *mantillas* draped over tall combs arranged amongst their glossy blue-black hair. They were descendants of the *hidalgos,* those blue bloods who had first come here from Old Spain to rule the new colony; ladies of birth and breeding married to

249

the wealthy *hacendados* of the surrounding country-side whose lands and holdings had somehow survived drought and war and other adversity. These women moved gracefully from stall to stall, perhaps languishing on the arm of an indulgent papa or escorted by a stern husband, or alone save for their ever-vigilant *duenna* and a young Indian serving maid in tow bearing a basket in which to carry her mistress's purchases.

The sultry air was filled with sunshine and the scent of flowers and fruits heaped in panniers of local tule reeds, roses and jasmine, vivid red and pink geraniums and oleander, fuzzy ripe peaches, sweet grapes just off the vine, and the newest crop, tangy oranges. The merchandise was varied, everything from egg-yolk yellow canaries and linnets in little reed cages to fringed shawls, table coverings, or altar cloths of fine Mexican drawnwork. The lace-makers' fingers were busy even now at some snowy piece of intricate work or other as they waited for their next sale. There were braided lariats and goatskin chaps fine enough to tempt any *vaquero* to empty his pockets, tall red earthenware water jars, basketware and pottery made by the mission Indians for even the most discerning house-wife's purse, and foods such as savory soup thick with meatballs and red peppers, or *frijoles*, or boiled rice, fresh tomatoes and onions, to make the mouth of a plaster saint water in sheer and undisguised delight.

Garrulous Señora Catalina spied an old friend amongst the throng and eagerly dragged Seraphina along by the elbow to be introduced to her. The woman seemed happy to see her old friend and anxious to talk with her at greater length. Accordingly, making her excuses and promising to return to Catalina's side very soon, Seraphina continued on alone, weaving her way between the marketgoers.

Vaqueros, colorful Mexican cowboys, were everywhere, and the sight of them in their goatskin chaps, their white cotton shirts, and braid-decked *sombreros* was such a familiar one that a little of her heartache over Joe melted away and she gazed at them with undisguised pleasure as they flirted and uttered lavish *piropos,* compliments, and made snapping dark eyes at the blushing *señoritas.* They—as proper young ladies must, according to Spanish custom—pretended great indignation at such boldness and haughtily turned their heads, only to glance coquettishly over their shoulders at the *vaqueros* seconds later and coyly flutter their dark lashes. It was an enchanting scene, the likes of which Seraphina had seen many, many times in the *plaza central* of Santa Fe. On Sunday mornings after church or on certain fine evenings, the young maidens of the *pueblo,* following the age-old, elaborate rituals of the courtship *paseo,* had circled the *plaza* in small groups under the watchful eyes of their *mamacitas* or other suitable *duennas,* their eyes modestly downcast and seemingly oblivious to the correct and nervous groups of young men moving in the opposite direction, whose hearts were in their mouths in terror of not being favored by some word of greeting, however small, from the *señoritas* who had captivated their hearts!

Soon, she thought, *soon!* It's just a matter of days now, and I'll be home at the Shadow *S,* with Tom and Courtney and Mama and Papa and Tío Joaquín and all the rest, and Joe and this whole, painful charade will be just a memory! It had been over a year since she had seen them all, and homesickness washed over her, filling her with a sudden eagerness to be gone, back to the beautiful Sangre de Cristo mountains that she loved, and to the Casa del Ombras where she had grown up. There the geraniums planted by Margita,

251

Papa's first housekeeper who was now long dead, still made brilliant scarlet masses against the mellow adobe walls, and the cypresses embraced the *hacienda* in the little valley like loving, cool green arms. There everything was safe in its familiarity . . . as she would be safe.

"Seraphina!"

The sound of her name being called in a loud voice dragged her back from her reverie. She spun about to see plump Señora Catalina beckoning madly to her from across the *plaza*.

"What is it?" she cried, picking up her skirts and hurrying toward her, for Catalina was of an indolent nature and rarely moved to agitation.

"Seraphina *mía,* I have something I must tell you!" Puffing and panting, Catalina bustled to meet her, her brown eyes snapping and bright.

Ah, more gossip, Seraphina decided, her alarm dwindling. "Very well, but please hurry now, Catalina, or I won't be able to find a new fan before the stage lea—"

"Perhaps you will forget all about that new fan once you hear what I have learned, *niña!*" Catalina cried. "Come out of the crush, do, and let me tell you!" Catalina drew her aside, to the walkway shaded by lacy pepper trees that lined the *plaza.* "Listen, *niña,* and listen well, for it is my thought that time is everything in this matter! My good friend, Señora Martinez, whom you just a moment ago met, is always the first in the valley to know everything that goes on at Rancho Fuerto—Señor Monroe's ranch. Her daughter, Ramona, is a serving girl there, you see, and somewhat of a gossip, alas, as is her dear mama. I have it from Señora Martinez—who heard it from Ramona—that Señor Monroe has learned of your husband's intent to make Las Campanas a working ranch once again, and that the news filled him with a terrible anger! He swore that the newcomers would not remain in the valley for so much as a single month if he had his way! Then he summoned his sons and bade them make ready their horses early the next morning. He planned to ride to . . . to Las Campanas, *niña!*"

"When was this?" Seraphina fired the words at the woman, grasping her so fiercely by her plump upper arms and shaking her so violently that the *señora* winced, though Seraphina was too alarmed by her news to notice.

"She said . . . she said this morning!" Catalina gasped, half shaken speechless by Seraphina's expression and her forceful grip.

"Damn!" Seraphina cursed, quite forgetting her sweet, retiring role for an instant in her alarm. She was only dimly aware of a shocked Catalina crossing herself with an incredulous expression as a result of her explosive curse as she asked, "Please, dear Catalina, have someone get my bags from the stage depot, would you? Take them and keep them at the inn for me until I return."

"Of course, *niña*. But . . . return? Where are you going?"

"To warn Joe—if I'm not too late! Oh, Lord, I can't be too late!" she added in a muttered breath as she hiked up her skirts and sped across the *plaza*, bobbing and weaving her way between the marketgoers and then racing on like a wild thing down the narrow streets, past the pungent cattle markets, to Reid's livery stables.

The sky was a perfect cup of vivid blue over the little San Juliano Valley that morning, the clouds that had massed upon the sawtooth ridges of the Sierras fluffy and white as newly shorn sheep. Way above the cloud masses, the sun shone, a winking golden *concha* that slowly spun and imbued everything with light as it revolved, a liquid, crystal-topaz light whose brilliance seemed absorbed by and reflected back from the glorious Sierras themselves in some magical fashion, so that rock formations and pines seemed to blaze with an inner green or golden fire.

Beyond the forested foothills, heat waves shimmered over the rolling land and an eagle wheeled far overhead in the cooler, higher currents, its massive golden wingspan spread, its bright, beady eyes scanning the dun-colored, undulating land and thorny chaparral far below for prey as it left the small canyon that was its home and where its aerie of ravenous young awaited its return.

All at once, the eagle spied a small creature far, far below, a plump young jackrabbit, alone and unprotected. With the wind rushing upward to meet it, it began the long, downward swoop to snatch up the rabbit in its massive talons. But while yet in mid-flight, the eagle became aware of Man's unwelcome intrusion into the valley yet again as five horses and their riders came over the curve of a rise, dust rising under their hooves. They were close to her prey—perilously close for the comfort of the ever-wary eagle, who could see the glint of the sun upon the shooting sticks they carried and which, to her, reeked of death. With an angry scream, she beat her wings furiously to regain height, caught an upward current of air, and soared away into the vast blue heavens.

"God Almighty, Pa, jest look at that eagle! Big 'un, ain't she, Pa?"

"Ain't no time for bird-watching this mornin', Stevie. We got pressin' business to tend to, boy," his father replied, shooting a sour look at his youngest and most exasperating son. "Yessiree, we got things to do, all right!"

"You aimin' to run 'em off like them Mex squatters, Pa, or get rid of 'em permanent?"

"Run 'em off this first time, I reckon." His father spat in the dust and shifted the quid of chewing tobacco to his other inner cheek. He grinned, but it was no more than a tigerlike baring of small, uneven teeth amidst florid jowls and never reached the pale blue eyes set deep beneath the heavy forehead and the welter of flesh below. He might have been a fine enough looking man at one time, but all claim to good looks had been lost long since over years of self-indulgence and mean thinking. "That is, 'less they ain't the real clever folks I reckon 'em to be, in which case things jest might get out of hand, if you catch my meanin'" He tapped his stubby finger alongside his nose.

Stevie grinned. "I catch it real well, Pa!"

His father shifted uncomfortably in the saddle atop the massive chestnut horse, rubbing his fleshy thigh. The musles were as slack as his suspenders after Sunday supper, he noted with disgust. "Roy, you and Jack go on ahead with Val. Stevie, you stay here with yer pa for a spell."

"Aw, but Pa—"

"Shut up, Stevie, and do as you're damn well told! You ain't gonna miss nothin'," his father snapped, a muscle working violently in his jaw as always when he was irritated—which was often. Ever since he had injured his leg years ago in an explosion, working a claim on the Comstock, he had had little patience and was quick to anger, quick to lash out. Not without cause, he reckoned. The pain had never left him, not from that day on, and every night since he had cursed the miner who had overloaded the charges that day, which had caused the cave-in and his injury. Not once in all those years had he stopped to consider that it had been his own fault, seeing as how the claim had been the other man's and technically he had been trying to steal from the new vein of gold the man had discovered days before . . .

"Leg botherin' you some, Pa?" his eldest son, Val, asked.

"A mite. Don't let it bother you none, boy. I reckon I'm used to it by now," he sneered. "You and your brothers ride on ahead and wait fer us by the bird rock. I'll rest up a while, and we'll meet you there."

"Right, Pa. Yaah!" Val spurred his horse down the rise, his brothers' horses following and kicking up red dust as they went.

"Ain't you worried that McCaleb fellow might be back 'fore we gets there, Pa?" Stevie asked, his ferretlike features anxious.

"Hell, no!" his father denied, clambering down from his horse with obvious difficulty. "Ain't no horse can git to the *pueblo* and back 'fore we get to Las Campanas. Quit your fussin', Stevie, and hand me that canteen."

"But what if he ain't gone to town, Pa?"

Harper Monroe drank greedily, wiped his lips on the back of his fist, and gave his youngest a withering look. "Now, where else in the name of God Almighty would he have gone, you pea-brained fool? He ain't got no stock to ride herd on or nothin', has he, now? Nor will he ever have, things go my way!"

Stevie shrugged. If his father said something was so, he wasn't dumb enough to question him about it a second time. That could prove mighty painful, he'd learned in the past.

Ming, despite the reassurances he had given Joe, was

nonetheless somewhat uneasy that morning. Much of the pride that had filled him when he learned Joe intended to entrust to him the safety of Peggy Kelly and the ranch house had dwindled when Joe had ridden out shortly after the golden dawn had broken, and he had realized how alone they both were out there, and how defenseless.

Before Joe left, he had repeated his urging that Ming be careful and keep an eye out for Monroe and his sons. Accordingly, the rifle was propped not two feet away from where Ming worked, within easy reach should the need arise. Joe had taught him how to load and fire it, and they had practiced his aim time and time again until Joe had been satisfied with both his accuracy and his handling of the rifle; yet he still did not feel completely comfortable with the weapon. Schooled in the Oriental martial arts from an early age—arts that Joe had observed with open-mouthed admiration in San Francisco—he had been taught that his body was a formidable weapon in itself; he had learned to summon all the inner, spiritual forces he possessed and to concentrate them into energy and strength, but more as a means of self-defense than attack. Of what use would his humble skills prove if there were gunplay? Fists and feet could work wonders close up, but they could do little against hot bullets spewed from a Springfield!

Ill at ease, stopping from time to time to gaze beyond the corral to the rolling, tawny land in the distance, he worked slowly at first, planing the wood before him carefully, running his palm with pride and pleasure over the smooth surface and eyeing with satisfaction the white curls of planed timber that had fallen like a lamb's creamy fleece about his feet. Since his first attempt at woodworking and the crude trestle table that had been the result—of which he was now heartily ashamed—he had learned a great deal. His current project was a secret labor of love, for it was to be a chair for Joe, a grand chair worthy of his beloved friend; a chair where Joe, after a hard day's riding, could find ease and comfort in the evening when he returned to Casa Campanas. As he worked carefully, steadily upon it, his uneasy thoughts were dispelled somewhat and he became lost in concentration on the work at hand.

So intent was he that he did not hear Peggy when she came up behind him bearing a mug of coffee and a kerchief-covered platter piled with warm, buttered biscuits for his mid-morning break.

"Here ye are!" she said gruffly. "This'll put some meat on yer scraggy bones, though I don't know, to be sure, why the divil it is I bother t'see ye fed, ye spalpeen!"

Her explosive words, rupturing as they did both the silence and Ming's intense concentration, had an effect she would not have anticipated in a million years. He flung about, and in the same lithe move he had leapt and twisted in midair and jackknifed his powerful heel against the platter in her hand. Platter and buttery biscuits all went flying. In shock, Peggy screamed and reflexively flung the tin coffee mug high in the air, splattering scalding coffee everywhere. She tottered and spun about, her apron clutched over her face, calling upon all the saints in heaven to deliver her from the hands of the heathen madman as she fled back toward the kitchens as if the hounds of hell snapped at her heels.

Too late, Ming realized he had erred—and gravely. He raced after her, youth on his side, and succeeded in overtaking her scant feet from the kitchen portal.

"Forgive me, Missie Peggy!" he cried, his arms outstretched in supplication, his dark, almond-slanted eyes filled with shame and remorse, for her face was as

258

white as a rice cake in the season of the Moon Festival. "You came upon me so silently that I thought . . . I thought . . ."

Peggy quivered, scowled, rumbled, and finally erupted like a small volcano. "Ha! Thought, did ye now? And what was it ye were after *thinkin'*, eh, you young . . . heathen, you! Leapin' at a poor body that way—scarin' her half t'death, why, 'tis lucky I am indeed t'have a stout Irish heart, else I'd be lyin' stone dead out there in that corral, an' only after needin' a foine wake to see me on me way t'blessed St. Peter's heavenly gate!" She snatched up the broom and brandished it at him. "Come on, then, young fellow-me-lad, if it's a tussle ye're after, I'm the woman for it! See if ye can take on a fightin' Kelly now I have me wits about me and me dander up!"

Mortified, Ming shook his head. "Please, Missie Peggy, no! I humbly beg your forgiveness! I would never have . . . I did not mean to . . ."

"I'm waitin'—and 'tis the cloth o'yer britches will soon be tastin' me trusty broom, I'm after thinkin'!" she taunted.

She advanced several steps, the broom held threateningly before her. Ming backed away, protesting and spluttering apologies as he went, so intent on holding her at bay he failed to see the pail of water at his back. He stumbled. His foot tangled in the handle, and he went down amidst peals of merry laughter from Peggy, flat upon his back in the dirty dish suds.

"Aha! I have ye on yer back, have I now. Well, I'd say this round goes fair and square t'the Irish, wouldn't you, me lad?" Peggy demanded, her blue eyes sparkling as, fists on hips, trusty broom now discarded, she beamed down at him.

He scrambled to his feet, his glossy black head cocked intently to one side.

Peggy, aglow with triumph, repeated, "Did ye not hear me, then? Or is it ye're too mortified t'admit I've won? I said as how I—"

"Yes, yes, Missie, I heard you," Ming agreed softly. "But never mind that for now. Listen! Someone comes! I can hear horses, can't you?"

Peggy could.

Chapter Sixteen

"Mornin', ma'am," Val Monroe said, leaning over his saddle horn and insolently tipping his hat to Peggy Kelly. "We're here to talk business with your husband, if you'd tell him we're here."

Eyes narrowed, Peggy stepped away from the kitchen and walked toward the five riders, ignoring Ming's anguished mutters for her to stay put. She was not deceived by Val Monroe's polite greeting. Friendly neighbors didn't make harmless visits armed to the teeth as was this litter of wolves, or she hadn't been born a Kelly!

"Mornin' to you, too, stranger," Peggy said in an equally civil, mild fashion. "But I'm not Mrs. McCaleb. I'm Peggy Kelly, her housekeeper. The McCalebs will be back any time now, if ye'd care to wait. Sure an' there's fresh coffee brewin', and biscuits just this minute brought hot from the stove, if ye'd like t'come inside."

Stevie Monroe brightened at the mention of biscuits and wet his lips eagerly as he glanced across at his father. "Can we, Pa, can we? I could surely go for a biscuit or two, my belly's grumblin' that loud!"

"Shut up, Stevie," his father growled. "We ain't here

261

fer neighborly visitin'!"

"Just what the divil are ye here for then, *Mister* Monroe?" Peggy demanded, fists planted on her hips.

Monroe looked down at Peggy, a malicious grin splitting his fleshy lips. "We-ell, ma'am, I came to deliver a message to McCaleb, but seein' he ain't home, I guess you'll jest have to pass on the message for us, won't ye? Val!"

He nodded to his eldest son, who trotted his horse away from the house toward the corral. Before Peggy realized his intentions, he had unlooped the lariat from his saddle horn. There was a whirring sound, and then the lariat snaked out, its noose dropping to hitch about a fence post. Val Monroe urged his horse backward to take up the slack, and in short order the new corral post that Joe and Ming had erected so recently toppled, the horses within it—including Seraphina's white gelding, Muraco—set to fleeing by Val's whoops and yells and hat waving. They galloped away toward the hills in a cloud of red dust.

Peggy, stunned both by the speed with which it had all happened and by their audacity, bristled like a furious Irish wolfhound. She looked to Ming and then back to Harper Monroe, two angry crimson spots flaming in her cheeks, her blue eyes hot and crackling with anger.

"Why, you accursed bunch o'divils! You stop that boy o'yours, Monroe, 'else I'll see t'stoppin' him for ye! In Mary's blessed name, stop that hooliganizing this minute, ye hear me?" She snatched up the fallen broom and brandished it as she rushed toward the eldest Monroe boy's horse, enraged that now he had begun similar tactics on yet another fence post. She was caught up in mid-stride by his brother, Roy Monroe, who leaned low in his saddle and scooped her up into one powerful arm, dragging her—screaming and

262

flailing wildly—across it before him.

"Why, if you ain't the orneriest old stew hen I ever did see!" Roy declared, panting for breath as he fought to hold Peggy still, for she continued howling curses at the top of her lungs like a banshee and writhing like a cornered wildcat to escape his grasp. He grinned and looked across at his father and brothers. "I'll take care of this old broody hen, Pa. She's a tough old bird, but I reckon I can handle her! You and the others see the rest of it done."

"What about him?" asked Jack, nodding toward Ming, who, frozen in horror, simply stood there, gaping.

"Who?" The older man spat in the dust. "You mean that there yeller hound dog over there?" Harper Monroe jeered. "Hell, we don't need to do nothin' 'bout that yeller pup, 'less it shows its teeth. Don't reckon it will, though. Them Celestial dogs ain't got no goddamned backbones, no how. Ain't that so, yeller boy?"

A muscle worked in Ming's throat and seemed to knot around it, threatening to choke him. A nerve pulsed at his temple, and his knees felt peculiarly rubbery and ready to buckle. Accounts he had heard of his people being gunned down or strung up and hanged for little or no cause by men such as these filled his thoughts. In spite of Joe's warning, in spite of everything, he had let him down. And worse, far worse, he was afraid, a coward, just as the heavyset man had said! The Monroes were here, as Joe had anticipated, but the rifle he had taught him to use with just such a moment in mind lay clear across the corral, out of reach, useless. He could do nothing to prevent whatever it was Monroe intended to do, or even to help Missie Peggy, not one thin lad against five of the tallest, biggest, meanest white men he had ever seen.

Shame overwhelmed him as, laughing scornfully, Monroe's other two sons quirted their horses toward the house, directing their mounts to trample the tender green shoots of the little vegetable patch Peggy had planted so lovingly soon after their arrival, leaving Jack, Steve, and Harper Monroe looming in a circle about him on their towering horses. With enormous effort, Ming squashed the fear that rose up his throat and threatened to choke him. No, these evil men would not destroy everything he and Joe had worked so hard to build. They must not be allowed to—no, he would not let them! Small he might be, yes, but he, Chen Ming, was of a certainty no coward! They would learn that the Chinese had backbones after all. He drew himself up proudly and folded his arms across his chest.

"My people are taught from when they are very young to respect their elders, Mistah Monroe," he said quietly, "so I may not respond to your insults. However, if one of your sons would care to accept my challenge on your behalf, I would be honored to take him on." He made a half-bow, inclining his dark head.

"Well, la-di-da! Ain't you got yourself a fancy way o'talkin', yeller boy!" Monroe crowed, rocking with laughter. "Any of you boys care to accept the yeller boy's *challenge?*" he mocked.

The two younger Monroes grinned but said nothing.

"Well, I guess they reckon your challenge ain't worth a damn, boy," Harper said at length, looking down at Ming. "Throw a rope over him, Stevie! We'll tie up this young yeller hound dog before his fancy yappin' and whinin' starts to gratin' on my nerves some. The rest of you, get to work!"

Stevie urged his sorrel pony toward Ming, who stood his ground. Outwardly he appeared calm, collected, but inwardly he was waging a major battle,

264

NO POSTAGE
NECESSARY
IF MAILED
IN THE
UNITED STATES

BUSINESS REPLY MAIL
FIRST CLASS   PERMIT NO. 276   CLIFTON, NJ

POSTAGE WILL BE PAID BY ADDRESSEE

ZEBRA HOME SUBSCRIPTION SERVICE
P.O. Box 5214
120 Brighton Road
Clifton, New Jersey 07015

endeavoring to regain control of himself, to vanquish his fear through his breathing, for in control of one's body and concentration lay the key to speed, agility, and strength, and thus power. He made no move to run even as Stevie's lariat loop shimmied over his head and coiled loose in the dust about his feet, but as he saw the one called Stevie signal his cow pony to back up and thence tighten the noose, he suddenly bent and grabbed the braided rawhide loop, gave a loud whoop, and flipped backward, head over heels, still holding it fast. He gracefully landed back upright, poised on the balls of his feet, several lengths away.

So agile and unexpected were his actions and the resulting sudden jerk on the lariat, that Stevie, not the brightest of the Monroe clan to begin with, never knew what hit him until, with a yelp of rage and pain, he was yanked forcibly from his pony's back. He landed on his nose in the dust with a sickening crunch, propelled there by virtue of his own rope and Ming's incredible gymnastics. Blood coiling from his nostrils in scarlet ribbons, Stevie staggered to his feet and lumbered toward Ming, enraged by pain, swinging back his fist as he came for a wild, driving punch that would have been vicious, had it landed.

At once, Ming darted forward and chopped the Monroe youth with the side of his hand. The chop slammed clean and true across Stevie's Adam's apple. He gave a single, choked gasp, no more, before Ming followed it with another left-handed chop to the opposite side, spinning like a top as he did so. Up came his feet—yell, twist, slam—and a deadly heel took Stevie square in the gut. His eyes bulged, he tottered, then he went down as if he had been poleaxed.

Aglow with satisfaction in the face of this small triumph, Ming bowed to his fallen opponent, then stiffened and turned slowly about at the ominous, loud click of a gun behind him. He found himself looking down the single, empty black eye of a gun barrel.

"You yeller son of a bitch! Look what you did t'my boy there! It's time you learned your place once and fer all time, Chinee!" Harper Monroe snarled, angered to see his son groveling in the dirt at the Chinaman's feet. Hell, a Monroe didn't grovel at any man's feet, least of all a yeller boy's! "A bullet in your belly'll show you who's boss 'round these parts, I reckon."

Savoring the moment, Harper Monroe slowly released the safety and, with great relish and deliberation, sighted down the barrel, leveled at the spot directly between Ming's eyes.

Ming stood very, very still, watching Monroe's hand, seeing every detail of the man's stubby, hairy-knuckled fingers as if they were larger than life. Scarcely breathing, he waited, the loud thud of his racing heart thundering in his ears. Everything seemed still and slowed in that moment when death looked him in the eye, as if the entire world was holding its breath, waiting for the deafening report that would hurl Chen Ming of San Francisco to his heathen Paradise. *I have failed Joe,* he thought, and there was a terrible aching in his heart, for how could he ever hope to make it up to him, dead as he soon would be? Better, perhaps, that he should die dishonored, than live with the knowledge that he had failed the man he admired more than any other in the world . . .

"Adios, yeller boy!" Harper murmured, and his trigger finger tenderly curled around the little tongue of metal that would soon make his farewell final.

"Pull it, and you're a dead man, Monroe!" came a cool, controlled voice from behind him.

Harper spun about in the saddle as if he had been gut shot, to see Joel McCaleb sitting tall and loose in the saddle of a rawboned paint pony that had had some

266

miles put on it, judging by the dust and lather that coated it. He wore a black hat with a braided white buckskin band about the crown above his shaggy blond hair, and the eyes that glittered back at Monroe from the shadow beneath the brim were as turquoise and frigid as a mountain lake in mid-winter.

Harper's pale blue eyes took his measure at a glance. He was not deceived by the man's casual, even mild, tone, or by his nonchalant handling of the forty-five in his grip, or by the spare, rangy build of him. The eyes, cool, all-seeing, said it all. Monroe had met McCaleb's type once or twice before, and he knew that beneath the friendly, easygoing outward appearance could lodge a killer as ruthless and cold-blooded and as lightning fast with a gun as any gunslinger. Hell, men like him could afford to act casual; they didn't give a damn if they lived or died and, having no fear of death, they held every ace in the goddamned deck! He wet his lips nervously. He'd always enjoyed putting the fear of God into those dumb squatters, enjoyed running them off, destroying everything they'd scraped together, but he was no fool, for all that. He wanted to live, to be around long enough to see his grandsons born, and to gain the same control over them he exercised over his sons. It was one thing to rough folks up some with his strong sons behind him to back him up, but quite another to attempt the same trick with a man like this McCaleb, a man who was holding a gun on him and looked like he knew real well how to use it, too! The stakes were too damn high.

"Drop the gun, Monroe—and hurry it up, mate. I'm getting impatient," Joe drawled, gesturing his forty-five in Monroe's direction.

"Sure, friend," Monroe agreed, licking his dry lips once more. He held his hand out at arm's length and released the gun, letting it fall to the dust with a dull

267

thud. Surely his boys would be back any second. Hell, he was thinking like an old woman! He didn't have a thing to worry about, not really, not if he just played it cool and easy and bided his time. "We were just havin' a little neighborly fun with your China-boy here, McCaleb," he said, smiling faintly. "You know how it is. Weren't nothin' meant by it, nothin' at all."

"I'm real glad to hear it," Joe said softly, urging the paint closer to Monroe's chestnut. "See, there's a rumor about town that you don't take kindly to newcomers. Silly of me, I know, mate, but I had this wild notion you and your boys just might have ridden out here today with the idea of running me off my land. Any truth to that rumor, eh?" He allowed his glance to shift subtly from Monroe to the others, while he awaited the man's answer. One of them, a dark-haired Monroe, had been holding a struggling Peggy Kelly but had now released her and was watching his gun hand, awaiting his chance, Joe guessed. Peggy stood quietly off to one side, but even from this distance, he could see the tears welling in her eyes. She appeared thoroughly shaken. Another, younger, fair-haired Monroe lay in the dirt, holding his face and whimpering as the blood gushed between his fingers from a broken nose. Bob Reid over at the livery stables in town had mentioned that Monroe had four sons. Joe's gaze narrowed. One, two, three Monroes in all, counting their father. Where in the hell were the other two—

"Well, well! Glad you could make it back in time t'meet us, McCaleb!" came Val Monroe's triumphant voice from off to Joe's left.

Joe's spine tingled. There was a gun leveled at his back; he knew it sure as breathing, without needing to turn and look. This one must have heard the commotion and circled around to make his move at just the right moment.

"Me and Roy here bin lookin' forward to meetin' you for some time now. See, folks in town bin talkin' about you, McCaleb! They reckon you might be the man to stand up to Pa here!" He snickered. "I say you ain't! I say you're as yeller as your China-boy over there!"

Joe's jaw tightened, but he said nothing. He groaned inwardly. He'd planned to bide his time and take care of the other Monroe boys one by one first, before tackling their father, but it had been apparent to him that Ming would no longer be around if he hesitated even a moment. Christ! Now they were in a pretty fix! How was he to—

"Put up your guns—and do it *pronto!*" came a woman's voice, and to Joe's—and the Monroes'—utter and complete amazement, a barefoot young woman with loose, waist-length black hair, clad in Mexican peasant garb of baggy white *pantalónes* and a looser tunic of bleached cotton belted with rope at the waist, stepped from the kitchen portal of Casa Campanas carrying an old-fashioned pistol.

The Monroes' mouths dropped open in unison as she padded out gracefully into the blazing sunshine and stood there, eyeing them calculatingly and with no trace of fear whatsoever in her cool, gray-green eyes.

She continued, "Seems I missed the introductions, so I'll make amends right away. I'm Seraphina McCaleb. Me and my man, Joel, have been looking forward to meeting you, boys!" There was a loud explosion, and the ancient gun in her fist spewed fire. Val Monroe's hat spun off his head with the impact, flew through the air, and landed in the dirt of the corral several yards away. The bullet passed through it and whined into the dirt, raising a small red dust fountain as it did so. "Shame on you, neighbor! Don't you know

269

you're supposed to take your hat off when you're introduced to a lady?"

"I'd take a guess these blokes have had about all the lessons in manners they care for, for the time being, Sera," Joe said grimly. "In fact, I'd swear I heard 'em say they were leaving right away. Isn't that so, Monroe?"

Gritting his teeth, Harper Monroe nodded.

"That's real smart of them," Seraphina said calmly, " 'cause I'd hate to have to use this little old pistol here to teach 'em some more manners. See, it's so goldarned rusty and everything, it's liable to shoot wide at just about any minute. I'd surely hate to shoot someone in the head next time, 'stead of in their hat!" She smiled sweetly.

"Okay, boys! Let's head for home!" Monroe said shakily, eyeing the sharpshooting Seraphina as if she were *loco*.

"We're real sorry you couldn't stay longer," Joe rejoined dryly. "But just the same, don't get it into your heads to come back. You do, me and my woman here'll be ready for you! Las Campanas is ours. We aim to keep it that way."

"You haven't heard the last of this, McCaleb, nosiree!" Monroe threatened, gathering his reins into his fists. "You've come out on top this time, but sooner or later I'll have you run out of my valley with your tail tucked between your legs jest like all the rest—or you'll be wishin' to God Almighty you'd never bin born!"

"I won't hold my breath, Monroe."

Monroe grunted. "Stevie! Mount up! The rest of you, git!"

"Comin', Pa!" Stevie staggered past Ming toward his pony, still clutching a bloody bandanna to his nose. "I'll fix you yet, yeller boy!" he muttered under his breath as he passed, his expression murderous. "I'll fix you real good someday!"

Ming, wearing a peculiar expression, averted his eyes, hung his head, and said nothing in reply as the Monroes dug spurs into their horses' flanks and galloped away, heading west.

After the Monroes had gone, Seraphina tossed the rusty pistol to the dirt, threw back her glossy dark head, and let out a wild rebel yell of sheer glee. "Oh, Lord, Joe, did you see their faces when I stepped out with that pistol drawn on them? Did you? Their expressions were worth a million dollars!"

"So they were," Joe agreed, but unlike Peggy Kelly, he was not smiling. "Why'd you come back here, Sera?"

Her gleeful expression faded. She frowned. "Why? Well, because I heard in the *pueblo* that Monroe and his sons were planning on paying you a visit, that's why! I'd hoped to get here in time to warn you. As it was, I'd say my timing was just about perfect." Her defiant expression challenged him to deny it.

"You would, would you?" He scowled, fair brows lowering over narrowed turquoise eyes that held no hint of warmth or joy at seeing her. "Well, I'd have to disagree! You ran out on me back in Los Angeles, remember, Sera? You made your choice, so why don't you just keep on running until you meet up with whoever it is you have waiting for you. See, as far as I'm concerned, you're bad news, Sera, you and all your kind. You lead a man on, get him so he's all torn up inside and doesn't know which way is up, and then leave him flat. I don't like the little games you play, love, and what's more, I don't need or want you around here. Go on back to the *pueblo*. We've been doing just fine without you."

Heated color filled her cheeks, and her eyes glittered. "Oh? Is that so, Joe? Well, I wouldn't call what was happening when I arrived doing 'just fine,' not by a long way," she scoffed, furious at him and at his casual dismissal of her. Lord, how his words stung her pride! The ungrateful, callous brute! But he was no fool. He must have realized that without her timely arrival, the situation would have culminated in tragedy. He was just so darned proud he couldn't bring himself to say thanks, or to acknowledge that she'd made all the difference to the outcome.

"We'd have worked it out without your interference, one way or another," he denied coldly. "Point is, Sera, you made your choice to leave me. What goes on here at Las Campanas now is no longer your concern. You'll get your share of the money all in good time, don't fret. Meanwhile, I suggest you hightail it back to wherever you came from. I've got work to do." With that, he spun on his heel and strode away toward the barn, a building that suited the warm climate and was more like a pavilion than a true barn, with its flat roof and corner posts and no walls.

"Damn you! How dare you tell me to leave? After all, half of everything here is mine. Maybe I've decided to stay and protect my interests!" she yelled furiously after him.

He halted and looked back at her over his shoulder. "Half of *almost* everything. Don't count me among your holdings, woman, because I won't be owned by anyone—least of all you. Far as I'm concerned, the only thing we have in common now is a name." He paused, then added grudgingly, "I guess you do have the right to stay, if that's what you want," he allowed with palpable reluctance. "I won't stop you. But get in my way, try to meddle in anything I plan to do, and I'll see you hog-tied and loaded onto the first stage to anyplace, so long as it's distant. Understand?" She gave a curt nod, which he returned before he continued on to the barn.

Seething, fists balled on her hips, Seraphina watched him go, her gray eyes narrowed as his lean, wiry frame moved away. She tossed her silky black hair irritably, but it was several moments before she was able to drag her attention from him and back to the others. She went to Peggy first. "That . . . that man!" she muttered. "You hear how he talked to me? He's got gall, I'll give him that!"

"Well, mum, if ye don't mind me sayin' so, animals ain't the only ones among God's creatures t'lash out and hurt when they're hurtin'. I fancy Mister McCaleb is still smarting a mite from the way ye left him. He's a terrible proud man, and one that finds it hard to forgive those that do him wrong—even when he loves them."

Seraphina resolutely ignored the latter and said waspishly, "Don't take his part, Peggy. You make him sound like one of your saints! We made a deal. Remember, I told you all about it? He knew well and good what he was getting into, and if he's feeling sour grapes now because he expected more, then he'll just have to learn to live with his disappointment. Now, how about you? Did the Monroe boys hurt you?" she inquired, putting her arms about the older woman and searching her drawn face with anxious eyes. It was a sincere gesture of affection and concern on her part, but a crafty one nonetheless, for it also served to redirect the conversation into areas she felt safer, less vulnerable, about. In other words, away from the subject of Joel McCaleb! Her ruse succeeded.

Sidetracked, Peggy scowled fiercely and shook her head. "Thanks be they did not, though to be truthful I *was* a wee bit frightened by the godless spalpeens! Animals, they are! Nothin' but spiteful animals!"

"You poor dear! Some hot coffee will set you to rights—maybe with a little slug of something stronger in it, if we can find any liquor," Seraphina suggested, smiling coaxingly. Poor Peg, and poor Ming! They must still be dreadfully shaken, she mused silently. "Ming? How about you?" she asked, turning to the unusually silent boy.

He shook his head. "No, thank you, Missie Se'aphina. I must go now, to help Joe mend the fences and track down the missing stock. I have failed him once already today. I must not do so again."

Seraphina's eyes widened incredulously, both at his words and at the flat, empty tone of them. "Failed him? Is that what you think? Of course you didn't fail him, Ming! Don't be so darn foolish! I saw how you handled that young Monroe—and it was the cleverest thing I ever saw, the way you had him flat on his nose in the dust like that!" She snapped her fingers. "You couldn't help it if they had guns. Nobody—not even your wonderful Joe—could have done anything to stop them from doing what they were doing, not staring down a gun barrel!"

Stubbornly, Ming shook his head. "No, Missie, you are wrong. I *am* to blame. You see, Joe taught me to use his rifle. He trusted me to make good use of it to protect Missie Peggy and the ranch while he was gone. I forgot the rifle and my duty, and when the Monroes came, I was helpless to stop them. I am not worthy of the trust Joe placed in me, nor am I still worthy of his friendship."

Seraphina grimaced and shook her head. "You're talking *loco*, Ming. Why don't you let Joe decide whether you failed him or not, instead of taking it all on yourself? Things like this shake everyone up, make you doubt yourself. You'll feel better by supper time, you'll see. Now, Peggy, how about that coffee? That long ride out from the *pueblo* was hot and dusty as perdition, and my throat's dry as a desert. I'll go tend to my horse, and then let's go inside."

274

"You do mean t'stay then, mum, despite what Mister McCaleb said?" Peggy asked hesitantly as they walked toward the *casa*. It was plain she hoped Seraphina's answer would be in the affirmative.

"I do," Seraphina said firmly. "I gave it a lot of thought while I was riding out here from Los Angeles, and I decided that since it's gone this far and lasted this long, I might as well be hung for a sheep as a lamb, as the saying goes!" She smiled enigmatically, then grinned.

Peggy grinned. "That might be a more fittin' description than you ever intended, mum!"

"How so?"

"Why, because your Mister McCaleb intends to run sheep on Las Campanas' land. But, of course, you'd be after knowing that already, would ye not, mum?"

Seraphina stopped dead in her tracks and flung about to face Peggy. "Sheep? *Sheep!* Lord, no, I had no idea!" For the second time that day she forgot herself and muttered, "Damn! I'd say I came back in the nick of time—and for more reasons than one!"

Each wrapped in her own thoughts, neither woman noticed Ming as he angrily scrubbed tears from his eyes with grimy knuckles and trudged off resolutely toward the barn.

Chapter Seventeen

Despite Joe's far from warm welcome, Seraphina was humming as she rubbed down her horse with a handful of straw. A feeling of satisfaction filled her that belied the morning's upsetting events. Was that because she'd finally made the decision she'd wanted to make all along but had feared making until the necessity of riding out here to warn Joe and the others had forced her hand? she wondered. Yes, she had a feeling that was exactly it! And even Joe's ornery attitude couldn't completely dispel that sense of rightness, of having come home after an endless journey, that filled her now. Peggy had been right about Joe's behavior, she suspected. He'd lashed out at her because of the blow she'd struck his pride by threatening to leave him for someone else. He'd get over his anger sooner or later. She was certain she could bring him around once she told him there was no one else waiting for her, and that she loved him; that she'd always love him, come what may! And then—she bit her lip here—then somehow she'd have to find the words to tell him the truth, all of it. It wouldn't be easy, far from it, but she had to tell him before he found out from someone else, or she slipped up and it popped out by accident. The truth always had a way of coming out, and she couldn't afford to run that risk. Then . . . well, then it would all be up to Joel. At least afterward, she'd know for sure if he truly loved her in return, or if it had just been William McCaleb's money and land he'd been after all along.

She moved around to the other side of her horse and continued her rhythmic grooming of the beast while she watched Joe over the animal's broad back. He was fond of Ming, that much was plain. About half an hour before, she'd heard him, in a patient, gentle tone, go to great lengths to convince the boy he did not blame him for the damage the Monroes had caused. Yet Ming had remained adamant that he was at fault. His temper already strained by his confrontation with her, Joe had impatiently told him to go inside the house and help Peggy prepare supper. He'd intended only to put the boy far from him in his bad-tempered mood, Seraphina guessed, but to Ming, heavily burdened with guilt as he obviously was, his clipped dismissal must have seemed a further indication that Joe, despite his denials, was harboring some resentment toward him.

Afterward, Joe had repaired the corral fence, working with a singular concentration, strength, and energy that she admired, until each post had been firmly reinstated in its footing, each rail renailed. The repairs were completed in half the time it would have taken most men, and his blue work shirt was ringed with sweat when he was finished.

She watched as he tidily hung his tools on the appropriate pegs in the barn, then untucked and peeled off his shirt, striding toward the pump as he did so. He worked the handle vigorously and ducked his head and bare shoulders under the gush to cool off. Feeling like a voyeur, Seraphina continued to watch him, the wadded straw in her now unmoving hand quite forgotten.

Sunshine transformed each droplet of water that clung to his streaming blond head to a sparkling diamond. Moisture made his lean, powerful torso glisten as if oiled and drew the eye to the play of powerful corded muscle beneath the taut flesh of his narrow waist, flat, hard belly, and lean hips. She shivered with sensual pleasure. It was like watching the way a young, healthy male animal moved, sure and knowing, yet with a lithe, pantherlike, masculine grace that did strange and wonderful things to her breathing. Lord, how I want him! she thought, her fingers knotting into fists, a knot of yearning bunching up in the pit of her belly. I don't know what it is about him, damn him, that makes him so much more exciting than any other man I've ever met, but I want him so!

"That poor beast is going to be rubbed down to the bone, you keep that up much longer," Joe observed dryly without looking around.

Flustered, she dropped the handful of straw as if it were red-hot, feeling as if she'd been caught peeping through a keyhole or something—which, after a fashion, she had.

"I reckon he deserves a good rubdown," she said, forcing her tone to sound nonchalant and succeeding only in sounding defensive. "He gave it everything he had on the ride out here, didn't you, boy?" She patted the horse's neck affectionately, and the chestnut tossed its head in pleasure.

Joe snorted, his disgust patent. "Where in the hell did you come across that getup and that antique pistol?"

"These?" She looked down at the loose-fitting white tunic and baggy *pantalones* she was wearing, with the pistol thrust into the rope belt, and she wanted to squirm in embarrassment. Although loose, she realized belatedly, they had been cut to fit a man's flat-chested, lean-hipped build, and on her they were baggy only about the waist and legs. The cloth, damp now with her perspiration, clung lovingly to her breasts and hips like a second skin and was almost transparent. The thin cotton accented her feminine curves more effectively than even a tight, low-cut gown could have done. As his mocking gaze raked her, she felt heat fill her cheeks and, to her horror, a telltale tingling as her nipples rose taut against the scratchy cotton of the shirt, right before his eyes.

In desperation and defense, she stepped away from the horse and walked toward him, crossing her arms modestly over her breasts to conceal the effect his gaze had had on her—though not soon enough, apparently, for Joe could not hide the twitch of a smile at the corners of his mouth that betrayed he had seen everything, any more than he could control the sensual darkening of his eyes.

"I borrowed them from Olivia Rodriguez when I stopped at her soddy on the way over here," she told him, the words tumbling over each other in a rush with her sudden edginess. "Let me tell you, it was darned awkward riding in petticoats and a gown! Hot, too. This was the only change of clothes Señora Rodriguez had to lend me. They're Esteban's, she said."

"I'd stake money he never filled them out the way you do!" Joe drawled. "Val Monroe just about gobbled you up with his eyes, once he'd gotten over his shock at losing his hat! Though I don't suppose you gave that a thought, did you?" There was a caustic edge to his tone that smacked of jealousy.

"To heck with him!" Seraphina dismissed the notion tartly with a defiant toss of her head. "What about the stock? You do plan to go after them?"

He nodded. "Now the corral's fixed, yes." He turned toward the house, his sweat-sodden shirt slung over his

279

shoulder, their conversation abruptly terminated.

"Wait up! I'd like to come with you, Joe. You know I'm good with horses. I could help you."

"I don't want your bloody help."

"Oh, quit actin' like a sulky kid and accept my offer, Joel McCaleb! You know as well as I do it's going to be hard work rounding up and bringing back four horses single-handed before nightfall. They'll be clear to San Francisco if you try it alone, and then where will you be?"

He spun about to face her. "Didn't I tell you to stay out of my way? You have a short memory!"

"But I won't be in the way, I swear it. Please, Joe?" she added softly and knew by the expression in his eyes, and with the instinct that all women are born with where men are concerned, that she had won this round. There was still a chance then. He wasn't as immune to her as he wanted her to believe! Her hopes soared.

He hesitated briefly, then nodded, eyes narrowed as he looked across at her. "All right. You've convinced me. I need a clean shirt. Saddle up, and I'll be back out as soon as I've had Peggy fix us some tucker to take with us."

"Food?"

"Well, like you said, it's not going to be easy, rounding up four horses that have scattered to the winds! I doubt we'll be back here before nightfall— maybe more than one nightfall, come to that." One shaggy brow rose inquiringly. "Still want to ride along?" he challenged, insolently looking her over through slitted eyes, as if she were a gaudy saloon girl, with no attempt made to conceal his thoughts or to hide the lust that smoldered in their darkened depths. If she wanted to come along, she'd do so on his terms, by God, he swore, and to hell with hers! After all, he hadn't been the one to go running after her—

"You bet!" she retorted without pause, meeting his eyes boldly and accepting the challenge in his tone. Oh, yes, she knew quite well what he was getting at, knew only too well, but she was not put off by his attempt to frighten her. He was as good as saying outright that if she came along, he'd expect her to make it worth his while. Well, so what? Wasn't that what she wanted, to be with Joe in that way again? She gulped, trying in vain to quell the fierce, hot stab of purely sexual excitement that had lanced through her with his words and the wicked glint in his eyes. A night, maybe two, alone with him! The prospect filled her with a strange, heady combination of excitement, eagerness, and, perversely, even twinges of dread. She'd have all the time she needed to try to bring him around, and perhaps even enough time to bring herself to tell him the truth. Time ... time to rekindle and recapture what it was they'd had that had ignited and blazed between them for those brief, idyllic weeks. It was an opportunity that seemed heaven-sent, and one she'd certainly not pass up, whatever his terms. But, could she hope to soften this new Joe, this bitter, hurting, proud man? She was suddenly uncertain, for the hard look was still there, in his eyes, for all that he'd capitulated. "I'll be ready and waiting," she told him far more firmly than she felt. Whatever the outcome, she had to try.

"Can you fix us a knapsack of tucker, Peg?" Joe asked, stepping into the flagstoned kitchen with two blanket rolls slung over his shoulder. He wore the clean blue and brown plaid shirt he'd changed into, with the long sleeves rolled up to the elbow to expose his tanned, wiry forearms. He glanced about him appreciatively. Christ! It looked more like home every day—

a *real* home, not some orphanage mockery of what a few pious old biddies thought a good Christian home should be like. Strings of onions and green and red peppers hung from the dark beams above his head, giving off their sweet, pungent aroma. Peggy was peeling potatoes at the table, and Ming crouched by the hearth, adding kindling to the fire. He didn't look up as Joe entered, nor as he spoke, which was unlike him. He'll get over it, Joe decided. He's just smarting because he feels he let me down, silly kid.

"Us?" Peggy echoed with bated breath, hardly daring to hope he meant what she thought he meant. She set her paring knife aside. "You mean . . . ?"

"Seraphina and me," he confirmed, reluctant to meet her eyes. "We need those horses, Peg. Someone has to go after them and round 'em up." He grinned his engaging, crooked grin, and his turquoise eyes gleamed. "But don't get it into your head that we've patched things up, though, Peggy, me darlin'! This is more of a momentary truce than a reconciliation!"

"Sure, an' I wouldn't presume t'think any such thing, sir!" Peggy scolded with a little sniff, then added slyly, "But half the loaf's better than none, I'm after thinkin'!" She beamed with obvious pleasure. "Now, let's have a wee look in the pantry and see what we can find fer ye. Truth is, sir, we've not much left in the way o'food. I'd been meanin' t'tell ye today we'd have t'ride into town for more supplies before the week's out. I've made a list, an' all, of what we're after needin'." She drew the crumpled list from her apron pocket and held it out to him.

Joe nodded. "Fine. But keep it until I get back, will you, Peg, then I'll see what I can do. Seems to me I'll have to see about hiring some hands to help about the place, too. I don't like the idea of riding into town and leaving you and the boy all alone again. And you can't

282

take the buckboard and go in yourself, not without a man to ride with you."

"Now, don't go fretting about it, sir. We'll work it out after ye and the missus get back, we will," Peggy suggested, wiping her hands on her apron. "Now, there's fresh bread here, an' a bit o'salt beef, an' a few biscuits that I baked just this mornin' before those divils rode up. Ye can take this coffeepot, too . . ."

Minutes later, Joe left Casa Campanas with the bedrolls, a bulging leather knapsack of provisions, the coffeepot, and two canteens filled with water. He found Seraphina already mounted. His own paint pony— which had been rubbed down and watered in his absence, by the looks of it—was saddled alongside her mount.

She still wore her Mexican outfit but had braided her silky, blue-black hair in two glossy plaits that swung down past the inviting curves of her breasts. The style suited her lovely, proud face, baring the exotic, high cheekbones and dark eyes that were the legacy of the Indian forbears she'd told him of. Christ! The full, glowing impact of her beauty struck him as never before as she sat there, loose and natural in the saddle, her back straight, her head slightly cocked, her full lips parted in a hesitant, inquiring smile. And the way her clothes clung to those supple curves . . . Even had he wanted to, it would be God-Almighty difficult to keep his hands off her once darkness fell and they lay side by side in the shadows!

The past days had been hard enough to bear without her; the nights had been hell, pure and simple. Then the memories had come crowding in, and he'd relived over and over again those times when he'd held her tight in his embrace at the adobe *posada,* with the perfume of flowers carried on the dew-damp air through the grilled windows. In those moments he'd longed to succumb to the fierce desires roiling through him, to haul her into his arms and— That witch! That lovely, maddening witch! Why was it always those moments he remembered so strongly, and never the hurtful time when she'd said she meant to go away, to that other, shadowy man who waited for her? Joe had no idea who that man might be, but he was a dead man if he came here to Las Campanas looking for Sera!

Inwardly, he sighed. Careful, Joe, old mate, you've been burned once already! You've seen what a woman like her does to a man. She'll smile at you, and all the threats you've made will thaw under the sunshine warmth of it. She'll flirt those dark eyes, and all the aching inside you these past weeks will ease and be forgotten as if it had never been. If you're not careful, you'll forget about the pain and remember only the pleasure—until the next time she kicks you in the gut and walks out on you. No doubt about it; he was a fool to be going anywhere with that scheming little gold digger, especially when his wounds were still raw and smarting. He deserved whatever he had coming to him, right enough, but he was taking her along nonetheless! Aye, he'd enjoy the lovely body she was so brazenly offering him, the little bitch, then coldly tell her to go! he promised himself. This time around he'd show *her* how it felt to be used and then set aside.

"Time's a-wasting, McCaleb!" she said huskily, breaking in upon his thoughts. "I brought along a couple of extra lariats and hackamores."

"Good." He lashed the bedrolls onto the horses, one behind her mount's saddle and the other behind his own. He added the knapsack and canteens to the paint's load and swung up into the saddle. "Yaahh, Jimbo! Git up, there, boy!"

Side by side under the vivid, peacock blue of the afternoon sky, they rode off across the tawny, rolling land toward the distant hills.

It was a little after sundown before they struck camp for the night beside a narrow creek fringed with cottonwoods and willows. Three of the missing horses were hobbled beneath a stand of pines alongside their own unsaddled mounts by the time the milky moon rose and the first star of evening glimmered in the dusky sky. Sharing the chores, they spread out the small feast Peggy had packed for them and made a pot of scalding black coffee. As the shadows deepened, they ate their makeshift supper.

"Three out of four. Not a bad day's work, wouldn't you say?" Seraphina declared, licking her greasy fingers. She frowned. "I wish one of those we'd caught up with had been Muraco, though. I've become fond of him these past weeks."

"My guess is he's headed higher into the hills after fresh grazing. We'll run across him tomorrow," Joe said, setting down his tin coffee mug. He stretched, twisting where he sat cross-legged upon the blanket to work the crick from his back. They'd covered many miles searching for the other three horses, and he wasn't yet used to spending long hours in the saddle. Sera couldn't be feeling much better than he did, he thought. First she'd ridden out from Los Angeles, and then followed that up with some hard riding throughout the afternoon and clear on into the early evening with him.

"Feeling sore?" he asked curiously, glancing up in the nick of time to catch her in mid-yawn.

"Not too bad," she denied, gamely stifling the yawn. "You?"

He nodded ruefully, eyes glinting in the glow of the camp fire he'd built them at sundown. "And how! I think I've got the saddle sores, 'stead of my horse!"

She laughed, but her laughter was swiftly silenced.

Soon she'd returned to hugging herself about the knees and gazing deep into the golden flames of their camp fire. What was she thinking? he wondered. She seemed edgy, despite her obvious exhaustion. He hid a wicked smile. She was probably afraid he intended to jump her at any moment, and throw her to the ground! And so he would, he mused—but not when she was prepared for it. Oh, no! Let her squirm for a while. Let her find out how it was.

Thank God he couldn't read her mind, Sera thought. He would have been astounded! With difficulty, she forced her attention back to the flickering of the fire and away from him. All day, the yearning inside her for him had mounted, until she was certain he must be able to read the naked wanting in her eyes. She had only to glance at him across the fire and her heart skipped a beat. She was mesmerized by every inconsequential move he made; looked for hidden meanings in every soft, drawling word he uttered; savored even the slightest, most accidental brush of his hand or lean body against hers. Lord, girl, you've sure got it bad! she scolded herself. You might as well go right on up to him and tell him: "Here, Joe, darlin', take me—I'm all yours!" Mmm. Despite the fact that the notion had been the most outrageous one she could conjure up, she was horrified to realize that all of a sudden it didn't seem anywhere near as outrageous an idea after all! No. It was nothing but the barefaced truth! Alone here with him, the velvet shadows wrapping them in intimate indigo darkness, the flickering glow of the fire playing jealously over their faces and bodies, it seemed all too direct and rational and matter-of-fact, for it was exactly what she wanted to do! You hussy! You wanton, shameless hussy! she upbraided herself, but with very little enthusiasm. Her decision to return to him after all those days of soul-searching had unleashed the full gamut of her emotions, including desire and love, where before she had kept a tight rein on them, believing their relationship must inevitably end soon. Now, all that had changed in some not-too-subtle fashion with her decision to come back to Las Campanas, and her hunger for him was voracious.

"Ready to call it a day?" he cut in roughly, intruding on her thoughts.

"I guess so. We should make an early start tomorrow."

"Right. Then let's bed down. Christ! The ground's like iron here. I'll cut some young pine boughs for you to sleep on. It'll be soft as a city feather bed."

His faintly mocking tone implied he doubted she could rough it, and it made her angry. Did he really think her so soft and pampered, so darn *useless?* Huh! "There's no need for that, Joe, really. I've slept out under the stars before," she said in a cool, casual tone.

"I want to, okay?" He gave her a knowing smile that was particularly wolfish in the light and shadow that played over his rugged face and gleamed in his turquoise eyes. "We might as well be . . . comfortable, eh, love?" His tone was loaded with innuendo.

"Right," she echoed faintly, and watched as he rose and drew his knife before melting into the shadows.

It seemed he was gone an eternity, though in reality it could have been no more than a few minutes. Needing to do something to busy her nervous hands and steady her thumping heart, she made her way down to the creek and rinsed their tin mugs in its cool flow. Moonlight drenched the creek in silver that winked with the chill pallor of ice. The night wind sighed amongst the cottonwoods and the willows, and she shivered; whether because of the chill or from her sense of what was to come, she didn't know. The dishes done, she made her way back to their camp fire, which was like a welcoming beacon shining through the darkness. But despite its ruddy glow, her feet were peculiarly leaden as she made her way toward it. There'd be no turning back, she sensed, not if they made love tonight. They'd reached a crossroad, and once she took that next step, she'd be committed to staying with him for as long as he wanted it that way. After all, she was the one who'd brought them back together again; she'd returned of her own free will. What happened next would depend entirely on Joe, and on whether he could forgive and forget her walking out on him before . . .

When he returned to their camp fire seconds later, he loomed out of the darkness at her side so suddenly, she could not stifle a small, shrill cry of alarm.

"A bit jumpy tonight, aren't you?" he observed, derision in his tone. "I didn't mean to scare you."

"Mean it or not, you did!" she cried, her hand pressed to her galloping heart. "You move like . . . like an Indian! Lord! My heart's thunderin'!"

He dropped the resiny pine boughs in his arms and moved slowly toward her. "Is it?" he asked, the timbre of his voice husky and loaded with more than mere concern; something dangerous and sensual that sent spirals of apprehension shimmying through her.

"Ye-es," she admitted shakily, flinching as he came to a halt scant inches from her.

"Let me feel it beating, Sera," he breathed, his tone smoky with desire.

She shook her head, feeling weakness flood through her. "No. I . . . no, Joe."

With reluctance, she forced herself to look up into his shadowed eyes. In the moonlight, naked desire blazed in their depths, shone out across the narrow chasm that yawned between them, and mirrored the desire in hers.

288

Before he had so much as moved to take that last, irrevocable step to close the gulf, she had anticipated his move, had known the moment she had longed for— and dreaded—had finally come. The sexual aura that surrounded him was a crackling, invisible force, yet one as potently felt as a bolt of white lightning stroked across her bared flesh. She wet her lips, suddenly, irrationally afraid of him, and of the intensity of her desire for him.

"I warned you, Joe, don't! Stay right where you are—"

"Shut up, Sera!" he commanded harshly. "Don't try to hide what you're feeling with words. It's too bloody late for that, don't you see, love? It's all there, in your eyes, for a man to read, if he's a mind to. I want you— and you want me just as bad! You're aching for me! Say it, Sera! Tell me you want me!"

"No, never!" she denied, shaking her head. "You're wrong. Never!"

He reached out for her. She skittered away from him like a green colt, but he relentlessly followed her away from the fire and into the darkness along the creek.

"Liar!" he challenged. "Admit it! That's really why you came back to Las Campanas, isn't it? You missed the way I made you feel, the things I could make you want so badly you couldn't think strai—"

"No! That's a lie! I . . . I wanted to protect my interests, that's all. I hate you!"

"The hell you do!"

He sprang toward her. His hand fastened around one long, dark braid, spinning her forcefully back against him. His breath rasped hotly against her cheek as he whispered, "The hell you do, woman! Like hell you hate me . . ." he repeated more huskily as, for a fleeting second, she remained pressed against him, making no effort to twist free and evade him. It was

289

long enough. He could feel her trembling under his fingers in that moment, feel the sweet, heady heat and perfume that rose from her body in that second.

"Soon you'll be naked in my arms, Sera," he whispered, "as naked as the day you were born, with only that witch's mane of black hair tumbling down about your shoulders. Oh, love, you'll wind your arms about my neck and beg me to make love to you! Then I'm going to touch you, kiss you everywhere, Sera, everywhere, and you won't stop me, no, love! I'll kiss you here, and here, and here." His rough hand slid down her body, grazing her breasts, her belly, and her thighs. "And sooner or later, sweetheart, like it or not, you'll be singing a different tune, oh, yes, love! It'll be, 'Please, Joe, please!' Then, love, you'll see!"

His ardent, husky threats sent shivers down her spine, their very roughness adding a delicious fillip of danger to his loving. He took her braids in his hands and unbound the ribbons that held them, combing the silken strands with his fingers until her hair fell in a rippling inky tide to her waist. "Naked, Sera. Think about it; imagine it. Soon you'll only have this to cover you." One hand winding through the ebony curtain to draw her closer, he whispered, "You want me, love," and stroked her cheek with the back of his hand. "You know you want me, and, by God, I'm going to see that you get just what it is you want!"

He lifted the silky, night black cascade of her hair and let it spill like water through his fingers, gleaming where the starlight stroked each shining strand. Starlight was there in her eyes, too—or was it the radiance of her desire glowing hot and fierce within each one like a lustrous light? "Don't fight me, Sera!" he breathed, cupping the soft curve of her cheek in a large hand. "Don't make it harder on yourself, love, because whatever you do, I'll still win in the end. I'll still have you!" He dipped his moon-frosted head low to capture her moist lips with the hard, demanding heat of his, savage in his need to possess her totally, to feel her grow weak and yielding under his caresses, and know that he'd won.

A thrill ran through her as their mouths touched, as his lips and tongue moved intimately against, then within, her own, an electric thrill that seemed to encompass every part of her. His tongue tip traced the line of her lips and surged between them to savor the velvet flower of her inner mouth in a way that made her knees grow weak and her heart thunder. As he kissed her, she sensed his touch at the lacings of her loose shirt, felt the cool of the night wind caressing her bared skin as he dragged it down from her shoulders and then undressed her completely, without finesse, without tenderness, but with a relentless sense of purpose that made her moan softly in unwilling surrender to his arrogance and mastery. She felt peculiarly unable—and reluctant—to halt him. Rather, standing quite bare and vulnerable now before him, his body's warmth radiating against her tingling flesh, his belt chafing against her belly, the longing she'd harbored since that morning mounted, becoming all but unbearable, every pore, every nerve within her craved him, were wide open and screaming with their hunger for him. She didn't care any longer about her pride, or if he should discover how very much she wanted him. None of that mattered anymore. She was his, had been from the first; his to do with just as he wanted!

As if wrapped in a magical spell where time and motion held no sway and surrender and desire were all, she sought and found his hand in the shadows and drew it up to encompass the soft weightiness of her bared breast, pressing the lightly furred back of his callused hand against her to urge him to fondle her. His roughened skin, his smothering, squeezing, arousing fingers moving over her sensitive flesh, made her shiver with delight as he traced each aching nipple, as he circled and pressed each delicate, swollen aureole. Goose bumps shivered up and down her arms.

"Oh, God, yes, you win, Joe! I won't fight you. I can't! You know that, damn you! Oh, make love to me, Joe," she whispered breathlessly. "I've missed . . . I've missed being with you this way so much. I lied to you, Joe! Believe me, there's no one but you for me, I swear it! There's no one waiting for me. There never was. Oh, Joe, stop . . . don't torment me any longer! Just . . . love me!"

Her husky, sensual pleas inflamed his senses as potently as her yielding nude body, held tight in the prison of his arms. He'd intended to shame her, to arouse her and then leave her, naked and imploring, without the release she craved of him. But his own scheme had proved his undoing. Strewth! What a fool he'd been to think for even a moment that he could pull it off! He could no sooner hold her bare beauty in his arms and forgo having her than he could cut off his right hand! Her warm, scented breath against his ear made his own breath catch thickly in his throat. The fragrance of her skin was a sensual perfume, all musk and woman, all warmth and dark passion and moonlight! And the madness—the wonderful madness of two who desire with a fierce, raging hunger and who love with a fiery need unknown to those of milder passions—possessed him.

With a low, savage growl from deep in his throat, he dragged her against him, his fingers rough, almost painful with his driving need as he coiled them about her upper arms and they bit into her flesh. His lean, wiry body hummed like a taut wire with his throbbing desire as he held her fiercely against its length. He buried his mouth in the fragrant mass of her hair, then took her lips time and time again, each deep and questing kiss seeming to touch and fill her to her very soul, yet still leave her thirsting for more.

The warm cradle of his palm and fingers encompassed first one aching breast and then the other, while his searing mouth plundered the damp hollows of her throat with the sizzling heat of a brand. Her breathing grew unsteady and shallow, each gasp rasping on the cool air like the trills of a night bird, as the feathery brush of his fingertips grazed her sensitive nipples with light, flickering caresses. She seemed to be slowly melting inside with his every teasing, tantalizing touch, bone and sinew dissolving into a liquid honey-fire that bubbled through her veins like molten lava.

Thrusting her down to the hastily spread blanket, her fragrance, and the resin scent of the young pine boughs heaped carelessly beneath it, heady and full in his nostrils, the breeze tousling and whispering breathy endearments to the fluffy cottonwoods above, he loomed over, braced upon his knees. He bowed his fair head to her breasts, thinking how pale and lovely they were in the starlight, their lustre that of creamy pearls crowned by twin rubies at their crests. He licked sensually at first one ruby peak and then the other, circling the tiny nubbins of taut flesh with his tongue tip, nipping each one with his taut lips until she cried out in anguish and implored him once more to ease her torment.

"Soon, love, soon . . ." he murmured huskily, stroking the velvety plateau of her belly, his palm gliding lower and still lower over her trembling flesh with erotic, circular movements that made her writhe in desperate delight, until at last he stroked the smooth satin of her thighs. He'd been holding back, reluctant to take her until he was certain she was ready for him, but all too soon the urgency of his desire overwhelmed him. The night was still young, and his need—and hers, he sensed—too urgent for further delay. There would be time enough later to love her at his leisure . . .

Breathing raggedly, he unfastened his clothing, drew off his wide leather gun belt, and knelt between her parted thighs, raising her hips to guide his throbbing length unerringly to their juncture as he gathered her up into his arms. To his delight, he found she was both ready and eager for him, and with a groan he lunged forward, burying himself in her moist sheath to the hilt. She cried out as he took her, arching upward to meet his driving hips. Her arms curled about his broad chest to embrace him, to keep him fast inside her. Head flung back, eyes closed, she surrendered to his mastery, transported by the male scent and feel of him as he rode her powerfully and soared with her to the heights of desire.

Their loving was brief and violent, an ecstatic, stormy mating that had little of tenderness about it but culminated in the exquisitely explosive release they both craved.

She was sobbing, "Oh, Joe, I love you, love you so!" in reaction to the shattering sensations ricocheting through her when he finally withdrew and stretched out beside her. He gathered her into his arms and drew the rough blankets about them both against the deepening chill of the night.

"Cry it out, love," he whispered, wise in the ways of women at such moments. He kissed the crown of her dark head, her nose, her tear-dampened cheeks, realizing with a bittersweet pang that he was lost all over again, sucked into a trap of his own making—and that he didn't give a damn, so long as there was a chance, however slight, that it might work out this time.

"I never wanted to care for you, Joel McCaleb," she wailed between hiccuping sobs, returning his now tender kisses. "It just happened, damn you, and now . . . now . . . it won't . . . it won't go away!"

He chuckled. "Well, if the truth were known, I can't say I ever wanted to fall for you, either, you scheming little witch. Or take you back, come to that. But then, who does get to choose these things? Lady Luck, that beautiful bitch, she's the one has the last say. Fact is, I love you, Sera, God help me. Always have; reckon I always will, whatever comes. All the people I've loved in the past have been taken from me, one way or another, and I swore I'd be damned if I'd let that happen again. It's too bloody painful. I stuck to it, too—until I met you. You came along, and damned if I could help myself!" He playfully twined his fingers in her black mane and growled, half in earnest, half in play, "This time, Sera, you'd better make bloody sure you want to be with me for keeps, because you ever leave me again, I'll find you and haul you back here somehow, I swear it—no matter what it takes. You hear me, woman?" he threatened.

"Oh, yes, I hear you, I do," Seraphina murmured, almost purring with contentment as she cuddled closer to him. She steadfastly ignored the nagging voice of her conscience that urged her tell him, tell him the truth, right now, this very second, before the moment was lost forever . . .

"Right. Now, where were we . . . ?" He pulled her close and traced the curve of her ear with a damp tongue tip, nuzzling deep inside until gooseflesh rose all along her arms and she squirmed under the ticklish torment. "Ah, dinkum! That's exactly where we were, I reckon! Just the ticket, eh, love?" Despite the meager light, she could tell by his tone that he was grinning.

In the shadows, her eyes flew open in amazement as

she felt him, hard and aching for her again, pressing against her thigh.

"So soon?"

"Why not? I've gone without you too long, for my liking! And this time, I'll even take my boots off!"

"McCaleb, you're an incorrigible rogue!"

"Not incorrigible, love. Insatiable's a better word where you're concerned!" he corrected teasingly, moonlight silvering his dusty blond hair and glinting wickedly in his eyes. "Now, shut up and come over here, woman . . . !"

Chapter Eighteen

Dawn broke in a flamboyant blaze of rose-pink and gold and ominous crimson across the Sierra Nevadas the following day, gilding the sawtoothed mountain ridges with liquid light and banishing the tattered remnants of the charcoal night sky.

The clouds were still gray, bordered with bands of gold, when Joe and Seraphina rose, washed up in the creek, and saddled their horses, heading out of their little camp before the first rays of the morning sun had sent golden arrows high over the mountains or dried the dew upon the grasses. Joe led the recaptured horses on makeshift hackamores behind his paint, while Seraphina, lost in a dreamy, introspective mood as a result of their ardent lovemaking all the night long, rode quietly beside him, a contented smile playing about her lips and shining in her lustrous, gray-green eyes.

Almost two hours passed before they found any trace of the white gelding, Muraco, and she had almost given up hope of ever finding him when Joe spotted the hoof tracks of a shod horse in the still-dewy, damp earth. They followed the tracks for a mile or more before spying the animal, drinking from another of the numerous small creeks that crisscrossed the dun-colored terrain. Apparently the gelding had been headed for higher ground and lusher grazing, as Joe had suspected, but nightfall and the threat of coyotes and cougars lurking nearby had forced him to pass the night in this small canyon in the foothills.

He lifted his ghostly head as the jingle of their bits reached him on the morning air and stood with water streaming from his mouth like liquid silver, his ears pricked back, until he caught their familiar scent. Having done so, he tossed his snowy mane and circled once, pawing the earth, before breaking into a trot with what seemed an almost nonchalant air and moving in a steady gait away from them, up the rocky canyon toward freedom.

Seraphina stood in the stirrups and called to him, but the gelding kept moving, his eyes rolling suspiciously now as Joe, astride his paint, circled around to one side of him, slowly uncoiling the lariat looped around the horn of his saddle. Seeing that her efforts to call the gelding to her had had no effect, Seraphina dug her heels into the chestnut's sides and came up around Muraco on the opposite side. Perhaps between them, they could head him off, and give Joe the chance he needed to rope him, she reflected.

"Careful, love!" Joe cautioned. "If he panics and decides to make a break for it, we'll lose him!" The canyon mouth was temptingly close now, and he could sense the horse's intent as surely as if it were his own. Any second now, Muraco would make a wild gallop for that narrow opening in his bid for freedom, and they'd have to start all over again. He gathered the lariat into his fist and slowly raised it, circling with his wrist to make it spin. There was a whirring sound as the braided rawhide bit the air, and then the running loop was slowly spinning toward the snorting gelding. It fell about his proudly arched white neck in the same instant he decided to bolt, which took up the slack and jerked the lariat taut. At once, Joe lashed the other end securely about the cantle and spurred his paint in hot pursuit, figuring to let Muraco run off some of his excess energy and tire out before reeling him in. With a whoop, Seraphina urged her chestnut after them.

The three horses erupted from the little canyon neck to neck and followed the willow-strewn banks of an *arroyo* for perhaps half a mile. The terrain grew more rocky as they began to climb higher through the foothills and up into the mountains proper, the air growing increasingly cooler with every minute. They thrashed through deep washes where violet-blue lupins and pastel-mauve larkspur made a gaudy carpet, and where the sculptor's tools of the sun, the wind, and rain had carved the rugged land into a wild beauty that was stirring and unique. Higher they rode, up into the dazzling light and the endless sky, until the twisting path of the wild sheep that they had followed led them to a broad, mountain *mesa,* where Muraco at last slithered to an abrupt halt, conceding defeat.

Blue wraiths of smoke pungent with the scent of burning sage rose from several cooking fires. The broad, sandy area was dotted with straggly wildflowers and twisted piñons, beneath which huddled several small adobe or redwood-plank Indian dwellings shaped like mounds, each one boasting a small, round entranceway close to the ground. Pink and grayish lizards slithered away from the paths of the flying hooves of their horses as they careened to a dust-stirring stop alongside the white gelding.

All about the little *ranchería,* the *mesa* was dotted with hardy sheep. People—old men, a few children, a solitary old woman with a half-finished reed basket in hand—and a few scrawny, yapping dogs came out to stare at them as Seraphina sprang down from her horse's back and ran to Muraco.

Now that he had accepted his recapture, the gelding obediently came at her call, nuzzling her outstretched palm for treats like a tame pup and tossing his head to show his indignation. She laughed and flung her arms about his neck, hugging him briefly before slipping a hackamore over his velvety nose and loosening and removing Joe's lariat. She grasped his rough-silk mane and vaulted astride him bareback, urging him to trot in a broad circle until he had calmed.

"There, you see? He knows when he's bested, don't you, clever boy?" she declared, patting his neck as they came to a halt alongside Joe.

The horse nickered as if in answer and eyed Joe with an almost cunning look. Joe grinned. The crafty horse was no fool. He'd known nothing but kindness from Seraphina, and had no doubt decided that recapture by his gentle mistress was by far preferable to another night out in unfamiliar territory, amongst predators that counted horseflesh a rare delicacy!

"Here, take this, will you, Joe? We really should apologize and pay our respects, don't you think?" Seraphina was saying.

Joe took the rope bridle she handed him as she slithered lithely down from Muraco's back. He swung about to follow the direction of her gaze and belatedly noticed the erect old Indian man standing watching them from beneath a *piñon* tree, his arms crossed over his chest. His face reminded Joe of a very old, very gnarled tree trunk, for a web of deeply etched furrows creased the mahogany skin. His nose was broad and somewhat hawklike. His eyes were dark, their intelligent gleam all but lost below a broad, prominent brow and the deep creases of flesh that encircled them. He wore a threadbare gray jacket in the fashion of another era, the metal buttons long since lost, the pockets torn, faded work pants belted with fraying rope, and moccasins. His gray hair, worn shoulder length, was neatly held in place by a patterned, blue cotton scarf bound about his brow and knotted at the temple.

"Forgive the rudeness of our intrusion into your village, Old Grandfather," Seraphina murmured, walking toward the old man with her head modestly bowed. "We have traveled many miles in search of the white horse, and in our great gladness to recapture him, we forgot our manners."

"You are forgiven, daughter," the old man responded with a faint smile. "For your white one's part, he seems happy to be reclaimed." He nodded at Muraco, who was trying to evade the hackamore in Joe's fist and nuzzle at her neck.

"As I am happy to reclaim him. Muraco is my friend, and my heart was saddened by his loss."

The old man nodded sagely. "It is my thought that he came back here, to where he was born, in search of safety, as we all try to return to that which is somehow safe and familiar when we are threatened in some way." He appraised the horse with knowledgeable eyes. "I am certain your Muraco is one of the horses we sold in the spring, to a white man named Reid. He lives in the *pueblo* of the Angels. The winds of fortune must have brought you, a woman of our blood, here to our camp in his pursuit. Tell me, daughter, who are your people?"

"Both the proud bloods of the red man and the white man run in my veins, as you must surely know, Wise Grandfather. My father's mother, Singing Wind, was the beloved daughter of the great *shaman,* Yellow Rock, who has long since joined the stars in the sky. Though his father was a white man, my father also bore a Cheyenne name. It was Tall Shadow. His family was of the camp of Black Kettle. For myself, I am known among the People by the name Star Dreamer."

"Ah. Yellow Rock of the Northern Cheyenne. That explains both your graceful bearing and your becoming modesty, daughter. Your great-grandfather was a man of wisdom and vision. I was already an old man myself when I heard the mourning chants that told of mighty Yellow Rock's passing, and of the great sorrow that befell Black Kettle's people at the Sand Creek that winter long past. Aiee! They were many who took the Star Path that day! And there have been countless other sorrows for the People since that time. Now we are all scattered as the dust of Mother Earth is scattered, whether Sioux, Crow, Cheyenne, Comanche —all of us! Our old ones lose themselves in the past, which can no longer harm them. Our young ones hold no hope for the future they fear in the white man's alien, hostile world, and so try to drown their failures and their anger in liquor. Their bellies grow fat, their muscles slack, their senses dull. Their skills as providers for their families are of use no longer, for what little wild game still remains lies beyond reservation lands such as these, and are forbidden to us. Instead, we wait like buzzards for the carcasses the white man sees fit to bring us! Gone are the hunters, the warriors, the wise men of the People. In their place are only empty shells, without pride or spirit or hope. Chinigchinich, who rules the heavens, has turned his back on us. We, who were many, are now few. Our god has forsaken his red children in their hour of need and turned his smile upon the white man." He sighed heavily. "But we will not speak of such sad things now. You are our guest, and Chief Tyonek's camp is honored by your presence, daughter. Food will be prepared for you and your companion. You will eat and refresh yourselves."

It was not so much an invitation as a command, and

Seraphina hid a sad smile at his still imperious tone as she beckoned to Joe to dismount and accompany them into the village. She would not refuse the old chief's hospitality, for to do so, however noble her intention, would shame him. Though it was obvious Tyonek's camp had fallen on hard times, he had retained much of his proud bearing and spirit, and would take offense at their refusal. In his youth, he must have been a warrior amongst warriors, she surmised; one who had struck terror in the hearts of the hated bluecoats when he took to the warpath, and who had counted many *coups*. Now he was an old and embittered man who had lived too long and had witnessed the gradual destruction of the Indian people, the slow and agonizing death throes of a once-proud race.

Memories came back to her as they walked between the dwellings to that of Tyonek, fragments of stories her father had told her of that dreadful winter morning over twenty years ago. That fateful day, the Colorado Third Company and others had attacked the village of old chief Black Kettle, which had peacefully surrendered itself to the officers at Fort Lyon and had camped along the banks of the Sand Creek at their instruction—only to become sitting targets.

Major Chivington, a former minister turned bloodthirsty, Indian-hating fanatic, who commanded the Third, had insisted there were hundreds of hostile warriors in Black Kettle's camp. As it transpired, the tepees had been occupied by women and children and old ones, for the most part. The massacre had continued nonetheless, even as the Union flag—given to the old chief as a token of peace between his people and the whites—fluttered limply over the sorry scene from above Black Kettle's tepee. Two of her own Cheyenne relatives had numbered amongst the fallen. The first had been Yellow Rock, her great-grandfather,

303

the old *shaman* who had told of the vision he had been granted by the Wise One Above, warning of the forthcoming attack, but who had not been believed. The second was wise Four Winds, her great-uncle, who had been slain while valiantly trying to defend the women and little children trapped amongst the sandy banks of the creek like fish in a barrel.

Her father had learned of the impending attack and had ridden furiously through the frosty November night to warn the Cheyenne, only to arrive too late to prevent the slaughter. There were times when she wondered if her father had ever forgiven himself for this, for when he told the story, his night-black eyes would glow fiercely like dark candles, and his hard, handsome features would grow bitter and as implacable as granite. It must have been far from easy for him, sharing two bloods, she reflected, for in taking the part of his mother's people, he would have been turning his back on his father's.

There had been an official inquiry in the months following the incident, for many good white men as well as red had been outraged by the atrocities they had witnessed that day. Her father had gone to Washington that August and had heard it all, her mother had told her, and he had returned withdrawn and brooding and sick at heart for some months afterward, for what good were inquiries, however well intended, when they could not restore life to those unjustly and brutally slain and mutilated? Their concern had come too late for them. The only purpose such hearings could serve was to ensure that such a dreadful thing would never happen again.

The massacre at Sand Creek had been the fuse to ignite the smoldering powder keg of the Cheyenne people into explosive action, sparking their participation in an Indian war of immense proportions, which had resulted in many, many deaths on both sides. For the Indian, these last, desperate, bloody battles served only to hasten the inevitable end. Those who survived the wars did so only to walk the heartrending Trail of Tears to first one of the white man's reservations, then another, and still another as the tide of white settlers grew rather than diminished, and even the reservation lands promised them by treaty after treaty fell prey to the white man's greed. On the reservations, they suffered a far more lingering death with the gradual conquering of their spirit, their will to live, their way of life, their freedom to roam Mother Earth at will, which was, to the People, the very essence and breath of life itself. There were those who took their own lives rather than face this; others who courted death and rebelled against the government agents' authority with violence in the following months, as had her father's cousin, the fierce and embittered, white-hating Scarred Hand. He had paid for his rebellion with his life and had found release at last at the end of a government noose. She had been only a tiny babe then, but the stories her father and mother had told had made the past come alive again in her mind many times since . . .

She and Joe sat across from Tyonek in his simple cottage of adobe bricks roofed with tule reeds and *brea,* while his lovely young granddaughter, clad in a warm, long-sleeved white blouse and long skirt with embroidered hems, bustled about preparing food for them. The little house consisted of only one large room. One side had a hearth for cooking and an area for eating; the other was obviously where the old man and the girl slept, rolled in their bright woolen blankets upon pallets of straw. Beautiful examples of the girl's expertise in basket weaving and pottery making were everywhere.

The old man's eyes followed his granddaughter with

pride and affection as she moved busily about the hut, and she returned his gaze with shy, fond smiles.

"She is all I have left now, my Izusa. Her name means 'the mountain snows,' for is not her complexion as white and fair as the snow? Her mother, my own daughter, Lomasi, brought great shame and sorrow upon myself and her people, for she turned her back on our village and her choice of the young men who would have taken her to wife, and left the mountains for the *pueblo*. She scorned the simple way we lived, you see, and vowed she would find herself a rich white man to take as her husband and live in a fine house with soft feather beds and silken clothes. Alas, Lomasi could find work only in a drinking place—a saloon where the white men came to gamble and carouse—for as a woman of Indian blood she was despised by the whites and considered no better than a dog. But, she was beautiful, a pretty flower, as her name promised, and despite her dark skin, the white men lusted for her. She was soon dishonored by the very same men who loathed her race! Too ashamed to return to our village and admit she had been wrong, she sought escape in the white man's liquor, and in bitterness she soon learned that she could survive in the white man's world only by selling herself to any man who wanted her for the night. She did so, in order to buy the firewater she craved.

"My granddaughter, Izusa, has never known the name of her father, though it is plain to all eyes that he was a white man, for she is very fair. When word reached me of my daughter's death in childbirth, I left these mountains and rode down into the *pueblo* myself, to bring back both her poor body and her little one. I felt only pity and sadness, not anger, toward my Lomasi, for she was not to blame. She had been born in troubled times, times when her people were like the white man's ships, without the anchors of custom and tradition to steady them. After our custom regarding those who have become one with the stars, we no longer speak her name in my camp, but Izusa has learned from the mistakes of her mother and is content to stay here. So, too, did I learn wisdom from the mistakes of my ancestors; I learned to forgive! I accepted her as my blood without condemnation, for there was once another Tyonek without such compassion or pity, a chief whose daughter shamed herself with a Spanish soldier, believing she was his lawful wife according to the teachings of the Christian *padres* at the mission. Only when it was too late and she was carrying his child did she learn she had been tricked. In anger, my ancestor cast her from him into the wilderness, where it is said her ghost yet wanders, weeping in shame and sorrow. When the chief grew old, it is said he grew to bitterly regret casting his beloved young daughter away. Aiee! I could not do this to Izusa."

Seraphina nodded. "This sad legend we have already heard from the Mexican *pastores,* the shepherds, Old Grandfather, for my husband and I are from Rancho de las Campanas, where once the Indian maiden you speak of met and was tricked by the man she loved."

"And have you seen the ghost of Little Owl there?" Tyonek asked curiously. "Have you felt the power of her ancient curse against those who dare to love in that place?"

Gooseflesh rose along Seraphina's arms, and the hair at her nape rose. She glanced at Joe, who shook his head. "We have seen and felt nothing, Grandfather," she denied. "It has been many years since those unhappy times. Little Owl's spirit is at peace now."

Yet even as she said the words, she recalled the first evening they had come to Las Campanas and how, upon opening the heavy portal, a white owl had flown out, startling both her and Joe. "Yes, she is at peace

307

now, I am certain," she repeated, yet her words sounded hesitant and unsure.

"And what will you do with the land, Husband of Star Dreamer?" the old man asked in faltering English, turning his grizzled old head to Joe and fixing him with a bright, dark eye that suddenly held a sly gleam in its depths. "Will you run many cattle there, as does the white maggot named Monroe?"

"No, Chief Tyonek. You see, I know very little of cattle," Joe responded frankly. "Instead, I've made arrangements with the shepherds of these parts. They're to go to the sheep fairs in New Mexico and purchase stock, the finest stud rams and breeding ewes that money can buy, to begin our flocks. The land is good for sheep ranching. In a year, God willing, they'll have doubled or more in number, if we have a good late-autumn and spring lambing. The *pastores* and I will graze our flocks on Las Campanas' land together, and share in the work and the profits after the old custom of *partido*. Do you know of this system?" He studiously ignored Seraphina's sudden tenseness beside him at this announcement, remembering only too well her opinion of sheep ranchers, voiced back in San Francisco over a luncheon table.

Tyonek nodded sagely. "I have heard of the system, yes. It is a good one, where all who labor share in the profits, as you say. But it is good only if the *patrón* himself is a fair and just man. It is my thought that you will succeed, for your eyes seem to me both just and fair. I see determination and honesty within them, and in your voice I already hear a love for the land that is now yours. Under your hand, Mother Earth will prosper and grow fat. Tell me, when will your flock reach here?"

"If the sheep drive goes as planned, next month. Yesterday, I commissioned Esteban Rodriguez and a

Basque fellow named Raoul Garnier—both knowledgeable about sheep and trustworthy men—to go down to Albuquerque to select and purchase the animals for me. You see, Chief, the one called Monroe would like very much for me to leave the San Juliano Valley, which he has sworn will one day belong entirely to him. Though I wanted to, I could not risk going down into New Mexico myself and leaving my woman and ranch at his mercy."

"You speak truly, for this Monroe is an evil, greedy man! He will be angered, as you say. My people were once shepherds. As you can see, our flocks are small now, and provide barely enough wool for the women to weave into the blankets they sell at the markets in the *pueblos*, but nonetheless, the old skills have not been forgotten. When it is time for the shearing and you have need of friends to help, send word to Tyonek's village. I will send as many of our young men as can be spared to help you shear your flocks."

"I am grateful for your offer of help, Wise Grandfather," Joe said, following Sera's lead in addressing the old man respectfully, "and give you my thanks. If there is anything I can do for you or your people someday in return, I'll do it. I give you my word and my hand."

He and Tyonek clasped hands. The old man grunted in satisfaction.

"It is well! Ayyahh! My Izusa tells me with her eyes that the food is prepared and we must soon eat or it will be overcooked and spoiled. Come eat, my friends!"

Later, as they were riding back down the mountain between the pines and junipers, Seraphina remarked, "So, sheep, is it, Joe? Peggy warned me as much, but I'd thought—hoped—I could talk you out of it, somehow.

309

Why sheep, for heaven's sake? Why not cows?"

"Seems to me a man should do what he knows best, Sera, wouldn't you say? And I know sheep."

"So it seems," she said dryly. "And you know how to ride and rope damned well, too! Tell me, Joe, did you learn all that roping and riding and sheep ranching back in Java?" she asked sarcastically, her brows arched. "See, from what I learned in my geography class, I had the wildest impression it was coffee beans and bananas and so on that they raised out there—not sheep!"

He grinned, his turquoise eyes twinkling. "And you're right. I spent some years in Australia, though. That's where I picked up everything I know about sheep."

"I see. Well, well! It seems there's a lot I still have to learn about you, isn't there, Joel McCaleb?"

"Oh, there sure is, love," Joe agreed amicably. "Tons of it! All of my wicked past may soon come to horrible light!" Though he said the words lightly, inside he was far from easy on the subject. Sera was too shrewd, too intelligent by far, to accept half-truths and evasiveness for overlong. He'd have to be very careful. "And while we're on the subject, what about your lurid past?" he countered. "According to Caldwell, you'd led a very sheltered life until old man McCaleb married your mother, his housekeeper. Then you tell me you have Indian blood, and Chief Tyonek not only knows your Indian great-grandfather's name but all of his exploits! You must have some very illustrious ancestors, love! And if I remember it right, you know quite a bit about cattle, too! Now, where'd that come from? Got any more skeletons in *your* closet?"

She flushed. "None that you need concern yourself with, McCaleb!" she countered tartly. "Getting back to where we were, you could at least have told me you'd decided to run sheep on Las Campanas' land, instead of letting me hear it from Peggy. Don't you think I deserve a say in what goes on there?"

"That short memory strikes again, love! At the time I made the arrangements, you—for all I knew—were rushing headlong into the arms of some fancy man you had waiting for you! No, Sera, love, I didn't think you deserved a say then, and I still don't now, even though you're back here with me. The range is my business. Yours is the house and such. I wear the pants around here, and I intend to keep it that way. That part of what I said still goes. Don't interfere, love."

She scowled. "McCaleb, you're not only arrogant, you're a pigheaded, opinionated son of a gun, and I'm having nothing whatsoever to do with your stinking sheep, not even if you beg me!"

"Fine! I'm real glad you made the decision yourself, love, because to tell you the truth, I was having trouble deciding exactly how to word telling you to keep your nose out of it!"

"Oh! You!" she hissed, obviously at a loss for further insults to hurl at him, or names to pin on him.

He winked and roguishly adjusted the brim of his Outback-style hat so that it shadowed his face at a jaunty angle and concealed the burning ardor in his eyes. How soon she'd forgotten the whispered promises, the soft and yielding side of her she'd shown him the night before. Now she seemed ready to explode, he noted, hectic color blooming in the pale gold of her cheeks, her gray-green eyes glittering. When she was angry, the emotion heightened her lovely coloring, making her beauty a vivid, voluptuous force that he found irresistible. And when all the fight was played out of her, when she was warm with surrender, she was even more magnificent! Was that her secret, her witch's spell? Her ability to be several different, fascinating

311

women all rolled deliciously into one, from giggling, tipsy temptress to tempestuous tiger? Whatever, the perverse urge to drag her from Muraco's back and make wild, hot love to her right there and then amidst the sagebrush and the chaparral filled him. He masterfully quelled the urge. Their loving would have to wait a while. He had to return to Las Campanas without further delay. If the Monroes had decided to return . . .

"Well," she continued, "don't say I didn't warn you! In a matter of months, your grazing land will be nothing but a dust bowl, and your precious, smelly old sheep will be dropping like flies from maggots and drought and starvation. When they do, don't come crying to me, McCaleb!"

"Don't worry, ma'am. I won't," he promised solemnly.

It was almost sundown before they spotted the looming landmark of the *campanario* of Casa Campanas ahead. The day had been one of blazing sunshine earlier. Yet toward afternoon, rain mists coated the Sierra Nevadas like a gray fleece draped carefully across them. The clouds to the east took on a violent, threatening, blue-gray hue. The scent of coming rain hung sharp and tangy on the air, like dandelion wine. As the sun bled over the edge of the mountains and darkness folded like a long, black wing across the valley, blue-white lightning ghost-danced upon the sharp ridges and the crackling of thunder drums ricocheted between the valley walls.

"We'd best get a move on, love," Joe warned Seraphina. "We're in for a fair old summer storm, by the looks of it!"

They gathered their reins in their fists and urged their horses into a gallop, the recaptured mounts thundering behind them. They managed to reach Las Campanas just as the dour sky opened up and unleashed the first torrents. They hurriedly dismounted and quickly led the horses beneath the *ramada* rather than to the open corral, and they were about to unsaddle them when Peggy came running out from the *casa* through the driving rain to meet them.

Seraphina turned to greet her and saw at once how pale and frightened she appeared in the sudden brilliant fork of lightning that lit up the sky.

"What's for supper, Peg?" Joe shouted over the drumming rain, his back to the woman. "Christ! I could eat a bear!"

"Shut up, Joe," Sera said curtly, disgusted by his single-mindedness. "Something's wrong! Look at her!"

Joe spun about and caught the pallor of Peggy's face as she reached them. "What is it, Peg? Did the Monroes come back?" he demanded.

"No, sir! T'be sure, it's not them! It's that contrary Chinee whelp ye left in my care! He's gone, Mister McCaleb, sir! Run away! He left soon after ye and the missus rode out yesterday mornin' and never came back. Curse his black heathen heart, I'll wallop the daylights out o'the seat o' his britches if he returns!" The worried wringing of her hands belied her fierce words and underlined the panicky edge to her tone, betraying her fear that he would not return at all.

"Oh, Christ!" Joe muttered, wishing the sudden, violent foreboding that had settled in his gut would go anyplace else.

313

Chapter Nineteen

The rock-strewn trail Chen Ming traveled was a long one, hard on the feet. Though it had seemed a good plan at the time, now Ming was beginning to wonder if he'd done the right thing. Though he'd covered several miles since evading Peggy and leaving Casa Campanas, the *pueblo* of the Angels was still many miles away and he was tired. His feet were sore and blistered. He sat down to rest for a while upon a boulder and removed his boots and emptied the dirt from them. Truly, his feet were sorry things to see! Used to going barefoot or to wearing the soft cloth slippers of his people, the heavy leather boots Joe had bought for him had raised huge blisters on his toes and heels, some of which had burst, leaving the skin beneath raw and exposed. He would carry the boots, he decided, and only put them on again when he reached the *pueblo*. To that end, he knotted the laces together and slung them over his shoulder before continuing on.

Drawing one of Peggy's biscuits from his pocket, he munched on it as he resumed his trek toward the Coast Range, which was a smoky blue ridge in the distance. As he walked, he thought how much he would have preferred a bowl of *mein,* noodles, and crunchy vegetables with *won ton*, spicy pork dumplings, floating in the soup, to the unbuttered biscuit. He considered also that impulsiveness was an unworthy trait. Perhaps he had done a foolish thing. Perhaps it had been unwise to leave Missie Peggy all alone at the ranch. Perhaps he should have waited until Joe's return before leaving. He sighed and shook his head. But then, Joe was not as easily fooled as Missie Peggy, and he no doubt would have discovered his disappearance and ridden after him. And then, how could he hope to prove himself to Joe, to redeem himself in Joe's eyes, when Joe considered him only a useless boy and would never let him out of his sight again? Peggy had the rifle, and it was doubtful that the Monroes would return so soon, after the way Joe and Missie Seraphina had seen them off the place. Everything would be all right; of course it would! And how surprised and pleased Joe would be to see him return with all the things they needed: flour and molasses and sugar and salted pork and beans and rice . . . The thought of it all made him feel hungry, despite the crumbling biscuit he'd eaten, and his belly growled.

No more than half a mile farther, Ming's head jerked up at the sound of hooves behind him. Joe? Had his disappearance been discovered so soon? Or was it someone else? The fine hair at his nape rose in alarm and a sick knot of dread lurched in his belly. He suddenly sensed, without the need to look back, that the approaching riders would not be Joe and Missie Seraphina, but the Monroes; he sensed it as surely as the fish senses the threads of the net that entraps it, or the rabbit the jaws of the snare that takes it and holds it fast for the killing club. Heart thundering so violently in his chest he thought for a fleeting instant it might erupt through flesh and bone, he halted and turned about to face the riders as they lashed their huge horses

315

into a gallop toward him. They were silhouetted by the sun against the horizon like great black demons on still blacker horses! It would do no good whatsoever to run, he realized helplessly, for they could easily ride him down on their devil-steeds.

The penciled list of provisions in his hand was sodden with his sweat when the enormous mounts careened to a halt inches from him, the lead script blurred and unreadable now. Chen Ming's nostrils flared. He could smell their sweat now, smell the leather of their saddles and bridles, smell the hatred that clung like a foul miasma about them, and see every detail of both horses and riders as if fear had heightened and expanded his senses in some uncanny way.

A hawk screamed as it wheeled in the blue of the sky far above, and Ming heard the sound and wondered if it sang his funeral song. Mouth dry as sand, he bit his lip and looked up at the three men, his eyes smarting with the grit their arrival had churned up.

"Well, heck, Val, jest look who's here! If it ain't that little ole yeller hound dog agin!" Stevie jeered, aping his father's manner of the day before. "I reckon he done broke his chain and wandered off from his kennel!" His smile did nothing to soften the horrific effect of the grossly swollen, discolored mess of flesh that was his broken nose.

"Yep. Reckon so," Val agreed, hunching forward over the pommel of his horse. "Don't look near so frisky now, do he?" He shoved back the brim of his hat and grinned nastily. "What's wrong, yeller? Ain't afraid of us boys, are yer? Why, we're all jest as nice and friendly as a litter of speckled pups!"

"Look at him, big brother! Reckon he is too scared," Stevie put in gleefully. "Reckon he's scared enough to piss his breeches! Know why? There ain't no petticoat t'back him up this time!"

"Say, li'l brother, I reckon you're right fer once! Ye know, I clean forgot 'bout that pretty little ole McCaleb gal, yessir!" Val frowned and seemed to consider his memory lapse. "Now, how in the world could I have forgot something fine like her? Surely ain't every day you see a woman built that way, all sweet and rounded where she's s'posed to be round, and trim as a whistle where she ain't! Hell, fairly made my mouth water! An' the way she come struttin' out with her little ole pistol leveled at me, her eyes sparking fire an' her voice jest cool as ice—now, that was somethin'! She filled out them Mex clothes so fine and purty, they was like a second skin!" He leered down at Ming. "Bet she makes your mouth get to waterin', too, don't she, yeller boy? Gives you real crazy ideas that make you all hot and bothered jest lookin' at her, don't she?"

Ming gritted his teeth and said nothing, though rage boiled inside him to hear Val Monroe speak of Missie Seraphina in that—that unspeakable, dirty way. He clenched his fists so hard against his thighs his palms hurt where his fingernails gouged into them, but the pain helped him to stay in control and so he welcomed it.

"I asked you if the McCaleb woman got you all overheated? Cat got your tongue, boy?" Val mocked.

Still Ming said nothing.

Val swung down from his horse and left the reins dangling as he ambled across to where Ming stood. He was swaggering, his thumbs hooked in his belt, his silver spurs jingling, his chaps flapping. The forty-five that rode low on his hip winked dully in the sunlight as he came. "I said, cat got your tongue, *boy?*" he repeated, his tone taunting.

Still Ming made no reply.

Seemingly from nowhere, Val Monroe's fist came

317

out, striking Ming full on the mouth. Blood sprayed from his cut lips. His head snapped back. A blinding white blur filled his vision. Aggh! Pain exploded through him yet again and still again as Val slammed his fists repeatedly into his face and belly. Dimly, through a haze of crimson, he sensed more blows, felt his knees give and buckle, then the sickening crunch as the hard earth rushed up to meet him. Dazed, only distantly aware of what was going on now, Ming heard Stevie's disgusted whining from somewhere far away.

"Heck, Val, you promised! You said I could fix him!"

"Then what you waitin' for, little brother? He's all yours," came Val's reply.

Ming heard the scrape of boots cross the dirt, again the jingle of spurs, the flap-flap of chaps, as someone walked toward him, and then he felt that same someone—Stevie Monroe, he guessed—squatting alongside him. He tried to sit up, but couldn't. Tried to see, but couldn't. Everywhere he looked was painted brilliant crimson, a shifting, slopping sea of crimson that made the gorge rise acidly up his throat. With a groan, he sank back down. Spiteful hands grasped his wrists and then lashed them cruelly together with a lariat before jerking him up by his hair to a sitting position. Still groggy, he finally opened one swollen eye as Val Monroe dashed a canteen full of water into his face to rouse him. The shock made him gasp and he moaned weakly but would not beg for mercy, no, not even now.

"Hey, Val, that's enough," someone protested, a voice Ming did not recognize. "Ain't no sense killin' him, fer God's sake!"

"Aw, jest shut up, Tallant, an' let little Stevie have his fun. The Chinee got it comin', after all, after what he did to 'im, right? An' if he winds up dead, well, I reckon

318

McCaleb will think twice 'fore he messes with the Monroes again!"

"Yeah! Come on! Wake up, yeller boy! You an' me're goin' fer a little ride!"

Stevie's voice. His was the last voice Ming heard before rending agony exploded through his body, centering in his wrists and shoulders before spreading out to govern every part of him. *They were tearing him in two!* After that, there was only a merciful blackness, from which he hoped he would never, never awaken . . . and much, much later, the blessed rain.

The rain drummed like a million tiny hammers upon the red-tiled rooftops of Casa Campanas. The gutters and waterspouts burbled and gurgled with their rushing burden, but their joyful song was drowned out by the roar of the rain and wind and the chattering of the thunder. In the *campanario* between the three silent bronze bells, the white owl that roosted there by day and hunted by moonlight blinked its round eyes and fluffed out its feathers irritably as the storm continued to howl and shriek and lash the *casa grande* with fierce, wet whips, rattling window frames and moaning through nook and cranny. There would be no hunting, not this night.

Below in the kitchen, the crackling fire of fragrant *piñon* logs in the wide stone hearth hissed and wavered momentarily as a trickle of rain leaked down the chimney, before returning to its former ruddy glow. From time to time, the narrow window was illuminated by blue-white flashes from the raging lightning beast without. The crackle and cannon fire of the thunder sounded nearer by the minute, great bolts exploding overhead as if a terrible battle raged nearby.

Joe swigged down the remaining dregs of the

scalding black coffee before him and pushed aside his unfinished platter of stew. None of them had much appetite, under the circumstances. His expression was tense, his clear, turquoise eyes muddied with concern.

"And he said nothing that would give you any idea of where he might go?" he asked the housekeeper.

"None at all, sir," Peggy answered. "After ye and the missus here left, I went back to preparing supper. The lad said as how he'd fetch in more kindlin' for the fire, since we were low. After a while, I thought it were takin' him a rare long while t'fetch the wood an' went lookin' fer him. Not a sight nor sound did I find! I came in and finished up about the house, and there were still no sign o'him. I waited outside by the corral 'til long after moonrise, gettin' wilder and wilder by the minute, thinkin' mayhap he'd decided to fell more timber up in the mountain—you know, fer the fine chair the lad's after makin' fer ye, sir?—but he never came back!"

"But, that was two whole days ago!" Seraphina cried. "Oh, Joe, something terrible's happened to him, I know it; I feel it in my bones! He was so ashamed, so upset that day, so certain you thought he'd let you down. He even told me he didn't feel he deserved your friendship."

"Aye, and he was uncommonly quiet after that, too!" Peggy added thoughtfully. "I wonder, now ye come to mention it . . ." She pursed her lips. "Now, maybe I'm clear off me head—an' if I am, I'll thank you t'tell me— but do you remember what it was ye said, sir, when I showed ye the list of provisions we was needin'?"

Joe frowned. "Not clearly. Something about not wanting to leave you and Seraphina and the boy alone while I went into town for them, wasn't it?"

"Exactly, sir! Now, I was wonderin'—since the lad took off right after that—do ye think he might ha'tried to walk into the *pueblo* after the victuals we were needin', by way o'tryin' to prove he was dependable after all?"

"I think Peg's on the right track, Joe," Seraphina agreed eagerly. "The way he was feeling, he'd have done anything to make up for letting you down. Do you still have that list, Peg?"

Peggy shook her head. "Now ye mention it, no, mum! When I went t'add something to it, it weren't in my pinny pocket. I thought as how I'd mislaid it, and didn't put much store by it—leastways, not until now. Oh, to my mind, this only makes everythin' point in the same direction we're after thinkin', mum!"

"I think you're right, too," Joe agreed morosely. "Christ! That bloody young fool! Anything could have happened to him out there! Let's hope he had the sense to give up and try to make it to the Rodriguez place instead of the *pueblo!*" With that, he stood and strode to the door, taking down a yellow slicker that hung from the peg next to it. "Sera, get me a storm lantern, will you, love? Peg, can you lay your hands on another slicker for the boy?"

"And one for me, too," Seraphina added.

Joe shook his head. "No. Just the one extra, Peg. I'm going alone—and no arguments from you, woman!" he cautioned Sera, whose mouth had already popped open to voice a protest. "The storm's bad, and doesn't look like it's about to let up any time soon. The last thing I need is to have you along to worry about, too!"

She grimaced, then smiled impishly in an effort to soften the grim expression he wore. "Oh, well, if nothing else, at least all of this has made you admit you *do* worry about me!" Her smile quickly vanished, to be replaced by an expression of concern. "Please be careful, Joe."

He slung the slicker about his shoulders and jammed on his hat just as Peg returned with the storm lantern

321

and the second slicker he had requested.

"Don't worry, love, I will. After all, I have you to come back to, don't I?" He winked and added in a lower voice as he chucked her beneath the chin, "Keep the bed warm, my little savage, and give me a big kiss to keep me going."

She stood on tiptoe and kissed him fiercely as he bent his fair head to hers, her arms curling tightly around his neck and twining in the small sea of dusty blond waves at his nape.

"Will that do you, you darn old sheepherder, you?" she asked huskily, her lips the color of a crushed crimson rose in the firelight as she pulled back and looked up into his face.

"Just the ticket, love," he murmured, stroking her cheek with the back of his callused hand. "Just the bloody ticket! A kiss like that, a man could walk through fire! G'bye, Peg. I'll be back by dawn, with any luck!"

With that, he battled open the door and, head down against the driving rain, forced his way through it and out into the raging black night. The door, slammed shut by the wind in his wake, sounded like a mighty clap of thunder, and somehow ominously final. Both women flinched at the sound.

"May St. Bridget an' all the Blessed Saints preserve ye an' the lad, sir!" Peg muttered under her breath, crossing herself.

"Amen!" echoed Seraphina. There was a huge knot in her throat that she could not swallow.

Neither of the women could sleep that night, too fraught were they with anxiety for Joe's and Ming's welfare. Instead, they brewed yet another pot of scalding black coffee and sat huddled by the fire in

322

blankets sipping it and listening to the howl of the storm outside or idly watching the writhing dance of the flames in the hearth, alternately lost in thought or quietly conversing.

"T'be sure, it's a terrible thing for a young lad to run away and leave no word o'where he's bound," Peggy said gravely. "I've heard o'mothers who lost their reason on account o'it—not that I'm that young whelp o'Satan's mother, thanks be!" She sniffed and drew from a cheerfully embroidered old flour sack at her feet a pair of knitting needles and a ball of cherry red yarn. "I said it before an' I'll say it again," she said, beginning to knit furiously, "if that young divil ever comes back, I'll give him a taste of my broom handle, that I will, and he'll be hard put to set himself down for a month or more!"

In the firelight, Seraphina could see the tears that misted the older woman's eyes. "You don't fool me, Peggy Kelly," she said softly. "Despite what you say, you're fond of the boy, aren't you?"

Another louder sniff from Peggy. "Fond o'him? Fond o'that heathen pup who hasn't a civil tongue in his head, nor an ounce o'respect for an older lady such as myself? What are ye thinkin' of, mum? Fond, indeed! Whisht!" The needles fairly flew in her hands, and her expression was one of extreme irritation.

Seraphina made no reply. Despite Peg's protests, the answer to her question was obvious. She slid down from the wooden bench and sat with her knees drawn up upon the colorfully braided rag rug before the hearth, which was yet another of Peg's cozy creations. Chin resting on her fist, she gazed into the fire, lost in thought. Peg's words regarding runaways had sunk home, however unwittingly she had said them. Did some mothers truly lose their hold on reason when their youngsters ran away without a word to them?

323

Could her own mother have lost her reason when Aunt Lucinda had returned from Europe last week and she learned that her only daughter had not been with her all these months, and, furthermore, that Aunt Lucinda had believed her safe at home on the ranch in New Mexico and had no idea where she might be, if not there? She bit her lip. Surely not. Such an idea was darn *loco!* Mama had always been so strong, so self-possessed, certainly not the type given to spinsterish vapors and flights of irrationality. Why, she could run the ranch as well as Papa, and often did so on the rare occasions he went away on business, or to visit his relatives on the Cheyenne reservations up north, for she knew every facet of the vast enterprise as well as he. Papa had said many times—and with obvious pride in his handsome black eyes—that his wife had learned ranching from the bottom up, riding herd and learning to rope and brand along with his *vaqueros,* earning their undying affection and respect in the process. She had accompanied him on the hard cattle drives up into Abilene or Denver and eaten trail dust for weeks on end without so much as a murmur of complaint. Surely such a woman couldn't lose her reason, not like one of those feather-brained, sissy heroines in the penny-dreadfuls, who had swooning spells at the first sign of trouble, however small. She tried to bolster her convictions with thoughts upon these lines, but nonetheless, no reassurances she could offer herself managed to totally convince her. When Joe comes back with Ming safe and sound, I'll send a telegraph to the ranch, she determined, telling them I'm well and not to worry about me.

They were both dozing, still sitting up, when the storm finally blew itself out. A bright, clear dawn came soon after. The joyous trilling of birds enjoying an early morning mud bath in the puddles and the brilliant beams of sunshine that lanced through the narrow kitchen window to touch their faces roused them.

Seraphina was the first to open her eyes, forgetting for an instant what she was doing there, sleeping in the kitchen. The fire had burned down to a heap of white ashes; the coffeepot had boiled dry. Peggy sat with her chin lodged on her chest, snoring slightly, her knitting hanging loose in her slack fingers. Memory rushed back to Sera, seeing her there. Of course! Joe and Ming! Maybe they'd returned during the night but had been reluctant to wake them! Oh, surely they had . . .

With a flirting of her long black hair, she jumped to her feet and flung open the heavy plank door, stepping expectantly through it and heading toward the corral and the barn, dodging mud puddles as she went. The morning air smelled fresh and clean. The sharp tang of rain-drenched earth was coolly delicious and bracing, waking her fully. Her expectant smile faded as she reached the barn. Muraco was there, just as she had left him, and he nickered in greeting. But of Joe's paint pony, Jimbo, and the chestnut horse he had taken along for Ming to ride, there was no sign.

"Damn!" she muttered, her hopeful smile replaced by a grim frown now. Hands on hips, she walked out past the corral and stood there in the open, shading her eyes against the bright morning sunshine to look toward the distant Coast Range for some sign of the pair. Nothing, nothing but the broad sweep of the tawny land, dotted with rough grass, with sagebrush and cactus and cottonwoods and a few late wildflowers that the night's rain had brought into bloom. No Joe. No Ming. Disappointed, she turned back toward the kitchen, where Peg was now up and about fixing breakfast of eggs and ham and thick wedges of bread and preserves. The smell of the food cooking usually made her hungry, but today it only made her feel slightly nauseous. She had a sneaking hunch she knew why this was so, and her anxiety for Joe deepened.

"Any sign o'them, mum?" Peg asked eagerly, looking up from her cast-iron black skillet as Sera came through the door. The light ebbed from her eyes as she saw her shake her head.

"Nothing yet, I'm afraid. Lord! I have to get washed up and changed, Peg. I feel as if I've been wearing these same clothes for a year or more—and a skunk would be insulted if he sat down by me right now!" She wrinkled her nose in distaste. "There's nothing we can do to help Joe or Ming, except to get on with the chores and such that have to be done and hope and pray they'll be back soon. I'll help you with breakfast and feed the chickens myself just as soon as I've washed up and changed."

"No hurry, mum. Ye go ahead an' take yer time," Peggy urged with little vigor. This morning, she looked tired and drawn. The anxiety in her eyes had grown.

Seraphina hesitated, then gave Peg a quick, grateful kiss on the cheek, thinking perhaps it was not such a bad idea if Peggy had something to occupy her mind other than worrying herself sick over Ming's welfare. "You're an angel, Peg. Thanks!" she cried and sped from the kitchen via another door that led out into the rest of the *casa* and thence to a large room that Peg had said last night would be hers and Joe's.

It was only upon reaching it that she realized her dilemma. All of her clothes, her soaps, linens, stockings, shoes, and underthings, were in Los Angeles, hopefully in the care of *Señora* Catalina, or else—shudder the thought—on a dusty stagecoach bound for Santa Fe, and growing further away with every passing minute! Still, Joe had brought his things out here with him, and surely he wouldn't object to her borrowing an item or two? Although she had no great fondness for parading about in men's clothing and

326

loved her feminine, frothy things in pastel colors trimmed with lace and threaded through with ribbons, *anything* would be preferable right now to dressing once again in the cotton shirt and baggy *pantalones* she'd worn for the past two days—even if they were laundered!

Joe's room. Oh, yes, spartan as it was under the circumstances, it was definitely his room. Despite his absence, his virile presence still filled it in some indefinable way. She stood in the doorway, feeling like an intruder. The whitewashed walls were bare, the dark angles of the *vigas* the only relief against the white. An Indian blanket of undyed wool woven with bright blue and red geometric patterns had been spread across the adobe floor. There was a rough, wide wooden bed, spread neatly with a similar blanket, with a clean, bleached flour sack stuffed with fresh straw for a comfortable, fragrant pillow. Upon the sea chest beneath the window he had arranged his toilet articles—shaving mug and pig-bristle brush, soap, razor strop and razor—lining them up like neat little soldiers. She crossed the room and picked up the items one by one, turned them over and looked at them, before lifting the shaving soap to her nose and drinking in the clean, masculine smell of it, a fresh, woodsy smell like pines in winter. It was a scent she'd always associate with him. "Lord, I love you so much, Joe! Be careful!" she whispered on the silence. "Even if you are planning to be a goldarned sheep farmer, and even if you're the bossiest, orneriest, most unreasonable man I've ever met, you're the only one who's ever made me feel this crazy way! That other one, the one that's s'posed to be here with you? Well, she couldn't ever love you the way I do, Joel McCaleb. It's Chuck she loves, you see, always has, and I just had to help them out!"

Feeling guilty for having revealed her innermost feelings and thoughts aloud, as if somehow his belongings could relay all that she'd said to him, she quickly set the soap back in its prescribed place and turned to Joe's clothing. How extraordinarily neat and clean he was, she thought, searching through a pile of tidily folded work shirts—quite unlike the cowboys she'd known, who thought a flag should be flown if they took a bath on any day but a Sunday and who expected bands to play when they laundered their clothes! She grinned. Well, this shirt will do just fine, Mister McCaleb, she decided, selecting the most faded blue one she could find. She was about to leave the room with it when she noticed a long-bladed knife sticking out from under the pile. She drew it out and looked at it curiously. It was obviously old, for much of the wooden handle had turned black with usage, but if she peered at it closely enough, she could make out a kangaroo etched into the wood, and the initials J.C. crudely carved beneath it. Not Joe's initials then. Had someone given him the knife? And if so, why would he bother to put it here, to conceal it, almost, instead of making use of it? She ran her thumb along the blade and yelped as a thin thread of blood appeared on the ball of it. Still sharp, too. Strange he wouldn't want to use it, but that was his business. She grinned. All the ranchers she'd ever known had fostered the opinion that sheepherders were a crazy bunch of men. Perhaps this was proof they were right. She snatched up a pair of coveralls and hastily left the spartan room, closing the door carefully behind her.

She had bathed and changed and joined Peggy for breakfast in the kitchen when both women heard riders approaching. They sprang to their feet and almost tripped over each other in their haste to be first through the door.

"Wait, Peg! Careful, now, we don't want to go courtin' trouble," Seraphina warned breathlessly, coming to her senses first. "Fetch the rifle Joe left from inside. It could be the Monroes back again, spoiling for trouble."

Peggy nodded and ran for the rifle. Together, with great caution, they moved away from the house and past the corral to see who their visitors might be. Seraphina all but bit her tongue in shock when she saw them, for, several yards from the corral, two tall Indians sat their shaggy ponies, watching silently as the women approached.

"Oh, Blessed Mary, we're to be scalped and ravished!" Peggy wailed, crossing herself.

"Oh, horsefeathers, Peg! All of that was stopped years ago! Look at them. They're quite harmless."

She headed confidently toward the two, smiling a warm welcome. It was only when she drew closer that she saw a third rider approaching, slowly drawing a *travois* of poles, on which lay a bundled figure.

The blood drained from her cheeks. "Oh, Joe! No, dear Lord . . ." She was off and running toward the third rider, totally ignoring the other two in her dread, her still-damp black hair flying out behind her.

The pony halted and she dropped to her knees in the dirt alongside the *travois*. It was with scant relief that she saw it was not Joe carried upon it, but Ming.

"Oh, my God, no!" she gasped as she looked down at him, for were it not for his mud-caked black hair, she would never have recognized him. Livid bruises mottled his face and both eyes were blackened and swollen shut. Twin trickles of blood had dried under his nostrils, leaving a rusty scab. She managed to control her shock and revulsion and pulled back the blanket that covered him, opening his shirt front to press her ear to his chest and listen to his heart. Thank

329

God, he was still breathing. They had that much to be thankful for. But the lean body beneath the torn shirt was little less bruised than his poor, battered face. Tears brimmed in her eyes and her throat was suddenly choked. Poor lad! Poor, poor Ming!

"Please, bring him up to the house!" she asked the Indian rider in Spanish. He nodded sympathetically and made a guttural clicking sound to his horse. The animal moved slowly on, dragging its unprotesting burden.

"Blessed Mother of God, no!" Peg cried, her hand flying to her mouth in horror as they reached the *casa* and she spied Ming's horribly battered face. "Is he—"

"No, Peg, he's still alive," Seraphina quickly reassured her, "but he's hurt bad." She turned to the Indians. "Please, would you help us carry him inside?"

The tallest man nodded gravely. *"Si, señora. We* will. When we found this one," he said, gesturing toward Ming, "he asked for the one named Joe. Our chief, Tyonek, told us of the woman, Star Dreamer, and of her great-grandfather, Yellow Rock, the Vision Seeker. He also spoke of her man, the one named Joe, and of the many sheep he will bring to the valley. So it was we knew to bring him here."

"But . . . what happened to him?"

The Indian shrugged. "Who can say for certain? Much of the time since we found him, he has slept the great sleep of the wounded and has not been able to tell us. We came upon him just after the storm began, as we headed for our *rancheria* in the mountains after hunting. It seemed he had crawled for some distance despite his great wounds, for the ground was churned up. Last night, we feared to move him, and so my brother rode up to our village to bring back Tyonek, our chief, and with him Satinka, our medicine woman. She cared for the worst of his hurts. Look!" So saying,

330

he drew back the blanket and showed Seraphina Ming's hands. Neat tubes of rawhide had been sewn around his wrists and halfway up his arms, then the skins soaked with water so that they would dry very tightly and hold the limbs firmly in place until the bones knit. "Both wrists were broken, little sister! It was Satinka's thought that the boy had been tied and dragged behind a pony by them. Thorns and dirt and small rocks were everywhere upon his clothing, you see." He shook his head, his black eyes grave. "Whoever did this thing was evil!"

Together, the three hunters carried the *travois* inside the *casa* and laid Ming down upon the same plank table that he had made himself with such glowing optimism weeks before. At once, Peggy was at his side with cloths and a basin of hot water and salve to bathe his wounds, clucking worriedly like a nervous mother hen. "Oh, ye young divil, ye poor, young fool!" she crooned tenderly. "What have they done to ye, me poor boyo?"

Seraphina turned back to the hunters, whose names, they told her, were Yakecen, Wichado, and Milap. Wichado, who stood taller than the rest, was the one she had spoken with. He appeared to be the leader of the three in his felt hat decorated with silver *conchas* and eagle feathers at the crown. "Wichado, we are forever in your debt for the great help you have given us this day," she told him warmly. "The boy is one loved by all of us here at Casa Campanas. Thank you for bringing him here. Will you eat and rest yourselves?"

Wichado shook his head. "Our thanks, but we have already eaten, little sister. Your offer of hospitality brings warmth and gladness to the heart of Wichado and his companions, who are your friends. I shall ask the Great Spirit to watch over Star Dreamer and those dear to her until she visits our village again. Now, we must return to the mountains. Farewell, little sister."

331

"Farewell, Wichado. And may the Great Spirit guard your path also."

With the quiet courtesy with which they had arrived, Wichado and his companions left.

"How is he?" Seraphina asked anxiously, going to Ming's side. Peggy had cut the clothing from him, and she saw the ugly bruises and cuts that marred his lean young torso and shoulders. There was little of his body that did not bear a bruise or a deep, angry graze or welt of some kind, and dried blood made the removal of his clothes difficult, the slightest shifting of his body eliciting a groan of agony from the boy.

"That medicine woman or whatever it was they were after callin' her did a fine job o'doctorin'," Peggy said grudgingly, "but he's terrible bruised an' such, and there's little fight left in him. I'm after thinkin' it couldn't ha' been a fall he took!"

As unemotionally as possible, Seraphina told her what Wichado had said.

"Dragged? Blessed Mary and the Saints! Why, who in his right mind would do that to this young divil? He's never so much as harmed a fly in his entire life, I'd warrant!" Peggy cried, ruddy color crimsoning her cheeks in her outrage and indignation.

"You're wrong, Peggy," Seraphina corrected. "Remember? He made a fool of that Stevie Monroe and bloodied his nose. That young rattlesnake didn't strike me as the type to forgive and forget, either! I can't be certain, but I wouldn't put it past the Monroes to have done something like this," she added grimly. "The cowardliness of it stinks of their brand, those yellow-bellied polecats! Lord, when Joe sees Ming this way, I wouldn't want to be in their boots, not for anything! Now, let's see if we can make Ming a bit more comfortable . . ."

Chapter Twenty

"Now come on, Joe, please!" Seraphina implored. "You can't ride out there and shoot the lot of them single-handed! Be reasonable!"

Joe swung about and glowered down at her as he buckled his gun belt across his lean hips. His eyes were molten, silvery-turquoise in the fiery white-heat of his fury. "Reasonable, you say? Christ! I ask you, Sera, were they *reasonable*? They attacked an unarmed, innocent boy, beat the hell out of him, then just for fun of it dragged him a mile or so behind their horses and left him to the buzzards? If you ask me, hanging's too bloody good for those bastards. I mean to make them suffer inch by inch, just they way they made Ming suffer, and nail their hides to a fence when I'm done, like the coyotes they are!"

He snatched up his hat and headed for the door he had entered not an hour before, after returning from his fruitless search for Ming. His anger and outrage had been terrible when he saw the unconscious, battered Chinese boy, and it had built still more when Ming had come to for a few minutes and managed with great difficulty—and even greater reluctance—to tell him it had been the Monroes who had attacked him, all the while imploring him not to go after them and endanger himself. Both Seraphina and Peggy had flinched as Joe cursed the Monroes foully and heatedly for what they had done in a violent tone they had never heard him use before. Then he had grown very quiet, and that, in some awful way, had been far worse.

He sighted down the nose of his black forty-five and squinted as he spun the gleaming barrel. Satisfied, he slid the weapon snugly into the holster at his hip. He did the same with the second gun, then said grimly, "I'll be back when I see this thing through."

She tightened her jaw, fear knotting up in the pit of her belly and squeezing tight in her chest. If anything happened to him . . . The thought made her feel sick and giddy with dread.

"Go on, then, you darned, hotheaded fool!" she screamed hoarsely at him. "Go right ahead and get yourself shot, if you're so damned eager to fill a pine box! They outnumber you five to one—but don't let those odds bother you none, Mister Joel McCaleb. I'll just tell our baby his daddy died like a man—a fool of a man, but a man nonetheless. I'm sure it'll be a real consolation to him when he's growing up alone." Her tone dripped acid.

"Baby? What baby?" His shaggy blond brows rose with an amazement that would have been funny at any other time.

"You heard me! You don't think I came back just to warn you that day, do you?" she taunted, hoping to convince him. "Hell, no, McCaleb! I wouldn't do that for a . . . a goldarned fool! But the baby I'm carrying will need a father, and I guess I was stupid enough to think no one but you could fit the bill. I was wrong. You go right ahead and walk out of that door, Joe. I'll find a replacement, don't worry. Papas are a dime a dozen, especially when there's a rich young widow for a wife—and one with Las Campanas for a fine dowry into the bargain! If me and our baby coming can't make you see sense, what about the land, Joe, your precious land? Who'll keep the Monroes off it with you gone, tell me that? Who'll stop them from making the entire San Juliano Valley theirs?"

She tossed her long black hair over her shoulders and faced him defiantly, blocking his exit through the door with her slender body. Her gray-green eyes were blazing, her fists planted on her hips. In his oversized shirt, and with the baggy coveralls rolled up about her slim legs, she looked barely old enough to be married, let alone carrying a child herself. She was though. She'd suspected as much for over a week now, though she'd tried to put it out of her mind, had hoped she was wrong, considering the way things had stood between her and Joe then.

Some of the fury dwindled in him. His shoulders slackened a fraction, and the tension ebbed from his features, to be replaced by wariness. "Oh, no, woman, that old trick won't work! And don't bother thinking up another one, because I've heard 'em all, sweetheart! You're just saying that to keep me from going. You're meddling again, aren't you, love? Hell, look at you!" he scoffed. "Your belly's as trim and flat as a ten-year-old's! It's my bet that you're lying, Mrs. McCaleb! Now, if you'll just step aside like a good girl, I'll be on my way."

"Over my dead body!" she spat. "Where's it written that a woman has to look like she's swallowed a . . . a melon, when she's only a month or so gone? I'm telling you, Joe, I'm pregnant! If you go through this door, it'll be over me, not around me, so help me God!"

He grimaced and shrugged, then strode to the door, grasped her by the waist and lifted her bodily aside before gently setting her down. "Didn't think of that,

335

did you, love?" A faint grin tugged at the corners of his mouth as he saw how furious she was, and he tweaked her cheek.

She angrily tossed her head away from his hand and her jaw came up. "Nope, I guess I didn't. Well? What are you waiting for? Go ahead, McCaleb, keep walking. There's no one stopping you now!"

He took a step into the doorway, then seemed to hesitate before going through it.

"What's wrong? Having second thoughts?"

His eyes narrowed as they flickered over her body, but in her baggy clothing, it was hard to tell anything. "Are you really carrying my baby?" he demanded.

"You'll never know, will you, Joe—leastways, not if you keep on going. You won't take more than a step onto Rancho Fuerte land before they fill you so full of hot lead you'll rattle like a pair of castanets! It seems they're smarter than I gave them credit for. They knew just how to bring you out, didn't they, Joe? They roughed Ming up for more than one reason, I'd bet, and I have a hunch just what that other reason was, besides revenge for poor little ole Stevie's broken nose. It was a trap, Joe, and Ming was their bait! And sure enough, you're ranting and roaring and just itchin' to ride off to Fuerte and deliver yourself to their doorstep, just like they planned!"

"I suppose you have a better idea?" he challenged, his fists balled on his hips.

She shrugged. "I don't know about better, but more sensible. Heck, yes! Go to the sheriff in town. Tell him what's happened and let him handle it. Don't play this game on the wrong side of the law like they do. Be better than them, Joe. Do it fair and square!" she implored him.

"Fair? There are no 'fair and square' laws to protect Ming's people's rights, Sera! Where have you been

336

living for the past twenty years that you don't know there's no justice in this land today for anyone but white men? Get your head out of the sand, girl, and take a long, hard look at things as they are! I've seen for myself how the Chinese are treated back in San Francisco, not to mention the Mexicans and the Chileans—yes, and the Indians, too. If a white man robs from them, murders their family, Christ, they can't even testify or call witnesses against him! It's my guess it's little different out here. I'd get more justice if someone stole my horse than those bastards would get for what they've done to Ming! My way is the only way, the only law those rattlesnakes understand: the law of the gun!"

"Won't you at least try it my way first?" she cajoled, her voice husky with fear. "Please, Joel? What have you got to lose by waiting? Then, if it works out as you say, I'll leave it up to you, I swear it! What difference can putting it off a day or so make, Joe? The Monroes will still be there. You can still ride to Rancho Fuerte if the sheriff refuses to take action."

He frowned. "Did you mean what you said . . . about the baby?"

She hesitated, then gave a nod. "Yes. At least, I'm pretty sure." She reddened. "My . . . you know . . . it's late, real late."

He stepped toward her, seeming enormously tall in that instant, dwarfing her as she stood there. Yet his expression was no longer hard and unrelenting, but foolishly tender and somehow awed. He tossed aside his hat and bent his head to hers, tilting her chin up so that he might plant a kiss full upon her pink lips. "I always wondered how it would feel to have a woman say she was carrying my child; that I was going to be a father. Now I know."

"And? How does it feel?" she asked, suddenly breathless with anxiety.

"Bloody marvelous, love!" He caught her about the waist and tugged her against him, kissing her fervently. His tongue tip parted her moist lips as he delved deep within her mouth, his palm caressing the flat expanse of her belly as he did so. "Christ, shouldn't you be lying down or something?" he asked anxiously when he had finished kissing her, then nodded toward the bed.

"That's the only good idea you've had all morning, Joe," she murmured seductively, taking his hand and leading him toward it. "The 'something,' not the 'lying down' part . . ." It might not be altogether honest, but if a full-out attempt at seducing him took his mind off going to Rancho Fuerte and getting himself shot, it would be well worth it. "I was so worried while you were gone, Joe," she continued in a small, frightened voice. "You can't imagine what went through my mind."

She unbuttoned the straps to her coveralls and shucked them off, stepping from them to stand a little shyly before him in his outsized blue shirt that only just covered her bare bottom. She moistened her lips and eyed him archly with her head cocked to one side as she started to unfasten the shirt, button by button. The sunlight streaming through the window and painting golden bars across the polished adobe floor caught the gloss of her hair and reflected bluish highlights. "When a woman loves . . . loves a man, she always imagines the worst, you know," she continued. "If he's even an hour or so late home, she thinks he's got his fool self killed falling off his horse!" She held out her arms to him, the shirt gaping open its entire length now, revealing a tantalizing glimpse of pale gold breasts tipped with dark rose buds, a trim waist just made to be spanned by a man's large hands, and sleek hips beneath. "Don't go, darlin'! Stay here with me. Make me forget all the worrying I did while you were gone last night, Joel, please, honey?" she whispered. "Make me forget the way that only you know how . . ."

He grinned wolfishly, his turquoise eyes raking her body, devouring her whole as she stood there. "Witch!" he muttered. "I know your little game—don't think I don't!"

She smiled and flirted her dark lashes at him, swinging the curtain of silken hair over her shoulders in a provocative gesture calculated to arouse him. Her nipples, barely covered, made tiny hillocks where they jutted impudently against the faded blue cloth of his shirt. They drew his eyes like magnets.

"So you know my game, do you, McCaleb? Then I guess I have only one more question to ask myself, right?" she murmured, stepping gracefully toward him and letting the shirt slide down from her arms and shoulders and fall carelessly to the floor in a crumpled heap while she stood, quite naked now, before him.

"What's that?" he asked heavily, his resolve dwindling, his breathing thickening as she curled her arms about his throat and pressed her warm, bare body to his hard length. He could feel his heart thudding rapidly against the crushed swell of her breasts, the taut buds of her hardened nipples rubbing erotically against his shirtfront.

"Are you going to fall for it, honey?" she breathed in his ear, darting her tongue along its outline.

Gooseflesh rose all over him and she felt his manhood thrusting hard against her belly as he retorted, "Christ! I reckon you already know the answer to that, woman!"

He lifted her into his arms and strode with her to the bed. Like she'd said, the Monroes would still be there tomorrow.

Much later, they lay in an intimate tangle upon the

339

rumpled blankets of Joe's wide, rough-hewn bed, which still had the scent of fresh pine about it. Joe's stubbly blond cheek rested just below the rounded swell of her breasts. His palm lay flat and possessive across her belly. His expression was intent, his eyes closed. Sera laughed softly as she caressed his fair head with idle, stroking motions.

"Of course you can't feel anything yet, silly," she murmured drowsily in answer to his comment moments earlier. "It's far too soon for that."

"I'm telling you, my son just kicked me, right here," Joe insisted, his tone a drowsy drawl that partnered hers. He tickled her in the spot he'd indicated, and she squirmed and writhed away from him.

"Oh, you just stop that, McCaleb! I'm too darned lazy right now for any more of your playing!" There was sleepy amusement in her tone, despite her scolding words. She yawned.

Joe chuckled. "And so you should be played out, you little wildcat," he teased, rolling from the bed and fastening a linen towel around his lean hips as he fetched the makings for a smoke. "You just about wore me into the ground! Keep that up, and I'll be an old man, worn out before my time!" He rolled his eyes and ducked as a straw-filled pillow came hurtling across the room, aimed at his head.

"Some gentleman you are!" she accused, snuggling deeper into the softness of the down-filled pallet. "It ain't right to kiss and tell, mister—or kiss and accuse, come to that!"

"I spoke only the truth, ma'am, so help me God," Joe said in his best western accent, coming across to stand beside the bed and look down at her. Her eyes were closed, but she was smiling.

"I know," she murmured, her tone smug as she drifted into sleep.

He smiled crookedly too, and bent to kiss her flushed cheek, brushing a raven-dark strand of silken hair away from her face. His wife. *His*. Christ! He could scarcely believe his luck! She was beautiful, intelligent, spirited, passionate, and fun to be with. And on top of all that, she loved him! Oh, yes, she loved him, all right. It was there in her eyes, in her lips, in her body when she surrendered herself heart and soul to him! Less than a month ago, he'd thought it was all over between them and had sought to drown out her memory in liquor, and now here she was, lying there sleek and content from his loving, their baby growing in her belly. And he'd almost been fool enough to risk losing all that by going after the Monroes with both guns loaded. He shook his head. "You're a bloody fool sometimes, Lightnin' Joe," he told himself.

If the truth were known, his happiness and love for Sera—coupled with the ownership of Las Campanas— scared him a little, way down deep inside, for he was unused to largesse of any kind. It was almost as if the newfound contentment growing inside him day by day was some mean trick of Lady Luck's, just another of that fickle bitch's sly ploys to lull him into a false sense of security while the winds of chance plotted his ultimate destruction. And, he feared his lucky streak was destined to run out, sooner or later, as all lucky streaks did. Christ, that was a damned sobering thought! After all, other people had their chance at happiness. Why should he feel he was in any way different, less deserving of happiness, than they? Hadn't he already had more than his fair share of hard times when he was even younger than Ming was now? Hadn't he paid Lady Luck her due, for Christ's sake?

He frowned, drawing deep on the hand-rolled cigarette between his lips, blue smoke spiraling from his nostrils. Maybe that was why he'd felt such protectiveness toward the boy from the start, such white-hot anger at the injustice of the beating he had received. Perhaps he'd recognized himself at that age in the proud, determined Chinese lad, and had wanted to save him from making the same mistakes he had made with his own life. And now, in a matter of months, he'd have a son to protect and care for, too! Aye, he was sure it would be a boy, he mused confidently, trailing his palm down over Sera's bare stomach with none of his former hesitation, for she was sleeping now and couldn't tease him for his fascination with her condition.

"It'll be different for you, son," he promised softly. "You'll have a mama and papa to love you and look out for you, a name that's all yours, and not one pinned on you like a stray pup, I swear it!"

Yet even as he made the vow, doubt slithered into his thoughts to gnaw at his confidence. He stood and walked to the window, his mind and emotions both in turmoil. What he'd promised the unborn babe had seemed simple enough a moment ago; it had been a promise given from the depths of his heart. But, what right did he have to give his son the McCaleb name as if it were his due? McCaleb wasn't his father's rightful name any more than Christmas was, but at least Christmas was his *legal* name, however much he hated it. And what about his and Sera's marriage? If it were somehow to come to light that he was an imposter, would they still be married in the eyes of the law, or would his son be born a bastard, as he suspected he had been himself? And then, that being the case, what about his right to Rancho de las Campanas? Something cold and dread-filled stirred and spread through him, chilling him to the marrow. The real Joel 'Mac' McCaleb had given him both his name and the inheritance that went with it, but the only *true* claim he might have upon the land was through his marriage to Sera, as the other beneficiary of William McCaleb's will, and their marriage certificate wasn't even worth the paper it was printed on! Christ, what an almighty mess! But, thank God, there was a way out of this, if he wanted to safeguard his—and thereby his son's—interests. He could marry his Seraphina all over again, this time with his real name on the papers. All he'd have to do was tell her the truth . . . All? Huh! Who was he kidding? It wouldn't be easy, not easy at all. And there was no guarantee that once she knew the whole story, her feelings for him wouldn't change. What woman would calmly accept the news that the man she loved was not only a liar, but also an imposter? Strewth! Just the thought of it made sweat break out on his palms and brow. Calm down, Lightnin' Joe, he told himself. There was no rush. He had a few months yet to work it out. Meanwhile, the problem of the Monroes was the one most urgently needing his attention . . .

He dressed and left Sera soundly asleep, going to the kitchen to see how Ming was doing.

"How is he, Peg?" he asked, nodding at the boy.

"Running a fever, sir," Peggy supplied, in the act of wringing out a cool cloth to bathe the lad's brow. "But his bruises have gone down a mite, I fancy."

"Has he come to again?"

"Aye, he has, once or twice. He asked for you, sir, and for water, and I gave him a little. For the rest o'the time, he's been gabbling on in his heathen Chinee, an' I'll be blessed if I can make head or tail out o'his gobbley-gook! He kept on saying as how he were awful sorry fer lettin' ye down, too, sir."

"Soon as he's able to understand, I'll have a talk with him," Joe promised.

Peggy snorted. "An' if you don't, then I will!"

Joe grinned his engaging, crooked grin. "Hate him,

343

do you, Peg?"

"I never said hated," she denied tartly. "But, does he make my blood fair boil with his cheekiness? Aye, he does that, sir!"

"Did you and your husband never have children?"

"That we did. Five in all, and not a one lived t'see its first birthday." She sighed heavily. "I fancy sometimes it were that what put Mister Kelly in his grave over-early. Wanted children powerful bad, that man did. I lost track o'all the waifs he brought t'me fer tendin' over the years. But, they grew up, got old enough t'tend to themselves, an' left. I tell ye, sir, there was an emptiness when they were gone that nothing else could fill. A house is just a place t'hang yer hat when it's without a child. With a family, it's a home." She set her shoulders and stood up, turning away so Joe could not see the suspicious dampness sparkling in her eyes. "Well, now, all this idle yammerin', pleasant as it might be, won't see the lad's broth cooked, now will it, sir? If you'll let me get on, I'll be after seein' to it, and to you and the missus's supper, as well."

Joe nodded and discreetly left her to her kitchen and her charge. Whether Ming knew it or not, he had one hell of a mother in Peggy Kelly—a Chinese son with an Irish mother, no less! Joe shrugged as he strode out to the corral. What the heck? Love was blind when it came to race, color, or creed; it was capable of surmounting and breaking down all barriers, thank God—which was just the way it should be. He only hoped the love between a man and a woman was strong enough to survive the harsh light of truth.

Chapter Twenty-One

Ming's fever broke during the night, thanks to Peggy's tender nursing of him, and by late morning it appeared the boy was on the road to recovery. He wouldn't be able to use his hands until the wrist bones knit, however, and so would require being fed, dressed, and cared for like a babe for perhaps as long as two months more. Peg seemed not to realize—or rather, to care—that she'd be hard-pressed to see to the boy and still continue her regular, arduous duties about the ranch house. But Joe, watching her carefully spooning broth into the boy and grumbling fondly all the while in her broody-hen fashion, understood only too well how difficult it would be, and he determined to see about finding a girl to help both her and Seraphina. He didn't know much about pregnant women, but it seemed to him Sera would need a great deal of rest in the coming months, and it was unlikely—being Seraphina—that she'd see to getting it when there was so much to be done about the *rancho* and no one else to do it in her place with Peg so busy. As it turned out, his wish was granted far sooner than he had expected, and without him ever having to leave the ranch at all.

Two days later, a wagon arrived bearing three men

345

and a slim, dark-haired girl sent, they told Joe, from the *pueblo* of the Angels by the shepherds he'd sent down into New Mexico to purchase sheep, Raoul Garnier and Esteban Rodriguez.

"My name is Gabrielle Garnier, Don José," the pixie-faced young woman introduced herself in delightfully Basque-accented English. "I am Raoul Garnier's only daughter. This handsome *hombre* here is my betrothed, Jaime Santiago, and the others are two of Papa's closest friends, Pepito Morales and Stefano Bartholomeo. They are all very fine shepherds and herders, and Papa told us you would soon have need of good hands here at Las Campanas, *oui, monsieur?* For myself, I go wherever Jaime and my papa go since the Monroes destroyed our home, and so, 'ere I am!" She shrugged her slender yet wiry shoulders and smiled. "There is always much work to do on any *rancho,* and I am a hard worker. Certainly I can help with the cooking and the cleaning, yes?"

"The Monroes did what?" Joe asked, startled by what she'd said.

"They burned us out—over a year ago, it was. My papa did not tell you this?"

Joe shook his head.

Gabrielle smiled. "He is a proud one, my papa. He does not like to tell others of his misfortunes. And I think . . . yes, I think that he is a little ashamed, too, though he has no cause to be. You see, they forced him at gunpoint to sign our land over to them. He was not afraid of them, or their guns, but they told him if he did not sign, they would harm me." She shrugged. "I am Papa's only daughter. What else could he do?"

Joe nodded in sympathetic understanding. So, that explained why Raoul Garnier had been so eager to help him; eager to see Las Campanas' range scattered with sheep. He also wanted revenge upon Harper Monroe, in any way he could get it without endangering his daughter. Were there more families scattered hereabouts who felt the same way, people who'd crossed Monroe and suffered because of it? Singly, they were vulnerable to the sheer numbers of the Monroes, but perhaps together they could make a stand, could do something . . . It would bear thinking about later, but first, he was determined to pay the sheriff in town a visit, as Sera had suggested.

He immediately liked Gabrielle Garnier and the three men with her, and he congratulated himself once again on choosing Raoul Garnier and Esteban Rodriguez as the men to go down into New Mexico to select the breeding stock for his flocks. He expected they'd choose the seed rams and breeding ewes as carefully as they had chosen the three new men.

"We can certainly use your help," a grinning Joe agreed in answer to Gabrielle's firm declaration. "Welcome to Las Campanas, Gabrielle, Jaime, Pepito, Stefano! We haven't much here as yet, but I hope one day, with your father's help, to make this *rancho* a place we can all be proud of!"

Gabrielle smiled. "So my papa said. He admires you very much, you know, for your determination to ranch here in the valley despite Monsieur Monroe. Please, from now on, you must call me Gabby, yes, as do all my dear friends? Gabrielle is much too formal! Jaime . . . ?"

Her betrothed, a dark-eyed, curly-haired Romeo who hung upon her every delightful word, obediently went around to the back of the wagon and let down the flap. Joe followed him, gaping in surprise. A cow and a calf were tethered to the rear, the cow's udder swollen with milk. In the wagon bed were piled small trees, their bushy roots swathed in dampened sackcloth, and numerous other bulky items. Atop them all curled an

347

enormously pregnant calico cat, which uttered a plaintive meow of indignation at their disturbance of her nap. She stood, arched her back, and stretched hugely, then sprang down to the dirt. Casting a disdainful, amber-eyed glance in Joe's direction, she flicked her tail and stalked aloofly away toward the house.

"I have a feeling I've just been judged and found wanting!" Joe said with a wry grin, nodding toward the cat.

Gabby smiled. "Lately she is that way with all males, human and animal alike, *monsieur!* Per'aps as a result of a distressing experience a few weeks ago with a handsome tomcat, who later proved himself unworthy of her affections?" She winked. "That is why my papa named her Madame, for she is a very aloof little lady. Nevertheless, our dear Madame is also an excellent mouser, and she and her kittens will keep your storerooms quite free of mice! Now, as for these," she added, gesturing to the plants, "they are for your future orchards, *monsieur.* There are orange and peach and other fruit trees, and also some plants for pretty flowers and vegetables, a gift to you and your wife from the Garnier family. And right here are the trunks of clothing that Doña Seraphina left in the care of Señora Catalina at the inn, who, by the way, sends her warmest greetings to you both. There are other things, too, things that you might have need of."

So it was that Gabrielle and Jaime, Pepito and Stefano—and, of course, Madame—joined their numbers at Casa Campanas. From the first, neither Pepito nor Stefano would consent to sleep under the *casa's* roof, superstitious about the haunting legend of the bells and of the ghost of the Indian maiden, Little Owl and her curse, which were known to one and all for miles around. Joe and the three men spent the next few days dismantling an old storeroom at the rear of the *casa* and in using the adobe bricks from it, as well as newly felled timbers from the mountains, to construct a bunkhouse for the new hands some distance from the main house and at a right angle to it, and for days the dun-colored, low hills resounded with the echo of their ringing hammers. Madame, not to be outdone, proved that she considered herself well and truly moved in by making a nest of wood shavings for herself in one of the storerooms and promptly giving birth to a litter of four tiny kittens, two of which resembled their proud mama, and two, possibly, their coal black, absent papa, though no one could be certain on that score, and Madame did not prove to be a lady who would kiss and tell.

When the bunkhouse was completed, the three shepherds moved their meager belongings into it, erected their post-and-rawhide beds, hung ornate saddles and bridles from the convenient wooden pegs, and seemed content to remain there forever. In the evenings, Pepito strummed his guitar, Stefano idly plucked his mandolin, and Jaime and Gabrielle sang both Basque and Spanish melodies, sitting cross-legged under the bright stars that seemed close enough to reach up and pluck like brilliant flowers, while a chorus of amorous coyotes yipped and yapped a harmony in the distance. It soon became a tradition that, weather permitting, almost every night after a tasty supper cooked by the three women and which everyone ate seated around the trestle table Ming had made, Joe, Seraphina, Peggy and a fast-recovering Ming would stroll out to listen to them, enjoying both their singing and the cool, sweet air of evening. It was on one such evening that Gabby mentioned that she and Jaime planned to be wed soon and told of their intention to ride into the *pueblo* for the occasion.

"Joe, couldn't we have the wedding here?" Sera asked, bright-eyed and eager. "They could have the service in the chapel, and afterward we could have our first *fiesta* at Casa Campanas!"

Joe grinned. "Sounds just the ticket, love, but it's up to Gabby and Jaime. Jaime?"

Gabby and her fiancé's delighted smiles were answer enough, and Seraphina and Peggy started planning the wedding and the feast immediately.

By now, Ming's injuries, save for his poor wrists, were almost a thing of the past. As Joe had promised Peggy, he'd talked to the boy, two days after Gabrielle and her entourage's arrival.

"It's about time we cleared the air about what happened to you, son," Joe had said, taking a seat by the boy's makeshift bed in the kitchen. His expression had been stern, his vivid eyes without their customary twinkle.

"Yes, Joe," the boy had agreed, swallowing and averting his own eyes.

"Taking off like you did was the stupidest damn thing you could have done. You left Peggy alone, and that was unforgivable. You have any explanations for it?"

Ming had gulped. "I have none, Joe. It was most foolish of me. I betrayed your trust, and I am sorry. It . . . it will never happen again."

"You're damned right it won't!" he had snapped. "When you're on your feet again, you and me have a little something we have to do out back of the barn, I'd say."

"Something? Excuse me, but I do not understand, Joe?" His almond eyes had been puzzled.

"You will, cobber—when I lay my belt across your britches the first time!" Joe had said grimly.

Ming had swallowed and bowed his head. "Yes,

Joe," he had said quietly but without resentment.

They had kept that appointment, too. Ming had moved even more stiffly for the next day or so, and had been more than willing to stand instead of sit. Yet after that, he had brightened, become more his resilient, old self, and Peggy had taken to cursing him again and calling him a damned, heathen whelp once more in her former "fond" fashion, which no one who had seen her tend him so carefully could any longer be deceived by. Seraphina, on the other hand, had been furious when she had learned of the whupping Joe had given Ming.

"How could you, Joe?" she had cried, tracking him down in the *ramada*—the shed—soon after.

"How could I what?" he had asked, though he had really known all along what had riled her so.

"How could you punish Ming? Lord! Didn't he go through enough at the Monroes' hands? How could you be so darn heartless?"

He had tipped back his hat and paused in tightening the girth on Jimbo's saddle, regarding her thoughtfully. "It had to be done, Sera. Can't you see he's better, almost his old self again now? As long as he kept on blaming himself for the Monroes' busting in here and tearing up the place that day, he couldn't stand his own guilt. It was eating away at him! My saying I didn't hold him to account only made it worse, because y'see, love, he still held *himself* to account for it. Now he reckons he's taken his punishment and can face me again. Sometimes, a man needs to be called to answer for his faults, just so's he can put them behind him and get on with living again." Like me with Ned Sullivan's death back in Sydney, he had added silently. Oh, yes, he still carried the scars of his guilt over that, and would 'til his dying day, he reckoned—just as the nagging doubts about his being here, under a false name, the lies he'd told Sera, still worried his conscience.

351

"Men!" she had snorted. "You're all plain *loco,* if you ask me!"

"That's not what you said last night, *chiquita!*" he had retorted, grinning wickedly. "If I recall, what you said was that I was *'muy viril, muy macho!'*"

She had flushed. He had been fast picking up numerous Spanish expressions from the new Mexican hands, and not a day had passed lately when he had failed to tease her with one or another of them. Well, two could play at that game! she had decided. *"Cojónes!"* Seraphina had insisted hotly and with great relish added, "I lied!" With that shocking comment and his deep laughter ringing in her reddened ears, she had fled back to the house.

Despite how it might have appeared on the surface, Joe had neither forgiven nor forgotten the Monroes. Nor had his intent to make them pay for what they had done to Ming been set aside. It had merely been postponed. Now, with the new flock scheduled to arrive within a week or so and hands available to protect the women in his absence, he figured the time was now or never for dealing with them. Telling only Ming and Jaime where he was going, for he knew Seraphina would either make some protest or insist upon coming with him, he rode into Los Angeles and went straightway to the sheriff's office.

Sheriff Tallant was a tall, beefy, gray-haired man. He appeared tough, an iron hand on the pulse of the *pueblo* and surrounding areas—or, at least, it seemed so at first glance. Joe soon had his real measure however, and saw the grit in him did not run any deeper than the fancy silk shirts and bandannas the man affected.

"The boy's a Chinee, you say, McCaleb? Surely you can't expect me to lock up the Monroes on account of a little tussle with a Chinee?" Tallant snorted. "Hell, I'd

352

be a laughingstock! Where've you been, boy, that you don't know the Chinees and their like don't have no rights in the eyes o'the law?"

"And what about my rights, since he's working for me? The Monroes put one of my hands out of action, for Christ's sake, and that makes me real mad. I'm the one making this complaint, Tallant, not him!"

Tallant's jaw squared stubbornly. "Don't make no never mind, McCaleb. Ain't a thing I can do. Now, why don't you jest go on back out to your ranch and forget all about it?"

"Hell if I will! I've been told I'm a stubborn cuss, Sheriff! I'm not leaving the *pueblo* 'til I hear it from you personally that you mean to do something about this."

"Then you'll wait 'til Hell freezes over, McCaleb!" Tallant spat, and a thin stream of yellow tobacco juice squirted into the brass spittoon in one corner of the office with a twang as it hit metal. Past near misses showed as yellow-brown stains all about the plank floor.

"Why don't you admit it, Tallant. You're so damned afraid, you're shaking in your fancy tooled boots! Afraid of crossing Monroe and his boys, like all the rest hereabouts!" Joel jeered softly. "Just exactly what hold does he have over you, sheriff? Your badge—is that it?"

Tallant blanched. "You'd best be real careful what you say, McCaleb!" he threatened. "I don't know what neck of the woods you're from, but men have been gunned down out here for less than what you're implying. I'm no yellow belly!"

"No? Then prove it! Go out to Rancho Fuerte. Bring Monroe and his boys in for questioning. Let a judge decide if they're guilty or not."

"Hell, the circuit judge ain't due through these parts for more'n a month yet. An' even if I wanted to, I couldn't get enough men together for a posse to go after the Monroes," Clem Tallant insisted lamely.

"More excuses, eh? Well, I can't say I'm surprised to hear them. Seems just about everyone around here has a streak of yellow running through him," Joe said darkly, "and it surely ain't gold! Thanks for nothing, Sheriff. You've answered my questions. I guess the only justice I'll get around here is what I make for myself!"

He turned on his heel and left the office, stepping into the dusty, narrow street, spurs jingling as he strode down it. He sensed Tallant's hate-filled eyes boring into his back, and the hair at his nape rose in prickling awareness. As he untied Jimbo from the hitching post and started to lead the horse across the street, he had the strongest sensation that Tallant might shoot him in the back, so angry had he been. But no bullet was forthcoming. He left Jimbo out front and turned into a noisy saloon on Cantina Row without incident, striding through the swinging half-doors and into the rowdy establishment. Weaving his way between the gaudy saloon girls and drinking and gambling patrons to the bar, he bellied up to it with a boot heel hooked over the brass foot rail.

Over a few warm beers, he did some digging into Clem Tallant's past and learned from the garrulous bartender that the sheriff had been elected to his office two years before solely by virtue of Harper Monroe's support and no little intimidation of the townsfolk. In the process, he also learned the answer to Monroe's dark influence over the people thereabouts. They had no recourse whatsoever to the law when he threatened them, for the law *was* Sheriff Tallant—and Tallant was completely in Monroe's pocket.

"Everything Clem has, he has Monroe to thank for," the bartender supplied, wiping his whiskey glasses. "His position here in town, his house, fancy schooling

354

back east for his daughter, Cissy, everything. When he came here a few years back, he and the little girl had nothing but the clothes they stood up in, and that weren't saying much. He'd struck it rich in the gold fields, see, then squandered the lot gambling and whooping it up back in 'Frisco. Expensive town, San Francisco, even in those days. There's many a man went broke just trying to live day by day. Tallant had lost his fight by the time he came here. Seemed like an empty shell more'n a man, and the little girl weren't much better. Monroe saw he could easily control him through her, and he set about making it so Clem would be so goldarned beholden to him, he'd never get out from under! He hasn't yet—though I've a hunch he'd like to, if he only knew how and could find the backbone to do it." The bartender grinned ruefully. "Hell, McCaleb, I'd like to find the backbone to stand up to'm myself, tell the truth!" He leaned on his elbows across the scarred bar top as he continued in a lower voice, "Seems about once a month, regular as clockwork, them Monroe boys and their hands come riding into town, whooping an' hollerin' an' shootin' wild, and they make straight for my place. When they leave, there ain't hardly a glass that ain't broken or a mirror that ain't smashed. And that Val Monroe, he's the worst of the bunch. Got a thing for one o'my gals, he has, name of Leila. See her over there, that little yeller-haired gal by the piano?" Joe glanced across the crowded room and spied the brassy, not unpretty, blonde. He nodded, sipping his beer. "Figures she's s'posed to wait on his visits inter town, Val does, an' he hears she's so much as looked at another man while he's been gone . . . well, you don't want to be around Val Monroe when he's taken by one o'his jealous fits . . . !" The bartender shook his head. "When he and his goldarned brothers light out o'Cantina Row, there's always one or other o'my gals that's been roughed up some. An' replacin' the things they bust gets to bein' real expensive, let me tell you. Heck, I'm lucky if I break even, most months! Find a way to checkin' Harper and his boys and their wild doin's, and you'll have yourself a whole *pueblo* full o'friends, McCaleb!"

"Amen to that, Bartender!" said a voice, and Joe spun around to see several men, ranchers, by the looks of them, seated about a nearby table, disconsolately playing poker. "If you could fix it somehow so Harper Monroe would leave us small ranchers be, stranger, we'd be mighty grateful. Ain't that so, boys?"

The men around the speaker grunted or nodded agreement.

"You've had trouble with him, too?" Joe asked.

"Sure have. My name's Tom Maxwell. This here's Mike Harvey, John Brown, and Dwight Miller's over here on the right. We've all had dealin's with Mister Monroe, and we've all come out the worse for them! He forced Mike here to sign over his land to him at gunpoint. John and Dwight came home to find their stock run off or killed and their womenfolk messed with. My woman"—he swallowed—"my little woman, Bethany, decided to stand up to 'em one day while I was away from the ranch house. The verdict on her killin' was accidental death. Sheriff Tallant told the coroner that it was his opinion my Beth had shot herself while foolin' with my rifle! I know better. Beth could shoot better'n any other woman in the whole damn county! Foolin', my eye! She was murdered by the Monroes! She's buried up there on the hill outside o'town. Mister, you might just be the only chance we got! You figure on a way, we'll back you every inch of it!"

"I'll keep that in mind, friends," Joe promised. "And if I come up with that way, I'll be sure to let you know."

Two could play at Monroe's game, Joe thought as he

paid for his drinks and left the saloon, the tinny plinking of a piano and the music of a badly strummed banjo ringing in his ears. Control, that was the key, as Harper Monroe knew only too well. Play on a man's weaknesses, and sooner or later he'd crumble, just as Clem Tallant had crumbled. It was only a matter of time. *What's your weak spot, Monroe?* he asked himself later as he spurred Jimbo out of town and headed back to Las Campanas. Your sons? A fancy woman, maybe? Certainly not your *hidalga* wife! No, he'd learned how deeply Monroe despised his poor Doña Anita from Seraphina. Then what? *What?*

Chapter Twenty-Two

He was still puzzling over the answer when he reached the Rodriguez soddy late that afternoon on the ride home to Las Campanas, having made only one more visit to the general store in the *pueblo* for supplies before he left. These he carried in bulging packs and heavy saddlebags lashed upon Jimbo's back.

Olivia Rodriguez came out to greet him, her youngest sons clinging shyly to her flowered skirts. Her handsome face split in a broad smile of welcome when she saw her visitor was Joe.

"Hola! Bueñas tardes, Don José!"

"And to you, too, Olivia," Joe rejoined, dismounting. "Everything okay here with you and the boys?" He was concerned about her and the boys being alone, with Esteban in New Mexico, but she had stubbornly refused to come and stay at the ranch house in his absence.

"Si, gracias. Everything is very well. So late you ride home from the *pueblo!* Come, *señor,* you must eat supper with us. I have fried *tortillas* and chicken with rice. I promise you, ees very good! Esteban say no other woman can cook like his 'Livia." She beamed proudly, and Joe, who had been about to politely refuse her

358

invitation, decided to accept. With Esteban gone, she was probably lonely. He swept off his white hat and, carrying it, ducked his head as he followed her through the low doorway.

There were only two rooms under the tule-reed and brea roof, but Olivia had done marvels with them. The dirt floors were cleanly swept and sprinkled with sand and sweet-smelling herbs. On the earthen benches that jutted out from the walls were spread colorfully striped woolen *serapes*. Strings of pungent scarlet chili peppers, hams and onions, leather ware and various bulging baskets hung from the smoke-darkened beams above. In a little niche garlanded with golden poppies, a statue of the Blessed Madonna, a loaf of bread in one hand, smiled benevolently down upon the little family in the gloom. It was small, perhaps shabby by some standards, but it was a home in every sense of the word, warm and welcoming; a place where love was a permanent guest. It struck an unfamiliar chord in Joe's heart and brought home as never before the barren wasteland of his own early years at the orphanage back in Sydney. Food had never been short, plain fare though it had been, but love—the touching, the holding, the simple warmth of true caring of any kind—had been sadly lacking. The orphans' bellies had been filled, while what he and the others had truly hungered for had been a filling and nurturing of the soul.

Aware of the dark eyes of Esteban's two young sons upon him, Joe ruffled their black hair. "So! Where's your little dog, *niños*? I don't see her about today?"

One of the boys gasped and excitedly replied in rapid Spanish, which Joe couldn't grasp. He and his little brother quickly disappeared outside, tumbling over each other in their eagerness to be first out and through the door.

Olivia laughed as she set platters of thin, perfectly round corn *tortillas* and savory *arroz con pollo* on the table before Joe. "My son, Ramon, said that his dog, Gitana, is with his older brother, tending the sheep," she explained, "but that his father spoke of *el señor* before he left and instructed him to do something if Don José or Doña Seraphina should pass this way."

"And what was that?"

"Ah, you will see shortly, *señor,*" Olivia promised mysteriously, her dark eyes twinkling. "I must not spoil my sons' surprise, eh? Now, eat!"

When the two boys returned, each carried a squirming black and white sheepdog puppy in his arms, two of the pups Joe had seen the children playing with the first time they had ridden to Las Campanas.

"For you, *señor!*" the eldest of the pair said solemnly, handing him a pup.

"And this one, too," the little one, Paco, not to be outdone, echoed, doing likewise.

"Papa said you will someday herd many, many sheep here, and that you will need good dogs to help you. These are the best in all of California and even Mexico," Ramon, Olivia's second son, declared proudly, "for they are the puppies of my Gitana and Papa's Chico, the best dogs ever. I have already begun their training, so they will be very little trouble to you. They know how to sit and how to roll over and almost everything!"

Joe grinned and tried to evade the small, enthusiastic pink tongues bent on laving his face as he tousled and scratched the two squirming pups that were all tail and paws. "I believe you, *niños,*" he said solemnly. "I reckon these are the best sheepherding pups I've ever laid eyes on. *Mil gracias* to you, and to you, too, Paco! I'll take care of them real well, and if you'd like, you can come on up to the *casa* from time to time and see how they're doing."

The little boys' almost-black eyes shone with pride as they nodded eagerly. They looked down at their bare, dusty feet and shuffled them with embarrassed pleasure.

"Now, let's see what we have in here," Joe said thoughtfully, patting his shirt pockets. "A gift like these two fine dogs deserves a gift in return, wouldn't you say? Ah! Here we go!" He drew from his shirt pocket several small canes of hard, boiled candy, which had the spicy smell of cinnamon and cloves about them. They were wrapped in twists of paper. He handed them to the older boy. "These are for you and Paco, Ramon. Mind you share them with your little brother, *niño,* but not until after supper, and then only—*only*—if it's okay with your mama, *comprende?*"

"*Si! Yo comprendo! Gracias, señor!*" the boys chimed together, seeing Olivia nod her smiling approval.

"*Muy bien, hijos!*" their mother praised. "Now, go and wash up for supper, and do it quickly!"

The two sped outside. Joe set the puppies at his feet, where they growled fiercely and worried his boots until they tired of their play and fell sound asleep in an untidy, furry heap under his chair while he finished his meal. "Your Esteban was right, Olivia," he said at length, pushing his empty plate away. "Your tucker is the best there is!"

Olivia blushed. "Nonsense, *señor!*" she disclaimed modestly, yet he knew she was pleased nonetheless. "*Chocolate?*"

He nodded, and she poured him a second cup of the thick, sweet brew her people favored above coffee, taking a seat opposite him to drink her own. "Esteban told me before he left that you expected trouble from

Don Monroe and his sons, *señor*. I saw them over a week ago, and then again yesterday, but they did not trouble us, although I kept our old rifle close by, just in case. Did they perhaps visit your *rancho?*"

Joe told her of the Monroes' "visit" and outlined briefly what had happened to Ming soon after. Beneath her olive complexion, Olivia paled.

"Aiee, *dios!*" she exclaimed, crossing herself. "*Pobrecito!* He will recover?"

"Yes, Olivia. Don't fret. He's almost as good as new already, except for his busted wrists," Joe reassured her, yet there was a grimness in his tone.

"Ah." Olivia nodded in understanding. "But you mean to settle the score with *señor* Monroe nonetheless, yes?"

"Indeed I do, sooner or later. Trouble is, Doña Seraphina wants me to do it by the law."

"Law?" Olivia grimaced. "Here? Pah! Impossible! What law can there be here when Señor Tallant, the sheriff, is known to everyone as Monroe's man. Such *hombres* do not respect or understand or uphold any law but that of the gun, or some force greater than their own! *La doña* Seraphina means well, but forgive me, *señor,* if I say that in this matter, she is wrong. If you would hold Las Campanas against Monroe and his sons, you must prove to him that you are *muy fuerte*— very strong—far stronger than he! Perhaps it would only need to be proved once for him to learn his lesson and leave Las Campanas and her people well alone? After all, even the biggest bullies are truly cowards at heart, yes?"

Joe nodded. "My thoughts exactly, *señora*. And the bigger they are, the harder they fall." He grinned fleetingly.

Olivia smiled in return, but then her smile quickly faded and was replaced by a weary sigh. "*Dios mío!* If only El Vengador were still living! Then . . . ah, then, *señor,* we would have someone to turn to for help!"

"El Vengador?" Joe echoed, frowning. "Who was he?"

"Those *gringos* who had cause to fear him called him a *bandito.* But to those he helped, why, he was a saint! He was an outlaw, *señor,* who made his hideout in an abandoned silver mine north of Las Campanas, deep in the foothills of the mountains. It is said that at one time he owned a *rancho,* but that his wife and little baby had been killed by men who wanted his land, his house razed, and so he took to the hills to avenge them, and others like them. From time to time, he would erupt from his stronghold and rustle cattle and rob the wealthy ranchers of their riches—only to return them to those to whom they rightfully belonged and from whom they had been stolen at gunpoint. A rancher who had had his stock run off would find it back in his corral one morning. Another whose little house had been razed would find timbers and materials for a new house awaiting him. You see how it went?"

Joe grinned. "This El Vengador—he sounds like a modern-day Robin Hood!"

"I am sorry . . . I do not know of this Robin Hood." Olivia declared, frowning.

"It doesn't matter, 'Livia. He was just someone I read about as a kid—a man like your El Vengador who robbed from the rich to give to the poor."

"Ah. I see. Well, that was how it was when I was a little girl. Aiee, *Dios,* how my brothers and myself loved to sit at our *mamacita*'s knee and hear her tell of El Vengador—it means The Avenger—dressed all in black as he rode his golden horse far and wide to right the wrongs done to others! But then, alas, El Vengador made his last ride. He was shot in an ambush, betrayed by one of his own men. He died, but his legend lives on.

Would it not be wonderful if El Vengador could live on also?" Her expressive dark brows arched inquiringly and her black eyes were bright and piercing as they met Joe's turquoise stare.

Joe frowned. "I understand what you're driving at. And I admit, it's an idea, Olivia, but it would be a damned difficult one to bring off. Still, I'll keep it in mind as a last resort." He rose, scooped up the pups, and tucked one under each arm. "I'd best be going now. Thanks for some fine tucker . . . supper . . . and for these little beasts. Esteban should be back any day now, but I'll have someone come by and check on you and the boys meanwhile. You take care, now."

"I will. Thank you. *Vaya con dios, señor!*"

He waved as he rode away, the pups tucked snugly in his saddlebags, Jimbo's hooves churning up a red dust cloud that quickly hid him from Olivia's view. Beyond his darker silhouette, the ruddy disk of the dying sun slipped over the sawtoothed rim of the indigo mountains and disappeared, leaving darkness and silence in her wake. The smiling silver moon and a sprinkling of tiny stars rose to take her place. Olivia crossed herself and murmured a prayer to the Madonna for Joe's success, and another to St. Christopher, the patron saint of travelers, asking that her Esteban be kept safe from harm until he returned to her, then she shooed the children inside their soddy for the night.

The sprawling black mass and the taller, dramatic *campanario* that was Casa Campanas lay just ahead of Joe. Lamps and candlelight in the windows made glowing golden rectangles against the indigo darkness, welcoming beacons that spelled home to Joe as no place had ever spelled home before.

Some distance still from the house, he reined in Jimbo and rolled a smoke, drawing in the fragrant tobacco aroma with leisurely enjoyment as he sat his horse on the crest of the hill, looking out across the land and the *hacienda* that was its heart with a warmth filling him such as he had never felt before this moment.

Inside Casa Campanas, Seraphina would be waiting for him, perhaps a little riled up that he'd ridden off without telling her, but with love and desire lighting her luminous eyes nonetheless. Either she'd be sitting by the fire in the kitchen with Peg, her blue-black hair falling in a loose curtain about her flushed face, or else curled sound asleep in his bed, warm, soft, and womanly as she drowsily awoke and came into his ever-eager arms. No doubt Peg would have a pot of something bubbling and ready for his supper, with mugs of scalding coffee and corn bread, and Gabby and Ming and the others would ask questions about his visit to the *pueblo* while he ate, or relay little tidbits of news about what had happened at the ranch in his absence, everyone talking and arguing good-naturedly at once as they always did. Above all, there'd be a warm welcome waiting, people who really cared about what he'd done and where he'd been, and who he cared about in return. Home. *His* home. The *casa,* the land, the people he'd come to consider his family, all his now.

Give up all of that because of his guilt, or because Harper Monroe was a greedy, land-grabbing son of a gun who wouldn't take no for an answer? He shook his head slowly, and the starlight glinted frostily in his turquoise eyes. No. No sir! He'd die before Harper Monroe claimed Rancho de las Campanas as his own, or ever again harmed so much as a hair from the heads of the people he'd come to love. "Vengeance is mine, saith the Lord" had been one of the orphanage's favorite Bible quotations, he remembered. "Vengeance is mine, too, this time, Mate!" Joe said irreverently, grinning broadly as he gazed up into the spangled heavens above.

He touched heels to Jimbo's flanks and rode on— rode home.

They had been asleep for about two hours when Sera was awakened by Madame's frantic meowing from somewhere far off. Still drugged with sleep, she yawned, rubbed her eyes, and shifted her position, hoping the sound would diminish. Instead, it increased, became louder and more squalling by the minute.

"Lord, Madame, I wish you'd keep your love affairs to yourself!" she grumbled, tossing back the sheets. "What a hussy you are! Isn't that new litter of kittens enough of a family for you?"

She staggered across the room in search of a shoe or some other missile to toss out the window in the direction of the sound, in hopes that she would frighten the cats away. In the darkness, she cracked her shin against the bedpost and swore loudly, hopping on one foot with the pain.

"What's up?" Joe asked groggily from the bed.

Through tears of pain, she saw a moving darker mass in the shadows as he struggled to a sitting position.

"What time is it?" He yawned loudly, turning to glance up at the window. "Christ! It's still pitch black out there! What's wrong?"

"I bumped my darn leg looking for a shoe to throw at Madame. She's out there somewhere, and feeling pretty amorous if her yowling's anything to go by! She woke me up. Just listen to that racket!"

"That doesn't sound like a lovesick cat t'me, Sera," he said after a few seconds. "She sounds more like she's been hurt!" He stood, grabbing up his pants from a chair back and sliding them on in one lithe move before striding to the window. "Christ Almighty! The storerooms are on fire!"

Seraphina spun about and hurried to the window even as Joe turned back and rapidly passed her, heading for the door and racing through it. The sight that met her eyes was like something from a nightmare. Flames were licking up from the storerooms at the far end of Casa Campanas, orange against the black bulk of buildings and shadow and distant mountains. The fire was not all, she realized, her eyes adjusting gradually, for in the moonlight she glimpsed men, several men on horseback. They wore hoods of white cloth pulled over their heads to conceal their identities, with slits cut in them for eyeholes. Their very anonymity was frightening. Two of them carried flaming brands, which they had obviously used to torch the storeroom, while the rest just milled about on their horses, whooping and jeering.

"You there in the house! This here is just a warning— a taste of what happens 'round these parts to them who reckon China-boys equal t' their own kind!" one yelled. "Next time, we fire the house!"

"We don't want you here, McCaleb! Take your woman and get the hell out of this valley!"

"Yeah, McCaleb, take your two-bit whore and go back where you came from!"

"And take that yeller-boy with you, 'fore we string him up!"

Sera bit off a terrified scream as she saw Joe race toward them from the house. He was unarmed, shirtless, and bootless; nevertheless he sprang at the nearest rider, grasping his arm and hauling him from the saddle to land in the dirt with a loud thud. Immediately, he swung a punch, fury loading his fists like lead shot. She didn't wait to watch anymore. The odds were too uneven. All it would take would be for one of the men to turn and realize Joe was out there and fighting, and they'd combine numbers against him and . . .

Hoisting up her nightgown, she flew from the room, racing toward the kitchen where Joe kept his rifle. Snatching it down from the rack above the wide stone fireplace, she fumbled in a box for cartridges and loaded it with shaking hands, all the while muttering under her breath to hurry herself, for God's sake, hurry, before it was too late.

Others were up now, Peggy with her hair in braids and a flannel robe thrown hastily over her nightgown; Ming looking ridiculously young in a striped nightshirt that, despite her fright and the giddy thump-a-thumping of her heart, still made her think incongruously of Wee Willie Winkie in the nursery rhyme. She thrust past them, gritting out as she went, "Stay inside; keep away from the windows; keep down!"

"What is it? Blessed Mary, what's wrong?" Peggy cried, starting after her.

"Vigilantes!" Sera yelled over her shoulder. "Joe's out there alone with them!"

Ming's face turned the color of ashes.

No sooner had she spoken than Sera was through the door and running around to the corral, cocking the loaded rifle as she went. Joe was still grappling with the man he had unhorsed, she saw, and the beast was sashaying about, reins dangling, hooves dangerously close to the two struggling figures in the dust. She raised the rifle to her shoulder and sighted down the barrel until she had a clear aim above their heads, squeezing off a warning shot that sounded louder than any crack of thunder in the night. A horse screamed in fear. The voices of the other riders changed from cocksure and jeering to anxious and cursing to be done and gone.

"Hell and be damned! They got guns! Light out, boys!" one man cried and wheeled his horse around, causing it to rear up in fright momentarily before he spurred it away. The other masked riders followed suit, except for one man who rode up alongside the two men still grappling in the dirt.

Before Sera could squeeze off another shot, she saw him kick Joe—who had the man pinned beneath him now—square in the head. Joe flew backward, as if poleaxed, and slumped to the ground. The rider reached down and gave an arm up to the other man, who got to his feet and vaulted up behind him on his horse. As the others had done, they wheeled about and rode away.

Sera raised her rifle a second time, sighted, and pulled the trigger. She saw the rider in back clutch his arm in silhouette, heard a yelp of pain, and knew with satisfaction that at least she had winged one of them before they had gotten away.

Peggy and Ming came running from the house then, their faces waxy moons in the gloom one minute, then lit starkly by the flames from the burning storehouse the next. Jaime and Stefano, awakened by the shouts and ruckus, came racing from the bunkhouse, still fastening their pants. They were bare-chested, as Joe had been.

"Stefano, Jaime, get buckets! Peggy, Ming, you too!" Seraphina snapped.

"What about Joe?" Ming asked. "Did they . . . did they . . . ?"

"No. He'll be all right. He's just out cold. Hurry with those water buckets!" she screamed, turning back now to the fire.

Half of the storeroom was already engulfed, she saw now. She made a mental tally, realizing with enormous relief that there was nothing inside that could not be replaced, only a few sacks of flour and navy beans, rice and such and—oh, no!—Madame's litter of tiny, newborn kittens, she remembered belatedly, misery bunching up in her chest. She looked hurriedly about and spied the calico cat then, crouched with her fur standing up on end by the corral fence. The cat was staring at the fire with fascinated, shining, hate-filled amber eyes. Every muscle in her usually lithe body was as tense as strung wire. There was something dangling from her mouth. A kitten, Sera guessed correctly, but there were no other furry little bundles to be seen anywhere about. Poor little things, she thought fleetingly. The mother cat must have been frantic to get back inside to save the remainder of her brood but had been unable to on account of the heat of the fire. It was a miracle that Madame's frantic cries had awakened her in time to save them all from being roasted alive while they slept! The realization of how very narrow their escape had been made her feel weak and trembly, and for a moment she was afraid her knees would buckle under. Yet, somehow, she managed to pull herself together and went to crouch alongside Joe, who was coming to.

"Are you all right?" she asked anxiously, reaching out to wipe away the smear of blood on his temple with the hem of her nightgown.

"I'll live," he said curtly, furious at himself for getting laid out. He jerked his head away from her hand and got to his feet, immediately heading to help the men returning from either pump or creek with slopping buckets.

They formed a living chain from pump to storehouse, passing buckets filled with water hand over hand to Joe and Jaime to throw on the flames. Joe used the first few bucketfuls to thoroughly damp down the other side of the storeroom, and in that way they were able to contain the spread of the fire to just the one portion of the outbuildings. Nevertheless, it took a grueling, backbreaking hour of frantic labor to completely extinguish the blaze. A rosy dawn was coming up over the mountains, lightening the charcoal sky, before Joe announced himself satisfied that there were no more smoldering embers, no stray sparks left glowing, that could restart the fire.

In the early morning light, Sera looked around at everyone's exhausted face, pale against smudges of soot or smoke or mud, and thanked God yet again that she and these few people who had become so dear to her had been spared. She picked up Madame and the single tiny black kitten along with her. "Well, we won," she murmured hoarsely, her throat parched from the acrid smoke that still hung in the air, "thanks to Madame. She woke me just in time! I'd say she deserves a big breakfast and an extra helping of cream, wouldn't you?" Tired faces grinned back at her wearily, and everyone nodded. Sera smiled. "Fact is, we all deserve a big breakfast! Clean-up can wait 'til later. It's not going anywhere," she said, grimacing as she nodded at the smoking, blackened ruins of the storeroom. "Come on inside, all of you."

A while later, over spicy *huevos rancheros,* heaped pan-fried hashed potatoes, pancakes, ham and coffee, Sera glanced across the table at Joe, who now looked like a desperado with a large sticking plaster stuck at a jaunty angle across his brow. "I guess you'll be riding into town later on to report what happened to the sheriff," she said, and she grimaced. "Damned vigilantes! I thought they'd outlawed all that years ago!"

"Wake up, Sera!" Joe growled, spearing a piece of ham on his fork and waving it in her direction for emphasis. "They weren't vigilantes, any more than

371

I am!"

She bit her lip. "You mean, you think it was the Monroes again?"

"Who else? Last night was just another attempt to get rid of us!"

"Then you have to go talk to the sheriff, Joe. I'll go with you. He'll have to listen to us! We'll *make* him listen."

"The hell he'll listen—or do anything about it!" Joe scoffed with conviction. "I rode into town to talk with him yesterday, about what happened to Ming, and he wouldn't do a damn thing!"

"Why on earth not?"

"He had several reasons. One was that he doesn't care for the Chinese and claims they have no rights under the law. Another was that he's in Harper Monroe's pocket and doesn't spit without asking Monroe's permission. And the last reason—well, that one's easy! Sera, love, our upstanding Sheriff Tallant was one of them tonight!"

"The sheriff? But they were masked! You can't be sure, Joe. Oh, surely not?"

"No? Then explain why he was wearing this!" Joe fished in his pocket and withdrew a piece of white cloth sewn into the shape of a hood. With a shudder of distaste, Sera recognized it as one of those worn by the riders. "I pulled this from the head of the man I fought with—the one you winged with that last shot. It was him, Sera! I'd stake money Sheriff Tallant's not using his left arm this morning—I'd stake everything I have!" He smiled mirthlessly. "Now, do you still think we should go to the sheriff and ask for help, love?"

As he saw her shake her head, Joe made a grim and silent vow: soon, very soon, El Vengador would ride again!

Chapter Twenty-Three

The moon was barely up two nights later when five men rode forth from a gaping black mine shaft that tunneled deep into the bowels of the mountain and turned their borrowed horses southwest, toward Rancho Fuerte.

Their leader rode a magnificent palomino stallion, lent him for this purpose from the Indian *rancheria* of old chief Tyonek, as were the other mounts as well. In the moonlight, the palomino's glossy coat shone with a pale, golden lustre and its sweeping mane and tail with the sheen of silver, as did the sparkling trim that ornamented its bridle and high-pommeled saddle. Its rider was dressed all in black, from the wide-brimmed hat he wore pulled low over his brow to the gleaming black silk shirt and the fringed, soft, black leather vest and pants that hugged his lean flanks and powerful legs. Above the triangular mask of the black silk bandanna that concealed his lower face, a pair of turquoise eyes burned with vengeance.

The five rode in silence until they reached a well-worn trail that wound out of the *pueblo* of the Angels, skirted Las Campanas' land, and scored the rough terrain beyond all the way to Rancho Fuerte. In the distorting shadow of a clump of oaks and cotton-woods, they reined in their horses and began their lonely wait.

"Here she comes—and right on schedule!" one of the men murmured almost an hour later, and all heads turned to watch as a single coach drew nearer and nearer, its steady advance revealed only by lanterns on either side of it that bobbed and danced eerily against the obsidian blackness, for the moon had modestly hidden her light beneath a veil of clouds.

"Ready, *amigos?*" asked their leader.

"*Si, señor!*" the four men sang out quietly, pulling up their own bandannas to conceal their faces.

"Tom, Dwight, you go across and take them from the other side. Mike, John, you're with me. Let's go!"

The coach driver let out a startled yell as the masked riders suddenly loomed out of the blackness on either side of the coach and grasped the traces, hauling on them to forcibly halt the racing team. He reached for the rifle alongside him, but a hand like steel closed over his fist and squeezed until he yelped with pain. The masked man took the rifle from him as easily as he might take candy from a baby and tucked it into the loop at his own saddle.

"No heroics, partner. Just sit quiet and easy, and no one'll get hurt. *Comprende?*"

Looking up into the black-masked face of the bandit, the coach driver gulped and nodded. The leader urged his horse alongside the coach, leaned down, and rapped loudly on the door. "Everyone out!" he barked.

After a few seconds, the door flew open and a young Mexican girl tumbled out, her shawl covering her face as she wept noisily and called upon the blessed Virgin to save her from ravishment. She was followed soon after by a lumbering Harper Monroe and his elegant wife, Doña Anita, who appeared pale but composed in the meager light as she stepped down elegantly from the coach without assistance from her husband. With the tall ivory comb in her upswept black hair, draped by a snowy *mantilla,* she was every inch a lady.

"*Señores,* it is my pleasure to inform you that this is a holdup! Your valuables, *por favor!*" the bandit leader growled.

The young Mexican girl, obviously a maid, uttered a shriek. "I . . . but I have nothing, *señores!*"

"Don't worry, *chiquita.* I am certain Don Harper will be more than happy to make a donation in your name. Will you not, *señor?*" The leader's turquoise eyes gleamed. Doña Anita, swiftly recovering her composure, was almost certain that he was smiling behind his mask.

"The hell I will!" Monroe growled, reaching inside his fancy evening jacket for the small pistol he carried there. His face was livid in the flare of the lanterns.

"It would not be wise to act rashly, *señor!*" the leader warned in a tone that brooked no refusal. Harper Monroe recognized the tone for what it was and drew out the pistol slowly, dropping it to the dirt.

"A wise man," the bandit chuckled. "And now, *señor,* what else have you for us?"

The four riders waited while Harper Monroe divested himself of a diamond stickpin, a roll of greenbacks, gold cuff links and pearl collar studs, all of which he tossed to the ground at the bandit's command.

"And now, the lovely *señora,* if she would be so kind," the leader requested in far gentler tones.

With a little click of irritation, Doña Anita tugged several heavily jeweled rings from her fingers and a weighty gold bracelet dripping sapphires from her wrist. "There. Now, take, them and be gone," she urged. "You are frightening my maid. Hush now,

375

Ramona, *pobrecita,* "she soothed, taking the girl in her arms.

"We'll be gone very soon, Doña Anita," the bandit leader promised. "But first, what of the necklace?"

"My necklace?" The older woman gasped as she reached to her throat to touch it. "Oh, no, *señores,* please, I beg of you! Take anything else you wish, but not this! The necklace . . . it was a gift from my papa shortly before his death. It . . . it is worth very little but has great sentimental value to me. Here . . . my wedding ring! Please, take this instead!"

Harper Monroe shot his wife a murderous glare, which she returned with a cool, withering glance.

"*Si,* take it," she urged. "It is made of gold, and very, very heavy, but it means absolutely nothing to me!" Her defiant expression challenged Harper to gainsay her.

There was a brief pause before the bandit leader spoke again. "I accept the ring, *señora,* and the charming plea from your beautiful lips! Keep your necklace and your memories, and let it be known that I am a gentleman who would never cause distress to so lovely a lady." He jerked his head, and one of his men dismounted and picked up the glittering hoard before vaulting astride his horse. The four rode off.

"*Buenas noches, señores* . . . and . . . *muchas gracias!*" So saying, the bandit leader nodded courteously to the ladies, then wheeled his great golden horse about and galloped away after his men.

"By the Blessed Virgin!" Doña Anita breathed, a little smile playing about her lips as she fingered the heavy silver crucifix at her throat. "He has returned from the dead!"

"Who's returned from the dead?" Harper muttered angrily, juggling with his shirt collar, which, lacking studs now, flapped loosely about his throat.

376

"El Vengador!" Doña Anita breathed, and sighed wistfully.

The following Monday, Esteban Rodriguez and Raoul Garnier returned from New Mexico, driving the newly purchased Las Campanas flock before them through the dun hills of the San Juliano Valley. Their long-awaited arrival was a red-letter day in Joe's life and forced him to postpone his burning quest for revenge upon the Monroes for the time being, as well as forgo his nocturnal forays.

Each day for the past week he had worked alongside his hands to dig several wells, mindful of the hot, dry summer months that lay just ahead. Then would the levels of the creeks and the San Juliano River that crisscrossed his spread drop drastically and his flocks be threatened with drought and starvation. Accordingly, he had determined to dig wells, wanting to take no chances on being left without a water supply for his animals. He had seen too many of the poor, stupid beasts die in that slow and agonizing fashion in the past—back on the arid sheep stations where he had worked in Australia—to want to see it happen here if he could possibly avoid it. He was riding between two such wells when he saw a dense, dusty red haze in the distance and caught on the already sultry morning air the faint shouts of the men on horseback that rode in and about it. Someone was moving a large number of animals, obviously. Was it Monroe's *vaqueros* and part of his vast herd, he wondered fleetingly? If so, they were running their longhorns clear across his land and, knowing Monroe, up to no good! He thought of Olivia, alone with only her two small sons, and his heartbeat quickened with apprehension. Had Monroe, infuriated by the attack on his coach and the rustling of several score of his cattle over the past week by the mysterious bandit, El Vengador, decided to take out his anger on still more innocent people?

But, wheeling Jimbo about and digging in his spurs to ride closer, he crested a low rise and recognized the cause of the dust cloud for what it was; not the dust thrown up by a herd of longhorns, but the dust thrown up by the cloven hooves of almost five hundred sheep—*his* sheep! And what sheep they were, he realized, excitement spreading through him as he rode nearer and saw at close hand the quality of the beasts.

Each animal was the best of its breed, Joe knew at a single, practiced glance, whether one of the several hundred aristocratic Spanish Merino ewes with their dense, creamy wool concealed under a thick coating of natural lanolin or the two magnificent, curly-horned rams that would sire the lambs dropped in the mild fall, or the handsome French Rambouillets with their far shorter fleece yet heavier, sturdier bodies that produced the best meat, the tastiest mutton.

"Yiihaa!" Joe let out a wild, Indian whoop by way of greeting and swept off his hat, brandishing it above his head in salute as he cantered Jimbo around the ragged perimeters of the large flock toward the rumbling chuck wagon that lagged behind it. Black and white sheepdogs—obviously close cousins to his own pups, which Seraphina had christened Picaro and Pia—had been set busily to rounding up the sheep, which had been startled by his whooping and had strayed from the tidy, close formation the clever dogs insisted upon. Now they snapped at the animals' heels and barked to add weight to their commands.

"Esteban, *amigo mio!* It's good to see you again, cobber!" Joe shouted, spotting the gentle Mexican striding alongside the chuck wagon. He carried his stout shepherd's staff in his hand, and a curly lamb, bleating piteously, was tucked under his arm. With his beard, a battered woven *sombrero* topping his shaggy black curls, and clad in loose, white cotton *calzones* and blouse, a striped serape slung carelessly over his shoulder as he plodded along on leather sandals, he could have stepped from the pages of a history book— or the Bible, Joe thought fleetingly and with a rare, fanciful turn of mind.

"Hola, Don José! Aiee, *gracias a dios,* it is good to be back!" Esteban, unusually talkative, responded with a broad grin. "Tell me, *patron,* how are my wife and my sons?"

"Muy bien, amigo!" Joe quipped. "They are very well. And as you can see, I've picked up a little more Spanish while you were gone. How were the sheep fairs?"

"Ho, there! McCaleb!" cut in a voice from the rear of the nearest wagon before Esteban could respond.

"Garnier! Get yourself out here, Raoul, you old scoundrel! Good to have you back, cobber! I'd say the two of you did fair dinkum, by the looks of things! They're a prime bunch, I'd say!" Joe gestured toward the milling flock as Raoul Garnier heaved himself down from the back of the chuck wagon, yawning hugely.

"Ah, *oui, certainement,* we did quite well for *el patron,"* Raoul agreed modestly, but with a twinkle in his dark eyes that made him appear very like a benign, enormously large gnome above his bushy mustache. "They said in Albuquerque, *señor,* that they would count it a very large favor if Esteban and I did not return to the auctions in the near future, *por favor!"* He threw back his great curly head, cradled his bulging belly with huge yet loving arms, and rocked with deep, rumbling laughter. "We drove a hard bargain, a hard bargain indeed, but in most cases, Joe, we got exactly what we wanted, and at a fair price, too! In others, we were forced to pay a little more than we'd expected. But the animals in question were well worth the higher price. Did you see the Merino rams yet?" Joe nodded, grinning. "And those buxom Rambouillet ewes?" Joe nodded again as Raoul bunched his fingers together and kissed them in true Gallic fashion. "I swear to you, Joe, my friend, they are so beautiful, I am half in love with each one of those curly-haired little darlings myself!"

Everyone laughed. Joe dismounted and, leaving his horse ground tied, he strode toward the camp fire and squatted down next to Esteban. Raoul Garnier joined them.

"So, tell me everything, partners. Did you lose many head on the way up here?"

"Three ewes simply dropped dead in their tracks the day before yesterday, I am sorry to say. I believe they were older than we were led to believe and the heat and the length of the journey was too much for them, yes? A pair of late lambs were carried off by coyotes another night. And we had to have the flock dipped and inspected for disease before we could enter California. But other than the usual things, it was an almost leisurely sheep drive," Raoul disclaimed airily. "By the way, we also acquired another couple of hands for you," he told Joe, gesturing toward two other men on the far side of the flock. "They seem to know sheep as well as we do, and they were keen on coming west. I thought you could try them and decide for yourself if you want to take them on."

"Sure will." Joe clapped both Raoul and Esteban across the back. "You did just bonzer—you did real well, my friends. I . . . I don't know how to thank you." His voice was husky with emotion.

"There is no need, Joe. The expression on Harper

Monroe's face when he sees your flock will be thanks enough!" Raoul said darkly, then added with one bushy black brow raised inquiringly, "Speaking of which, Joe, we heard some most interesting news just outside of town. Something about the outlaw, El Vengador, having returned to the valley?"

Joe nodded, smiling innocently. "Damned if I haven't been hearing the same story, Raoul! But you know how it is 'round these parts—if it isn't one story, it's another. I guess folks have gotten bored with Indian princesses and bells lately and have hit on a new tale, wouldn't you say?" He met Raoul Garnier's intent, searching gaze with an engaging, crooked grin that caused the older man to throw back his head and roar with laughter.

Raoul clapped Joe across the back. *"Mon ami,* what I would say is, *whoever* El Vengador might be, he's my kind of fellow!"

Joe smiled and nodded. "And mine, too! Well, my friends, we're on our way," he continued, unable to keep the rising excitement from his voice. "Let's forget about Monroe and his doings and drink a toast to the future. Pour the coffee, Esteban, *mi amigo!*" He took up a tin mug and held it out to Esteban, who filled it with the scalding, thick black liquid from the steaming coffeepot.

Raoul grimaced. "A toast? Here? With *café* instead of a full-bodied red wine? Pah! Forgive me if I am unimpressed, *señores!*" He snorted disdainfully.

"Shut up and drink, friend," Joe urged, the broad, crooked grin tugging at the corners of his mouth more uncontrollably. "Coffee now, to wet the head of our new enterprise . . . and something a little stronger, a little more to all our likings, later, mates, home at the *casa.* My treat!"

"Ah. Well, in that case"— Raoul Garnier filled a

third enamel mug for himself—"I propose a toast. To the new McCaleb sheep ranch, Rancho de Las Campanas! To our worthy *patron,* Don José, himself, and to us, his humble shepherds." He inclined his head in a courtly fashion. "And last, but by no means least, to those beautiful, beautiful sheep!" He held the mug aloft. "To you, my delectable, darling girls, and to your lovely little hooves of pure gold!" He brandished the mug, then drained the contents in a single swig. The others followed suit.

Oh, yes, Joe thought, they were truly on their way! The vow he'd made himself months ago, under the moonlight and tossing palms upon a tiny island named Java, was finally coming true. He'd finally amounted to something. Who'd ever have thought it possible, way back then? He ignored the insistent voice of his conscience as it whispered in his ear that everything he had accomplished thus far was founded on lies . . .

"Oh, come on, Val, surely I can't have changed that much since last summer!" Cissy Tallant simpered, eyeing Val Monroe coyly from beneath the brim of her stylish navy blue hat with the small, sassy ostrich plume that danced in the breeze. She hoped fervently that the handkerchiefs she had wadded into her bodice beneath her breasts to enlarge and lift her small bosom didn't slip at the wrong moment. "Why, it's only been a year since I was home the last time!"

"Year or not, you surely have changed, Miz Tallant," Val argued, leering, his gaze wolfishly devouring the generous swell of bosom that threatened to spill over the lace-edged bodice of her sprigged blue gown. "Yessir, Cissy, you've filled out, and then some! Last year, I reckoned I'd seen broom handles with more curves to 'em than what you had, gal!"

Oh, but you haven't changed a bit, more's the pity, Val Monroe, Cissy thought, her seductive smile slipping a little with his insulting comment. You're still a loud-mouthed, ignorant cowboy! But though her fair complexion turned an indignant, blotchy crimson, she forced herself to smile even as she bit back the scathing retort that had sprung to her lips. Be quiet, you little idiot. Isn't this better than nothing? she warned herself. Any sign of Val's noticing her, in whatever way, was far better than the indifference he had shown her whenever she had returned from back east in former years. Why, those times, she practically had had to strip naked and jump up and down to get him to even acknowledge she was alive—and she intended that Val Monroe would one day do far, far more than merely notice her.

Her baby blue eyes hardened as she slyly glanced across at Val as they skirted the crowded central *plaza* of the *pueblo* of Los Angeles, crowded with stall holders this market day. He was good-looking, she supposed, in a sharp-featured, foxy sort of way, and probably the brightest of the Monroe litter, as well as the meanest. But his attributes as a man weren't what gave him his allure as far as Cissy was concerned, no sir. It was his father's money, pure and simple, and the power and control Harper Monroe wielded over the ranchers and folk hereabouts by virtue of it and the force he employed. As Val's wife—and she fully intended to become Val's wife in the not-too-distant future—all that loot and prestige would one day be hers! Harper Monroe might have her daddy in his pocket, but he'd never have her in there along with him! She smiled smugly as she tripped along, swinging the basket of purchases she had obtained at the market. She knew folks here in town laughed behind her back at her aspirations to marry Val, thinking a lowly sheriff's daughter didn't stand a chance of catching him, no, none at all. Well, that just went to show how little those fools knew, she thought smugly. She had more than just a vague dream that Harper might approve of their tying the knot; she had his spoken approval!

Last summer, old man Monroe had given one of his famous *fandangos* in honor of her return from school for the holidays—an annual gesture that would have seemed generous to a fault to an outsider, but which Cissy had recognized long ago as yet another of Harper Monroe's means of controlling folk. The *fandango* had been in full swing, everyone dancing, laughing, and talking with a brittle eagerness peculiar to Monroe gatherings of any kind, when Harper himself had surprised her and Val alone together in a secluded orange arbor in a distant corner of his *hacienda's* grounds. That she'd pursued Val all evening and at last had cornered him there had been only too obvious. Sakes, yes! She had been in the very act of unbuttoning the front of her gown and flagrantly offering a disinterested Val a sampling of her none-too-impressive charms as part of her all-out seduction attempt when the old man had stumbled upon them. When Val had gratefully used his father's intrusion as a chance to escape, Monroe had chuckled and limped his heavy way toward where she sat upon the stone bench furiously trying to rebutton her bodice with fingers that shook with shame and rage. Tears of frustration had glistened in her eyes.

"Mister Monroe!" she had cried, endeavoring to appear distraught. "Thank goodness you happened along just when you did! Why, your son tried to . . . to have his way with me!"

The rancher had grinned nastily. "The hell he did, missy! I ain't blind, even if I am half lame. I saw what you were up to, yessir! Val's as hot-blooded as the next

384

boy—takes after his pa that way, I reckon—but it weren't him doin' the chasin' this time, was it, eh, miss? Oh, you gave it a good try, little gal, I won't deny that, but it didn't work, did it?" he had said scornfully, his pale blue, piggy little eyes gleaming with mockery. "See, honey, my boys ain't partial to scrawny women. You went fishin' with the wrong bait, if'n you was hopin' t'hook Val. Now, his pa's different. He's older, smarter'n them boys o'his are. He learned a long, long time ago that ye don't look a gift horse in the mouth—not even a skinny little ole filly, if ye catch my drift? Now, you come along over here to me, baby blue eyes! Let an old bull who knows what he's about show ye what that young calf couldn't!"

So saying, he had suddenly sat down heavily beside her and his powerful, burly arms had snaked out to encircle her waist, dragging her half across his lap before his meaning had registered in Cissy's stunned mind. As his moist lips had smeared themselves over hers, she had all but gagged and tried to break free, but then cold common sense had prevailed, coupled with a rising excitement, and she had gritted her teeth and endured his embraces. Why not? she had asked herself. If not the son, then why not the father? After all, it was Harper Monroe who held the purse strings; he who called the shots. And he despised his Mexican wife, Doña Anita; everyone knew that. Maybe . . . just maybe . . . she could take that snooty woman's place. What was the saying? It was better to be an old man's darling than a young man's slave? Yes, that was it! Now, that would be something, wouldn't it—Sheriff Clem Tallant's little daughter as the *patrona* of an enormous spread like Rancho Fuerte! So, instead of struggling, she had given a sigh of resignation and melted into the old bull's arms, submitting to, and even returning, his hateful kisses and moaning loudly in feigned delight when his fumbling, stubby fingers had roughly plunged into her bodice to explore the small breasts she had so eagerly offered up to his son, Val, minutes before.

"Why, Mister Monroe, you're so right! I never realized that an older man such as yourself would be so deliciously virile—and so very much more *skilled* at making love to a woman than a mere boy," she had murmured, fluttering her curled, sandy lashes coyly as she gazed up into his florid face and wriggling and squealing enthusiastically as he tweaked her nipples.

Her flattery had acted like a spur dug into the old man's broad rump. He had all but thrown her down on her back across the stone bench and had shoved her skirts and the many layers of petticoats beneath clear above her waist before reaching for the drawstring of her drawers and yanking them down with more force than tenderness or expertise. "Oh, Mister Monroe, you really shouldn't!" she had cried in what she had hoped was a reasonable facsimile of maidenly protest. "My father . . . ! Why, whatever would he say?"

"Clem?" Though breathing heavily with lust, Monroe had managed a snort of derisive laughter. "Why, little gal, he'd offer your sweet young body up to ole Harper on a golden platter, if he thought it would do him some good!"

His hands, sweaty now with his excitement, had soon found their circuitous way beneath layer upon layer of clothing to her flesh, and her skin had crawled as he had poked and prodded. Though she had gritted her teeth and hidden it well, making no protest, his words had stung, for she had known in her heart that every hurting one of them was true. Her father *was* a spineless yellow belly who owed all he had to Harper Monroe, and would have done anything to stay in his good graces, including handing his daughter over to him on a platter!

Ironically, it had been those selfsame words that had at last brought her to her senses—and in the very nick of time, too. If she gave herself to Monroe, what guarantee would she have that she would ever become Mrs. Harper Monroe, she had reasoned? What else would she have left with which to barter her way into the position she intended to hold, if she let Monroe do what he so obviously intended to do with her body? Nothing, nothing at all! There'd be no divorce, that much was certain. Doña Anita, damn her, was too soaked in her pious Catholic faith for that. No, perhaps on second thought it would be better if she played hard to get, played Harper off against his son for a while. At least that way, she could be reasonably sure of getting one or the other of them in the end.

"Oh, Lord, Mister Monroe, stop! Why, what on earth are we doing? What can we have been thinking of?" she had cried, suddenly endeavoring to shove him from her. "In my . . . excitement . . . why, I clean forgot that you're a married man! And heavens, what have you done to me . . . and to my clothing? I must have been so carried away by your kisses and . . . and *everything* that I almost let you . . . ohhh!"

She had given a small, anguished cry and had turned her face away from him as if to hide her mortification and upset. "Oh, Mister Monroe, do you see how dangerous you attractive, older men are? Why, you drive an innocent girl to sheer madness, so she doesn't hardly know what she's doin'! Please, sir, you mustn't take advantage of my . . . my innocence!" she had squealed, writhing to free herself from his weight as he made a lunge across her to pin her to the bench.

She had succeeded and jumped to her feet, her skirts falling modestly down to cover her as she did so. Acting flustered, she had attempted for the second time that evening to fasten the tiny buttons that closed her bodice, while a wheezing Harper had lumbered, scowling and panting heavily, to his feet. Would he be angry over her rejection? she had wondered, swaying a little as she stood there, her hair mussed, the sweet scent of orange blossoms so heavy on the night air they made her feel downright queasy. But to her surprise, his thwarted scowl had faded and he had thrown back his head and laughed.

"Hell-an'-be-damned if you ain't good, li'l Miss Cissy Tallant!" he had roared. "Yessiree, honey, you know how t'play the game all right! I guess that fancy schoolin' I footed the bill for taught you a heap, huh? Heck, if yer pa had your guts, honey, he wouldn't be under my thumb the way he is!" He had limped toward her, his lame leg dragging more noticeably than usual, his pale eyes narrowed shrewdly now as he tweaked her cheek. "Tell yer what, Cissy, honey, if you can rope and hog-tie my boy into marrying up with you, I won't stand in your way. Fact is, I'd welcome you into the family with open arms, seeing as how you and me are two of a kind!" He had nudged her painfully in the ribs. "It's 'bout time Val settled down some and saw t'breeding me some grandsons, anyways. Go to it! Bring ole Val t'heel, gal. Don't care how you do it. That's your problem!" And with that, he had tottered off, rumbling with laughter as he went.

Lord, how she loathed that sly old man, even while knowing that everything her father had, her own schooling and fancy clothes, the very house they lived in, came directly or indirectly from him. Somehow, that made it worse, knowing she was beholden to the man. So, he thought to get her into the family as Val's bride and find himself with an ally, perhaps a convenient mistress on the side, and a mother for the future, snotty-nosed little Monroes, too, did he? Well, he'd be wrong! Cissy Tallant was nobody's ally but Cissy Tallant's, and Harper Monroe wasn't getting any younger. Some fine day, he'd find out just how much she'd learned from his example, but by then, it would be too late! Little Cissy Tallant, Sheriff Tallant's golden-haired, blue-eyed little girl, didn't intend ever to be hungry or poor or looked down on as she had been as a child, nor would she be beholden to anyone, ever again, whatever it took—

"Now, that's what I call a woman!" Val suddenly exclaimed and whistled through his teeth.

His exclamation jerked Cissy back from her reverie. The mere thought of Val eyeing any woman but her— or that brassy slut over at the saloon that he was sleeping with—filled her with rage and something akin to panic. "What woman? Where?" she demanded, looking about wildly.

Val nodded across the *plaza* to where a slender woman was laughingly haggling with an old Mexican *señora* over the price of her baskets of oranges. Her luxuriant blue-black hair tumbled loose and shining across her shoulders and full breasts and was held away from her lovely profile by a pair of small silver and turquoise combs that caught it back gracefully above her ears. She wore the *china poblana,* the traditional Mexican dress of a simple *camisa* of bleached cotton, its low, gathered neckline and puffed sleeves embroidered with brilliant flowers, the red and green swirling skirt lifting to flirt the frothy white petticoats and the trim pair of ankles beneath as she laughingly went up on tiptoe to caress the cheek of the ruggedly handsome, shaggy-haired stranger she was with. Now, he was surely something, so tall and tanned and fair! Her gaze left the attractive man with reluctance and returned to the young woman, drawn back against her will. Staring intently, she frowned, her pointed little nose wrinkling like a curious ferret's. There was something awfully familiar about her and about her pose, gazing up at the man, and for a moment Cissy was quite at a loss as to where she could have seen her before.

"Who is she?" she asked, jealous of the hungry eyes Val was casting on the dark-haired woman. "Some little *muchacha* from the *cantina* you've been keeping company with?"

"Jealous, Cissy, honey?" Val drawled, malicious humor in his eyes. It was no secret to him that Cissy was out to put her brand on him, and he enjoyed provoking her when the chance arose.

Cissy flushed darkly, a color that ill became her strategically lightened blond hair. "Should I be?" she retorted, far more waspishly than she had intended.

"Depends," Val bantered, enjoying the angry glint in Cissy's eyes. "Right now, that sweet young thing's a mite out of ole Val's reach, what with her man watchin' out fer her like a hound guarding a juicy bone. But, happen there'll come a time when he won't be, and then . . . wheeee! Watch out!" He grinned. "Heck, Cissy, don't know as how a man could keep himself from hankerin' after a sweet, spirited little thing like that!" He nudged Cissy in the ribs. "And I'll bet she don't even have to stuff nothin' down her bodice, neither, not like some! Yessir, everything 'Phina McCaleb's got looks to be the real thing, and nothing but!"

Cissy's eyes filled with outraged tears. She was about to whirl away and run back home and leave Val standing there—he could rot as far as she was now concerned—when the dark-haired young woman turned around and waved to an elderly Anglo woman who was coming across the square. Cissy saw her face for the first time. Her baby blue eyes widened in disbelief and she gasped, remembering as clear as if it were yesterday a certain Boston drawing room last July, and a certain couple she had interrupted in a fond embrace, only to be hastily ejected from the room by the woman's threats.

"Wh . . . what did you say her name was?" she demanded, fighting the rising tide of excitement building inside her.

"McCaleb. Seraphina McCaleb. Her man—that tall son of a bitch with her—inherited the Las Campanas spread a couple of months or so back. They run several hundred head of stinkin' sheep there. Pa don't like it, neither, don't like it at all. Tried to run 'em off a couple of times, he did, too, but McCaleb didn't scare easy. You know Pa, though. It's jest a matter of time."

Cissy muttered agreement, but she'd heard Val's comments with only half an ear, too busy digesting what he had told her earlier, what it could mean, and how she could best use what she knew to her own advantage. *Seraphina McCaleb?* Huh! Who did she think she was fooling? Whoever and whatever else the woman across the square might be, she wasn't *Seraphina* McCaleb, no, sir!

"Well, Val, honey," Cissy said sweetly, indicating her half-filled basket, "I do believe I have everything I'll be needing for my little visit. If you're ready, we could take the buckboard out to Rancho Fuerte now. Lord, I'm just dying to see your dear papa again after all this time! We have *so* much to talk about." They did indeed—more than Val could have dreamed of, thanks to what she had just seen. Cissy had a hunch she now knew a surefire way for Harper Monroe to rid the valley of the McCalebs—or at least, one of them—if that was what he wanted to do. And who knew what form the old man's gratitude might take?

"Sure, Cissy, anything you say," Val agreed, deceptively amiable. "And maybe you an' me can have ourselves a nice little ole *siesta* down by the willows 'long Squaw Creek, if the drive gets to being too hot for you?" He arched his brows and winked slyly. "Maybe we could cool off with a skinny dip—an' if I'm a real good little cowboy, maybe you'll give ole Val a chance to find out if all that's you or not." He tugged sharply at a ringlet of her blond hair and nodded at her swelling bosom, all but popping from the low-cut neckline of her gown. "Hmmm, baby blue eyes? What do you say?"

Stabs of excitement darted through the pit of her belly, and Cissy was dry mouthed and weak-kneed as she mumbled prissily, "Why, Val, whatever kind of girl do you take me for! After all, I'm the sheriff's daughter, and I do have a certain reputation to maintain."

"Oh, heck, I know jest what kind of a girl you are well enough, Cissy Tallant!" Val soothed slyly, wetting his lips and thinking not of Cissy at all, but of McCaleb's pretty woman. "But it ain't like we're strangers, now is it, honey? 'Sides, I've been thinkin' on settlin' down lately, you know what I mean . . . ?"

Cissy did. She smirked from ear to ear. "Oh, Val! I think I do . . . if you mean what I think you mean."

"Why don't you just come along with old Val and find out," he hedged.

He grasped her elbow and all but hustled her to the waiting buckboard, caressing her scrawny buttocks mechanically as he helped her up into the vehicle. Hell, Cissy was built like a scrawny old stewing chicken, all bones and gristle, and he tried to think longingly of hot little Leila over at the saloon, ready and waiting for him any time he chose to whistle. But seeing McCaleb's woman's soft curves and long, slim legs had driven him wild, and thinking about Leila was useless. That Seraphina had blotted from his mind his desire for any other woman but her. He looked back over his shoulder toward the *plaza,* in time to see Joel McCaleb tucking a crimson rose in his smiling wife's glorious black hair. Nor could he fail to see the tender smile she flashed him in thanks—an invitation in her glowing eyes. "Go ahead, neighbor. Make the most of what time you have left," Val said jealously under his breath. "One fine day, she'll be smiling up at me that way, that sweet young thing!"

The green water of Squaw Creek reflected puffs of snowy cloud and the azure sky like a tranquil mirror. Cissy, sniffling, huddled on the reedy banks, her blue eyes reddened from weeping, her complexion blotched and ugly. Chipmunks mocked her with their chatter nearby as she jabbed her bare toes into the water and angrily dispelled the peaceful reflection of sky and clouds. Val Monroe scowled as he towered above her, tucking in his shirt and buckling his belt.

"Stop it right now, you hear me, gal? Hell, didn't I tell you I was sorry?" he growled, angrily retrieving his hat and jamming it on.

"Sorry doesn't mean a damn to me!" Cissy snapped. "I . . . I gave you the most precious gift a girl has to give the man she loves, and what do you do . . . ?"

"I didn't mean nothin' by it, Cissy. I done told you that once already, gal! The name just . . . just sorta slipped out. Reckon it was seeing her in the *plaza* this mornin' put me in mind of it."

"At precisely *that* moment? Huh! Who do you think you're foolin', Val Monroe? You were making love to me, but you were wishin' all the while it was her!" She flung aside the scratchy old horse blanket they had lain on and began dressing, dragging on her disheveled clothes with hands that trembled. Tears blinded her eyes; tears of rage and hurt and shame commingled. "Damn her! Damn that Katie Steele, always buttin' in

393

where she ain't wanted—first at school, an' now here! Oh, but she'll be sorry she caught your eye, Val Monroe, I swear it! I'll tear out that long, black hair of hers and scratch up her face real good. She'll be so darn sorry she'll wish she'd never bin born!"

"Katie? Who in the hell's Katie?" Val demanded, confused.

"Katie? Oh! I ... I meant your precious little Seraphina," Cissy amended lamely.

"You said somethin' about her and school. I heard you. And you called her Katie. You know McCaleb's wife from back east, Cis?"

Cissy looked evasive. She busied herself with her clothing, reluctant to meet Val's piercing glare. "So? What if I do? Don't mean nothin'. I was just talkin' mad," she covered, but her tone rang false.

Val, cunning as always, sensed she was lying and, leaning down, knotted his fingers in her damp blond hair and tightened his grip painfully so that she yelped as he dragged her closer to him. "I asked if you knew her!" he growled. "Don't lie to me again, gal, and make out you don't!"

"You're hurting me, Val! Please, let me go!" she wailed, trying to writhe free of his hold.

"Tell me, then!" he threatened, still maintaining his grip.

"There's nothin' to tell, honest—oww!"

Tears spilled down her cheeks, making rivers in the powder and paint there as he tugged viciously at her hair, grinding out "Liar!" as he did so.

"All right, Val, please, stop that, an' I'll ... I'll tell you. I'll tell you everything!" she wailed. "I was fixing to tell your pa, anyways!"

Val released her and straightened up, all ears. "Then you'd best tell me instead, hadn't you, Cissy, honey? See, I don't hold with the women I bed down with

394

keeping secrets from me—and I can be a real ornery son of a gun if I find out they've lied to me."

She nodded, shaken by his violence, by his hard, cold expression; frightened of what more he might do to her if she tried to talk her way out of this one and he found out later she'd been holding out on him. She'd heard whispers of how he was with that Leila woman, and they'd scared her. Besides, there was a good chance she'd lose him if she didn't give in. "It's about your precious Seraphina," she ground out bitterly through clenched teeth. "That half-breed teacher's pet and I . . ."

Val leaned forward to catch every last word.

Seraphina seemed unusually quiet on the ride home to Las Campanas that afternoon, Joe thought, stifling a yawn. Too many sleepless nights were beginning to take their toll.

"You're the silent one today, love. Cat got your tongue?" he asked, drawing Jimbo alongside her white gelding and reining him in to a walk to match Muraco's gait.

She glanced up, startled. "Mine? No! I was just thinking. I'm sorry. What did you say?"

Joe grinned. "I didn't! Christ, love, you must have been a mile away! Not feeling under the weather, are you?"

"No, really. Fact is, I feel just fine," she denied.

He couldn't contradict her, not looking as radiant as she did today. The child she was carrying agreed with her, and health and vitality seemed to shine out from every pore. Even in her condition, she rode her horse with the easy grace of one well-accustomed to the saddle, despite the fact that her full skirt was hitched up about her thighs. The Mexican clothing suited her still-slender, yet seductively rounded, figure, the vivid colors of the embroidered flowers and the glowing crimson of the rose he had tucked into her shining black hair setting off her pale gold complexion, the lustrous gray-green sparkle of her eyes, and the moist coral of her lips that seemed always to tempt his kisses.

"Can't argue with that," he drawled, his turquoise eyes devouring her hungrily. "You look more than 'just fine,' woman—you look good enough to eat! Fact is, I can hardly wait to get you home and into bed!"

She laughed and looked away, a little embarrassed by the wicked sparkle in his eyes and by his frankness. "Oh, you!" she scolded. "Don't you ever think about anything else, McCaleb?"

"Nope!" he rejoined, and they both laughed.

Joe jockeyed Jimbo closer to Muraco and leaned down from his saddle. He wound his hand in her long, raven black hair, tugging her gently to him by the silken tether. He kissed her deeply and sweetly, drowning in the sensation of his mouth moving over her soft lips, her delicious taste under his tongue tip, her unique, lily of the valley scent in his nostrils as she returned his kisses, and he felt the telltale hardening of her nipples against his chest in response through her thin blouse. Then Jimbo shied at a gopher hole, and they were torn abruptly apart.

"Damned horse!" Joe growled huskily, his eyes dancing with deviltry. "I should take my gun and shoot him stone-cold dead, moving at a moment like that! Bloody son-of-a-gun animal's got the worst timing I ever saw!"

"It's just as well," Seraphina said, though her eyes lingered tenderly on Joe's mouth as if mesmerized by its shape. "Any moment, the buckboard'll be coming over that rise. You wouldn't want Ming and Peggy to surprise us, now would you?"

"Woman t'tell the truth, I wouldn't give a damn!" Joe denied fiercely. "Besides, it's about time Ming furthered his education in that direction, 'stead of plaguing me for that piece of land he's hankering after all the while. When I was seventeen, I was chasing petticoats, not weeds!" He shook his head in mock disgust as he drew the makings from the small, flat tin in his shirt pocket and rolled a smoke. He winked as he licked the gummed tissue strip of paper.

"Joe . . . ?" Seraphina began after they'd ridden on for a while in amiable silence.

"Mmm?"

"You remember when we were buying the oranges from that old woman, there was a buckboard that passed us?"

"What of it?"

"You don't happen to know who that woman was with Val Monroe, do you?"

"Woman? Didn't even notice he was with one, love. See, when you're around, I have eyes only for you! Besides, I was too fired up with wanting to wring his neck, if you recall, to notice who he was with. If you hadn't stopped me . . . !" He shrugged. "Why're you asking? Did you think you knew her or something?"

"No, not really. She probably just reminded me of someone I used to know."

"I'm sure glad it wasn't a man. I'm real jealous these days, Sera," he teased.

"Don't I know it!" she rejoined, but there was something in her expression, which Joe, had he been looking at her in that moment, would have recognized as anxiety. She bit her lip and continued, somewhat quickly, "Oh, I can't wait 'til the wedding tomorrow! It'll be such fun, Joe, what with all the food and the dancing and everything, and I do think Gabby and Jaime make a perfect couple, don't you?"

"Almost as perfect as you and me. Did I tell you I plan on giving them a pair of my best ewes as their wedding gift from us? In a few years, Jaime should have quite a tidy little flock of his own, enough to make a good living for him and Gabby."

She nodded. "It's a fine system, Joe. And the *pastores* all respect you as their *patron*. I didn't think you could make it work—"

"—not with all those 'stinking sheep'?" he accused laughingly.

"Despite those 'stinking sheep'!" she agreed, shame-faced. "But you proved me wrong, and I'm real glad you did, darlin'. You should have a good first lambing in the fall."

"*We* should, Sera," he corrected. "But it will mean work, hard work, for everyone. Next month, we'll have to get down to building lambing pens and see the ewes herded into the foothills for better grazing during the drier summer weather. That way, we can make sure we'll have only healthy lambs born in the fall. Chances are, some if not all of the creeks will dry up, and we'll be glad of all the time we spent on digging the wells then."

She nodded in understanding, then added, "But you'll need more men before then, men with guns. All those defenseless lambs and laboring ewes will draw the coyotes and the buzzards like flies!"

"We'll have all the men we need before shearing time," Joe said confidently. "Tyonek has offered to help, and now that folks have seen we're not afraid of the Monroes and mean to stay put come what may, they're more than ready to come to work for Las Campanas."

Seraphina smiled tenderly. "I'm real proud of you, Joel McCaleb! These past months, you've worked so darned hard, done so much in so little time."

"You mean that?"

398

"Of course I do, you darn fool!"

"Well, then, I figure a little reward's in order, wouldn't you agree?" He tipped back his white hat and winked wickedly.

"Definitely," she agreed solemnly, knowing only too well the reaction her response would bring. Delicious tingles of anticipation prickled in the pit of her belly.

His shaggy brows rose in delighted surprise. "You would, would you? Well, well, woman, I'd say today's my lucky day! Last one home is a lousy dingo! Yeeaah, Jimbo! Get up there, boy!" He kicked his horse into a gallop and Seraphina, laughing helplessly, urged Muraco after him at a slower, safer pace, dust churning as they rode.

By the time they reached Casa Campanas and Joe's wide bed, she had completely forgotten her uneasy feelings earlier that afternoon—as well as the woman with Val Monroe.

Chapter Twenty-Four

That night, El Vengador embarked on a raid more daring than any he had attempted before. Alongside his four masked companions, he rode boldly onto Rancho Fuerte land, to the place where Don Harper's *vaqueros* were grazing the herd.

The *vaqueros,* mindful of the recent outbreak of rustling that had already claimed several hundred head of Señor Monroe's cattle, were more than usually vigilant that night, yet El Vengador and his men were upon them before the first sentry shouted an alarm, which was abruptly cut off.

"Mike!"

"Here!"

"Take the east flank! Dwight, you've got the west. We'll stir 'em up some, and cut the herd down the middle!"

"Okay!"

El Vengador's men spurred their horses around the restless, milling animals, which were uttering indignant bellows now. The *vaqueros* rode the fringes of the herd to meet them, kicking their sturdy little *bronchos* into a gallop.

"Stay where you are and no one'll get hurt! Monroe's

cattle ain't worth getting yourselves killed for, *hombres*—and neither is he! Now, reach!"

The Mexican drovers reined in their mounts, confused both by El Vengador's words and the gleaming black forty-five angled in their direction. *Dios,* but *el bandito* was everything they had imagined —a towering *gringo* dressed all in gleaming black upon a prancing palomino stallion! one *vaquero* reflected nervously. And as he had said, they were not so eager to die! One by one, they dropped their weapons and raised their arms above their heads in surrender.

El Vengador nodded in satisfaction and covered them until his men had cut several hundred head from the herd. Tom Maxwell rode up to him.

"We're ready to move out."

The bandit leader grunted. "Good. You and the boys drive 'em down south—and do it *pronto!* Don't let up 'til you're safely across the border. You know what to do next. I'll be seeing you when you get back."

Tom's blue eyes twinkled above his mask. "You surely will, El Vengador!" he murmured. "Sure you can handle them?" he asked, nodding toward the *vaqueros.*

"I'm sure. Now, move out before any of Monroe's boys get wind of what's going on."

With a nod, Tom wheeled his horse's head around and galloped off after the rustled cattle and the others. El Vengador jerked his gun barrel toward the fascinated *vaqueros.* "Dismount, *amigos,*" he ordered. "I'm going to have to take your horses and your guns. Can't have you singing out an alarm, now can I? You over there—what's your name?"

"Me? Paco, *señor!*"

"Well, Paco, you gather up the guns and dump 'em in the creek. The rest of you, unsaddle your horses."

When it was done, El Vengador rode his palomino across to the *vaqueros'* mounts and, with a lash or two across their rumps with his reins, sent them scattering toward the hills.

"Gracias, señores!" He saluted them with an upraised arm and was about to ride away himself when someone sprang at him from the darkness, fastening his arms about his booted leg and trying to drag him from the saddle. He kicked out and caught a glimpse of the man's face in the moonlight. Turquoise eyes met muddy brown for a burning instant that seemed endless, then he broke free and spurred his horse after the others.

It wasn't until much later, in the dark hours just before dawn, that he discovered the knife he carried in his boot was missing. For a moment, fear of discovery reared its ugly head, but then he relaxed and quickly continued changing from his outlaw garb into his usual work clothes. No one could tie the knife to him, he realized. The initials carved into it were not the ones he was known by here. If anything, the false clue should serve to throw Monroe off his trail! He tethered the palomino just inside the entry to the shaft, saw it watered and fed, replaced the brush that hid the entry, and rode home on his paint.

The women of Casa Campanas had outdone themselves in preparing the adobe ranch house for Gabrielle and Jaime's wedding. The little chapel beneath the *campanario* had been thoroughly swept and the stone altar spread with a beautiful cloth of white lace and drawn work that had been Gabrielle's Spanish mother's. A statue of the Madonna in her sky blue robe and a large silver crucifix, both Peggy Kelly's, had been set upon it. The light that lanced in narrow bars through the two arched windows high above was reflected in flashes of silver fire off the cross,

402

winking light that vied with the flickering luminescence of the elegant white tapers in wooden candlesticks that flanked it.

In tall, red earthenware *ollas* at the foot of the altar, Seraphina had arranged the Castilian roses and wildflowers she had bought at the market in the *pueblo* the day before, or else gathered in the foothills of the Sierra Nevadas early that morning while the dew still clung to each petal and the rising sun had made each drop reflect light like a fiery topaz jewel. There were lupins and Indian paintbrush, wild dog roses, and the satin poppies that the Spanish explorers had called 'cups of gold,' which would always poignantly remind Seraphina of Southern California for, like an undulating bolt of orange-yellow satin unrolled across the hills, they bloomed everywhere in the brief spring and early summer.

So, too, had she and Gabrielle carefully blown the yolks and whites from several eggs and replaced the cleaned insides with fragrant perfumes and colognes and confetti, stoppering them afterward with melted wax. These would later be divided amongst the young female guests. At an auspicious moment during the festivities, the young women would break the eggs upon the heads of the young men they admired while their backs were turned, and then quickly hide themselves. It fell upon the men to try to determine who had played the fragrant trick upon them. If they guessed correctly, they earned the honor of acting as escort to the lovely *señorita* for the remainder of the evening. It was, Gabrielle had explained, a silly yet popular game played at *fandangos* here in California, especially on the occasion of a wedding, and great fun. Since, unlike the customary bull- and bear-baiting and cockfighting popular amongst the men at *fiestas,* it was also harmless, Seraphina had eagerly gone along with the preparations, filling an egg destined only for Joe's shaggy blond head with her own favorite lily of the valley fragrance.

The kitchens had not proved large enough to handle the preparations for so lavish a feast, and so Joe had seen to the digging of a huge pit and the construction of a spit outside in the *patio,* the courtyard, upon which to roast a whole steer provided by the bride's proud father, Raoul Garnier, for the occasion. By noon, the succulent aroma of barbecued beef and mesquite smoke filled the sultry air, along with numerous other aromas that made everyone's mouth water in anticipation. There were baked and glazed hams, fried chicken, spicy *chorizos,* potatoes, and *frijoles.* There were golden ears of buttered corn and pots of simmering beans, tangy salads of sun-ripened tomatoes and onions from Peggy's own vegetable garden. Sardines had been brought inland from the blue waters beyond the Coast Range, and there were also *tortillas* and pastries and fresh-from-the-oven loaves of golden bread, which the bride herself, along with Seraphina, had baked after the gathering of the flowers shortly after sunup.

The entire house gleamed. The floors of each room, whether adobe or red tile or plank, had been scrubbed and buffed until they shone as richly as oiled leather. Still more flowers in colorful Indian pottery-ware bowls or exquisitely woven, water-tight tule baskets brightened gloomy corners, and though lacking in furniture, the cavernous rooms had been made to appear both cozy and attractive by means of many colorful, geometrically patterned Indian blankets hung where they would create the greatest impact against the stark, newly whitewashed walls. The wrought-iron sconces had been taken down and dusted and supplied with plump, new, ivory candles, and all of the dishes and platters—both the few Joe and Seraphina possessed themselves and others loaned from Señora Catalina and Gabby—had been washed and polished until they reflected images like mirrors.

"I just hope everyone comes after all this work," Seraphina said anxiously, for this was the very first time she had ever been the hostess at such a large gathering. According to custom, no invitations were ever sent out for a *fandango*. All those from the surrounding *ranchos* attended or did not, according to their fancy, so the reputation of the hostess was the only guarantee that anyone would come. "Harper Monroe has a big *fandango* planned for today, too, by all accounts, Joe. Señora Catalina said it's a yearly thing he does, to celebrate the sheriff's daughter's homecoming from school for the summer holidays. What if everyone's so afraid of offending him they go to Rancho Fuerte instead of coming here?"

"Then it's their loss, *querida,"* Joe said patiently, "and good riddance to the lot of them who're too bloody yellow to do what they want to do with their lives." He smiled grimly. "Must be mighty crowded in Monroe's pocket by now, I'd say! Where do you want this, love?" he asked, indicating the huge black stewing pot he had brought into the kitchen.

"Set it down in the corner over there, will you? And Joe, we need more kindling inside, when you have the time. The *tamales* still have to be steamed." There were stacks of them lined up upon the scrubbed table, all rolled tidily in their corn-husk jackets like little soldiers in uniform.

"I'll see to it," he promised. "Where's the blushing bride?"

Seraphina smiled. "Where else? In her room, fussing with her hair and her wedding gown, and wondering if she isn't making an awful mistake by marrying Jaime!

405

In fact, she's doing what just about every bride does on her wedding day—act nervous as a green colt! She'll be all right, though. Peg's clucking around her like an old mother hen, bless her! How's the groom bearing up?"

"He's groggy but likely to live, I think, though I did wonder about that last night! I rode ho . . . I woke up a while before dawn, and there was Jaime staggering around the corral drunk as all get out, yipping and howling at the moon like a coyote! He looked over at me when I took him by the elbow t'take him back to the bunkhouse and he said, real sad-eyed, 'Don José, my friend, my freedom is about to come to an end! It is all over!' as if he were contemplating the end of his life, for Christ's sake, instead of marrying the girl he loves!" It did not occur to Joe that he had felt exactly the same not too many months ago, when faced with the prospect of marrying Seraphina. Love had softened the sharp, uncomfortable edges of memory in his case.

"And I would hope you told him otherwise?" Seraphina demanded, indignation in her tone.

"Well, I *would* have, love . . . I'd have told him all about the wonders of wedded—and bedded—bliss, if I'd had the chance, but—!"

"But why didn't you?"

"Because the poor bloke passed out on me—faded dead away at my feet! Couldn't wake him for anything, so me and Stefano had to drag him inside to his bunk. Got himself a bonzer headache this morning, he has, too, and looks sort of green about the gills. Got anything that'll take care of it?"

His wife nodded. "Of course. I'll send him out some herb tea just as soon as these chickens are in the pot."

"Just the ticket!"

She dropped the skillet with a clatter then, and she noticed that he winced.

"Care for some of my herb tea yourself, Mister

406

McCaleb?" she asked, her dark, winglike brows raised inquiringly, a suggestion of fond amusement in her eyes. The men had begun some serious drinking soon after sundown the evening before, and they hadn't shown any sign of quitting even long after moonrise, when she had turned in for the night. She had a hunch Joe was feeling somewhat under the weather and green about the gills himself.

Joe grinned. "Nah, love, I never touch the stuff," he denied scornfully as he left the kitchen, pinching her bottom on the way out as she bent over.

By noon, everyone from Casa Campanas and several guests from the *pueblo* and surrounding *ranchos* who had wanted to witness the service, among them Señora Catalina and Olivia and Esteban Rodriguez, Joe's *mayordomo,* had assembled in the little chapel within the adobe ranch house. The heady fragrance of the pink, white, and crimson roses and the pungent smell of incense from the early-morning Mass filled the air.

As the priest, who had ridden out to the ranch from his church in Los Angeles, offered a last blessing for the newly married couple, Seraphina gazed up at the freshly whitewashed walls of the little chapel where once, not so very many weeks ago, the accusing eyes painted upon them had so disturbed her. Her gaze traveled still higher above, to where the three lovely, silent bells hung in the *campanario*—silent, so legend said, because the beautiful bronze trio were destined never to ring until the curse of the Indian princess, Little Owl, had been finally laid to rest and two who truly loved had been united in marriage in this very chapel. Would Gabrielle and Jaime's wedding here, in this place, release Las Campanas from the ancient spell under which, at times, she yet seemed to slumber?

407

Holding her breath, Seraphina realized with a start that it was all over. The service was over, but for several moments she had subconsciously been waiting for a sudden, silvery clamor to peal forth from the *campanario,* a sign that Gabby's wedding was indeed blessed. There was none, of course, and a sad little sigh escaped her. She and Joe had not been married here in this place; nor, if the truth were known, had they ever truly been married at all, not lawfully, for it was not her own name she had signed on the marriage certificate in San Francisco but that of another young woman.

A shudder of foreboding washed over her. Surely, under the circumstances, she and Joe should be vulnerable to Little Owl's curse, if she believed in such superstitious nonsense. *If.* Ah, but there was the difference, surely! She *didn't* believe in it, she told herself sternly, and therefore it was nothing more than a delightful, if melancholy, old legend . . .

"Ding dong!"

She glanced up sharply into Joe's smiling face, the blood draining from about her mouth. "Oh!" she gasped.

"Sorry, love, didn't mean to startle you," he apologized softly, staring down at her pale, lovely face and taken aback by the dazed, almost shocked, expression in her haunting, gray-green eyes. *Madonna eyes,* he thought fleetingly, moved by the unexpected sadness in their luminous depths at that moment and wondering at its possible cause. "Say, you weren't really expecting the bells to ring, were you, Sera?"

Taken aback by his uncannily shrewd insight, she tried to look indignant but succeeded only in looking guilty. "Of course not! What do you take me for? A silly, romantic fool?" she hissed.

He shrugged noncommittally. "Well, just in case you were wondering, Ming and I checked them two days

408

ago. They're perfectly ordinary bells, except for one very important difference," he whispered.

"What's that?" she couldn't resist asking, despite her irritation with him.

"They have no clappers—you know, the parts that strike the bell to make the sound? That's why they've never rung, see, love? It has nothing to do with Indian curses or legends or anything like that, I'm afraid! I wanted to fix them up for the wedding today, but there was no time."

She nodded but did not appear entirely convinced, he thought. By way of reassurance, he squeezed her hand and was startled to find it as cold as ice. "Y'know, you look lovely enough this morning to be a bride yourself, love," he murmured, caressing the tip of each chilly little finger in an intimate way that sent warmth seeping back through her. "Know what I'd like to do right now? I'd like to unfasten all those blasted little pearl buttons one by one and . . . !"

She blushed, smiled, yet scolded him. "Shh! We're in *church,* Joe! Behave yourself for once!"

"I'll try," he promised solemnly, but the wicked glint in his turquoise eyes refused to be dimmed even in the hushed gloom of the chapel.

"Bravo!" someone shouted, splintering that hush, and Seraphina glanced up just as Jaime Santiago lifted his radiant bride's white lace *mantilla* away from her pixie face and bent his dark, curly head to kiss her for the first time as her husband.

All at once, the people in the chapel exploded into life again, the *pastores* flinging their best, silver-trimmed *sombreros* into the air and whooping as cries and shouts of congratulations went up. The new Señor *y* Señora Jaime Santiago, both smiling broadly, exchanged tender looks. They clasped hands and ran from the chapel and out into the brilliant sunlight, showers of rice and rose petals raining down upon them from the dozens of guests gathered outside in the courtyard waiting to wish them well.

"Music! Wine! Everyone, dance! Be happy!" roared Raoul Garnier, beaming with pride and pleasure as he gazed at the flushed and happy faces of his only daughter and his fine new son-in-law. He gave Gabby a great bear hug about the shoulders and kissed her soundly on both cheeks and mouth. Then, to everyone's amusement, he did the same to a red-faced Jaime. The fiddlers and the guitar- and trumpet-players eagerly struck up a merry Mexican melody, lively, romantic music that seemed created especially for weddings. Jaime, stars in his dark eyes, resplendent in his groom's finery of bolero jacket, scarlet sash, and ruffled shirt, form-fitting pants and stilt-heeled boots, took his Gabrielle by the arm and led her out into the courtyard, where the dewy-eyed bride and groom danced to the first melody alone.

Tears of happiness for the couple misted Seraphina's eyes, for he was so handsome, she so glowing in her heavily embroidered white gown, the traditional Basque coronet of white flowers and the snowy lace *mantilla* framing her heart-shaped face. As they danced about the courtyard, many of the guests went up to them and pinned onto, or tucked into, their clothing gifts of money, a Spanish custom to assure prosperity and good fortune in their married life together. The money-festooned pair offered their thanks to the company and were further rewarded by enthusiastic clapping and cries of *"Bravo!"* when they had finished dancing. Then everyone, it seemed, joined them in the second dance.

The dance had not quite ended when the fiddlers suddenly stopped their enthusiastic sawing, their unfinished notes squalling like shrieking cats on the sudden quiet that had fallen over the courtyard. So, too, the trumpets were abruptly silenced. A hush fell upon the crowd as all heads turned toward the wide double gateway in the fortresslike *casa* walls; all eyes grew riveted upon the little party of Indians who sat their shaggy ponies there between them.

A whisper of unrest and dismay rippled through the gathering like the wind through a field of ripened wheat. *"Pah! Indios!"* The words, uttered with disgust and contempt, trembled on the lips of many, for what good intentions could these scavengers, these lazy, good-for-nothings, have toward those of Casa Campanas on such a day? No doubt they were beggars, come here to ask for handouts!

But to everyone's surprise, Joe stepped forward from the crowd, Raoul Garnier at his elbow. Both men were smiling broadly as they approached the party, and Joe had his hand outstretched in obvious welcome to Chief Tyonek, who watched him approach with an impassive expression.

"Greetings, Wise Grandfather!" Joe declared in his newly acquired Spanish. "We are honored that you and those of your *ranchería* have come here to Casa Campanas today to join our celebration of this occasion! Chief Tyonek, this is the father of the *señorita* who was wed today, and also my friend. Raoul Garnier, Chief Tyonek."

The old chief nodded and, in the style of the white man, reached out to clasp the hand Garnier extended to him in a firm handshake. "When a daughter marries, it is a joyful time for a father, for in the joining, he gains a son," he pronounced solemnly. "And soon, if the Wise One Above wills it, grandchildren!" Now Tyonek's black eyes twinkled. "It is my wish that your grandchildren will be many, and also your winters in which to enjoy them, friend Garnier!"

411

Raoul threw back his massive head and gave a great rumble of laughter that shook his prodigious belly. "And mine, Chief!" he roared, tugging at his mustache and heartily slapping across the back the fragile old man, who had dismounted from his pony. "Gabrielle, *ma belle fille,* come, greet your guests!"

Gabrielle and Jaime came forward to meet and greet Tyonek and those of his *rancheria*—Wichado, Yakecen, and Milap among them—who had accompanied him. Gabby exclamed in sincere delight as she accepted the beautifully patterned baskets of tule reeds, the woolen blankets, the silver and turquoise ornaments, and the fine new *ollas,* which they had brought the couple as wedding gifts.

"Grandfather Tyonek, my husband and I thank you for everything, from ze bottom of our hearts! Please, come with me. You have ridden so far, and now you must eat and rest and enjoy the music," Gabby urged Tyonek, though for once she seemed shy and uncertain of herself. "There is plenty, more than enough for everyone," she declared, overcoming her shyness.

"We will share your feast," the old chief agreed amicably. "But first, our medicine woman, Satinka, wishes to see the young one who was injured two moons ago."

"He means Ming," Seraphina explained to Gabby, smiling as she came forward tugging a suddenly tongue-tied Ming by the elbow. "Old Mother, this is the one. Look at his wrists! The bones are straight and strong, thanks to your healing. We have great love in our hearts for you, and for what you did for him that awful day."

Ming nodded solemn agreement, though his almond eyes widened at first sight of the frightening old woman who had suddenly thrust herself forward from behind the Indian men, for she resembled nothing so much as a

412

scrawny scarecrow adorned by various-colored rags, all twiglike arms and bony legs. Animal claws, pouches, feathers, bone whistles, and other tinkling talismans hung from her person and from the waistband of her skirt. Bright, cunning, slanted black eyes gleamed back at Ming from a nut brown, weathered face that appeared to have sunk in about the mouth from lack of teeth. Like a squash left too long in the sun will rot and sink inward, he thought as she grinned broadly. He gulped. "I am most grateful, Missie . . . Missie . . . ?" Embarrassed, he gave up and repeated lamely, "I am indeed most grateful for your help that day."

The old medicine woman nodded toothlessly, grinning and cackling with laughter. She gave a whoop and clapped a clawlike hand on either side of Ming's head, dragging it down to plant a smacking, gummy kiss full upon his lips. She reeked of garlic and musty herbs and the unspeakable contents of her amulets, but to Ming's credit, he made no attempt to escape her poisonous embrace, much to Joe's amusement. The woman muttered something excitedly to Tyonek, and the chief smiled as the old crone batted her eyelashes in Ming's direction.

"Mother Satinka tells me she finds me she finds you very pleasing to look upon, Little Yellow Brother, and that it is many, many winters since she has embraced so handsome a young brave! She asks if there is already one who shares your blankets?"

"Huh?" Ming queried, mystified.

"Is there a woman who shares your lodge?"

Seraphina jabbed him in the ribs, trying hard not to laugh. "Wake up! Mother Satinka is doing you a great honor, Ming. She . . . she wants to know if you're . . . you're married!"

Panic flared in Ming's dark eyes. "Why?" he squeaked,

his voice breaking.

Seraphina grinned, laughter bubbling up from deep inside her. "Why do you think?"

Ming's almond-shaped eyes widened, becoming as round as saucers in his dismay. He shook his head slowly from side to side. "Oh, no, Missie Seraphina, please . . . Joe . . . I cannot!" he whispered, his voice strangely hoarse and strangled sounding all of a sudden. "I cannot!" He gave a jerky nod to the old woman, muttered something, and bolted.

"Our little brother said that he is overwhelmed by your offer, Mother Satinka," Seraphina explained politely, lying through her teeth, the corners of her lips twitching, her eyes dancing merrily, "but he regrets that, according to the customs of his people across the Great Waters in the west, he is far too young to take a woman to his blankets, however much he may admire her wisdom and her beauty. He asks your understanding and acceptance of his customs, however strange they may seem to you."

Satinka cackled with raucous laughter and crowed something outrageous, and probably salacious, to her chief, who translated, smiling as broadly as all of them were now, "Satinka says that she understands, but promises she will wait—though very impatiently—until he is older, to share his blankets!"

Raoul Garnier, chuckling himself, declared, "Enough, all of you! You are indeed scoundrels, *mon amis,* for teasing the poor boy so! No doubt he will not dare show his face again this day! Come, follow me to ze tables! You've come a long way, Tyonek, and an empty belly is a most uncomfortable thing, *n'est-ce pas?"* He winked broadly and patted his own, definitely not empty, belly, before taking Tyonek companionably by the elbow. He led the old chief and his shy, lovely granddaughter, Izusa, and the others to the groaning tables.

After a few moments more, the dancing and music got underway again, the tension having been dispelled as everyone followed Joe's and Raoul's leads and accepted the Indians as the welcome guests they were.

"I do believe our Ming is growing up," Seraphina whispered, going on tiptoe to murmur in Joe's ear.

"Why? What did the lad really say before he cut and ran?" Joe asked with a grin.

"That he liked Izusa real well, but would never, *never* marry the ugly old she-demon!" She chose that moment to draw her cologne-filled egg from beneath her skirts and dash it against Joe's head, laughing as streams of the fragrant lily of the valley perfume and damp confetti cascaded over his shoulders.

"What the—"

"A local custom, *Don José!*" she crowed. "It means you've been chosen as my escort for the evening!"

He grinned and shook his streaming head. "Does this mean I don't stand a chance with pretty little Izusa?" he teased.

"Try it, McCaleb, and you'll be sorry," she threatened.

"Don't worry, woman!" he retorted, tugging her close and claiming a quick kiss. He sniffed. "In small doses, that perfume smells pretty enough, but in quantity . . . Strewth! Smelling like this, even my horse won't want to know me!"

They were separated soon after, Seraphina dragged away to perform introductions, serve punch, and attend to her other duties as hostess, Joe called away to the corral to see to the wild mustangs, the *bronchos,* which Tyonek's braves had rounded up and herded down from the foothills. The riding of these spirited animals would be the main attraction of the small *rodeo* he had planned for entertainment that afternoon, along with the inevitable horse races and exhibitions of roping and riding that were customary at any *fiesta*, as well as the less pleasant but customary cockfight Raoul had arranged and upon which most of the menfolk had wagered bets. Seraphina saw that Señora Catalina's plate was filled and stopped by to exchange a few words with her.

"It is a lovely *fiesta*, Serafina *mía!*" the widow exclaimed, patting her hand fondly. "You should be most proud! The food is *magnífico!*" She glanced over her shoulder, as if to make certain they were not being overheard. "Many of your guests were expected to attend the *fandango* at Rancho Fuerte today, you know, *niña*. It is a mark of their respect and liking for Don José and yourself that they have risked Don Harper's anger and have chosen to come to Las Campanas instead."

"And what of you, Catalina, and your poor cousin, Doña Anita? Do you not fear for her if Don Harper is angered?"

Catalina sighed. "I do indeed. But, for many years now, Anita has been forced to fend for herself against him. Were I to have gone there, there would have been little I could have done to help her, other than offer a sympathetic ear." She brightened. "And so, I decided I would come to Las Campanas instead, and visit *mi amiga* Serafina. Forgive my indelicacy in asking, *niña*, but . . . there is a certain look about you . . . Are you not with child?"

"I am," Seraphina confessed, blushing.

Catalina clapped her hands and beamed. "A baby! Oh, how wonderful for you and Don José!"

"Thank you, Doña Catalina! But now, if you'll excuse us, I'd like the honor of this dance with my

416

future son's mother!" came a voice to Sera's right, and she looked up to see Joe standing there.

"I'd be delighted, sir," she smilingly accepted, offering Catalina an apologetic smile. He took her arm and led her out into the sunlight of the courtyard.

The last time he had danced with her had been at their own wedding, Seraphina recalled as Joe's arm slipped snugly around her waist. He drew her close and turned her fluidly in time to the strains of the waltz that seemed to lift them up and carry them away on its lilting tide. They'd come a long way since San Francisco, she thought, and yet they had come absolutely nowhere! She rested her cheek against Joe's broad shoulder as they waltzed, drawing a little comfort from his wiry strength, his masculine warmth and nearness. But even their closeness was not enough to dispel the melancholy that had tangled gloomy webs about her spirit more than once already that day. Although they had their mutual love for each other, she strongly believed that many of the other things that a marriage should be founded on, such as honesty and truth, were lacking. Joe had no inkling that she'd been less than honest with him. Oh, dear lord, yes, there were too many lies, half-truths, she had told him. Her heart ached, and the gaiety of that shining day was dimmed by sadness. She should have told him the truth long ago; she knew that. The minute she had found out the implications of William McCaleb's will, she should have set her cards on the table. By saying nothing, by leaving it this long, it had grown so hard to tell, she'd never be able to do it! She was only human, after all, with human failings. How could any woman tell the man she loved that she was not the woman he believed her to be; that she had lied to him and, furthermore, that because of what she had done, the very land he had grown to love, had worked for and fought for, had

417

risked his life for, was not his? And it could *never* be his, not if William McCaleb's will was legally binding. Without Joe's marriage to Seraphina Jones, Las Campanas became instead the property of the First Presbyterian Church of San Francisco, to be disposed of or retained as they wished. Damn! How she regretted the day she'd recklessly agreed to help Chuck when he'd come to her at the Boston Academy! What a little fool she'd been to let herself become so enmeshed in this whole business! But she had, and now here she was, paying the price for her recklessness; in love with Joe, carrying Joe's baby when they weren't even legally married! And her poor family had not the slightest idea of where she was, or even if she was alive or dead! Just the thought of all the grief and heartache she must have caused them these past weeks made her stomach heave and her knees feel weak.

"Please, honey, I have to sit down for a spell!" she pleaded, looking up at Joe and seeing him through a mist of tears. "Why don't you ask the bride or Catalina for the next dance while I sit out?"

Joe frowned, concern deepening the sun furrows that winged outward from his turquoise eyes. "What? Shall I fetch a doctor, love?"

"No, no, of course not! It must be the heat and all the excitement this week. I'll be fine after a little rest, really, Joe," she insisted, smiling bravely on the outside but close to tears on the inside. It was as if all her worries, her fears over her deceit, had reached their culmination on this one day, filling her with a sense of doomed hopelessness that was overwhelming.

Despite her protests, Joe escorted her to a shady spot beneath a towering cypress tree where she could watch the festivities from the comfort of a wide wooden bench close to the opened gateway. Through it wafted a cooling breeze, which fanned her flushed cheeks. "Sit

418

yourself down here, love," he ordered, "and put your feet up. I'm going to fetch you a cold drink and something bonzer to eat. That'll set you right up! You've been so busy seeing to everyone else, I'd bet you haven't eaten a thing all day yourself, have you?"

"No, but I really don't want anyth—"

"Shh. I'm the boss around here, *el patron,* remember, little mama?" he teased, gently stroking her flushed cheek with the back of his hand. Before she could protest further, he strode off in the direction of the laden tables, weaving his way between the colorfully gowned, dancing couples. She was left alone.

For several moments, she simply sat there, lost in her thoughts, oblivious to the gaiety, the music, the laughter, the vivid blue skies above the *casa* and the air of *fiesta* everywhere about her. Then she sighed and scanned the throng for Joe, needing a glimpse of his dear face for reassurance. She was unable to spot him amongst the guests, but he'd be back soon, as he'd promised—

She stiffened, fear leaping through her as cruel fingers like steely traps suddenly clamped over her bare shoulders and dug in painfully.

"Don't scream, sweet thing," came a harsh voice against her ear. "Don't scream, don't try to run. Just stand up and walk with me through the gates, easy now. If you behave yerself, you won't get hurt. Nor will anyone else."

As if in a horrifying dream, she obeyed the anonymous voice, rising and turning and walking between the heavy wooden gates and out beyond the *casa* walls with the mechanical movements of a puppet. But once outside, she swung around and caught a fleeting glimpse of Val Monroe's leering face before he grasped her wrist and twisted her arm up cruelly behind her back, spinning her around. The pain made her whimper. Another half-inch, and the bone would snap, she sensed, feeling sick and faint.

"So, you seen me! Well, now you know who I am . . . and I know exactly who you are, sweet thing! That's only fair, ain't it?" he jeered.

"You're *loco,* Monroe! You must be, to come here today! If Joe sees you, he'll kill you!" she hissed at him. "Now, let go of me and get off my land!"

Val chuckled, breathing heavily down her neck and making her flesh crawl. "That would be a mite too easy, now wouldn't it, honey? You and me both know you've got guts, but you'll have to do more than threaten to get rid of me this time, sweet thing. A whole heap more."

She gritted her teeth, her eyes blazing. "If you mean what I think you mean, you dirty snake, you really are *loco!*"

He laughed softly, regretfully. "Oh, honey, I just wish that could be so! I'd show you a real fine ole time of it! But that's not why I'm here. I came to bring you a message, see, from my pa. He ain't too fond o' you and yer man today, no siree. Seems folks'd rather ride out to Campanas for their *fandango* than visit Fuerte. Got heaps o'chow fixed out there, and only a handful o'folks t'eat it. Yep. Pa's *real* unhappy 'bout that so soon after them danged rustlers made off with nearly half our herd. Say, you wouldn't know of anyone who lost themselves a knife, now would you?" He casually drew a hunting knife from his belt that she recognized all too well. The initials J.C. were carved into the wooden handle, alongside a kangaroo. "It belongs to that bandit, El Vengador," Val continued. "If'n I ketch up with him, I'll use it t'slice him inter little pieces!"

"I've never seen it before," she lied, her heart pounding. Oh, Lord! Joe was El Vengador, she knew it! And if Val found out . . . ! "If that's your message, you've delivered it. I'll pass the word on to our guests

420

about your pa's . . . disappointment."

His eyes glittered as he smarted under her jibes. To even the score, he jerked hard on her arm, smiling as the move elicited a gasp of pain. "Oh, but that ain't it, gal," he breathed. "There's more. A heap more."

"O-ohh?" she gritted.

"Yessiree! Pa told me to be sure an' tell you he knows *all* about you, little gal!"

"Good for him! Now, if that's all you've got to say, I'll be getting back!" She tried to wrench away from him, but he jerked her arm up again so roughly that the bone ground against the joint, making her cry out. Beads of sweat sprang out on her brow and upper lip.

"Sometimes, *Katie,* honey, you're a mite too plucky for your own good. Now, stand still! I don't want to hurt you 'less I have to." His eager, breathy tone belied his denial.

"What did you call me?" she asked, realizing suddenly what it was he had said.

He flung her about to face him, relishing the ill-concealed dismay in her expression.

"There! Now you're listening up real nice! I called you *Katie,* sweet thing. Katie Steele. That *is* your real name, after all, ain't it?" His tone was definite, final.

Only a slight flicker of her black lashes betrayed her as she insisted, "Maybe you've been out in the sun too long, mister? Or got some *loco* weed mixed up in your feed? You know damn well what my name is! Seraphina McCaleb."

"Really, sweet thing?" He grinned wolfishly. "Cissy Tallant didn't seem to think you were who you say you are, not at all."

A strangled cry broke from her. "Who?" she breathed.

"Little ole Cissy—Sheriff Clem Tallant's daughter."

"Tallant? *Cissy*—Cecilia Tallant's the sheriff's

421

daughter?" Lord, she knew she sounded like a dim-witted fool, but it wouldn't sink in, somehow.

"That's it! Cissy told me you and she went to school together back east, and that she'd know you anywheres, sweet thing! She told me all about you, an' all about your pa and his Injun blood and his ranch, and all about what good friends you were with Seraphina Jones—the *real* Seraphina Jones, that is. 'Course, we just *had* to tell my pa all about it. Hell, it was too good a secret to keep! He rode into town and sent a wire or two to friends of his up in Frisco, and a little while later we knowed all about you and McCaleb and his grand-daddy's money and what you done. You lied, sweet thing—and that trustin', upstandin' man of yours don't even know it, do he?"

She bit her lip and knotted her fists to keep from screaming and flailing at his hateful face. Her heart's loud thumping hammered in her ears. *Cissy Tallant.* There was no point in denying it, not if that spiteful little cat had recognized her. How could she have been stupid enough to miss the connection between Sheriff Tallant and sneaky Cissy, his daughter? When had she seen her? In the *pueblo* yesterday? Yes, it had to have been then . . .

"You've made your point, Monroe," she managed to say finally, sounding far calmer than she felt. "What is it you want from me?" She knew without a shadow of a doubt there would be a price for his silence, and she had a hunch about what it would be. Damn! She'd sooner die . . . !

His gaze wolfishly raked her, as if his hungry, leering eyes could peel away her clothes and see her stripped naked beneath them. "Oh, there's no time for what I'm really wanting, sweet thing," he said so softly she had to strain to catch his words, his tone loaded with regret, "so I guess I'll have to settle for less. My pa wants

McCaleb out of this valley, and soon. Looks like we're in for a long, hot summer, an' he wants the water Las Campanas has for our herds, and the land and the wells your man dug with it. He's gotten real tired o'waitin'. You know he's tried everything to budge your man, but nothin's worked. Pa figures he's got one last shot at it— through you, honey. He reckons he can use you to get McCaleb out of this valley once an' for all."

"How?" she demanded, her voice hoarse with fear.

"Anyone with eyes can see the man's crazy about you, Miz Katie-Seraphina! Heck, I can't say I blame him, neither." His snake eyes glittered again and he licked his lips, his hand hovering out as if he intended to stroke her breast. He thought better of it, however, and the hand fell slack against his side. "But . . . just supposin' you weren't around, honey. What if you up and left him flat, without a word to anyone about where you'd gone or why or with who, and you never came back? Sweet thing, I reckon that'd kill him surer than a bullet in his belly! It'd take the heart and the fight clean out of him. And then . . ."

"Then you and your family of stinkin' buzzards could add a little pressure, move in on him hard, and Joe would leave Las Campanas?" She shook her head, her eyes glittering with scorn. "You're a bigger parcel of fools than even I took you for, if you believe that would work! You're underestimating a man who's worth fifty—a hundred—times what you and your litter of coyote brothers are worth! Joe loves this land! It means as much—maybe more—to him than I do. And he's awful proud and awful stubborn, too. Even if I agreed to do what you said, he'd never leave. Never, you hear me?"

"You think not? Well, you do your part real nice, an' jest let us worry about that, sweet thing."

The hand was back, hovering inches from her

423

breasts. He stared at the swell of them as if mesmerized, and her flesh crawled.

She snorted with disgust "You're *loco* if you think I'll help you!"

"An' you're *loco* if you think we'd just ask, all pretty and nice!" He leered. "Oh, no, hon, we ain't askin'. We're *tellin'*. 'Less we hear word in the next day or so that you've hightailed it for home—New Mexico, weren't it?—your precious Joe is gonna meet with a real nasty accident, a long and lingerin' sort of accident, if you catch my drift." He grinned. "Either way, we'll win. And don't think we can't do it. Your Joe can't stop us, neither. Hell, we fixed that yeller-boy he's so darned fond of but good, didn't we—an' we can do the same to him. Only takes a second when his guard is down out there on the range, or when he's sleepin' by the camp fire, and it'll be all over with for your stinkin' shepherd an' his stinkin' sheep," he mocked. "I'd say you wouldn't want that, right, sweet thing?"

She swallowed, feeling sick to her stomach. "And if I don't do it, you'll tell him everything?"

Val nodded. "Either way, you stand to lose him, honey. Men ain't partial to lyin' women, see. Leastways if you do what we want, he'll still be alive." He quirked his brows and scratched his jaw. "Sort of."

He stood watching her face, watching the play of emotions flickering across her face like night moths. Lord, if she weren't a looker! His gaze dropped down to savor again the firm thrust of her breasts against the pleated bodice of her rose-pink gown; the sleek swell of her hips and the long, lean line of her flanks hinted at by the garment's folds. The ache in his groin grew and spread out until it was all he could do to stand there, doing nothing. Every fibre of his body ached with the lust to throw her down on her backside in the dust, throw up her fancy skirts, and have her; to burn the

424

hankerin' for her out of his body and soul once and for all, and wipe that cool and mocking expression, that undisguised contempt for him, from her eyes. Learning from Cissy that she had a dash of Injun blood had only whetted his lust, not dulled it as Cis had hoped. Hell, every man knew that when you had yerself an Injun woman, it was like riding a bucking bronc or wrestlin' a mountain cat, they were that hot fer a man—any man! "I'm waitin', gal," he said unsteadily. "Will it be yes or no?"

He almost held his breath for the few endless seconds it took her to answer, hoping perversely that she'd say no.

But at last she nodded and murmured faintly, "Yes." Then again, stronger and with hatred sparking at him like embers from her burning eyes, "Yes, damn your souls! I'll do it." She had to! She knew only too well that the Monroes were more than capable of making good their threat. After all, Joe was only one man against the five of them, his shepherds gentle, non-violent men incapable of providing the assistance he would need to meet the Monroes in another confrontation. Even the thought of Joe wounded or dead made her feel faint and cold as death herself, she loved him so! "Well, you've got what you came for, Monroe!" she said woodenly. "Now, get your slimy carcass the hell off this land, before I get reckless and yell for help!"

With a final leer, Val Monroe tipped his hat to her and strode to his horse, which had been feasting on some of Peggy's vegetables where Val had left him ground-tied. His spurs jingled and his chaps slap-slapped as he went. He swung up into the saddle with a creak of leather and gathered the reins in his fists, looking down at her.

"To tell the truth, honey, I was kind of hoping you'd say no," he said ruefully. "See, I figured a young

425

widow-woman like you would be needing some company real soon, with McCaleb dead, and I reckoned ole Val to be just the one to give you a little comfortin'."

"Monroe!"

"Yeah, sweet thing?" He leered down at her.

What she said next drove the sly grin utterly from his lips and made the blood drain from about his mouth, leaving it a white, pinched slash in his foxy, tanned face. Scowling and tight jawed, he lashed his reins across his horse's rump and spurred the poor beast away toward Rancho Fuerte.

Only when he was no more than a distant cloud of red dust did Seraphina let her knees do what they had willed for so many endless minutes, and she sank slowly down to the ground outside the tall adobe walls of Casa Campanas.

Joe, who had noticed her missing and come in search of her, found her there moments later, too numb for tears—and far too afraid of Val Monroe's threats to tell.

Chapter Twenty-Five

Joe lifted Sera and carried her to their room, setting her down carefully upon the wide bed. Peggy hovered at his elbow, making concerned clucking noises.

"Is she all right, sir?" she demanded. "Shall I send one o'the men t'the town fer a doctor?"

"There's no need. Doc Wilkinson is here at Casa Campanas, Peg. Fetch him, would you?" Joe asked tersely.

Doc Wilkinson came, expecting some dire emergency judging by his expression as he entered the room, a result, Joe guessed, of Peggy's excited and all but incoherent babblings for him to hurry himself. The doctor's grim expression softened after he had carefully examined Seraphina and pronounced her fit, other than for her quite obvious fatigue. "You know how women are, Joe," he said reassuringly when he was finished. "They get all fired up and fluff out their feathers when there's a party in the offing, and just about run themselves into the ground preparing for it! In my opinion, your wife will be just fine after a good night's sleep, but I'll leave a bottle of tonic for her to take anyway. It can't hurt." He turned to look down sternly at Seraphina over his gold-rimmed spectacles.

"As for you, young lady, you take things easy for a spell, you hear me? You wouldn't want to lose that little baby, now would you?"

She shook her head and smiled wanly.

"Good. Well, if you don't need me any longer, I'll be going back to the *fiesta* now. Wonderful party, Joe! Haven't had myself such a good time in ages. I'll look in on her again before I head on back to town. How's that?"

"Just the ticket. Thanks, Doc. You've taken a load off my mind," Joe murmured, walking the doctor to the door and herding Peggy Kelly through it along with him. Under protest, Peggy left in the doctor's wake.

"Well, love," Joe said seconds later, coming to sit beside Seraphina and taking her hand in his, "It looks like you'll live! Christ! You gave me a scare! Thought I'd lost you for a minute." His crooked grin denied the tension about his eyes. "I couldn't take losing you, Sera. Not now." His tone was husky, loaded with emotion.

She reached up and straightened the lapels of his coat, smoothing down the ruffles of the formal, Spanish-style shirt beneath in a caring gesture. "Don't talk *loco!*" she murmured, endeavoring to keep her tone light though the effort it took to reassure him at all, to lie yet again, was great and weighed heavily on her heart. "We all feel that way when we're faced by losing someone. But somehow, despite the grief, we manage to go on when we do, don't we? So would you."

"Can't say I agree with you, love. There's a world of difference between just *existing* from day to day and real living," Joe said with feeling. "That's what it would be for me, without you. Existing. Nothing more." He leaned down and gently pressed his lips to hers, kissing her so tenderly she felt as if she were melting inside. "I hate to leave you, love, but if you're sure you're all

428

right, I guess I'd better get back to our guests," he said with obvious reluctance as he stood up.

"Men! You're all bad liars, Joel McCaleb!" Seraphina teased gently. "I know exactly where you're headed—and it has nothin' to do with our guests. To the cockfighting pit! Come on, 'fess up! How much have you wagered—and on whose bird?"

He grinned. "Only five bucks—but it's a sure thing. One of Raoul's best cocks."

"Nothing's a sure thing, when it comes to gambling. Oh, go on with you, then! Don't look so darned guilty!"

"I'll send Peggy in to sit with you, shall I?"

"Don't be silly! Let her enjoy the *fiesta*. Lord knows, she's worked hard enough this week! Honest, Joe, there's no need to fuss over me. I'm feeling much better, really I am."

"You're sure?"

"I'm positive."

With her reassurance, he left her alone.

To Sera's surprise, she dozed for an hour or so after Joe left, yet it was a far from restful sleep. She dreamed about the Indian princess, Little Owl, and fancied she saw her, her belly swollen with child, wandering aimlessly through the desert regions north of the Sierra Nevadas' sawtoothed range, her long, black hair matted with dirt and dust, her fringed, buckskin garments torn and dirty. In her dream, she ran after Little Owl, but when she reached the crest of a sandy hill, the lovely Indian maid had vanished and only a blinking white owl, perched among the twisted branches of the thorny chaparral, remained where she had been. The owl opened its beak upon spying Seraphina, seemingly to give a low whoot or twitter of protest at her intrusion upon its roosting place, but the sound that came forth from the bird's throat was undeniably human; it was the bitter, soul-wrenching weeping of a young girl as she mourned her handsome, heartless Spanish lover's betrayal and grieved for the cruel father who had abandoned her, made her an outcast, and left her to die. The eerie sound made Seraphina's flesh crawl.

"Please, oh, my father, let me come home! Let me return to the lodges of our people! I thirst, oh, how I thirst, Father! My belly cries with hunger, and without food and shelter my babe and I shall surely die!"

In the manner of dreams, Seraphina was at once apart from and within the young girl. She felt the pain Little Owl felt; the huge swelling of her tongue and lips with thirst; the mindless craving for liquid of any kind; the gnawing hunger in her belly and the merciless blaze of the relentless, spinning white orb of the cruel sun upon her bared head and arms. And she felt—dear Lord!—she felt the flutter of Little Owl's babe in her womb, the faint stirrings of the new life that would undeniably culminate in death even before its true birth—or was it the butterfly stirrings of her own child, hers and Joe's?

In confusion, she tossed fretfully, grinding her fists into the pillows, imploring Little Owl's father to relent and bring his daughter safely home to their *ranchería*. "She must come home, don't you see? And I . . . I must go home, too . . . yes, it's the only way! Oh, Joe, darlin', be careful! Please, please, be careful!"

In her dream, she heard suddenly a clamor of bells in the vast, empty desert, echoing, echoing far across the burning white sand, reverberating amongst the spiny cactus and the blood-and-ochre-colored canyons. It was not the sweet, joyous pealing of the bronze bells in the *campanario* of Las Campanas, but a harsh, ugly sound, so loud and violent and demanding that the very earth trembled with the strident clanging, and even in her dreams, her ears pained her so badly she

430

covered them with her palms to blot out the sounds. From nowhere, Satinka, Tyonek's medicine woman, appeared and began an eerie dance, her multi-colored rags flying about her like the bedraggled feathers of some grotesque, enormous bird, her scrawny brown arms and legs working like frantic pistons as she jiggled and jerked, clicking her gourd rattles and cackling her incantations to Chinigchinich:

"You have broken the laws of our people, my pretty, and shared the robes of a man not of our people without benefit of marriage. Such is forbidden, as well you knew, and so, you must pay. The price is death, Little Owl! Come, O Great Chinigchinich! Come in the guise of our brother the bear, or the mountain lion or the clever raven, and slay her! Make this most wicked maiden one with the many stars above. Come! With claw and teeth, with beak and fang, with fur and feather, come! Come! Come!"

Seraphina was abruptly jolted awake by the violence of her visions; by the awful chanting of Satinka that echoed over and over in her mind; by the bells' violent jangling, and by her own cries and the conflicting emotions battling inside her. She wept with relief to find it had all been nothing but a horrible dream. Bathed in perspiration, she lay very still, waiting for the wild tattoo of her heart to steady to an even throb. Lord! Little Owl, the bells, the desert wastes and frightening Satinka—they had all seemed so real! Too real by far . . .

Her eyelids fluttered open. With a sigh, she saw that she was quite safe in her and Joe's room. Familiar shadows filled it, cool and restful and infinitely soothing. The sky, framed by the wrought-iron grilled window, was paling to a gentle amethyst pricked with tiny white stars and a full round moon that was the creamy, waxen color of a yucca lily. The chords of a guitar carried from the *patio,* and along with the intricate melody plucked from it by loving fingers, a rich male voice rose in harmony. It was a song she knew; a *corrido,* a ballad of love won and lost such as lovesick *caballeros* were wont to play when serenading their sweethearts below flowered casements on romantic, sultry evenings such as this. The music became louder, yet no less sweetly melancholy and stirring as it came nearer and nearer, until at last she realized the musician was directly below her own casement. She rose and went to the window, though still half asleep, and looked out.

There stood Joe in the silvery moonlight, jacketless, his white hat held in his hands, singing as she had never imagined he could sing. Beside him, grinning as he strummed the guitar, was Stefano Bartholomeo, one of Joe's *pastores.*

"Serafina, *mi corazón,* I am faint with love for you!" Joe declared dramatically when he had finished singing, and he heaved a long, drawn-out sigh to add emphasis to his impassioned declaration.

Faint with love? Ha! It was not love that had made him so, but a little too much *pulque* or whiskey or beer, she thought, hiding a fond smile. But she did not voice her thoughts, for the dear, romantic silliness of his serenade to her touched her deeply, whatever its origins, for Joe was not normally overly romantic by nature. He was courting her, she realized, courting her as he had never had the time to do before their travesty of a wedding . . . but it was too late! She smiled sadly, yet she said with forced lightness to her tone, "Indeed, *señor?* Then I must confess that your boldness has quite set my maiden's heart aflutter! Will you not scale my casement and join me?"

Joe, grinning broadly, summoned a stern look and continued the playful dialogue, "For shame, *señora!*

For you to so immodestly invite a man to your chambers . . . ! Why, it is not what I expected of you! What would your *mamacita* say? Or your so-vigilant *dueña?*" And slyly, he added, "Or your jealous husband?"

She grinned impishly. "Just climb on in here, Joel McCaleb, and let me worry about him!"

Stefano let out a great roar of laughter and wrung a rousing final chord from his guitar. "The *'señorita'* is wooed and won, *patron!* Enough! *Buenas noches, Don José!* And to you too, Doña Seraphina!" So saying, he gave her a gallant half-bow, saluted, and strolled away, leaving Joe standing before the casement.

"Well?"

"Well what?"

"Are you going to let me in? Strewth! I feel like a bloody fool standing here alone in the moonlight!"

"I'll . . . think about it!"

"Hmmph. Fickle, aren't you, love? And to think I wasted my time learning that song and persuading poor Stefano to play for me!" He scowled, pretending to be angered.

"Oh, all right, I guess you've earned it!" she teased and, leaning over, she unfastened the grill and swung it open. Joe clambered inside the room easily. At once he growled fiercely and caught her about the waist, pulling her close, burying his face in her cloud of midnight hair, then kissing her throat, her cheeks, her eyelids in a display of ardor that bordered on the feverish.

"Whoa!" Seraphina implored him. "You'll take my breath away, Joe!"

"That's the plan, love—to sweep you off your feet! See, I got to thinking earlier, after I left you, just how empty my life would be without you; how much I need you beside me and how little time we had for courting. I

433

made myself a promise. From now on, I plan to make every moment we spend together count!" His turquoise eyes glowed with determination.

Oh, Joe, don't! she silently implored. *Don't! I can't bear it!* Yet she said none of this aloud. Instead, she smiled and twined her slender arms about his neck, playing with the thick waves of dusty blond hair that curled about his nape, caressing the strong column of his neck and his broad, hard shoulders.

"Then what're you waiting for?" she murmured, seduction in her smoky tone. Yes! One last, glorious night together, and then she must leave Casa Campanas—or else jeopardize his life by staying. Come what may, this would be a night to remember, to hold and cherish for the remainder of both their lives, she vowed silently.

She took his hand and led him to the bed, tugging at him to sit down upon it. With eyes that were like radiant stars in the half gloom, she plucked the hat from his hands and tossed it aside, then reached for the buttons of his ruffled white shirt. One by one, she unfastened them to bare his broad, tanned chest, her fingertips tracing the hard curves of muscle beneath taut flesh, or else idly outlining circles in the golden pelt there, teasingly following the tapering forest down to where it vanished beneath his belt. She leaned forward to press a kiss to his lips as she unbuckled it, raining still more flirtatious kisses across his muscled chest and shoulders and to his flat male nipples, which hardened beneath the moist assault of her tongue and became rigid little nubbins of dark rose flesh.

"I wasn't so drunk I can't remember what I said that first time in San Francisco when you made love to me. I still feel the same way. You really are a beautiful, beautiful man, Joel McCaleb!" she whispered huskily.

Joe groaned and reached out to draw her into his

arms, but she playfully backed away and laughed softly, deep in her throat, as she evaded his embrace.

"No, *señor!*" she teased sternly, reaching up to pluck the pins and combs from her hair. "Patience for one moment more, *por favor . . .*"

She shook free her midnight hair, letting it stream in ebony cascades about her shoulders, and then she lingeringly unfastened each one of the tiny, pearly buttons that fastened the bodice of her rose-pink gown until the garment slithered down about her waist. She stepped from it and gracefully picked it up, tossing it across a chair back with a swish of silk. Her eyes holding Joe's willing captives, she set one dainty foot upon a chair seat and reached to her lacy garters, sliding them slowly down her firm, golden thighs and her long, slim legs, before doing the same with each one of her black silk stockings in turn. Her seductive undressing made the breath rasp against Joe's chest, until he was breathing as if he'd run a mile flat out.

"Christ, Seraphina!" he whispered huskily. "There should be a law against the way you make me feel!"

"There probably is . . ." she retorted softly, stroking up the long length of her legs and then her thighs with lazy, lingering fingertips, knowing full well that his eyes hungrily followed the motion of her hands. "But I'm in the mood to break a few laws tonight. Aren't you, darlin' . . . ?"

She eyed him archly between strands of shining black hair as she peeled off the last stocking, her lashes like dusky fans that flirted and fluttered, promising untold delights. Her moist pink lips were parted in a delicious little half-smile. She pointedly held the gossamer stocking out at arm's length and let it fall in a silky puddle at his feet beside the first, with the rest of her frothy lingerie. Joe's eyes still jealously, smolderingly, following its whispering path.

She had never looked more lovely, more seductive, than when she sashayed barefoot across the room to him moments later, clad only in her white, lace-trimmed corset and lace-edged drawers. She stood before him, eyes downcast and feeling suddenly shy for some unknown reason. "Would you ... would you care to help me with the rest, mister?" she invited him, her hips swaying ever so slightly.

Dry mouthed, he silently nodded. Lace straps and silk-encased stays fell away under his deft fingers, leaving her delightfully bare-breasted before him.

"Christ, Sera!" he exclaimed, gathering her breasts into his keeping as if they were golden apples he feared to bruise in the plucking. She gasped at the fiery heat of his mouth as he sampled each delicate, rosy fruit, her fingers knotting in his fair hair as his tongue tip danced in lazy, maddening circles around and around the sensitive flesh until her knees threatened to give way.

She closed her eyes and stood there before him, breathing shallowly with rising passion as she surrendered to his lips and his touch, until at last he drew her between his knees where he sat upon the bed, and dipped his fair head lower to nuzzle her hardening belly, savoring its smooth, velvety texture. After what seemed an eternity, he hooked his fingers inside the waistband of her pantalets and slid the lace-trimmed garment slowly down over the smooth lines of her sleek hips and thighs and ankles, drawing a shaky, husky breath as each inch of her flawless body was revealed. He lifted her free of them, at last, and she was bared completely. Drunk on the sight of her nude loveliness, he hauled her roughly across his thighs and held her prisoner there while he kissed her deeply, his mouth a hungry savage against her own yielding, quiescent lips.

Yet soon, mere surrender was not enough for Seraphina. She matched his hunger measure for

436

measure with a desperate hunger of her own, arching her slender body against the hard strength of his, moving her mouth eagerly, greedily, against the flaming, demanding heat of his mouth, even as she strived to bring her hips close against his hardness. His strong hands grazed her back, tracing the delicate bumps of her spine down to the taut swell of her derriere. He cupped and stroked her there, and then his hands moved down to caress her thighs.

"Who's impatient now, my lovely?" he breathed, tracing her ear with his tongue tip. "You teased me, sweetheart . . . drove me crazy . . . now it's my turn to tease you! Do you like this, little love? And this . . . ? Tell me, sweetheart, tell me what it is you like?"

"Everything, Joe, everything! Your kisses, the way you hold me, touch me!" A shiver of delight ran through her. "Oh, Lord, Joe, enough! Now! Please!" she begged. She could bear his sweet torture no longer, and again and again she implored him to hurry, to end this tender torment.

But laughing softly, he refused. With a languorous touch that delighted her senses even while driving her desire to fever pitch, his fingers explored the silky inner columns of her thighs, rising, oh , so *damnably* slowly, in ever-widening circles up the trembling columns of sensitive flesh until, at long, long last, he brushed aside the curling midnight pelt at their joining and delved deeply within, interspersing each intimate caress with kisses that mounted in their intensity.

"Damn you, Joe, now! I want you *now!*" she gasped, the pleading words torn from her in her passion.

In answer, he set her down momentarily to shrug off his pants, and then stretched out, lifting her astride his hard flanks. He wound her long, black hair about his hands and his throat and pulled her head down to his. "I love you, Sera," he whispered huskily, gazing deep

437

into her eyes in the moonlight.

She gave a great sob, tears spilling down her cheeks as she began to move upon him, welcoming him deeply into herself with a long, drawn-out cry of delight.

It was with a combination of ecstasy and despair that she made love to him that glorious last time. Joe's hands were everywhere, twining in her hair, caressing her breasts, stroking her shoulders, her belly, and her long, lovely thighs as she moved her hips to take him deeper and still deeper into her. She could never get enough of him, never! she thought desperately. How could she condense into a single, fleeting night the lifetime of love and passion she wanted so much to share with him? The emotions careening inside her—passion, yes, but also love and a deep, overwhelming grief that after this night, they would never be together again—built until the pulsing heat that surged through her like a hot, demanding flood ready to burst through a dam could no longer be contained. She became very, very still, her head flung back, her long, lovely ebony mane sweeping his upper thighs as shuddering rapture possessed her, lifted her on silver-feathered wings. Through the stillness, she felt an answering throb deep within her as Joe gained his own release, and little cries broke from between her parted lips to mingle with his muffled groan.

"Oh, Joe, I love you so, yes, yes, I . . . love . . . you, too . . . I . . . ohh!"

She fell forward across him, exhausted, her cheeks flushed and wet with her tears, her gray-green eyes luminous. He brushed aside her dampened hair and kissed her closed eyelids, the moist hollows of her throat, cradling her sleepy weight upon his own and wanting to hold her there just that way the whole night long.

"Good night, little love," he whispered. "Sweet,

sweet dreams . . ."

"Good-bye, Joe, my darlin'," came her sleepy reply.

Good-bye? He grinned fondly at her slip and wrapped his arms about her to draw her closer, not dreaming that this would be, could be, their last night together.

But when he returned from riding the ranges of Las Campanas the next evening, it was to learn that the woman he had called wife, his lovely Seraphina, and her white gelding, Muraco, were both gone. The opal wedding band he had slipped upon her finger on their wedding day rested upon his empty pillow like an accusation.

Why? For Christ's sake, *why?* Where had he gone wrong? he would ask himself over and over in the ensuing days. But there would be no easy answer to his questions. And along with her loss would come the discovery of a yawning emptiness, a chasm in his heart and soul, his very life, where she had once been. It was an emptiness that no amount of wealth or land could ever hope to fill.

Chapter Twenty-Six

Katie Steele squinted against the New Mexican sunlight drenching the mellow adobe walls, thinking the ranch house was exactly as she remembered it. Or was it? The dark cypresses still curved loving, protective arms about the sprawling *hacienda*. The beautiful Sangre de Cristo mountain range still loomed grandly as a backdrop behind it. But something *had* changed. *Me,* she realized with a sudden flash of maturity and wisdom that brought a self-conscious little smile to her lips. *Casa del Ombras hasn't changed. I have!* It was sure strange how events could alter you in so brief a spell, so that you scarcely remembered yourself as you'd been then; the difference that a broadened experience of life made, making you feel alien in places you'd known and loved for years. But it was true, she acknowledged. She wasn't the same. She'd longed to come back after so many months away, to return to the security of the only home she'd known since birth. But now that she was finally here, it no longer seemed like home. Tears misted her eyes as she stood there, her single carpetbag at her feet, her long hair, which had been carelessly caught back from her face with a length of ribbon, limp and dusty from her travels, her gown a wrinkled disaster now. It was as if she were caught in some frightening sort of limbo, her identity uncertain. She was not Seraphina Jones, but she was not Katie Steele, either—or at least, not the same naive Katherine Steele who had left here to go east for her last year of schooling! Who was she, then? Some nameless third person who'd come into being as a result of her masquerade . . . or had she simply grown up? Lord! She'd played the part for so long, she'd forgotten how to be herself!

"Katie? Katie!"

She turned slowly about to see her mother standing before her, dressed for riding. She wore her corn-silk hair swept neatly up under her smart, flat-brimmed Spanish hat with silver braid about the brim and crown, and her willowy figure, still slender and firm as a young girl's at thirty-seven years of age, radiated health and vigor and efficiency. Clothed in a tailored, western-style shirt and divided suede skirt, she carried a quirt, which she tapped against her high-heeled riding boots. Dear Mama, so self-controlled, so poised, so . . . so perfect, she thought with a grimace. At least that much hadn't changed. Her mother still made her feel gawky and schoolgirlish by comparison.

"Katie, honey, what's wrong?" Striking, slanted green eyes narrowed as Promise Steele walked slowly toward her daughter, wanting to wrap her arms around the silent girl and hold her close, but unable to. Her heart went out to the girl, for she appeared so very young, so bereft and vulnerable standing there, all alone. Katie, dear Katie, her only daughter and the eldest of her three children, had never welcomed displays of affection, holding herself aloof from the boisterous hugs and kisses the boys indulged in. Promise could not break the ingrained habit of twenty years of restraint. It was like a wall between them,

441

however badly she wanted to send it crashing down in ruins . . .

"Hello, Mama," Katie managed finally, feeling ten years old all over again and wondering why it was she could not show her mother the warm rush of affection that had swept through her on seeing her again after so long, despite the twinges of resentment. "I'm home," she announced unnecessarily, at a loss for words.

"So I see," Promise agreed gently, a fond smile teasing the corners of her mouth as she reached out to brush a damp strand of black hair from her daughter's cheek in an instinctive gesture of caring. How like Luke she is, she thought, so very remote at times, so very proud. And how much like my own dear mama, too, in other ways! But she said nothing of this. Instead, she picked up Katie's bag and took the young woman by the elbow. "Lord, I'm glad to have you home with us at last, Kate! It's been so darned long. Come. Let's go inside, honey. You must be worn-out."

Despite the fierce heat of the summer sun outside, the Casa del Ombras was cool and shady within. The vast rooms echoed the sound of their footsteps. Half barrels of bright flowers and potted plants added life to the most unlikely dark corners, banishing the church-like grandeur of the place. On the walls hung vivid woven Indian blankets, a polished spread of massive longhorns, and several landscapes done in primitive earth tones that captured the stark yet vivid beauty of New Mexico. Over the wide stone fireplace hung several hunting rifles. The tiled floor shone like fine old polished leather, and the furniture was solid and comfortable, much of it fashioned by her father or brothers from timber grown in the foothills of their own lands, the Shadow *S* Ranch, or by her grandpa Courtney, before his death three winters ago.

Katie sighed, wishing with all her heart that he were

still with them. He'd have understood better than any of them about why she'd taken 'Phina's place, and about Joe, and everything. He always had. The bond that they'd shared since she'd been a baby had been a strong one, and there had been nothing she could not unburden herself of to the grand old white-haired gentleman, nothing that could extinguish the love for her that shone in his gentle green eyes. His easy Southern drawl as he offered her advice or simply urged her to confide her fears or problems to him had always been like a balm, soothing her wounded pride, or her hurt, or stilling her childish anger.

"He's still with us, Katie," her mother softly cut into her thoughts with an intuitiveness that surprised her. "In the spirit, if not in the flesh. You don't have to look so bleak and . . . and desolate. Sit yourself down, honey, before you fall down. Mmm. You look a trifle peaked to me, though I'd say you've gained a little weight since we saw you last, so it's probably just the journey, right? Can I have a cool drink brought for you? Some lemonade, or iced tea, maybe?"

Katie flushed guiltily at her mother's mention of her gained weight, feeling color suffuse her face. She laced her fingers together in her lap over her hardening belly in a revealing, cradling gesture, then unlaced them again when she realized what she was doing, wondering how on earth she was ever going to find the words to tell them. "Some lemonade, please," she responded absently, aware that her mother expected some reply.

"Lemonade it is, then. While I see to it, I'll send a rider out to the east line camp for your father. He and the boys're mending fences out there. They'll be real glad to hear you're back." Promise Steele removed her hat and set it on a table, tucking back the fair tendrils that had escaped her smooth chignon. "There! That's more comfortable. Lord, it's hot today! You settle

443

yourself and I'll be right back."

"No, Mama, please!" Katie cried after her as her mother headed from the room in the direction of the kitchen. "Don't . . . don't send anyone after Papa, not . . . not just yet. See, I was hoping all . . . all the way here that you and I could . . . could talk? Alone. Just the two of us?"

Promise nodded, returning slowly to her daughter's side and looking down at the bowed dark head she yearned to stroke. "I'd say it was time, Katie, yes," she agreed, taking a seat beside the young woman. She reached out and tilted Katie's face by the chin, green eyes meeting gray-green eyes moist with tears in a searching gaze. "We've had quite a drought here in New Mexico," she murmured. "How was it in Southern California?"

"You . . . you knew!" Katie cried, and realized suddenly that she should have guessed as much, since her mother had asked no questions about Aunt Lucinda or her trip to Europe or her lack of baggage, or anything else, come to that.

"We did. We've known for quite some time where you were, honey. Let me see, it must have been back around December of last year that Chuck came and told us where you were. He was worried that he hadn't heard from you. He and Seraphina had been married for about five months by then—oh, but of course, you'd already know about that."

Katie nodded, looking quickly away from her mother. "Yes. Yes, I did," she whispered, hanging her head. "That . . . that was what started it all."

"So Chuck explained! Darn that boy and his madcap ideas! He always was a rascal, leading you into scrapes left, right, and center! Still, I'll give him credit for coming to his senses at last and having the foresight to let us know what the two of you had cooked up. And

444

why," she added.

"He told you that, too?" Katie said, her voice tinged with bitterness.

There was a pause before her mother spoke again. "He had to, Katie. If not, how could he have explained the rest of it?"

Katie nodded dumbly, too shaken by this news to speak.

"None of it was necessary, you silly, dear girl," Promise said gently, drawing Kate's chilly hand between her own. "Your papa and I love you dearly, Kate. You had only to come to us, tell us how pressured you felt, that you had no wish to marry Chuck, and that would have made an end to it."

"No!" Kate cried, springing to her feet and shaking her head in denial. "That's not true! Oh, Mama, I know it was never intended, but have you any idea how it was to listen to you and Pa—and even Tom and Court-ney . . . everyone!—spouting on about how it would be when Chuck and I were married, day in and day out? Do you have any idea how pressured we felt? Or how trapped and misunderstood? But we didn't want to disappoint you or let you down, truly we didn't, not you and Papa, nor Uncle Cay and Aunt Carol. We . . . we just didn't know what else to do, and so Chuck decided he'd run away with 'Phina and put an end to it once and for all."

"But I can't believe that it never once occurred to you to *try* to tell us how opposed to marrying Chuck you were—to at least give us the chance to see things your way. We love you, Kate, you *and* Chuck, as much as if he were our son, too. We only wanted your happiness, child! We would have understood."

"Would you?" Katie accused, whirling about to face her mother. "Would you really? Mama, you have no idea how strong you are, how in control of everything

445

that goes on here at the Shadow *S*. I've seen you, seen how you twist Tom and Courtney about your little finger, and Tío Joaquin, and even Papa—though I don't think he even realizes it until it's too late! Oh, I don't deny that you love us all dearly, Mama, and that all you do is in our best interests, but Mama, we all have to grow up someday. We have to learn to make our own choices and sometimes, yes, even our own mistakes in the process. You can't protect us all our lives by choosing for us. We have to find out for ourselves! If I'd come to you, told you I didn't want to marry Chuck, you'd have agreed that it should be my choice—and in the next breath you'd have been pointing out what a pity it was, seeing as how he was so perfect for me, and how our families had always been so close, I just know you would! And, sooner or later, I'd have given in, just like you planned from the first."

Promise Steele smiled faintly. "You make me sound real intimidating, honey. I'm almost afraid of myself!"

Katie had the grace to look chagrined but remained firm nonetheless. "I'm sorry, Mama, I don't mean to hurt you, but it's true. And so"—she shrugged—"when that telegram came, tellin' of William McCaleb's death, I saw how that could destroy everything Chuck was hoping for—and all that I was hoping for, with Chuck safely married to someone else—and decided to take 'Phina's place and claim her inheritance for her. See, I'd thought that way, if Uncle Cay was real angry about Chuck marrying someone else, at least they could get a start together somewhere with her guardian's inheritance to fall back on. There didn't seem much harm in it, not at the time, truly there didn't. McCaleb's lawyers hadn't seen 'Phina in years, not since she left San Francisco to go to school over two years before, and we're enough alike in coloring at least that I didn't think there'd be much chance of them finding out I was an imposter. It all seemed so easy until—"

"—until you found out that a condition of Mister McCaleb's inheritance was that his ward should marry the grandson he'd never seen," her mother finished for her.

"You know all about that, too?" Katie breathed, gray-green eyes widening with astonishment. "How?"

"Your father, Katie. He was beside himself with worrying about you! He contacted Edward Caldwell in San Francisco, and that's how we found out that you went through with it and married that . . . that man!" *And more about him besides—much more than you'd ever imagine or want to know, honey,* Promise recalled grimly. But she only stood and came across to stand before her daughter, placing a slim hand on each of Katie's shoulders as she added, "Oh, yes, we knew all about that part of it, too!"

"And you didn't try to stop it—to stop me?"

Promise shook her head. "No. We didn't, much as we'd have liked to. If we had, we'd have been doing exactly what you just accused me of doing, wouldn't we? Trying to manipulate you into doing what we wanted, rather than allowing you to live your own life the way you want to. You're twenty, Kate, and like you said, not a child anymore. You made your choice back in Boston, right or wrong. We didn't approve of what you were doing, but we knew if we stopped you, you'd resent our interference and be terribly angry—perhaps even decide to leave home for good, with hard and bitter feelings on both sides. But even though we agreed to leave you be, we didn't once stop worrying about you these past months, nor did your father or I ever leave off wishing you'd end all that foolishness and come on home to us! We hoped when you were ready for us to know, you'd see to it, and here you are."

Katie remained silent for several moments to let all

that her mother had said soak in. All these months, she'd fretted that they'd find out she wasn't in Europe, and they'd known exactly where she was all along but had done nothing to force her to come home! The knowledge stunned her. She'd said that was what she wanted, hadn't she—the freedom to make her own choices? Well, they'd given her all the space she had needed, so why the heck did she feel so darned angry all of a sudden, angry at *them?*

"You know that my marriage to Joe isn't legal then? That we're not really married because it wasn't my name I signed on the marriage certificate?" she snapped, all trace of weariness gone and replaced by that building irritation. She saw her mother nod. "And you still sat back and did nothing? What kind of parents are you?"

Her mother shook her head. "You can't have it both ways, Katie! You said you wanted the freedom to live your own life, right? The opportunity to make mistakes is a part of that freedom, honey; you said so yourself. You do feel that . . . marrying . . . your Joel McCaleb was a mistake, then?"

Katie shrugged. "I . . . I don't know anymore. See, it was never meant to be a real marriage," Katie revealed, misery in her tone. "It was a deal we made between us. Joel . . . he wanted McCaleb's inheritance, and so did I, for Seraphina's sake, so we agreed to get married only to fulfill the stipulation in the will. We'd planned to sell the ranch and split the proceeds, then go our own separate ways. It . . . it seemed such a simple solution at the time. But we didn't reckon on the Monroes, and no one daring to buy the land because of them. And I didn't figure on Joe . . . on Joe's deciding to keep the land and work it himself. Nor on . . . nor on . . ."

"On falling in love with him?"

Katie nodded, her shoulders slumped and tears

streaming down her face now. "Yes! Oh, yes! And what's worse, I'm . . . I'm having his baby, Mama, and he still doesn't know the truth! He has no idea that I'm not really Seraphina Jones and that we're not really married and that Rancho Campanas isn't truly his!" She flung herself across the room at her mother's feet and rested her head on her lap, sobbing. "Oh, Mama, tell me what to do, please, Mama? Tell me how to make it right? Joe's in danger, real danger, and I left because I had to, because I love him so and I couldn't take the chance that Val Monroe would . . . would kill him! But if he ever finds out—if he ever learns the truth—he'll hate me for it, I know he will! He'll lose everything he's ever wanted once I tell him who I really am. Oh, Lord, Mama, tell me what to do!"

"I can't, honey," Promise said gently, though her heart went out to her daughter. She smothered a groan. Oh, Lord, Katie was carrying that . . . that Joe's baby! What a tangle this whole business was fast becoming! Her lips thinned. What sort of man was he, anyway? Was he as concerned about being as honest with her Katie as she was about being honest with him? Obviously not, judging by the sound of things, that sidewinder! It was tempting to tell her daughter to forget all about him, that he was a liar and a cheat and no damn good, but she couldn't do that. It might have the very effect she dreaded, and drive her straight back to him. Besides, Kate had to decide this for herself. "Whether you go back to Joe or stay here is something you have to decide for yourself. No one can decide what's best for Katie Steele except Katie Steele." As she stroked her daughter's long black hair, Promise's lovely face, which had only the faintest suggestion of age lines starting at the corners of her eyes and mouth, was strained with her concern. How well she remembered falling in love with her Luke in the months that followed their explosive first meeting—and the fear and misery, the literal heartache of not knowing if he'd ever come to love her in the same way. And then, she had caught him in a lie—such a lie—and had been given ample reason to believe that she could never come to trust him again. But for them, it had all worked out happily. Could she deny Katie the chance to try, simply because of her own feelings of animosity toward this Joe she'd never even met, and especially since those feelings were based on hearsay? "Let me tell you a little story, Kate, a true story," she said at length. "It might help you to decide what to do.

"See, your grandmother, my own mother, Mary, came from a well-to-do family, the Senator Samuel Haverleighs of New York, as you know. Your Aunt Lucinda, her sister, was, of course, a Haverleigh before she married your uncle, Bernard Downing, of Boston. Things were different back then. I guess Mary must have led quite a sheltered life, as did all the young women of her circle in those days, and your great-grandfather, Samuel, did most of the thinking for his two young daughters.

"When Mary was still quite young, she met a handsome, green-eyed soldier at a ball one evening, and it was love at first sight. He wanted to pay court to her, but her papa wouldn't hear of it. They were Northerners, you see, and the young man was from a monied old family of the South, the Fontaines of New Orleans. The tide of unrest between North and South was brewing even way back then, you see, and Samuel Haverleigh would not entertain the idea of a Southern husband for his Mary. But despite his opposition, the two young people met in secret and fell deeply in love. The result of their trysts was that Mary found herself with child." Promise looked down into Kate's now rapt face and smiled before continuing. "Before she should

450

announce her condition to her Courtney—yes, the young man was your grandpa Courtney, Kate!—her papa learned of their meetings and used his connections in the city to have the young soldier sent back down to Louisiana. Mary was desperate and in her anguish she confided her secret to one of her father's servants, an Irish groom who had long been sweet on her. The man, Patrick O'Rourke, was a good sort, tender hearted where his pretty Mary was concerned, and offered to take her away, to marry her and save her from disgrace, and to give her child his name. Mary took the easy way out and ran away with him. That child was me! Until I was sixteen years old, Kate, I believed Patrick O'Rourke was my true father. He was a rascal, but an endearing one, and I know he loved me as much as he would have loved any daughter he'd fathered.

"Shortly before she died, my mother told me all about Courtney, and about how she had wasted her entire life pining for a man she could never have. I understood why she told me what she did, but I could never, never understand her meek acceptance of her lot. Had I been in her shoes, I would have left New York, no matter what it cost me, and found my Courtney somehow! I could not have given up until I heard from his own lips if he loved me still or no. And, if he proved unworthy and told me he did not, I would have made a new life for myself and my babe somehow and put the past where it belonged—behind me. I would not have done as your grandmother did, and marry a man I knew I could never come to love, and quite destroy his chance for happiness—and my own— by forever comparing him unfavorably to my first love! That's what my mother, Mary, did, though I loved her dearly despite it. And why, why did it have to be that way? Because she lacked the courage and the determination to fight for the man she loved!

451

"It wasn't until after she'd passed on that I finally met my natural father, and that was quite by accident, soon after Carol and I had escaped from the Comanche camp and been taken to Fort Lyon. Colonel Fontaine was a rebel soldier who'd been taken prisoner and was about to be sent to a prison camp to wait out the war. After the war ended, he found me and came here to live with us, as you know, God rest his soul. We were lucky to have many good years together to make up a little for those we'd spent apart. I know he loved you dearly, Kate, for you always reminded him of his Mary, whom he'd lost." Promise Steele stood up. "Well, honey, I don't know if what I've told you is a help or not. The decision is still yours, whether you go back to your Joel and level with him, or hide away here with his child and raise it in bitterness and regret. Whatever you decide, your father and I will back you up all the way. Your papa might have a notion to go after Joel McCaleb with a shotgun at first, but he'll come around in the end!" She leaned over and hugged Katie tightly, kissing her flushed, damp cheek, wishing she could protect her from heartache as she'd done when Katie was a little girl, but knowing she could not. "We love you, Katie, come what may. Don't ever forget that! Now, I'd best go tell the boys and your father that you're home." So saying, she left Katie alone.

Katie couldn't resist a smile through her tears after her mother had left. "Oh, Mama, whether you realize it yourself or not, you did it again with your little story!" she murmured, fondly exasperated. Then she frowned. Everyone—Grandpa Fontaine, her papa, Aunt Lucinda—had always said she was like her grandmother, Mary O'Rourke. Were they right? Was she like her, deep down inside—lacking the conviction and the courage to fight for the man she loved? Had she, perhaps, taken the easy way out and secretly enjoyed letting her parents control her life all along, even while bemoaning the fact? It was something she'd have to think about—along with thinking about Joe. Oh, Lord, Joe! She bit her lip in sudden fresh anxiety. Had her departure really saved him from the Monroes—or made him all the more vulnerable?

Chapter Twenty-Seven

Ming halted in the kitchen doorway, his dark eyes anxious as he looked across at Joe. Since Missie Seraphina had left him again, his Joe was a changed man. The laughter in his turquoise eyes had died, leaving them cold and empty. He rarely smiled now, and both Peggy and Gabby gave him wide berth, hurrying past him with their eyes averted. He was silent most of the time, too, speaking only when forced to do so, and the change in his personality had affected his looks. His hair and beard had both grown long, shaggy, and unkempt, and he seemed not to care if the clothes he wore gave him the disreputable air of a bandit, Ming thought, sighing heavily.

"Don't look at me that way, boy!" Joe snapped sourly, glancing up from his half-emptied bottle and shot glass at that inopportune moment. "I don't like it, and I won't bloody stand for it either, y'hear me, cobber?"

Ming nodded, nervously wetting his dry lips, wishing he possessed the physical strength to wrest the whiskey bottle from Joe and smash it against the wall; to force him to see what he was doing to himself. In that moment, Ming hated Seraphina with a passion, his

454

hatred born of desperation over his dear friend's rapid and steady decline. It was all her fault, Ming thought angrily. It was just like the first time Missie Seraphina had left Joe and they'd come to Las Campanas, and he'd sought comfort and forgetfulness in a liquor bottle. Only this time, he showed no signs of coming out of it.

"There's someone to see you, Joe," he said hesitantly, for these days one could not be certain how Joe would react to anything. "Edward Caldwell from San Francisco is here. He has another man with hi—"

"Caldwell, is it?" Joe cut in and laughed bitterly. "Good ole Edward from Frisco!" He took a long swig of his whiskey, wiping his lips on the back of his fist. "Well? What the devil does *he* want with me, eh, Ming? T'make sure me and Sera are still married, still the happy little lovebirds we once were? To see for himself that we're taking good care of William McCaleb's goddamned land?" he jeered. "Tell him to go to hell!" He waved his hand in Ming's direction in a dismissing gesture and drained his glass to the last drop. "Whiskey's just the ticket, mate," he told no one in particular. "It's the only bloody thing you can rely on in this life! Beats the hell out of women!"

Ming frowned. "Please, Joe, I . . . I think you should see him. He has a briefcase with him, and many papers, too. It . . . it sounds important, Joe."

"It does, does it?" Joe scowled, then got unsteadily to his feet. "All right then, Ming, little cobber, you've won. Lead the way," he muttered. "I'll see him, though what good it ll do, I don't know."

Almost dizzy with relief, Ming took Joe's arm and helped him to make his way down the *corredor* to the enormous parlor of Casa Campanas.

Edward Caldwell was looking out of the window when Joe reeled into the room. He turned about with an expectant smile of welcome wreathing his kindly face, a smile that vanished and was replaced by an openmouthed frown of consternation when he saw Joe. His blue eyes narrowed as they traveled up and down the length of the man who stood—with obvious difficulty—before him, taking in the unkempt beard and long, dusty blond hair, the haggard face and hollowed, bloodshot eyes, the wrinkled shirt beneath the leather vest. Was this the same Joe he had met and both liked and respected little more than six months ago? The change in him was staggering!

"Why, Joe, your friend here didn't tell me you were ill! Son, you should have said something!" Caldwell exclaimed, casting a disapproving eye upon Ming, who still hovered by the door. "Come on, Joe, have a seat before you fall down, man! What is it? Some tropical disease from your days in Java? Malaria, maybe?" He shoved a chair in Joe's direction, recoiling as the reek of whiskey reached him and with it, understanding. Eyebrows raised, he glanced inquiringly back at Ming and saw the boy shrug and hang his head, obviously reluctant to admit to an outsider such as himself that his beloved Joe was not ill but very drunk.

"How long has this been going on, Ming?" Caldwell demanded sternly, pressing Joe down into a chair.

"Ever since Missie Seraphina left, Mister Edward, sir," Ming revealed, "he has been as if a demon had taken over his body! He is not the same Joe, not anymore."

"Mrs. McCaleb left him? Good God! When?" Caldwell queried.

"Six weeks ago, sir. And it's all her fault that he's this way! It is just that . . . that he drinks to . . . to forget, you see? Truly, sir, he cannot help the way he is now! It . . . it has not been easy for him, you understand? He

456

loved Missie Seraphina very much and did not want her to go. The day he learned she had gone was very terrible. And . . . and the Monroes, they have been causing plenty much trouble since she left! Twice they have ridden into the flocks and scattered the sheep. They poisoned one of our wells, too, but luckily Joe discovered it before the sheep came to water. And another time they . . . oh, sir, there have been so many troubles! But Joe will be all right; you'll see. Time will help him to forget, and so will Chen Ming—as he once helped me when I was in need of a friend. He'll be himself again soon." Ming's jaw came up in a familiar gesture of determination and obstinacy that Edward Caldwell remembered remarking upon at Joe's wedding. The boy's devotion to Joe was touching, but right now it wasn't helping him any.

"No one's blaming you, Ming. You can fill me in on the details later, son. Meanwhile, find Mrs. Kelly and have her make a good, strong pot of black coffee and bring it in here to me, will you?"

Ming nodded and left. Joe gave a mirthless chuckle as the boy went. He fixed a bleary eye on Caldwell. "So, Edward, still playing the good Samaritan, are you, cobber? It won't work, y'know! I'm past bloody redemption, I am!"

"Pull yourself together, Joe, and listen to me!" Caldwell ordered sternly. "There's someone here to see you—someone you met a while back."

For the first time, Joe noticed the other, white-haired man by the window. He carried a cane hooked over his left arm, and there was something vaguely familiar about his profile—or so Joe fancied—which was a young one, despite his white hair. But the bright sun that streamed in through the window blinded his bloodshot, smarting eyes. When he tried to focus, the images moved in and out, and he could not place the man. Too many whiskeys and too many sleepless nights had taken their toll. "'Fraid I've forgotten your name, mate," he drawled, slurring the words. "Refresh my memory, will you, there's a good bloke."

"I'd be glad to," the man said, stepping across the room and out of the sunlight. He leaned heavily upon his cane as he walked. He was smiling, but it was a sad smile nonetheless as he stopped and looked down at Joe. "My name's Joel McCaleb."

Joe's head jerked up, and the blankness, the nothingness, in his eyes wavered. The ruddy flush caused by the fiery whiskey paled somewhat in his bearded cheeks. "Joel McCaleb?" he breathed. "Christ Almighty, it can't be!" He shook his head slowly from side to side. "Nah, mate, I don't believe in ghosts! You can't be Mac! Mac's dead, that poor sod! I left him six feet under, back on Christmas Island!"

"Wrong, Joe. I'm here, and I'm very much alive— thanks to you, pal! It was a long, hard road to recovery, but I made it. Except for this bum leg of mine and a few prematurely white hairs, I'm as good as new. I can never repay you, Joe. You saved my life back then." Mac's voice was husky with emotion, his cornflower blue eyes moist.

Joe had risen to his feet in astonishment at hearing— and seeing—Mac alive, living and breathing, before him. Now he sat down again with a jolt.

"Strewth, Mac! I left you for dead that morning! Hopworth—the doctor, remember?—he thought you were dead, too!"

"And so I was—almost. It was touch and go for over two months. I had some pretty grave internal injuries, and the odds of my recovering were almost zero. Henry—Doc Hopworth—didn't see much point in telling you I'd survived. He still expected me to give up the ghost, you see, and he figured since you'd gone through my dying on you once, there was no point in putting you through that a second time. By the time he was certain I was out of the woods and would live, you'd been taken to the Sandwich Isles to recuperate." Mac grinned ruefully. "Come on! Say *something,* Joe, or I'll think you'd rather I'd stayed dead!"

"Christ-Al-bloody-mighty, *no,* mate!" Joe breathed, staring at Mac's face as if he had indeed seen a ghost. "I . . . it just won't sink in!"

"You'll get used to the idea," Mac reassured him. "And while you are, we'll get some coffee into you, and you can fill me in on what's been going on with you since we parted ways. The ranch looks damned good, Joe, from what I've seen of it! And there's big money to be made sheep ranching in America these days, so I'm told, if you're not afraid to work hard for it. Congratulations, Joe! You did what you set out to do, friend. You've turned over that new leaf and used what you've learned to make something of yourself. I'm glad to hear it, real glad. It couldn't have happened to a finer man."

Joe's mind was fighting off the fuzziness the liquor had caused, despite the effort it cost him. Notwithstanding his condition, the ramifications of Mac's being very much alive had not been lost on him. Through the liquor's numbing haze, he struggled to make sense out of confusion. Christ! With the real Joel McCaleb alive, where did that leave him? "Does Edward know?" he asked softly.

"He does," Mac confirmed, "and he was pretty upset when I explained the switch to him, too! A real stickler for doing things by the book, is Edward. It looked a bit sticky for a while. But we put our heads together and discussed all the angles, and we've come up with a solution we think you'll find acceptable, Joe. Here, drink this down, and if you're feeling better in a little while, we'll show you what we've put together." He thrust a cup of steaming coffee—brought in by Ming while they talked—into Joe's hands.

"A solution? You mean charity of some kind, don't you, Mac?" Joe said with a bitter twist of his lips that only barely resembled a grin. He set the coffee aside untouched. Mac's resurrection had already sobered him considerably. "You know me better than to think I'd go for that, surely?"

"No, not charity, Joe; nothing like that, believe me! Damn it, Joe, I wouldn't insult a friend by offering him charity, and you know it! What I am offering you is a contract, isn't that so, Edward? A simple business proposition."

"That's true, Joe," Edward agreed. "When Mac heard about the conditions of his grandfather's will, he realized what a terrible obligation he'd put you under by urging you to take his place. His survival changed everything, except for one notable point. He still wanted you to have Las Campanas, but *in your own right,* if that was still what you wanted, no strings attached. Since the stipulations in William McCaleb's will weren't met, under the circumstances the land and the town house and the financial bequest became the lawful property of the First Presbyterian Church of San Francisco. Mac arranged to purchase the house and land from the church. Since they have little use for so many acres, they were more than happy to make a swift sale so that they could have the proceeds accessible to further their good works. The result is that Mister McCaleb—er, Mac, rather—has arranged a mortgage for you with a reputable bank in San Francisco. He has also generously agreed to guarantee the loan himself—"

"Ah, so you have, have you, Mac, old cobber?" Joe said in a jeering tone. "What are you—my fairy

460

godmother or something? Did you come into another inheritance, is that it? Strewth! It sure sounds like charity to me, mate!"

Edward frowned. "Now, see here, don't take that tone, Joe! Mac's only trying to help, after all. I don't think you realize just how generous Mac is being, or how fortunate you are, under the circumstances. Why, what you did could have resulted in your arrest and a lengthy imprisonment! Mister McCaleb's a successful businessman in his own right, with a most profitable coffee plantation of his own back in Java—land that fortunately was unscathed by Krakatoa's eruption. Let me point out that he's under no obligation to do anything—"

"Please, Edward, that's enough," Mac cut in, knowing Edward's preaching attitude would only further chafe Joe's smarting pride. "Joe and I have a great deal in common—more than I would ever have guessed from our brief acquaintance. Like me, he has his fair share of pride. Right now I'd bet money he feels like he's been offered a handout, right? Not so, Joe! The note on Las Campanas will have to be repaid to the bank—with interest—by you and you alone, if you accept my offer. All I've done by guaranteeing the loan is to demonstrate to the bank my good faith that you *will* pay it back, seeing as how you're just starting out in a new country and something of an unknown quantity. You can't hold it against me for wanting to do that much for you, after what you did for me, surely? I owe you my life! My guaranteeing the loan is a damned poor exchange for that. Take all the time you need to think it over, Joe. There's no rush. Edward and I will be staying in town until the end of the week. You can reach us there at any time." He came forward and extended his hand to Joe in farewell.

Joe gritted his teeth and shook it. "Thanks for all

461

you've tried to do, Mac. And believe me, I'm bloody glad you made it! I . . . I know you mean well, but don't be surprised if you don't hear from me. Two months ago, I would have taken you up on your offer like a flash, but now . . ." He shrugged. "Las Campanas was never mine. I knew that deep down inside all along. I guess I was just trying to fool myself. Your grandfather meant for you to have it, Mac. You . . . and Seraphina. I was just tempting Lady Luck by taking your place and pretending I was you." He smiled bitterly. "Nothing ever comes easy for the Joe Christmas's of this world, does it?"

"Nothing worthwhile ever comes easily to anyone, Joe," Mac pointed out. "That's a lesson life teaches all of us, sooner or later."

To Ming's surprise, Joe didn't return to his bottle after the two men had left Casa Campanas. He swigged down the entire pot of coffee, cup after cup, and disappeared into his room, asking Ming to bring him some kettles of hot water. An hour or so later, he emerged looking refreshed and far more like his old self. He had trimmed his hair and shaved off his beard, and the denim shirt and pants that he wore under a black leather vest were clean. The remoteness still lingered in his eyes, but it was a start, at least, and Ming's spirits soared.

"Are you hungry, Joe?" he asked eagerly.

Joe glanced at the youth and saw the anxiety in his expression. He reached out and rumpled the boy's straight, blue-black hair. "Y'know, mate, I reckon I am," he agreed. "Hungry enough to eat a bear!" He allowed the boy to drag him to the kitchen and dish him up a heaped platter of Peggy's Irish stew.

Ming chattered on and on while he ate, the words

tumbling one after the other from his mouth like water gushing from the pump. He talked about how well the sheepdog pups, Picaro and Pia, were doing under Stefano's careful training, and he described with bubbling enthusiasm the few acres he had been plaguing Joe to lease him, with the intention of planting citrus seedlings upon them.

"Imagine, Joe, trees filled with oranges and lemons and grapefruit! The climate is very good for such fruits, I understand, and the rainfall . . ."

Joe said nothing except for an occasional grunt of agreement until Ming broached the subject of leasing the land from Joe, then he said with great gentleness, "Ming, there's something you should know—about me, and Las Campanas." In as few words as possible, he told the boy what he had done, and about taking Joel McCaleb's place. "So you see, son, I'm no hero. I'm an imposter, nothing more. A fake. A phony. Las Campanas isn't mine to lease you, son—not even one square foot of it!"

"But . . . but the real Mister McCaleb—he wanted you to have Las Campanas, did he not?"

"He did," Joe agreed. "But what I did was still wrong, still against the law; you understand? The land was meant to be his from the beginning, an' I can't stay here, not under any condition. Truth is, Ming, it's a relief that it's all finally out in the open. It gets to being like a weight around your neck, living a lie. Soon, I'll be leaving here, to make a fresh start on my own somewhere else—"

"No!" Ming cut in heatedly. "You love this place, Joe! You can't leave! You can't!"

"I don't have a choice, son. I have to leave. But I'll talk to Mac—the real Mister McCaleb—and I'll ask him about those few acres you wanted. Maybe he'll come up with a way—"

"No! You're lying, Joe! You *do* have a choice. I heard that man—and he offered you the chance to stay. It was you—you who turned *him* down! Why? Because Missie Seraphina isn't here to share it with you? Is that why you are going away, letting everything we worked for fall apart, because of her? I hate her for what she's done to you! I used to believe that you were the bravest man I had ever met, Joe—the kind of man I would have been proud to call father, or brother, or friend. But I see now that I have been blind, that it is not so. You are weak! When the land came easily to you, like a ripe lichee plucked from the tree, you would never have given her up. Now that you have learned that you will have to work for Las Campanas if you wish to keep her, you say you must go! I do not understand this. I no longer understand you! I know only that you have changed since we left San Francisco. You once spoke to me of accepting responsibility for my actions, and I was filled with shame for having let you down. But what about you, Joe? What of your responsibility to all of us here? Is that of no account? Will you leave us behind without a second thought? I believe that you are a coward, Joe! A coward!" Overwrought, furiously scrubbing tears from his cheeks with his knuckles, he spun about and fled the kitchen, leaving an astonished—and severely chastened—Joe gaping after him.

After a few moments, Joe sighed heavily and drew a deck of cards from his shirt pocket, idly shuffling them. While he was cleaning himself up earlier, he had toyed with the idea of teaching Ming to play poker—a belated attempt on his part to give the youth some badly needed attention. God knew, he'd given him damned little of his time lately, since he'd taken to the bottle in an attempt to ease his misery over Sera. Now, with Ming's impassioned outburst, it was doubtful if they'd ever be able to mend things between them before

464

he went away.

He was still sitting there at the table, numbed by the day's unsettling events, when he heard the hoofbeats of a furiously ridden horse approaching the *hacienda*.

Absently tucking the deck back into his breast pocket alongside his tin can of tobacco and papers, he jammed on his hat and strode quickly from the ranch house to the corral, just as a mounted Jaime Santiago careened up to it and slid to a halt.

Gabby left the henhouse, setting aside the basket of eggs she had been gathering as she came out to see who the rider was. Peggy, hoeing the weeds that threatened to choke her precious vegetable patch, stopped and shoved back her bonnet, wiping her perspiring face on a corner of her apron as Jaime slithered down from his horse's back and began excitedly to tell Joe what had happened.

"You must come quickly, *señor!*" he cried. "There is trouble—much trouble!"

"Where?" Joe barked, heading for the *ramada* and his horse at such a rapid stride, the far shorter Jaime almost had to run to keep up.

"To the northwest, *patron!*"

"Northwest it is. Mount up. You can tell me about it while we ride," Joe instructed curtly, notching Jimbo's girth.

Joe shoved back his hat and mopped the sweat from his brow with the red bandanna from about his throat. Cursing the white-hot noonday sun that blazed down on him from directly above, he looked at the scene of wanton slaughter all about him. His expression grew more and more thunderous as his mental tally of the number of dead animals rose.

As Jaime had warned him on their furious ride here,

close to thirty head of his sheep lay scattered across the dun-colored hillside, their heavy Merino fleece stained rust with blood. The coppery stench of it hung in the uncannily still, sultry air. Each one of the animals' throats had been slit, and from the looks of things, buzzards had already staked their claims on the remains. The huge birds now perched in nearby trees, watching the two men sullenly with bright, beady black eyes, their obscenely full bellies resting on their roosts.

He drew his gun and fired at the birds, sending all but one of them rising in a screaming black and white pall as fury rose through him in an acid flood that was bitter as bile in his throat. Damn the Monroes; damn them all to hell! The senseless, wanton slaughter of the innocent, harmless beasts angered him even more than the financial loss of the animals themselves.

"Christ!" he muttered under his breath, battling away the greedy flies that swarmed all about, metallic blue pests gorged with blood. He nodded at the slaughtered sheep. "They'll be stinking in an hour or so in this damn heat. Round up Stefano and a few others to give you a hand, Jaime, and pile the carcasses over there. Then get some kerosene and burn the lot of them. It'll be faster and cleaner that way."

"Si, señor," Jaime said in a melancholy voice, hanging his head. He rubbed at the knot on the back of his skull. "I . . . I am sorry, *señor patron.* But there was nothing I could do! As I told you, I heard Gitana bark once last night, then a yelp, and then only silence. Earlier, just after moonrise, I had heard coyotes in the distance. I thought that perhaps one had come down from the hills to scavenge. The little dog didn't come when I whistled, so I left the campfire to go to see what was keeping her. I found Gitana over there, lying by the tree. As I knelt down to see to her, they jumped me from behind and clubbed me! It was daylight before I

466

came to."

Joe nodded, leaning low in the saddle to clap Jaime across the back and reassure him. "I understand, Jaime. No one's blaming you. On second thought, find Stefano and have him see to getting rid of the carcasses. You go straight on up to the house and have Gabby or Peggy take a look at that lump on your head. You've the makings of a regular goose egg from the looks of it, cobber, and I don't want that wife of yours riled at me for not seeing it cared for!"

Jaime shrugged. "It is nothing, *señor*. I will tend to it after I have done what must be done." He frowned. "You will go after them, *señor*? You will make them pay for what they did? For what they have been doing to us these past weeks?"

Joe's turquoise eyes met Jaime's trusting brown ones, and he nodded slowly.

"I must. This shows how desperate they are. The next time, I've a hunch they won't stop at killing sheep!"

With those ominous words, he wheeled his horse about and set him toward the west, where the sun was just beginning its descent. Sooner or later, he'd have to hand Las Campanas over to Mac. But for now, the responsibility of dealing with the Monroes lay squarely at his door, and he would deal with them face to face, not as El Vengador, nor as the imposter Joel McCaleb, but simply as himself, a man fighting for justice. There would be no masks, no lies, to hide behind, not this time.

"This'll be my parting gift to you, Ming," he muttered, "my last responsibility, so t' speak! Paying them back for what they did to you is long overdue. Too bloody long!" Seraphina had stopped him from going after the Monroes before, begging him not to repay violence with violence. He'd listened to her,

467

remembering all too well that last fight back in Sydney and Ned's unfortunate death. But Sera wasn't here to stop him now. And Ming had called him a coward . . . What did he have to lose? Nothing, came the answer, nothing at all.

Grim faced and granite jawed, he rode on toward Rancho Fuerte.

Chapter Twenty-Eight

It was late afternoon before he had crossed over from Campanas land to the Monroes' range, uprooting and breaking down a portion of the fences he had raised himself weeks ago in order to do so.

The drought was bad here, too, he saw at once, the grass sere and yellowed almost to white. The water level in the creeks was low—far lower than the blessed San Juliano River that ran through Campanas and offered life-giving water to the flocks. A heat haze shimmered over the cracked, hard earth, distorting gnarled cottonwoods in the distance and making them seem as if they were dancing. Once in a while, a dust devil would swirl up and then die away as furiously as it had risen. The electrical tang of a coming storm hung in the air, he fancied, but whether it was real or a result of the mounting tension crackling within himself, he was uncertain.

Joe rode on, a man alone; a man who knew what had to be done to end the Monroes' tyranny in the valley; a man whom many would have called a fool—or a hero. Joe didn't think of himself in any of those terms. He was simply doing what he felt he had to do; what had been left undone for far too long. He should have ignored Sera that day, should have gone after the Monroes and ended it—one way or another—there and then. Instead, he'd let them get away with what they'd done, and as a consequence they'd grown even bolder. Sometimes, the only way to meet force was with greater force, to fight fire with fire. Christ! Simply doing nothing hadn't worked—nor had going by the law! Sheriff Tallant was as rotten as the rest of them, no more than a pawn in Monroe's hand. Joe harbored no illusions that justice would come from his direction, and so now it was all up to him. He'd use force, or cunning, or both; whatever it took to engineer a final confrontation. The outcome would be up to fate— solely in the hands of Lady Luck herself.

"'An eye for an eye,' Jimbo," he murmured to his horse. "That's what it says in the Good Book! Let's see if a taste of their own medicine will force those rattlers out into the open. That'll do it, for starters." Yes. Out in the open, that's where he needed to get the Monroes. Away from their *casa grande,* which could serve as a fortress for them to hole up in indefinitely while he sweated out the wait, his resolve growing weaker by the minute . . .

Gaining the next rise, he spotted the red dust cloud he'd been looking for, and knew that the Rancho Fuerte herd lay just ahead along the banks of a creek, which was little more than a dry wash now, after weeks on end of hot, rainless days. Sure enough, moments later he saw them: hundreds upon hundreds of longhorns milling about and pawing the hard earth, bellowing for the blessed water that never came. Dun and yellow hides, red and black, their numbers spread out for as far as Joe could see, meeting the hazy gunmetal gray and blue of the distant horizon in a restless, moving, dark blur. From here, the whistles and yells and the cracking of the whips used by the

470

vaqueros and cowboys could be as plainly heard as gunshots, and once in a while, Joe caught the sparkling wink of a bridle or a silver spur in the brooding light.

He reined in Jimbo beneath a clump of spreading oaks, where the shade would conceal him, and he dismounted, leaving the horse ground-tied while he crouched down to survey the scene below.

About the chuck wagon, some of the cowboys had congregated for the usual early supper and were squatting in the dust, smoking or eating their chow with spoons off tin platters. The savory aroma of beef stew and biscuits and beans wafted up to where Joe squatted, reminding him that he'd be missing his own supper.

A slow grin started at the corners of his mouth and spread to glimmer wickedly in his eyes. He tilted back his hat, feeling excitement beginning to quiver and dance through him, making every nerve and muscle hum like plucked wires.

"Strewth! You'd have to be *loco* to try it, Lightnin' Joe!" he warned himself, but he knew nonetheless and without a shadow of a doubt that he would put his plan into action despite the risks. It had all the audacity of his bold entry into Tea Rose's brothel to rescue little Mei Ling—and the smack of danger to it that was like a heady shot of whiskey in his veins! He could just imagine the Monroes' reaction when they found out. Old man Monroe would bust a blood vessel, then come running, thirsty for revenge! Which was just how he wanted it . . .

His mind made up, he grasped Jimbo's reins and vaulted astride him, turning the paint's head toward the herd. Bold as brass, he dug in his spurs and galloped the horse down the rise, raising funnels of dust in his wake as he headed straight for the chuck wagon.

Several heads turned as he rode up. He gave a half-nod of greeting to the dust-caked cowboys as he passed. They looked curiously at him, but made no move to stop him, for the most part returning his nod with nods of their own. A cautious scrutiny of the men hunkered on their haunches over their supper settled his remaining misgivings. Not a sign of a Monroe anywhere—yet!

"Take my horse, son," he ordered, springing down from the saddle and casually tossing the reins to the *remuda* boy, a pudgy Mexican youth.

"*Si, señor,*" the boy agreed readily, taking Jimbo's reins and leading the beast toward the string of spare or resting horses as he would have done for any returning cowboy. Joe grinned his thanks and took off his hat, dusting it off on his chaps as he made his way to the rear of the chuck wagon.

"Evenin', mate," he greeted the cook. "Dish me up a plate of grub, will you? Damn if I couldn't eat a bear!" He grabbed up a metal platter and a spoon, and confidently held it out to the man who, after a moment's hesitation, ladled him out a portion of stew and beans, slapped a biscuit down in the middle of the mess, and looked at him long and hard.

"Ain't seen you before, stranger," he asked suspiciously. "Passin' through?"

"Nah, mate. I signed on with the boss this morning. Christ, that Monroe's an ornery so-and-so, ain't he? Reckon I'll be moving on before long."

"Ornery ain't the word, stranger!" the cook returned with a grimace. "He's about as pleasant as a dog with its fool head stuck in a tin can—and that's on one o'his good days! The boys call me Cookie. Ain't too original, but it serves." He held out his hand, and Joe juggled with his meal and his spoon to take it and shake it in return. "And you'd be . . . ?"

"Folks call me Lucky," Joe supplied, grinning

innocently. "And I surely hope I am!"

Cookie grinned back. "Pleased ter meet you, Lucky. You from hereabouts? You sound like you're from back east somewheres?"

"Nah, mate. I did some cattle ranching back in Australia. That's where I'm from. I heard about the ranches over here and decided to give America a chance, see the world, like. But it's no easier over here than it was there, more's the pity. Trail dust still tastes the same in the back of your throat, and a dollar spends just as bloody fast in a saloon here as it did back in Sydney!" He shook his head ruefully. "That's the only reason I signed on." He tapped his pockets. "As cold and empty as a doxie's heart!"

Cookie laughed, wiping his hands on his gravy-and-grease-spattered apron. "Hell, I reckon Lucky ain't no luckier here than he was back there, then!"

Joe laughed. "That's it, mate! Say, who do I see about cutting fifty head from the herd? The boss told me he'd sold the government some beeves for their railroad workers, an' he promised 'em delivery before sundown. That cuss told me to make damned good and sure I see that they get there on time, too!"

"Where's there?"

"The way Monroe told it, the government's laying ties thataway." He pointed eastward. "Is that right?"

"If that's what the boss said, then I guess that's how it is," Cookie said in a guarded manner and his blue eyes slid away from Joe's direct gaze like butter on a hot griddle. "The person to see about cutting out those beeves is Hank Walker over there. He's the ranch foreman." His final tone implied their conversation was at an end.

"Thanks. Will do, mate," Joe agreed, "just as soon as I get me another plate of that stew under my ribs. Best bloody tucker I've had since Sydney!"

His words returned a reluctant grin to Cookie's face. The barrel-shaped man ladled him out another helping, then left Joe to his own devices while he set about mixing another batch of biscuits. Obviously, at least one of Monroe's hired hands didn't approve of the boss and his doings, Joe thought. The knowledge was heartening. If one was against him, chances were there were others who felt the same.

He ate slowly and with relish. He hadn't been lying. Cookie's tucker was as tasty as it had smelled from up in the shade of the oak tree a while ago, and the Irish stew he'd gulped down at Ming's urging in the kitchen of Casa Campanas seemed a lifetime away already. He'd take his own sweet time, and then sidle on up to that Hank Walker and see about getting those "beeves" for the "government workers" cut out of the rest of the herd!

"Hank Walker?" he asked minutes later, offering his hand as he looked down at the man Cookie had pointed out as the ranch foreman.

Walker glanced up, ignoring the proffered handshake, and Joe knew as he met his muddy brown eyes that the foreman was Monroe's man, body and soul. In that instant, he also recognized the muddy brown eyes that met his.

"Yep. I'm Walker. Who're you?" he demanded, looking Joe up and down with unconcealed suspicion and dislike.

"My name's Lucky. Mister Monroe hired me this morning—told me to ride out here and see to delivering some beeves he sold the railroad. Said you'd see about it, or he'd know why." He grinned insolently.

Walker wiped his lips on the back of his hairy fist and set his coffee mug in the dirt. He was grinning himself as he stood up and tucked his thumbs in his gun belt. "He did, did he? Where was it you said he signed you on?"

"Up at the house."

"You say so, partner?" Walker whistled softly through the slight gap in his front teeth, fixing Joe with an intent gaze. "Well, that's real clever of the boss, seeing as how he went to Monterey yesterday morning and ain't due back until after suppertime this evenin'!" The grin widened. "Now, how's about singin' a different tune, *McCaleb*—or should I say El Vengador?"

"Hell and be damned!" Joe said softly. "I figured you looked stupid enough to fall for it! But I guess appearances can be misleading, eh, Walker?"

He sensed the coming blow before Walker's fist had scarcely knotted knuckles, and he quickly ducked. The punch glanced off his shoulder, but he countered it with a hefty slam of his own fist into Walker's beefy belly. Walker doubled over with an undignified groan, cradling his guts while Joe caught his breath.

"Better lay off the biscuits from here on, mate," Joe advised solemnly. "You're a mite flabby about the middle and too sluggish on your feet for fist fighting. Next time, stick to the yellow-bellied games you know best, cobber. Like firing storehouses with a hood over your head to hide behind. Or roughing up a young boy who'd never done you a second's harm. Or cutting the throats of a man's stock."

"You ain't callin' me to account fer none o'that!" Walker growled, straightening up and wincing as he did so. "Your quarrel's with Monroe, not me. Have it out with him and his boys."

"That's exactly what I mean to do," Joe agreed, his tone mild, his manner pleasant. "And you're going to see that I get to talk to them—out here. Send a rider to Fuerte, Walker!"

"And if I won't?"

Like magic, a forty-five seemed to appear in Joe's

475

fist, large and black, cold and threatening. Joe cocked the trigger and aimed the barrel at a spot midway between Walker's groin and belly. "Won't?" He laughed softly, the fading light reflecting like fire bursts in his turquoise eyes. "Hell! There's six good reasons right here that say you will!" He glanced over his shoulder at the wide-eyed circle of faces now watching him. "Or we can be fair about it, and make it one for each of the first six of you who think differently. Any takers?"

There were none.

Chapter Twenty-Nine

It was a full moon that rose that night, the kind of silvery moon that drenched the hills and gulches with a cold, ethereal light. Cottonwoods huddled alongside dry washes became twisted old men in its sheen. Willows seemed maidens washing their long, silvered hair over the gleaming water of the creeks. It was the kind of moon that made a coyote melancholy and set him to a full-throated, lonesome yipping and yapping on distant hills; the kind of moon the white owl from the *campanario* of Casa Campanas favored for her hunting as she drifted over the gray and silent range on snow-feathered wings.

But the owl was not the only creature hunting. There was another who watched and waited; another who knew that success or failure meant the difference between life or death for him that night. On a nearby ridge, where he could watch the herd from a place within range of his guns and in sight and earshot of the camp fires, Joe lay on his belly in the cover of a random formation of boulders and thorny chaparral, and waited and watched.

He'd collected his horse from the *remuda* and ridden off after leaving Walker, doubling back after a spell to take up position here, where he coud observe the goings-on. He'd left Walker a message to give the Monroes. A message? Hell, no. He smiled grimly. It had been a challenge. He intended to hear it delivered.

It was over an hour before he heard horses and knew the Monroes were coming. Sure enough, they came spilling over the rise like rats pouring from a rotted log, Val and the old man in the lead, Jack and Roy trailing after them, Stevie bringing up the rear alongside the hand Walker had sent to Casa Fuerte for them. Joe's fist tightened over the butt of his forty-five, and something like fever swept through him for an instant, shivering down his spine, burning hotly behind his eyes and in the pit of his gut. His finger caressed the cold little curve of the trigger lovingly. Five tall hats. Five tall silhouettes etched sharply from the surrounding terrain by the cold, silver moonlight. Six lead bullets; one for each of them; and one for luck. He could pick them off one after the other, so simply it would be like shooting sitting ducks at a carnival! He could . . . The last one of them would be dead before the first even toppled from his horse. His finger tightened a fraction on the trigger. He could . . . He could . . .

"Cold-blooded murder's not your style, Joe; I know that, and so do you."

After all these months, Joe swore he could hear Sarge Murphy's voice in his ear—the police sergeant, Sean Murphy, who'd had a soft spot for him back in Sydney; the same man who'd given him the chance to escape after Ned's unfortunate death.

"You're right there, Sarge, my old cobber!" he whispered ruefully on the night wind. His right hand, the one cradling the gun, relaxed marginally. The knot of tension between his shoulder blades loosened somewhat. Eyes narrowed, he watched as Harper Monroe lumbered down from his horse, and he heard his gravelly voice clearly from where he lay.

"If you brung me out here on a wild-goose chase, I'll nail your goddamned hide to a fence post! Where in hell is that son of a bitch, Walker?"

Walker wet his lips. Joe caught the slick sheen of his spittle in the patchy light as he did so. "Ain't no wild-goose chase, boss, honest it ain't! McCaleb was here! He said t'tell you if you thought he was gonna be easy pickins' like the Chinee boy, t'think again. Said he'd be ready and waiting fer you and your boys out there somewheres"—he jerked his head toward the moonlit range that ringed the camp fires—"if you had the guts to go get him before . . . before he got you! Said if you wanted him out of the valley, this was your chance. Your *last* chance."

Harper Monroe's fleshy lips split in a smile, revealing the wolfish gleam of small teeth within. "The bastard's got himself a sense of humor, I reckon, Val. Who in hell he think he is, fixing to take on the five of us on our own range?" His smile widened. "Shoot, it ain't hardly worth the effort, goin' after a goldarned fool like that!"

"No, he ain't worth it, Pa," Val agreed softly. "But Rancho Campanas is! With McCaleb six feet under, and a signed bill of sale for his spread in our pockets, the government contract's as good as ours. Just think on it, Pa! We won't need to make no more cattle drives to them stinkin' cow towns from here on in, not with a railroad runnin' nice and easy past our own spread! It'll make life as sweet an' simple as spittin'!"

"And we won't have to sweat over finding water for the herd each summer, not once the Campanas water rights are ours, Pa," Stevie pointed out.

Monroe scowled. "I don't need spelled out to me what I already know, fool! Jack, Val, you boys take the west range. Me'n Roy'll go east. Circle around some, try to flush him out. We'll meet up along Canyon Aguilar. You spot McCaleb, give us a signal—three shots, say. We'll do the same. Let's go! I aim to be sittin' down to breakfast at my own table come sunup—with McCaleb taken care of once and for all."

Up on the ridge, Joe caught Monroe's final words. He grinned and gave a shrug. Hell! Every man was entitled to dream, even Harper Monroe . . .

"Pa? Who do I ride with, Pa?" came Stevie's querulous voice.

Monroe snorted. "You stay put, boy! You don't move your butt more'n an inch away from this camp, you hear me?"

"I hear you," Stevie said sullenly.

Joe watched as they split up and rode off before he slithered backward down the ridge on his belly to where he had left Jimbo, then he mounted up himself, heading directly for Canyon Aguilar. Let the Monroes ride around in circles all night, if that was what they wanted. He'd be rested up and ready for 'em by the time they showed up . . .

Dawn was breaking. The rising sun was tinting the sky with a gold-and-rose-dipped paintbrush from beyond the Sierra Nevadas. Cream-colored clouds streamed across the sky, driving charcoal clouds in dark herds before them. It looked to be a fine day, Joe thought, and stretched himself with a yawn. He'd reached the canyon in less than an hour the evening before, and had taken advantage of the long wait ahead of him to catnap, knowing the rain would wake him in good time, and it had.

The storm he had sensed the afternoon before had broken in the wee hours, cloud masses obliterating the silvery moonlight and making everywhere black as pitch in the brief lull before the thunder crackled, the lightning flashed, and rain began pelting the hard, cracked, dry earth, which drank it thirstily. The cowboys would be hard put to control their thirsty herd in such a storm, Joe had mused, snug and dry himself in the lee of a rocky outcropping. He had doubted he would need to worry about the Monroes' getting help from their crew, under the circumstances. At ease then, he had drawn his little tin case of tobacco and makings from his shirt pocket and lit up a smoke, smiling a little as he imagined the Monroes floundering around in the wet and darkness, cussing him out. It had made a pleasing picture.

The hours had passed on leaden feet. He had shifted position from time to time after the rain ceased, reluctant to have boredom or a crick in his muscles dull the humming readiness that sang through him. Once in a while, he had taken out his deck of cards and riffled them idly from hand to hand in the darkness, needing something to busy himself, for more than once that long night, thoughts of Sera had returned to haunt him, and memories had sifted through his mind like falling stars, each one painfully vivid, painfully real.

Why? he had wondered for maybe the thousandth time. What had he done or said, left undone or unsaid, that last night they'd been together to make her leave him without a word or an explanation or so much as a go to hell? He'd replayed that last day over and over in his mind but had yet to come up with an answer. He knew only that it was not until she was suddenly gone from his life that he'd realized how deeply he'd come to need her over the months. That was the way it went, he had thought heavily. You never guessed how much you cared for someone until she was gone; never told her how much you cared. And, by the time the emptiness engulfed you, the grief released you, it was too damn late. That's how it had been with his Aunt Polly. He'd never been the able to find the words or the actions to hug her, to kiss her rouged cheek and tell her how he felt. They'd frowned on such demonstrations of affection at the orphanage, on the grounds that it made a boy unmanly and soft, and it had been hard for him to overcome his reservations. It was only when they'd lowered Aunt Polly's coffin into the dirt that grief had unlocked his tongue, but by then, of course, she hadn't been able to hear him. He'd tried to be different with Sera, tried so bloody hard to tell her, with words and kisses and with his love making, just how he felt. Maybe he hadn't tried hard enough . . .

He cussed angrily under his breath. Christ! His train of thought was draining the fire out of him, dousing it. It was time to be moving about, setting up for the Monroes, not dwelling on Sera. She belonged to his past now, not the present—or the future, either, if he had one. He got to his feet, stomping the pins and needles from them, and took off his hat. With a crooked grin, he set it atop a broken branch and began clambering over rocks and working his way higher up, toward the farthest inside rim of the canyon. By the time the Monroes realized their error, they'd be caught deep in his trap.

Katie leaned against one of the wooden pillars of the *corredor* and sighed heavily. Lord, it was no use, no use at all! No matter how she tried, she couldn't put Joe from her mind, couldn't sleep nights for thinking about him. Six weeks she'd been gone; for six weeks she'd fought the urge to hightail it back to Southern California and Casa Campanas, telling herself he was better off without her, safer without her around, too. But still her conscience nagged that if she loved him, really loved him, and he loved her, they were better off facing the Monroes together, side by side. There was only one thing holding her back; would he want her there when she told him she wasn't Seraphina? Did he love her enough to put his love for her above his love for the land? Maybe—just maybe—he'd understand, would be willing to accept her simply as Katie Steele, the landless woman who loved him, and start afresh someplace else. She knew in her heart that what she was doing—staying here at the Shadow S—was cowardly. But it was easier to hide and not face up to the possibility that Joe's answer to her question would be the one she dreaded hearing—easier than asking him outright and finding out once and for all—

"Having trouble sleeping?"

She glanced up, seeing her father standing there in the moonlight enjoying a smoke. The tobacco aroma reminded her painfully of Joe.

"I guess so, Papa," she confessed, shrugging. "It was so hot in my room. Not even a breath of air! I figured it would be cooler out here."

He came toward her, his hair so black it took on a bluish hue in the starlight, his broad shoulders blocking the amber haze that spilled from the French windows of the bedroom beyond, which he and her mother shared. He reached out and tilted her face up to his, gazing down at her with concern in his night black eyes. The familiar faded silver of an old, old scar at his temple, shaped like a small arrowhead, showed pale against his deep tan.

"Quit tryin' to fight it, Katie," he said in his deep voice. "You're losing the battle, honey."

Her lower lip quivered. Tears rushed to fill her eyes. "I don't know what you're talking about, Papa. It was hot. I woke up and came outside for some air. That's all," she insisted.

"You're just like me, Katie. A damned bad liar!" Luke Steele murmured, tugging a wayward strand of his daughter's hair. "What's he like, this Joe of yours?" he asked, surprising her with the suddenness of the question.

"Joe? Well, he's . . . oh, I don't know! Different, I suppose. He's not like anyone else I've ever met, that's for sure."

"Different? How?"

She escaped his arms and walked away from him down the *corredor,* her head bowed in thought, hugging herself about the arms for a few long moments before she answered him. "It's hard to explain. I . . . I was attracted to him the very first time I saw him. I remember thinking how vivid his eyes were, and how I liked the way he smiled—sort of crooked, you know?— a way that made me want to smile, too. I couldn't say he's handsome; not really. But there's something about him that . . . that kind of makes my heart do flip-flops inside me when I look at him, or he looks at me—" She broke off, embarrassed by her frankness. "Oh, Papa, you don't want to hear all this silly nonsense!"

"Try me," Luke said with a smile. "Go on. What else?"

"We-eell, this may sound kind of crazy, but sometimes I got the feeling when I was with him that there were two Joes: the one he let everyone see—you know, a real tough *hombre* who could talk mean and ride and shoot better than most men, and who didn't give a darn about anyone or anything, sort of as if he had a giant grudge against the world—and then . . . then there's this other Joe, the Joe who's gentle and funny and silly, and even romantic, sometimes. I often got the feeling that deep inside, he wasn't half as tough and independent as he'd have liked me to believe, nor as rough and rugged. He wanted a woman to love, and a home, and a family. It sounds corny, but I guess . . . I guess I felt he needed me, to love me and to be loved by me. Am I talking *loco*, Papa?"

"If talking as if you're in love with this Joe means you're *loco*, then I guess I'd have to say you are, honey," her father replied, laughter in his eyes. "So, if that's the case, what are you doing here?"

"I told you about those men—the Monroes? I can't go back and run the risk of Joe's getting hurt, maybe killed."

Luke Steele sighed. "Or run the risk of leveling with him, maybe?"

Even in the shadows, he saw the blush that rushed to her cheeks. "That too," she admitted.

"Your Joe sounds to me as if he's man enough to deal with the Monroes—and anyone else he might have to deal with, like you, maybe! Kate, why don't you trust him to handle the situation, and to handle the truth when he hears it from you? Go back to California. Don't wait even one more day! Find out just what you're up against. Wondering and worrying is always worse than knowing, and you can't run away from it forever."

"You're beginning to sound a lot like Mama!" she teased. "She didn't send you out here to talk to me, did she?"

Luke grinned and kissed his daughter's brow. "Not this time. She only gets to manipulate me when I want to be manipulated. Didn't you know that? Good night, honey. I'll see you in the morning."

"Papa . . . ?" she called after him as he opened the French door to go inside.

"Yes?"

"Make it early in the morning, Papa. I . . . I have a train to catch."

"Good girl, Katie." He turned to go once more but

paused when he saw her frown again.

"Papa, one more thing. What about the baby—what if . . . if it's all over between us? What if he tells me to hightail it out of there?"

"I don't reckon for a second he will. But just supposing he does"—Luke grinned—"maybe I'll come to California with you. I have a shotgun that might just change his mind *real* fast!"

"Oh, you . . . !" she scolded, and blew him a kiss.

Luke was still grinning as he slipped inside his room. Promise awaited him in their bed, her long, corn-silk hair tumbling loose over her bare shoulders. There was a familiar invitation in her sparkling green eyes, an invitation he'd been about to take her up on when he'd heard Katie outside in the *corredor* that circled the courtyard.

"Did you talk to her, Luke?"

"Weren't you listening?"

"I don't eavesdrop, mister!" she declared indignantly, aiming a down-filled pillow at his head, which he deftly avoided. "Do you really think she'll be on that train in the morning?"

In the act of unbuttoning his shirt, Luke reached out and tweaked her cheek, his midnight eyes shining with amusement, his darkly handsome face smiling broadly. "Not listening, hmmm? I reckon so."

Promise frowned. "I hope we did the right thing, urging her to go back to him. Oh, Luke, what if he's all wrong for her? What if he was really just . . . just using her all along? You didn't tell her about that Mister Caldwell, and Mac McCaleb, and what we found out?" He shook his head. "Then she still only knows that it was through the lawyer that we knew where she was?" He nodded. "Then maybe we should tell her before she leaves?" Promise suggested.

"Not the way I see it. They both have to level with each other for it to work out right." He shucked off his pants and strode across the room toward her, stretching out alongside her on the bed. "Now, *desperada,* quit worrying. Katie will sort things out; she's no fool. It seems to me we had something else in mind a while back . . . ?" His rough, tanned hand grazed down over her rounded shoulder to caress a full breast, and by the shiver of anticipation that rippled through her warm body pressed close to his, Luke knew he now had his wife's fullest attention.

"Did we? Now, what was it? You'll have to refresh my memory, darlin'," she murmured, her voice husky and teasing with passion. "I'm not as young as I used to be, and I keep on forgetting." Her green eyes glinted in the shadowed room.

"I'll remind you, *desperada!*" Luke promised.

Chapter Thirty

"And where the divil might you have been, young fellow-me-lad?" Peggy demanded as Ming endeavored—without success—to sneak in through the kitchen door unnoticed. "Everyone else had the decency t'come t'table when supper was ready, but not you, oh, no!"

"Forgive me, Missie Kelly," Ming mumbled, "I . . . I was whittling, and I forgot the time."

"Ah. So, whittlin', was it? On the chair you were after makin' fer Mister McCaleb?" Peggy asked, her tone a little gentler now.

Ming shook his head. "No. I . . . the chair will not be finished now, not ever. Joe's going away. He won't need it."

"Going away? From Las Campanas? And why ever would the poor, troubled man want to do a thing like that, when 'tis plain he's in need o' his friends?"

"You must ask Joe," Ming said, tight lipped. As far as he was concerned, the subject was definitely closed.

Peggy eyed him shrewdly. "You sound a wee bit sorry for yourself, ye young divil. Did ye cross words with the mister, then, lad?"

Ming grimaced. "Far worse than that, I fear. I . . . I

called him a weakling, and a coward, too! I was mad at him for wanting to give up the ranch, you see, and the words . . . the words just came out!"

"Aye, as they've an inclination to do when we're angry," the housekeeper commiserated. "Don't worry yourself sick about it, Ming, lad. When he comes in, you can explain and tell him you're sorry. Mister McCaleb will understand."

"I sure hope so." Ming suddenly glanced up sharply. "When he comes in, you said? Where is he?"

Peggy shrugged. "I don't rightly know. He didn't come back to the house for supper, you see. All I'm after knowing is that there was trouble today, out at the west grazing. Those Godless spalpeens, the Monroes, slaughtered some of the flock in Jaime's charge—slit their throats, those poor, dumb beasts! He rode in around noon to tell Joe about it. Mister McCaleb looked powerful angry when he heard, too! Straightway, they rode off together."

Ming nodded. Frowning, he turned and started back toward the door he had just entered.

"And where are ye off to now, I'd like t'know? You come back here, my lad! What about your supper?" Peggy demanded, fists planted on her hips.

"I'm not hungry," Ming muttered and darted out of the door before she could stop him.

"Heathen ruffian!" Peggy grumbled as she cleared away the supper dishes, covering a dish of warm apple pie with a clean cloth and setting it in the cool larder for Ming to eat later on, when he found his appetite. "Why I worry about that boy is a blessed mystery, an' that's a fact!"

It was soon very apparent to Ming that no one at the ranch house knew where Joe might be. Nothing they said should have alarmed him unduly. There had been trouble with one of the flocks just that morning, after

489

all. Perhaps, Gabrielle suggested sensibly, Joe had decided to ride from pasture to pasture and check on the safety of each of his *pastores,* his shepherds, and their flocks, in turn. Ming had to admit it sounded not only feasible, but probable, knowing Joe. Nonetheless, he could not rid himself of the gnawing sensation in the pit of his belly that told him it was not that simple; that something was wrong, badly wrong, and that that something involved his Joe. Acting on his hunch, he decided to ride out to where Jaime Santiago's sheep grazed, which was the last known place Joe had been heading. He would find out for himself!

Unaccustomed to saddling a horse—or riding one, come to that!—Ming selected a docile chestnut gelding from the corral for his mount. Despite its apparent gentleness, it took Ming over half an hour to first catch the wily beast, then lead it to the *ramada* where the tack was kept, then slip on the bridle and fit the bit into the gelding's mouth and heft the weighty saddle up and over its back. A few more minutes passed as he fumbled to tighten and buckle the girth strap. Grasping the reins somewhat gingerly in his fist, he tucked his toe into the deep stirrup and swung himself astride. To his delight, the gelding stood quietly while he mounted, and when he touched his heels to its flanks and clicked for it to move out, the gelding started off at an ambling gait well suited to his lack of expertise, before breaking into an alarming, bone-shaking trot as they passed the corral and headed due west.

The moon was up, round and full and white as the translucent rice cakes his mother used to make for him, he noticed, thankful for its light, for otherwise he would have been quite unable to go out in search of Joe. There was the metallic tang of a coming storm in the air, however, that promised the full moon and the light she shared would not last for long. He shivered.

The scent of rain reminded him of the night he had lain, beaten and only half-conscious, waiting for someone to find him, while the storm crackled and flashed overhead. It had seemed a lifetime before old Chief Tyonek's hunters had gently lifted him onto their *travois,* and the old medicine woman, Satinka, had salved his wounds . . .

He had not gone far when a rider materialized on the rough trail ahead of him, going in the opposite direction. At first, he thought it was Joe and almost cried out in relief. But as the rider drew nearer, he recognized the bulky silhouettes of man and massive horse as those of Raoul Garnier and his sturdy mount, returning from a visit to the *pueblo.* He had left the morning before and knew nothing of the lawyer and the other Joel McCaleb's visit, nor of the slaughtered sheep. Ming greeted him and quickly told him all that had transpired since his departure.

"I do not know why I am so worried about Joe, Mistah Garnier, but I am! It is simply something I feel in here, and here." He touched his belly, then his heart. "I cannot explain it."

Raoul nodded, his ruddy face concerned now. "It does not pay to deny such feelings, Ming. And you do not need to tell me how it is. I am Basque!" he added simply, as if that explained everything. "We understand and accept that there are things such as intuition that serve to warn or guide us." He frowned. "But you must not go looking for Joe alone. It is far too dangerous for you out here at night, *mon ami.* We will go together."

Though he would never have admitted it, not to anyone, Ming almost wept in relief.

Jaime Santiago's tiny campfire shone out like a beacon as they approached it much later. Beyond, dotted across the hills like grubby-white, enormous mushrooms in the moonlight, were Jaime's portion of Joe's flocks. Save for an occasional plaintive baaing, the sheep seemed calm and content, but the shepherd was obviously nervous. He leapt to his feet as they rode up, his club in hand. But the black and white sheepdog beside him, Gitana, neither growled nor barked an alarm at the new arrivals. Rather, she whined softly and wagged her plumed tail to and fro eagerly. Reassured, Jaime let the hand that wielded the stout club fall slack at his side.

"Señor Garnier! And you, too, Ming? What are you doing here?" he exclaimed. "My Gabrielle . . . there is nothing wrong, is there?"

"*Non, non.* Gabrielle is very well, *mon fils,* you may rest assured on that score. And it is high time you called me Papa, instead of Señor Garnier!" Raoul exclaimed, dismounting as he greeted his son-in-law. "We rode out here because we are concerned about Mister McCaleb. No one has seen him since you rode up to the house this afternoon. Do you know where he is?"

Jaime frowned. "He did not return to the *casa? Dios mio!* But he left many hours ago!"

"Did he tell you where he was going?" Ming asked urgently.

"He did not say . . . no, not in so many words. But . . . but I asked him if he intended to deal with the Monroes—if he meant to call them to account for the slaughter of our sheep. And he said . . . he said that he must!"

"Then he rode to Rancho Fuerte, alone?" Garnier pressed.

"*Sí,*" Jaime confessed dolefully. "Alone—and with a look in his eyes such as I have never seen before, or ever want to see again." The shepherd shuddered.

Ming and Raoul Garnier exchanged glances that spoke volumes.

"I hope to God we are not too late, *mes amis!*" Raoul said softly, putting Ming's dread into words.

"Nor too few!" Ming breathed, his heart thudding with fear. They needed help, but who would help them?

He looked up as a ghostly white form glided overhead, its wings silvered by moonlight, its shadow drifting slowly over the ground. He caught the low, melancholy hoot of the hunting owl as she passed over them, and fragments of the haunting legend of the Indian maiden whispered over and over in his mind. His almond-shaped black eyes glittered. He knew just where he could go to find help for Joe—to Tyonek, and old Satinka . . .

The air was pure and crystal clear up on the rim of the canyon that morning. Joe could see for miles. The earth smelled rich and fertile after the rain, so rich he could almost taste its tang on his tongue. The eerie rock formations all about him, whether rust or ochre or brown, were washed sparkling clean. He felt a curious calm inside him; no trace of fear, but rather a quiet acceptance of whatever was to come—acceptance, and a determination to win.

It was a little after dawn when he spotted the first horses moving slowly toward the canyon. A grim smile played about his lips. From the way their mounts were moving, heads down and dispirited, Harper Monroe and son had done some rough riding during the night! He held his position until the horses entered the mouth of the canyon.

Harper Monroe reined in his horse and shifted uncomfortably in the saddle.

"Val!" he yelled, cupping his mouth. "Jack! You boys here?"

" . . . here? . . . here? . . . " came the answering echo.

"They ain't here, Monroe!" Joe yelled back, ducking down into his rocky roost. He waited until the echo was silent again. "But I am!"

"...am...am..."

Harper Monroe spun about in the saddle, deep-set eyes darting nervously to left and right, up and down, trying to judge from which direction the sound had come. "Show yourself, McCaleb!" he shouted. "Maybe we can talk this out!"

He heard only a low ripple of laughter in reply, mirthless laughter that was thrown back at him time and time again by the towering canyon walls to mock him.

Cussing under his breath, Harper Monroe waved Roy back. "Go get him, son," he commanded softly. "I'll keep him talkin', give you a chance t'figure where he's got himself holed up."

With a curt nod, Roy slithered down from his horse's back and, drawing his gun and bending low as he scuttled crab-style across the hard dirt and rubble, he made it to the rocky canyon wall.

"I see you, Roy!" Joe taunted, his voice sounding curiously disembodied by the echo to Harper Monroe's ears. "I can pick you off any time I like!"

"Then go ahead, McCaleb! Try it!" Roy Monroe snarled back, bracing his belly over an enormous boulder and leveling his gun as he scanned the opposite canyon wall. "'Less you're yeller, that is," he added.

"That old trick won't work, Roy," Joe retorted scornfully. The echo repeated "...Roy...Roy..." after him. "I wasn't born yesterday! You'll have to come looking for me, if you want me."

He picked up a small rock and hurled it as far left as he could. There was the dull sound of rock striking rock, then a small landslide as dislodged rubble showered down. At once, both Monroes spun toward the sound, guns up and blazing spurts of yellow fire. The bullets whined off rocky surfaces, and the sound of the reports repeated over and over like a drawn-out crack of thunder.

"Not there, boys! Care to try again someplace else?"

Monroe swore foully and lumbered down from his horse, using the animal's body as a cover until, his crippled leg dragging, he managed to stow himself safely under a rocky ledge, close to the ground. He settled down for what promised to be a long wait, taking a swig of water from the canteen strung over his chest. Sooner or later, Val and Jack would be along. Between the five of them, McCaleb didn't have a hope in hell! He tipped back his hat and slowly scanned the canyon walls, carefully sorting out rock shapes that looked more like men or large, supernatural beasts than the formations shaped by time and weather that they really were. Nothing. His gaze swept on, then back to a point that had drawn his attention. He squinted against the dazzling light as something white caught his eye again, just a flicker, but enough.

"Roy!" he hissed, pointing. "Up there!"

Roy looked, a grin squirming its way up between his lips. "I see it, Pa," he rasped back. "Damn fool shoulda took his hat off!"

So saying, Roy worked his way back, out of sight and range of where the white hat they had spotted showed against the darker rocks, scrabbling and sliding around and then up, heading toward it. Meanwhile, his father kept up a steady stream of insults and taunts, designed to fix Joe's attention fully on him instead of Roy's climb. From time to time as he felt inclined, Joe answered him in a lazy drawl that stuck in Harper's craw. Then came utter silence.

Nothing he said could induce that bastard McCaleb to speak! Monroe realized. The silence grew and swelled and squeezed in all about him until Harper Monroe felt the first churnings of fear start up in his belly and the slow sliding of sweat down his spine.

From his position several feet above where he had conspicuously lodged the white hat, Joe pressed himself back against a rock and held his breath as he heard Roy climbing steadily up toward it. Heard him? Strewth, he would have had to have been deaf not to, for Monroe's third son was panting like a blue-heeler after a ten mile kangaroo hunt on a hot summer's day! Joe grinned as he slipped into position, his blood singing with excitement. Only another few feet, just another few, and old Roy would be wondering what in the hell had hit him!

Monroe's son squirmed his way between two massive boulders, wanting to holler out loud that McCaleb was a darn fool and good as dead, for he could glimpse the white hat clearly below him and it would be an easy shot, straight through the head, easy as taking candy from a baby! He drew his forty-five from its holster and sighted along the barrel. He crooked his index finger around the trigger and started to squeeze, but then white and scarlet stars exploded through his mind and pain tore through him as Joe dropped a heavy boulder directly onto the back of his skull from still higher above.

Roy Monroe came to to find himself bound hand and foot and sitting upright, a red bandanna stuffed in his mouth—and the white hat perched atop his own head! He was propped against a boulder. He could see every last detail of the canyon bed far below and the *arroyo* that ran through it, and he could make out his father, still hunkered down under his rocky ledge. Sweat broke out on his palms and slithered down his back as he saw a rider coming up fast into the canyon. McCaleb had help on the way and hell, he had no cover, none, not even a rock or a bush! He was a sitting duck up here in the open! There was a better than even chance he'd be plugged by his own family in the cross fire if he couldn't get rid of the gag and yell for them to hold their fire, that it was now Roy, not McCaleb, under the white hat, and for God's sake not to shoot—

"Not much fun being helpless, is it, mate?" Joe gritted softly. "I'd guess that's how those ranchers and their women felt with you boys holding a gun on them—innocent, hardworking people like 'Livia Rodriguez and her boys. I guess that's how my young friend, Ming, and Mrs. Kelly felt the day you no-good dingoes rode up to Casa Campanas, or the night you fired the storehouse. I guess that's how just about everyone you've messed with has felt! So. How is it, mate? Is it still fun when you're the one in hot water?" The only answer was a series of coughs and gurgles from Roy Monroe as he tried desperately to spit the gag from his mouth. "Have fun, Roy," Joe said grimly. "I'll be back for you in a while—if your pa don't finish you off first!"

So saying, Joe left him. One down, four to go. The odds were dropping, and in his favor!

"Roy! Shee-it! Where in hell are you, boy?" Harper Monroe yelled from his hidey-hole. The echo threw back the word *"boy"* over and over, but there was no answer from Roy, and Harper's fear mounted.

Joe grinned mirthlessly, hearing the edge of panic that laced Monroe's voice as he clambered down the series of boulder steps behind the man's rocky covering. Basking pinkish gray lizards and an old rattler, startled by his intrusion, scampered or slithered away, unseen by Joe. All his thoughts were on Monroe and his revenge. Let the old man sweat! Let him taste fear, sharp and foul, on his tongue, he thought with grim satisfaction! Let him wallow for a while in how it feels to be the victim, rather than the hunter!

He was ready to jump Harper Monroe when he heard the Monroes' horses nicker a greeting to other horses, and he froze in his tracks. He cautiously poked his head up over a rock, even as the clatter of hooves and the sound of his own name, loudly called, rang out through the canyon, and the rider Roy Monroe had spotted from his vantage point minutes before careened to a halt almost level with his hiding place.

"Joe! Where are you, Joe? Val Monroe's coming!"

". . . coming . . . coming . . ."

Sweet Christ. It was Seraphina! She was alone, for the time being, but he could see the dust of other riders approaching in the distance. Val Monroe and some of the cowboys from Fuerte, he guessed, but he had no time to think any further as he saw Harper Monroe below him edge the nose of his gun out from under the rocky ledge, figuring to take a shot at the young woman.

"Get down, Sera!" he roared, and his gun cleared leather in the same breath. His bullet took Monroe in the hand, spinning the gun from his bloody grip. The man's own aim had been thrown off by Joe's roar so close behind him, and Joe leapt and landed full weight upon him before he had time to recover his weapon and try again. He ground Monroe's face into the dirt hard, then quickly stood and rolled the weighty man over, looking him full in the face with turquoise eyes that blazed hatred.

"I've been waiting a long time to do this, mate!" he rasped before he slammed his clenched fist squarely into Harper Monroe's face, feeling bone and muscle give like water beneath his knuckles. Never had a punch felt so damned sweet! Monroe's piggy little eyes glazed, and then his head lolled sideways as he lost consciousness.

498

A grim smile of satisfaction flitted across Joe's face as he straightened up, but it was a smile that was short-lived.

"Interfering again, eh, love?" he asked, striding quickly to Katie's horse and yanking her bodily from the saddle. "You're like a bad penny—you always show up when you're not wanted!" He started back up the rocky incline toward where he had left Roy Monroe bound and gagged, almost dragging her along behind him.

"Damn you and your pride, Joe," she panted, hard put to keep up with him as she scrambled over sharp or slippery boulders. "Can't you say you're glad to see me, just this once?"

"I'm not," he retorted, hustling her up a steep, craggy wall ahead of him. "Leastways, not right now! Hurry it up, love! Val Monroe's coming!"

Katie shivered with distaste. The mere mention of that slimy sidewinder's name was enough to make her double her speed. Seconds later, they crouched side by side behind where Roy Monroe still perched, struggling desperately to free himself.

"Sweating now, are you, Roy, old son?" Joe mocked. "Go ahead, mate! Sweating's all you'll be doing, this time around." He jerked his head toward the canyon floor. "Here comes your big brother."

Katie could see Val Monroe below, entering the canyon. He was alone, and he held his horse to a walk. They watched as he spotted his father sprawled in the dust beneath the rock ledge and swung down from his mount to check on him. Obviously satisfied the man wasn't dead, he straightened up, squinting warily about him, scanning the rocky walls.

"McCaleb!" he yelled, slowly drawing his gun. "You here?"

". . . here . . . here . . ."the canyon answered.

After a lengthy silence, Val Monroe spat. He was about to remount his horse when a shot whined on the still air and threw up a funnel of dust between his feet. He spun backward as if plugged, scrambling for cover.

"That answer your question, Monroe?" Joe yelled from his rocky roost.

Val Monroe swung about, trying to gauge the direction from which the bullet had come. His eyes narrowed as he spotted the flash of white that was the hat perched atop Roy Monroe's head. Taking careful aim, he squeezed off a shot. It missed, the bullet chipping a rock scant feet away from Roy's bound hands, but it was close enough to put the fear of God into Roy Monroe. Through his gag, he sobbed like a baby, tears streaming down his narrow face.

Joe's smile was mirthless as he slithered over to him. "I'm going to give you just one chance, Roy," he told the man. "Just one, mind. Sing out loud and clear and tell your brother to drop his guns, you hear me? You say one word out of line, and my next bullet has your name on it. *Comprende?*"

Roy nodded weakly, sweat still pouring off him. He was a decidedly greenish color as Joe roughly yanked the gag from his mouth.

"Go ahead. Say your piece," Joe ground out.

"Va . . . al!" Roy croaked.

". . . al . . . al . . ." the canyon mocked him.

"It's me, Roy! Hold your fire! McCaleb's holdin' a gun on me, Val! Don't shoot!" he yelled. There was silence broken only by the echo, by the nicker of Kate's horse far below, and the indignant scream of a hawk wheeling far above in the blue sky.

"Did . . . did you hear me, Val? For God's sake, say somethin'!" Roy pleaded.

"I hear you, little brother!" came Val's snarled reply.

"McCaleb says . . . says to throw down yer guns! Do

500

it, Val, for God's sake, *please!*" He was obviously uncertain that Val would consider his life worth saving. So much for brotherly love, Joe thought with macabre humor.

Roy died a thousand deaths in the endless minute it took Val to comply. Joe watched with satisfaction as Val Monroe stepped from hiding and unbuckled his gun belt, tossing it to the ground at his feet.

"Kick it away from you!" Joe ordered, standing now. Val obediently did so. "That's real smart of you, mate," he approved grimly, stepping out into the open. "I'm coming down to get you. You and me and Roy here and your pa are going to take us a little ride—to the marshal up in Monterey. Seraphina's here beside me. She'll be holding a gun on Roy here, so if there's any funny business on your part, poor ole Roy won't be laughing over it for too long. You hear me, Monroe?"

"I hear you, you son of a bitch!" Val Monroe snarled.

Joe handed one of his guns to Katie. "You heard what I said?" She nodded. "Do you think you can do it?"

"Yes," she said without hesitation.

"Good girl."

"Joe . . . ?" she called softly after him as he started the downward climb.

"What is it?"

"Be careful, Joe!"

He nodded and disappeared.

Katie edged forward until she had a clear view of the canyon floor. Her attention was riveted first on Val Monroe, then on Joe in turn, as she saw him clamber surefootedly down toward the man. He had almost reached him when she caught a sudden blur of movement off t Joe's left. Oh, Lord, no! Harper Monroe had come to!

501

"Joe!" she screamed, recklessly standing in her fright. "Look out!"

Joe jerked around a second too late. He felt the rush of hot air as Harper Monroe's bullet nicked him in that same instant and a blaze of fire swept through his shoulder. He fell the remaining few feet and rolled over and over, yet in almost the same breath he was up and on his feet and charging for Harper Monroe, leaping the last few feet in a flying tackle that sent the crippled old man reeling. Joe gripped Harper's fist in both his own and grappled him for the gun. The two men rolled in the dust, furiously fighting for possession of the weapon, first Harper on top, then Joe, then Harper. And then, suddenly, there was a deafening explosion between the two of them as the gun went off. Katie screamed once in terror, then held her breath in an agony of waiting. Both men sprawled on their backs on the ground. Both men lay still. Oh, dear God, which one of them . . . ? Her tears of terror turned to tears of relief as she saw Joe slowly get to his feet and look dazedly around him; saw the dark stain spreading across Monroe's belly that had to be blood. It was only then that she remembered Val Monroe. She frowned, craning her neck as she looked frantically back and forth below her. Val was nowhere to be seen, so where the devil had he gone?

"Lookin' for me, sweet thing?" came his mocking voice at her back. Chills raced up and down her spine as she turned slowly about to face him.

Joe realized immediately where Val must have gone. His heart began a slow and ominous thudding as he started climbing back up toward Sera. Could she have remained cool and calm while he grappled for his life with Monroe? His hopes plummeted as he recalled the frantic scream with which she'd alerted him. Now, he doubted it. More likely than not, Val Monroe was up there, and Sera helpless to get away from him, he realized grimly and with a sinking heart.

Sure enough, as he eased himself over the last boulder, he saw Val Monroe not twenty feet away from him, with Seraphina held tight around the throat, the barrel of his gun digging hard against her temple.

"Throw down yer gun, McCaleb!" Val ordered, "or this sweet thing's deader than a doornail!"

"I told you, you crazy fool, it's no use!" Katie gasped against the choking pressure of Val Monroe's forearm across her windpipe, her fingers clawing at his hands. "There's help coming, for Joe, and for me! Clem Tallant's had his badge taken away from him and half the town's on its way here, howling for justice and your hide. If that's not enough, Chief Tyonek's on his way with his braves. So you see, even if you kill me, you won't get away with it! They'll fill you so full of lead you'll rattle!"

"Jest you shut up, sweet thing! I ain't no greenhorn t'fall for your bluff. McCaleb, you step on over here. Hell, I've been waitin' t'meet you face t'face again fer a long, long time! Did your pretty woman here tell you how it was with us the day of the *fiesta,* McCaleb? Did she tell you how it was between us while you were dancin' and prancin' and *fandangoin'* about?" He leered at Joe, his tone loaded with innuendo. "Hell, I had her all warm and willin' in my arms, down on her back in the dust, an' she was just a-beggin' me to give her some o' my sweet lovin'! Did she tell you 'bout that, partner?" he asked softly, caressing Katie's temple with his gun barrel. "Yessiree, McCaleb, she was just *pantin'* fer it, and so, hell, what could an old cowpoke like me do? It ain't nice to say no to a little lady, now is it?"

"You dirty liar!" Katie screamed, reckless in her outrage. "He's lying! It was never that way, never! It's you I love, Joe!"

503

"You're a dead man, Monroe!" Joe seethed, his eyes now so pale and cold they were like slits of blue ice. He cocked the safety of his forty-five with an ominous click.

"Go ahead, McCaleb, do it!" Monroe goaded him, smiling broadly. "Use that gun, and this sweet little thing'll be turning cold before you clear leather!" he spat back. "I'm callin' the shots this time, remember? Draw your weapon, real nice and easy, and toss it clear over here t'me. And hurry it up, you son of a bitch!"

There was an edge of panic to Val's voice now, for he could hear horses coming up fast from the east; he could see the dust cloud they were churning up as they drew nearer. The McCaleb woman hadn't been bluffing as he'd figured, he realized. Help was really on the way for her, and for her man. He licked his dry lips. First Jack, that yeller-belly, had run out on him, and now it looked like he was gonna be cheated out of dealin' with McCaleb. Hell and be damned if he'd let that happen, not after comin' so close! "The gun, I said!" he repeated. "Move it!" He cocked his gun, and Katie flinched as if he'd struck her.

She'd seemed calm under the circumstances a moment before, but now Joe saw the terror that filled her widening gray-green eyes, saw how her hands trembled with fear and how her pale gold skin had drained of color. Her expression tore at his heart—the heart he'd tried so desperately to harden and close against her. There was no way he could shoot Monroe before he could squeeze off a shot, he acknowledged, feeling a great weight fill his chest. If he didn't do what Monroe wanted, Sera was as good as dead.

"All right," he agreed softly. "Let her go, and I'll throw down my gun."

"No way, partner! The gun first."

"The girl first."

Val Monroe shook his head. "You don't have the say-so, McCaleb. I got the girl, see. I say who goes first."

Monroe held the trump card all right, Joe realized bitterly. He had to trust him to let Seraphina go. He had no choice.

"Right." He tossed his forty-five across the dirt. It landed with a dull thud at Val's feet. Horses were entering the canyon now, many horses, and Joe could hear shouts on the still air.

"Untie my brother!" Val rasped quickly.

Joe did so.

"Okay, Roy, now git, you goldarned fool!" he snarled, and Roy, rubbing chafed wrists, needed no second urging. He began scrabbling down the rocky incline toward his horse. When he had mounted up, Val turned his head to dart a glance over his shoulder at the fast-approaching riders, and then in the same instant he unexpectedly shoved Katie hard in Joe's direction. Taken by surprise, she lost her balance, stumbled, and fell into his arms, even as Val broke and sprinted for cover. Over Katie's shoulder, Joe saw Val Monroe raise his gun, leveling it at her defenseless back.

"You got your skin! You don't get your woman, too, McCaleb!" he yelled, and fired.

Joe reacted without thought for himself, without weighing anything but the desperate need to save his woman, the woman he loved—would always love! He flung her sharply, brutally, aside, as far and as hard as he could.

Sprawled in the dirt, her palms bleeding, a stunned Katie looked up at him. There was hurt, confusion, fear in her eyes. "Please, Joe, don't! Monroe lied! You have to believe me, Joe, you must—"

And then she knew why Joe had hurled her aside,

505

knew only too well it hadn't been hatred or rejection on his part. For even as she glanced up—even as another shot whined out and finished Val Monroe—Joe's arms flew up and wide open. His body jerked like a puppet yanked by a string. He traveled backward a step, then two, before he dropped like a stone to the dust and lay still, felled by the bullet that had been meant for her.

Chapter Thirty-One

Katie knelt beside Joe, shaking her head slowly from side to side in shock and disbelief. Her gray-green eyes were blank and emotionless, her expression stunned. She hugged herself about the arms and began to rock back and forth. Her lips were parted, but no sound came from them.

Ming looked toward her, and then back to Joe's still form, and then he was running up the slight incline, ignoring Raoul's shouts to come back.

Scant feet from the pair, he slithered to a halt and simply stood there, unable to believe the truth of what he was seeing. He looked down at Joe, feeling grief well up inside him in a hot, choking flood. His chest and throat were filled with it, filled to bursting, to explosion point! He wanted to scream, to tear out his hair, to gouge out his eyes and assuage the agonizing pain. But he could only stand and stare with eyes that refused to believe what they were seeing, and a tongue too tied to put it into words and make it real.

Joe's body was spread-eagled face up in the dirt. His vivid turquoise eyes were closed. His shaggy, dusty blond hair sprayed across the red earth. His emptied forty-five was beside him where he had tossed it at Val

Monroe's command. On the left side of his upper chest was a large, neat hole. The scorched edges showed black against the checkered cloth of his shirt pocket. He'd been shot straight through the heart.

The tiny flicker of hope that Ming had kept alive as he scrambled frantically down over rocks and boulders guttered and dimmed. There was no hope, no doubt. Joe was dead.

Raoul blinked back tears, a knot of grief in his own throat that refused to be swallowed as he glanced at the girl, then back to the lad. He could do nothing for her. She was lost in her grief for the time being, rocking, rocking soundlessly. She had her father to comfort her, but the Chinese boy . . . ? With Joe dead, he had no one! He saw Ming's bony shoulders begin to heave, heard the dry sobs that finally tore loose and racked him, and Raoul's heart went out to the lad. He strode heavily across the dirt to comfort him, while Jaime and Tyonek, old Satinka and several braves, who had followed them deeper into the canyon after shooting Val Monroe, looked on, their expressions appalled, anguished.

Grim faced, a nerve pulsing beneath the white scar at his temple, Luke Steele went to his daughter and lifted her up into his strong arms, carrying her from the scene and back to where their horses waited. She made no protest, nor did she say a word. To all intents, she was as lifeless as Joe.

"Come away, *mon ami,*" Raoul urged the boy hoarsely, taking him by the shoulders. "You did all you could for Joe in trying to bring help, believe me. He would have been proud of you, my little friend!" The boy suddenly flung his arms around Raoul's enormous belly and buried his face against the Basque's shirt-front. Raoul soothed him while he wept, tears filling his own eyes as he added sadly, "Oh, so very proud, my poor little fellow . . ."

Satinka clambered down from behind Tyonek's horse and scampered across to Joe's body. As always, she was cackling like a madwoman, jerking her bony arms and body—swathed in the usual assortment of rags—wildly about, causing the amulets and tiny cone-shaped bells that hung on rawhide thongs at her wrists and about the hems of her skirt to tinkle. She hopped and swooped and gyrated across the dirt and rubble, finally flinging herself down upon her scrawny brown knees beside the body. Muttering some incantation or other she leaned over and pressed her ear hard to his chest, her eyes brightening and gleaming like wet blackberries as she listened for what seemed an eternity before straightening up. She turned and said something in her Gabrielino tongue to Chief Tyonek. Raoul saw the old chief shake his head.

"What did she say, my friend?" Raoul asked, curious. Did the old Indian crone plot some dark magic to bring Joe back to life, or some awful ritual to be worked over his body? He would permit neither! he decided at once.

"It has been said many times in her lifetime that Satinka's mind has been touched by the hand of the Great One, and that she is not like others. This I now believe, for she told me in our tongue that the one named Joe yet lives!" He shook his grizzled old head. "I told her that she is a foolish old woman; that no man can survive a bullet to the heart! I told her to speak no more of such things while our hearts are still heavy with grief. Instead, I bade her chant a song of mourning for his spirit, which has gone to become one with the stars above."

Raoul nodded soberly. "Thank you, my friend." His shoulders sagged, and a heavy sigh escaped him. "Well, I suppose all we can do now is take him home to Casa

509

Campanas. Will your braves prepare a litter of some kind for his body?"

"We will. Wichado! Yakecen!" Tyonek commanded.

Raoul Garnier plucked Ming's arms from about his body and looked down into the youth's reddened, swollen eyes. "It is all over with here. We must go now. Come, *mon ami.*"

Drained for the moment by weeping, Ming nodded mutely and turned away from the Basque. "Yes. I will come. But first . . . I . . . I must say good-bye to him." He stumbled a few paces, then stopped. His head snapped back and fury replaced the misery in his eyes. "No! Make her get away from Joe! Do not let the old she-demon have his body for her spells!" he cried, and before anyone could halt him, he flew across the dirt toward where Satinka had again taken up a position squatting alongside Joe's body. He tore at her arms, trying to drag her away. "Don't touch him!" he yelled, his almond-shaped eyes ablaze.

Satinka cocked her head to one side. She reached out and, with a bony claw of a hand, trapped Ming's wrist, tugging it down toward Joe's body. His eyes widened in horror as he guessed her intent. He tried to break free, but the old crone was surprisingly strong and would not release him. Down, down, with a grip of iron, she forced his palm down, to lie flat upon Joe's chest, covering the round, black wound there. His hand trembled wildly in her grip, like a trapped bird.

Ming recoiled, disgust, fear, nausea filling him. "No!" he kept repeating hoarsely. "No! No, please, old woman! Don't make me!"

In answer, Satinka muttered something and gave him a toothy grin. She shook her head and pressed a finger across her lips to bid him be silent. "Feel, Yellow Brother," she urged, and tapped her hand in the air, as if patting a little drum. *"Feel!"*

510

For a second, her eyes held him like rheumy magnets, held him so tightly by horrified fascination he could not look away. The tension flowed from him, and, in the stillness, in the calm that replaced it, he felt beneath the sensitive flesh of his palm a definite vibration; a strong and steady thump-a-thump-a-thump like the invisible drum Satinka had played—and something cold and hard between his hand and the throbbing.

Fingers shaking with emotion—with a mixture of dread and joy and disbelief—Ming slipped his hand inside Joe's shirt pocket and withdrew the contents.

He could have recognized them by touch alone, without the need for eyes, for he had seen them so many times. There was the small, metal tin in which Joe always kept his makings for a smoke, and his deck of cards, well thumbed and worn. They were familiar items, save for one added, yet vital, difference: straight through both sides of the flattish tobacco tin was bored a neat, black hole. The hole continued on through several of the top playing cards and then . . . then Ming found the bullet, lodged snugly within all but the bottom card in the deck, the card that had been closest to Joe's chest and which was miraculously unmarked in any way!

"Chrrrist Aaalmighty! Who the hell kicked me, cobber?"

Ming's smile grew wider and then still wider as Joe's eyes opened. He stirred. He groaned and shifted position. Ming was smiling so broadly now his almond eyes had become lemon-peel slits and had almost disappeared beneath his cheeks. Satinka had been right all along! Joe was alive!

Joe groaned again and finally managed to mumble a few more words. Though they were, for the most part, only cusses, they were music to Ming's ears nonethe-

511

less! Ming felt like whooping and dancing around like a madman. Satinka met his shining eyes and nodded sagely, giving a smug little cackle of merriment that she had been proved correct.

"Nobody kicked you, Joe," he told Joe eagerly as his friend struggled to sit up. "It was Val Monroe's bullet. It struck you—right here." He pointed to Joe's chest.

"Strewth!" Joe exclaimed in disbelief, pulling out his shirt to inspect the damage. The neat hole with its burned edges was exactly where Ming had said it was. Joe was amazed. "Then how come I'm still here?" He frowned. "I . . . I *am* still here, aren't I, mate? We're not both . . . ?"

Ming vigorously shook his head, holding up the tobacco tin and the deck of cards. "No, Joe, we are not both dead! The bullet must have been slowed as it went through the can, see, and then finally lodged within the cards!" he guessed as Raoul and the others now crowded excitedly around. "If you had been another step closer, Val Monroe's bullet would have had the range to kill you! You see, Joe, you see? All of the cards are notched, save for this one."

Joe ran his hands through his dusty blond hair, and there was wry amusement in his turquoise eyes as he clambered heavily to his feet and shakily took the card from Ming. His chest felt as if it had been kicked by an ornery mule. There'd be one hell of a bruise there in a few days, but that was a small price to pay for his life. He looked down. "That one?" He snorted and shook his head, grinning his crooked grin as he looked around the circle of smiling faces. "I should have guessed it, cobber! This beautiful bitch has been flirting with me since the day I was born! See, Ming? It's Lady Luck herself, God bless her!"

Joe held up the card. It was a queen—the Queen of Hearts. And, to Ming's eyes, she seemed to be winking.

Turning at the sound of an exultant cry, Joe let out a wild whoop and spread his arms wide as Katie flew across the rubble toward him. Her black hair was loose and streaming behind her, her face aglow with joy. Her slender arms twined fiercely about his throat as she reached him, and as their lips touched, as his strong arms and warm, vital body pressed tightly to hers confirmed the truth of her hopes, she clung to him as if she'd never, ever let him go again.

Luke Steele planted a hand on each of his daughter's shoulders. His night black eyes were troubled as he gazed into her lovely face. "It's now or never, honey. You'd best tell him and get it over with."

"I know, Pa. And . . . and I will, I promise. Thanks for coming back with me."

Her father nodded. "I couldn't let you come back here alone, now could I?" He grinned. "Besides, if I hadn't, your mama would have strapped on her gun and come in my place!" He ducked his head and kissed his daughter's cheek. "It'll all work out, Katie. You'll see."

At that moment, the door opened and Joe stepped into the room. He was still putting on his shirt as he entered, and as they broke apart to turn to look at him, Katie saw astonishment, then anger fill his face in rapid succession.

"Hell! I guess I don't need to ask why it was you left me again, do I, Sera?" he said softly. "But I would like t'know why you came back—and with him in tow." His turquoise eyes crackled. He clenched his fists, only his self-control preventing him from striking out at the man he was convinced was his rival.

"Joe, stop it! It's not what you think!" Katie protested, indignation in her eyes.

"Isn't it?" Joe taunted. "Well, why don't you explain how it is—and in the process, explain *him,* too!" He'd sworn once that he'd kill any man who tried to take Sera from him, and he was close to doing just that as he looked across the room at the tall, black-haired, handsome man who met his gaze unflinchingly with eyes that were so dark brown they were almost black. "Christ, Sera! Couldn't you do any better? He's old enough t'be your father!"

Luke Steele grinned. "Tell him, honey," he urged.

Katie shot him a beseeching look. "I will. But . . . I'd like to do it alone, please?"

Luke nodded. "Sure, honey." He picked up his hat from the table as he exited, adding over his shoulder, "Good luck! I reckon you might need it!"

"Well? Tell me what?" Joe snapped jealously when Luke had left them alone.

Katie's shoulders slumped. She sighed. "Tell you that he not only looks old enough to be my father, he *is* my father!"

"Your father?" He snorted. "You expect me to believe that?"

"You'd better, Joe, because it's true! Fact is, if you're feeling up to it, I've been wanting to talk to you for quite a while. I guess now is as good a time as any!"

He nodded, buttoning the blue-checkered shirt at the cuffs as he turned to face her. Above his breastbone was a large, livid bruise, she noticed. "Well? Talk away, love! And, when you're done, there's something I have to tell you before I leave. Something I should have told you a long, long time ago."

Katie nodded. ". . . I guess it's high time both of us 'fessed up," she agreed huskily and gnawed at her lower lip, wondering how best to tell him. "Joe . . . I'm not lying, not anymore. Luke Steele really is my father. And I'm . . . I'm not who you think I am!" The words, too long bottled up, came out in a breathless rush. "I'm not Seraphina Jones. I'm not William McCaleb's ward. My name's Katie—Katherine Star Dreamer *Steele,* to be precise. The *real* Seraphina is a friend of mine from the Academy back in Boston. A real good friend. You see, last July, she was planning on running away and getting married, but then . . . then she heard her guardian had died and she'd have to come back to San Francisco to sort out his affairs. It meant the end of everything she and Chuck, her sweetheart, had planned! And so, I decided—"

"—and so you decided to take her place?" he finished for her.

She gulped and nodded, adding in a faint voice, "Yes, I'm afraid so! See, I didn't know then about the stipulation in William McCaleb's will. If I had, maybe I wouldn't have . . . but that's beside the point! Once I'd heard about it, I realized the only way to get Seraphina's inheritance for her was to go through with the marriage. And then, when I finally met you, your suggestion that we get married and then go our separate ways was so exactly what I'd been hoping for, I thought everything would turn out just perfect, without anyone's getting hurt or anything. I didn't bargain on your deciding to keep Las Campanas, or on the Monroes, or on—"

"Or on what?" he asked, suddenly tense.

Color filled her cheeks. "Or on your making love to me and getting everything so confused!" She grimaced. "Oh, hell, Joe, this is the time for confessions, right? I didn't plan on falling for you, either, darn it! All of this . . . mess . . . is my fault. I should have told you who I was before."

He nodded, adding softly. "Finished?" The anger had left his expression, to be replaced by something curiously akin to relief.

"I guess. Except to tell you that because of me, Las Campanas can never be yours, Joe. You see, Seraphina is married to Chuck now. I'm . . . real sorry, Joe. There's no way you can carry out your guardian's last request!"

"He wasn't my guardian."

"What?"

"I said, he wasn't my guardian, Sera . . . I mean, Katie. I'd never even heard of William McCaleb until last August." As briefly as possible, he told her of Krakatoa's eruption, the tidal wave, about saving Mac McCaleb's life and taking on his identity at his urging, all of it. She appeared stunned when he was through.

"But . . . that means you're an imposter, too!"

He grinned ruefully. "I guess it does. We were both playing a game of liar's poker, love—and neither one of us held the winning hand!"

She shook her head vigorously. "That's not true, Joe. We're still the same people, and I still love you, Joe, darlin', whether my name's Seraphina or Katie or Mildred or Anna or—"

The door opened again, and Edward Caldwell poked his head in.

"Oh, er, excuse me, Joe! We didn't mean to interupt you two, but we do have some business left to attend to, if you recall, and I really must be getting back to San Francisco. We'd been hoping to hear from you before this, to be honest, but when no word came, Mac and I decided to ride out to Las Campanas and see if you'd made some decision on the matter."

"That's quite all right, sir. Why don't you both come on in?" Joe gave Katie a long, intent look and turned toward the door as Edward entered, followed by Mac McCaleb.

"Well, Joe," Mac said, smiling across at Joe, "Edward and I have presumed that no news meant

516

good news! Sign right there, where I've marked, and Rancho Campanas will be yours." Mac McCaleb smiled as he limped toward Joe, drawing out a pen and gesturing to the papers, which were spread across the table behind him, unnoticed until now. "And then, I think a celebration would be in order, wouldn't you say, Edward?"

"Indeed, yes!" Edward Caldwell agreed happily. "And I must say, it's all turned out very well, despite the somewhat . . . the somewhat . . . unorthodox . . . way things were!"

Joe, who had stalked across to the window, spun to face them. Katie saw that his tanned fingers were clamped so tightly over the edge of the table that his knuckles were bleached white. His turquoise eyes blazed with a wild, blue-green fire she'd never seen before. His expression put her in mind of how a fugitive's might look when cornered by his pursuers. There was a desperate quality to it, and more than a hint of fear. She bit her lip. His strange, remote behavior of the past two days—behavior that had made it so terribly hard for her to confront him sooner—had been neither her imagination nor the result of guilt on her part, she realized belatedly. Something was still eating away at him, something that even their mutual confessions hadn't eased. But what? The rest of the Monroes were safely in Monterey jail, awaiting a circuit judge and a trial. Harper and Val Monroe were dead. Ming had redeemed himself in his own opinion and in Joe's by fetching Tyonek and his braves to come to their aid in the canyon, so what on earth was left for him to be so grim faced and evasive about? Men! They never made sense, no matter how hard you tried to understand them . . .

"So! The pair of you think it's all turned out bloody well, do you?" Joe was saying. "Well, that's just

517

dinkum, because I don't!" He snatched up his hat and headed for the door. On the threshold, he turned back to face the three of them, white about the mouth. "Unorthodox, you said, Caldwell? Why don't you say what you really mean for once, mate, and tell us exactly what it is! What I did was *illegal*, and you both know it. But then, what else would you expect from a bloke like me, eh, Mac, my old cobber?" he demanded bitterly. "You know how it was before I met you. I told you the whole bloody story that night on the beach, remember—about Ned Sullivan's death and why I had to get out of New South Wales in a hurry? Chances are, my parents, whoever they were, were laggers—convicts—or descendants of 'em. All that bad blood . . . strewth! It would have been a bloody miracle if I'd turned out straight, wouldn't you say? And you're offering to guarantee a loan of that size for a man like me?" He shook his head. "Sorry, Mac, if I say you're off your head! Christ! I don't even trust myself! Why in the hell should *you* trust me? My answer's no. Mac, Edward, thanks. No hard feelings, but I'm not interested." So saying, he left the room.

Mac and Edward exchanged shocked glances.

"What the devil's gotten into him?" Mac wondered aloud, visibly upset. "The Monroes are all in jail up in Monterey. Sheriff Clem Tallant and his daughter have been run out of town . . . why, for the first time in his life, he's got everything going for him, and he throws it back in our faces! Damned if I understand him at all!"

"No. But I think I do," Kate said softly. "If you gentlemen will excuse me, I'm going after him."

"And the contract?"

"Leave it there, please," she asked, gesturing to the table. "And wait a while, if you would? If it works out the way I'm hoping it will, your ride out here won't have been for nothing. Now, I must go and change.

Please, make yourselves comfortable gentlemen, and I'll have Peggy serve you some refreshments."

Moments after she had left Mac and Edward, she was running out toward the *ramada*. As she waited while Ming hefted the heavy saddle over Muraco's back and tightened the girth strap for her, she wondered if anything she could say could possibly sway Joe, considering the mood he was in. A fleeting memory of his face that first time they had come here, to Las Campanas, filled her mind. She remembered the glow in his eyes, the dawning pride and love of the land he had regarded as his in that moment. He couldn't have changed that much; she just knew it! He'd loved Las Campanas then. Inside, there was a better than even chance he still did. She intended to use that knowledge—and the certainty that he loved her—for all it was worth. She set her jaw and mounted up, swinging Muraco's head around toward the direction of the bird rock and digging her heels in his flanks to urge him on. She believed she knew just where she'd find Joe.

Her hunch was correct. He was sitting Jimbo atop the slight rise where they'd reined in their horses that first time, awestruck by the grandeur of Casa Campanas silhouetted against the dying sun. He was smoking as he gazed out over the dun-colored land, which was scattered now with the tallow-hued bulks of Esteban Rodriguez's portion of the Las Campanas flocks.

He didn't turn around as she slowed Muraco to a walk and came up behind him. But he obviously knew she had followed him, for still without turning around, he said softly, "You shouldn't have come after me, love. You're only wasting your time."

"Am I?" she asked, drawing her horse level with him. "Sorry, Joe, but I'd have to disagree."

He tilted back the brim of his hat and grimaced with wry amusement. "Still the same old Katie, eh? Still fighting for lost causes! You never learn, do you, love?"

"I don't happen to think you're a lost cause," she said quietly. "But then, I could be wrong."

"When it comes to Joe Christmas, you would be, Katie love," he said bitterly. "Biggest bloody lost cause of them all since the day he was born!"

"Ah. Feeling sorry for yourself, are you, Joe? Go ahead, wallow in it, drown yourself in self-pity, if it makes you feel better. After all, your Lady Luck didn't come through for you this time, did she, darlin'? You've got good reason to feel sorry for yourself! She left you high and dry just like she does the rest of us—faced with the prospect of having to work for what we want, maybe work damned hard, too! But I guess you wouldn't know what I'm talking about, would you?" she challenged.

He bristled before her eyes, his own turquoise ones narrowing against the weathered tan of his complexion, his lips thinning. "That's enough! I know what you're trying to do, Kate, but it won't work. Sorry, love, but I can't make a go of the ranch. I was a damned fool to ever think I could! See, I've tried to make something of myself before." He shrugged. "Going from sheep station to sheep station and back again, slogging at it day in and day out, didn't get me anywhere—'cept in trouble."

"So you just gave up and waited for life to hand you everything on a platter! And it did, too, didn't it—in the shape of Mac McCaleb and a smoky old volcano erupting and William McCaleb's inheritance! But then Mac showed up alive, and your easy way out was gone, popped like a soap bubble. Lord, Joe, how you must hate Mac for being alive, for showing up here!"

He scowled, and she knew by the tightening of his

hands upon Jimbo's reins that her words had needled him. He pinched out the butt of his smoke and tossed it aside.

"You're saying I wanted Mac dead? That I was glad when I thought he'd died?"

"Weren't you? Wasn't that why you pretended to try to save his life—so you could lay claim to his grandfather's inheritance?"

"The hell it was!" he growled. "If you'd believe that of me, woman, then you'd believe any damn thing! I no more wanted Mac to be dead that morning than I wanted Ned Sullivan to die after that fight we had!"

"Of course you didn't, Joe," Katie agreed gently. "I knew that the minute I heard your story, because I *know* you! Because I know that underneath all that toughness, you're not a bad person. Oh, a bit hot tempered, maybe. A little eager to use your fists instead of reason, sometimes—but not a bad 'bloke,' as you'd say. There's an awful lot that's worthwhile about you, Joe Christmas, if you'd only shrug off that chip on your shoulder. That's . . . that's why I love you so, I guess. You took Ming under your wing when he needed help, and little Mei Ling, too. And what about Chief Tyonek, and the shepherds? You're kindhearted and you've a good head for business, darlin', so don't sell yourself short. You know how to get things done and how to make people respect you and want to do their best for you. If you doubt me, just look around you! Raoul, Esteban, Jaime, Gabby, Peggy, Ming—to them, you're *el patron,* whatever your real name is. They *trust* you, Joe! They believe in you. Now you have to learn to believe in yourself! You came here, and you stood up to Harper Monroe, not for your own benefit, but for all the little people around here he'd been walking over for too darn long. And you've already started Las Campanas on the road to becoming a fine

521

working ranch again—just look around you! Forget about your bad start in life. None of that matters anymore. It's the man you've *become* that really counts—and all of us here at Las Campanas need that man. Mac's offering you a chance to make your dreams come true—the right way! Don't throw it all away, Joe! If you hightail it out of here, if you let someone else take over Rancho Campanas, you'll be letting down all those people who believed in you! Most of all, you'll be letting down yourself, and me, and our baby, too, Joe."

"You'll be better off without me; both of you will," he said heavily. "You'll find another man—one who'll give you and our child the kind of life you were meant to have."

"But we don't want another man, Joe, nor any other kind of life than what we could have here, with you. Our baby will need his father, and I . . . oh, Lord, Joe, I need you! Don't make us suffer because you're afraid to accept your responsibility. Don't condemn our son or daughter to growing up never knowing his or her pa, the way you did. Joe, I've said it before, but this time I want you to hear it loud and clear: *I love you, Joe,* and there'll never be anyone for me but you. I love you with everything I have inside of me, with every breath I take and every beat of my heart! I swear it before God, as I swear I'll never leave you again. No matter how rough things might get in the future, or how black things might look for a while down the years—because there'll be hard times as well as good, like in any life—it'll be you and me, Joe. Side by side. Together. Always! For God's sake, sign the paper, Joe! Sign it and give us a future."

Shame filled him as he looked into her eyes, for they were filled with pleading and the moistness of unshed tears. "I can't do it, Katie! I just . . . can't. I guess . . ." he began hoarsely. "I guess deep down I've always been afraid of making a commitment to the future, whether it was staying with one woman or building a dream. Not afraid for my life, but afraid of *failing*. I can't do it because—strewth, Katie, I guess I'm still afraid!" His voice cracked at the end. His tone was choked and strangled sounding with the supreme effort the confession had cost him. He abruptly turned his face from her and adjusted the tilt of his hat so that she wouldn't see the moistness in his own eyes. Men didn't cry, not real men, he thought, disgusted with himself, certain if he looked back he'd see contempt in her expression, contempt for his weakness.

But there was no contempt in Katie's eyes or in her tone as she reached out and lightly touched Joe's shoulder. There was only love. "You don't have to be afraid, Joe, not anymore, not of anything. There's the two of us. That's all we need, Joe, you and me. Together we can do anything. I just know we can! There's no such thing as failure—not as long as you never quit trying. Please, Joe?"

Slowly he turned back in the saddle to face her and saw the tears brimming in her gray-green eyes, the grave beauty of her lovely face as she gazed imploringly back at him. Her expression tore at his heart. Christ! What a fool he'd been to think he could ever give her up, turn his back on her and ride away. He'd known it really from that moment in the canyon when he snatched her from the path of the bullet. It wasn't the land that meant so much in his life, not anymore. It was Kate and their future together. He couldn't stand to lose *her;* he knew that now. If he rode away from Las Campanas alone, he would never be anything but a broken man, without the woman he loved, his beautiful Katie.

"I reckon you've convinced me, love," he said at length. "And, since I don't see how I can go on living without you, I reckon I'll have to try to make a go of it. Will you marry me if I stay, Kate?" he asked, his voice sounding stronger, more like his old self now. "Will you marry me because you want to, pure and simple?"

"Do you have to ask, Joe Christmas, you darned fool?" she whispered, tears streaming down her cheeks—tears of relief and happiness now. "Of course I'll marry you—heck, I'll even sign my real name on the certificate!" she teased.

He threw back his shaggy blond head and laughed deeply, and when he looked at her again, she saw he was grinning his old, familiar, crooked grin.

"Come here, then, Katie Christmas," he growled, and shook his head. "Christ! What a name!"

Katie laughed. "Will Shakespeare said it better than anyone—what's in a name, anyway? We're not roses, that's for sure, but whether I'm called Seraphina Jones or Katie Steele, or you're called Joe Christmas or Joel McCaleb, we're the same people inside, right?"

"Right, love." He leaned down to coil an arm about her waist, then dragged her clear of her horse to sprawl across his saddle. His arms tightly about her, he gazed into her eyes for a second or two, as if unable to believe his luck. Then he lowered his head to kiss her, a kiss that she returned so wholeheartedly they were both breathless when it was finished.

"There, you darned kangaroo cowboy! Now do you believe I love you?" Katie gasped, hanging on to her hat for dear life with one hand, and to Joe with the other.

"I guess I'll have to, love." He winked, toying with a tendril of her black hair. "That kiss was just the proof I needed!"

"I'm glad to hear it, mister," she retorted teasingly, "because that one little kiss is going to have to last you for quite a while—at least until we get back home and get the paper signed for Mac and Mister Caldwell. And

524

then, well, then there's the matter of the wedding! I'd like to be married in the spring, with the wildflowers in bloom, and all our friends, new and old, beside us. Why, it could be over two months, maybe more, before we get the banns read and you get to do more than kiss me!" She eyed him archly.

Joe groaned as she untangled herself from his arms and slipped back onto Muraco's back, for he already wanted her—wanted far, far more than a single kiss. "You drive a real hard bargain, shady lady!"

"You betcha, Joe Christmas!" she retored with a cheeky grin, evading like quicksilver the hand that came out with the speed of greased lightning to try to trap her wrist. "Yah! Get up there, Muraco!"

She gave Muraco his head and lit out across the dun-colored, rolling lands toward home, the gelding's white mane furling, his silvery tail streaming in the wind, as was her flowing black hair.

"It'll be worth the wait, love," Joe murmured softly as he jammed on his hat and spurred Jimbo into a gallop after her.

Chapter Thirty-Two

The little chapel of Casa Campanas was filled with
the fresh green fragrance of wildflowers and Castilian
roses on the day Joe and Katie were wed the following
spring. She wore a gown of pale blue silk. A *mantilla* of
snowy lace, held in place by tall ebony combs chased
with silver and turquoise stones, hid her luxuriant
black hair. Joe was tall and ruggedly handsome in a
tailored suit of dark gray, a satin vest the same hue as
Kate's gown beneath it.

Their guests were few, under the circumstances.
Only Kate's family and her and Joe's dearest friends
had been invited. Promise Steele, looking far from
grandmotherly, stood with Joe's son, one-month-old
Nathan, sleeping cradled in her arms. Alongside her
stood her two tall sons. Tom, the elder of the two who
was as darkly handsome as his father, stood quite erect
and motionless while the solemn vows were exchanged,
while Courtney, who had inherited the corn-silk hair
and green eyes of his mother, fidgeted and yawned and
loosened his starched formal collar and wished with all
the impatience of any fourteen-year-old boy that all
this sissy nonsense would soon be over.

So, too, had Kate's "Uncle" Cay and "Aunt" Carol

come from Colorado to be there. Their son, Chuck Bushley, and his wife, the real Seraphina, and their baby boy, Daniel, were seated beside them. Peggy was crying noisily into a scrap of handkerchief, while Gabby, several months gone with child herself, looked up coyly into her Jaime's face, no doubt remembering their own wedding day. Raoul Garnier, Edward Caldwell, and his wife, Lavinia, were there, too, as, of course, were Chen Ming and his *shao-mei-mei*, little Mei Ling, sent for two weeks earlier. The little girl looked even more like a petite Oriental doll today in her brand new *cheong-sam* of rose-pink silk. She would not be returning to the Donaldina Cameron Home in San Francisco, but would stay with her dear brother, Ming, at Casa Campanas, under the watchful, motherly eye of Peggy Kelly, until she was old enough to help with her older brother's ambitious plans to become the first Chinese millionaire in America—a plan he intended to fulfill by planting citrus trees upon the several acres of land Joe had agreed to let him farm in the southern part of the Las Campanas rarge, and selling the fruit.

Olivia, Esteban, and their three sons, who were all scrubbed and had had their hair neatly slicked down, were there too. By the little altar stood Luke Steele, as dark and proud, as tall and straight as any arrow, relieved at having done his part and given his lovely young daughter away. Joel 'Mac' McCaleb, Joe's best man and his closest friend, set his cane aside for the moment as he handed the opal wedding ring to Joe and looked happily on as his friend slipped it upon his bride's slim finger.

". . . by the power vested in me, I now pronounce you man and wife," the priest declared with a flourish and closed his prayer book with a final thud. "Mister Christmas, you may now kiss your bride!"

527

Joe's heart felt filled to bursting as he looked at all the smiling faces around them, then down into his Kate's radiant eyes. He cupped her face in his large hands and lowered his lips to hers.

It was a lingering, sweet kiss, a chaste kiss. But it was, nonetheless, a kiss that said everything she'd ever wanted him to say, Katie thought dreamily. She tilted her head and gazed up into his turquoise eyes. Simultaneously, there came a sudden burst of sound from the *campanario* high above them.

A thrill ran through Katie. "Oh, thank you!" she whispered tenderly. "This makes everything just perfect! We've ended that silly old curse, Joe. There's nothing but happiness ahead for us now!"

Joe nodded, his shaggy brows coming together in a puzzled frown. He looked over Katie's shoulder to where Ming stood, his almond-shaped eyes also wide with surprise. He cocked an inquiring eyebrow at the youth, who gave a vigorous shake of his head in reply. But if Ming hadn't, and he hadn't, then who the blazes . . . ? Joe shrugged. Who or how or why didn't matter. Like Katie'd said, Little Owl's curse—if it had ever existed—was now ended. A new life was beginning for them, a life filled with hope and achievement, with the joy of sharing and togetherness, and most of all, with love!

He gathered Katie in his arms and kissed her again and again, while the bronze bells in the *campanario* rang out for the very first time.

The glad message pealed across the flower-strewn hills of Rancho de las Campanas, to the farthest reaches of the Sierra Nevadas' sawtoothed range.